MIDWINTER FAE

A PROCESSION OF FAERIES ~ 2

DAYLE A. DERMATIS   DIANA BENEDICT

LEAH CUTTER   LESLIE CLAIRE WALKER

ERIC KENT EDSTROM   RON COLLINS

REI ROSENQUIST   KAREN L. ABRAHAMSON

DEANNA KNIPPLING   ANTHEA SHARP

MARCELLE DUBÉ   DEB LOGAN   T. THORN COYLE

JAMIE FERGUSON   KRISTINE KATHRYN RUSCH

REBECCA M. SENESE   STEFON MEARS

BRIGID COLLINS   ALEXANDRA BRANDT

Edited by
JAMIE FERGUSON

COPYRIGHT

On the day of the shortened sun
A battle between two kings has begun.

The old year dies, and the Oak King rules
We celebrate with logs of Yule!

But the Holly King is defeated, not dead
To Caer Arianrhod he heads.

Until Midsummer, when they battle again
And the Holly King will once again reign...

CONTENTS

INTRODUCTION

Midwinter Fae, the second volume in the series *A Procession of Faeries*, is a collection of stories about faeries and Midwinter, the day with the shortest amount of daylight and longest night of the year.

There's quite a bit of mythology and faerie lore related to this celestial event. Midwinter is associated with Alban Arthan, a Druidic festival held at the winter solstice that celebrates the defeat of the Holly King, who signifies the old year and the shortened sun, by the Oak King, who signifies the new year. The Holly King is associated with the wren, and the Oak King with the robin, and there are many historical events and celebrations involving both.

I love faery stories, and found the stories in this collection a pure delight to read. I hope you enjoy their magic as well.

—Jamie Ferguson
Editor

THE MADNESS OF SURVIVAL

DAYLE A. DERMATIS

S uddenly awake, I stared into the darkness, all senses straining to figure out what had woken me.

The clock LED gleamed just past midnight. The trick-or-treaters were snuggled in their beds, the partiers hadn't yet stumbled home. Only the faint occasional hum of a car broke the silence. Santa Barbara in autumn was just barely cool enough to close the windows at night, and I had a light comforter pulled over Shawn and me.

Eva was sleeping through the night now, but I was still breastfeeding, the milky scent clinging to my body.

Had Eva made a noise? I listened, heard nothing.

A mother's instinct was what pulled me from beneath the covers. Barefoot in a pair of cotton pajama pants dotted with flowers and a pale pink tank top that didn't remotely match any colors in the pants, I walked to the bedroom doorway. I didn't need to turn on a light.

In the bed, Shawn stirred. "Alis? 'kay?"

"Just checking on..."

Framed in the doorway, I smelled it. Tasted it.

Faerie glamour.

Spun sugar, too sweet. Like walking through cobwebs the consistency of cotton candy.

"...Eva," I whispered, fighting through the strands. Then I could move at normal speed again (How long had it taken me to get from the bed to the doorway? How long had it taken me to even wake up?), and I ran into the next room. Hit the light switch shaped like a sheep. Three long steps to the crib.

Some disconnected part of me noted that the wail emerging from my lungs sounded unearthly. Inhuman.

Despairing.

◠

W inter Solstice in Santa Barbara, California. A balmy 50 degrees on the longest night of the year. Never a wish of snow in the air, and I wouldn't have been surprised if some fool had been out surfing today.

I've lived here for twenty years and it still seemed wrong. My very ex-husband, Shawn, who'd spent his whole life in Southern California, thought it was normal to wear shorts on Christmas Day. Didn't see anything wrong with wrapping strands of lights around a palm tree.

Now, as my motorcycle slipped through the dark, arid streets, I ached for the fresh linen scent of snow. My ex had said snow stayed in the mountains where it belonged, and we could visit it. I'd said I wanted our daughter to know the magic of waking up on Christmas morning and seeing the great white flakes drifting down.

But then Eva was gone, and my ex soon thereafter. Death of a child is hard on any marriage, but when you can't explain why you're reacting the way you are...

When the Fae take a human child, they leave a changeling. Sometimes that changeling isn't a living thing—that explains, for example, SIDS. To the human eye, there's a baby who died an unexplained death. To anyone able to see through Faerie glamour, all that lies in the crib is a bundle of twigs.

I could see through the glamour. Thankfully I was smart enough not to tell anyone past my first, initial hysteria—a hysteria that was chalked up to a mother's fresh grief.

Sometimes the Fae leave one of their own Faerie children, which will be sickly and pale because we don't have the right food in the human world, although fresh, whole cream and oats and pomegranate seeds, and leeks sautéed in butter, will help. That's apparently what happened with me, when I was taken as a child—which is why I was able to fight my way out, sending my faerie doppelgänger back home. I imagine she fared better than I did.

Then again, the Fae are cruel and capricious, and may have taken out their anger at losing me on her.

As far as I know—as far as any of us know—children exchanged for bundles of twigs never return.

It's probably madness that lets me believe I'll see Eva again. I desperately hope she won't be broken; hope that because of my own experience and understanding, I'll be able to ease her through the transition.

Most of us are some level of broken.

The madness that allowed us to survive in Faerie.

We—the group of us that ride together and protect children from the Fae—have hints of leftover magic. Our motorcycles make no sound to the human ear, seem to have a dusting of *don't-look-here* about them, allowing us to slip in and out of traffic, make our way through the city without notice. Or, if someone does notice us—someone who also has the mark of the Fae upon them, perhaps—they forget quickly.

The rheumy-eyed homeless man, grey in his tattered tweed coat and unraveling fingerless gloves, eyes me from his spot tucked into the bank steps as I idle at a stop sign. He turns to his companion and says, "Did you see—?" and then I'm gone and his companion asks, "What?" and he shakes his head and mutters.

Joe-Joe, who survived being conscripted into the Wild Hunt, opines that the bikes are ensorcelled faerie steeds. Sometimes I feel as though mine's alive—I can't say why I have the habit of running my hand along her chrome flanks as if soothing her—but I'm not sure.

My time in Faerie taught me to question everything, believe nothing.

My motorcycle was a small cruiser, comfortable and low enough for me to plant my feet firmly on the ground when needed. I called her Asfaloth, like the horse Glorfindel rode in *The Lord of the Rings*, who carried Frodo from the Ringwraiths.

Fast, brave, and able to outrun evil.

You might think I'd shy away from a name like that, but Tolkien's Elves are nothing like the Fae. And besides, the steeds were never malevolent.

If magic is real, I had to believe there was good magic.

We're like the Lost Boys and Lost Girls, like war-torn orphans in a country we've never seen before. We've had experiences few people understood—few people would even believe were real. You can't explain to a psychiatrist that your PTSD isn't from a tour in the Middle East, but in the wars between Light and Dark Fae, between Good and Evil, and you never volunteered to serve.

That the howl of a dog sends you into a sweating, trembling panic, not because you'd been bit, or menaced by a stray pack, but because the sound is a pale echo of the hounds baying in the Wild Hunt—and you'd angered the Queen and had been ensorcelled to run *as* one of her jet-black hounds.

We couldn't find empathy from anyone except those who'd experienced the same thing. Slowly we banded together, a gang from the outside, perhaps. But a family from the inside. A family made up of the ragged, the broken, the formerly bespelled, helping one another heal.

And protecting children from being taken like we were.

∾

I pulled up in front of a California bungalow home, a gabled, two-story construction painted a classic sage green with brick red and cream accents. Fat square wooden columns, narrowing as they rose, held up the wide porch roof. Fragrant pink flowers spilled from baskets hanging along the eaves. This late at night, the only light on was the porch light, shaped like a lantern.

I was off my bike and backing away, chanting "No, no, no" before I even realized I was doing it.

I knew this house. Knew who lived there.

Joe-Joe was already there, and Parvo, and Sunny. Joe-Joe, the nominal leader of our group, was the one who came over to me, holding out his hand as if to sooth a skittish horse; then, once he was sure I wouldn't bolt, resting his hand gently on my shoulder.

"Alis? What's up?" he asked.

Joe-Joe rides a Harley, and looked like a typical rider except that he's smart enough to wear a full helmet, not one of those little Nazi-esqe beanies with a spike on top that wouldn't protect a watermelon being thrown down on the pavement. He was tall and burly, with scraggly hair and an even scragglier beard. If you could get past that, though, his hazel eyes were kind, always kind, despite a hint of despair behind them.

He had been in Faerie the longest of all of us, and has the knack to know which kids the Fae will be targeting. He's the one who tells us where to go. I don't know how many jobs we all had tonight, in Santa Barbara and down the coast into Ventura and Oxnard. As with Halloween and the Summer Solstice and the equinoxes, it was one of the busiest nights of the year.

Certainly enough for all of us to have one, maybe two rescues to handle.

We work in teams of two, one person outside in the hopes of stopping the Fae if they came that way, or distracting anyone else who might try to enter the house, and one person inside, the last line of defense for the child against the kidnappers.

I unbuckled my own helmet and tugged it off. The cool breeze ruffled my hair. I kept it in a dark tight braid, because nothing tangles hair better than wind when you're riding. All those movies and commercials where a woman removes a motorcycle helmet and shakes her head and her perfect hair comes cascading down? Bullshit.

Even my braid probably looked like ass right now, matted down, wisping out. I shoved the bangs off my forehead, took a deep, deep breath.

Eased the air out through my teeth, counting down, calming.

"I don't know if I can do this," I said.

Joe-Joe waited. Patient. I'd talk when I was ready.

But he also knew, just as I did, that it was nearing midnight on the Winter Solstice, the longest night of the year and one of the times when the Veil between the Worlds is thin, and the Fae come out to play and steal their latest crop of toys.

We didn't have much time.

Inside, little Noah, age 4, slumbered peacefully away, unaware of the fate that would befall him—unless we got inside and stopped it.

Inside, my former best friend, Grace, slumbered peacefully away as well, trapped in the cotton-candy gauze of faerie glamour.

We had been friends pretty much since I'd returned from Faerie. She'd never been. Our mutual love of folklore, myth, and fantasy stemmed from different desires: she wanted to escape the real world, whereas I wanted to understand the world I'd escaped from. She never knew about my past.

Which was probably why she turned her back on me after Eva was taken. Pretty much everyone did, because who wanted to stick by a woman who insisted her dead child wasn't dead? Eva's death was ruled as SIDS; any questionable charges against me were dropped. I pulled my crazy together, just barely, but by that time Shawn had filed for divorce and taken off, and even Grace, my oldest friend, mumbled something about "nothing in common anymore."

Which translated to "I have to protect my own child from the crazy."

And now I was expected to protect Noah? Was this irony, or design?

We don't know how the Fae choose children.

Not many people escape from Faerie, so my own situation was especially unusual, a returnee—an anomaly—who then has child taken by the Fae.

This...gang/family/group had spent a lot of time helping me with the guilt that the Fae had taken Eva as payback for losing me. Whether or not that was true, I still suffered the guilt.

The Fae were capricious, cold, but in some ways, not calculating. They held grudges, oh, yes they did—their feuds lasted centuries— but by the same token, they moved slower than humans did. My time with them was a blink of an eye, like owning a goldfish.

There was no way to know.

Question everything, believe nothing.

Now, while I dithered, Noah could be lost.

No matter how Grace felt about me, no matter that a two-decades-old friendship had shattered in flames, I couldn't do that to Noah.

I couldn't do it to any child, but especially not to one I knew and, despite everything, loved.

Joe-Joe waited, patient, for my explanation.

My hands shook. I wanted to rest them on Asfaloth's tank, soak in the warmth, the safety. Astride her, I felt invincible. Like I could outrun my fears.

I understood now I had to face those fears.

"I'm okay," I said. Deep breath in through the nose, out through the teeth. Had the temperature dropped? I dug my hands into the pockets of my brown leather jacket for warmth and solidity. "I know the people who live here. We...have a history."

"You sure?" he asked, his deep voice rumbling with sympathy and support. "Sunny and I have another house nearby, but Parvo can take point, or we can swap..."

I shook my head, stripping off my leather gloves. Parvo was like *that* uncle, the one who's normal most of the time, but you know he's skittish and you avoid certain topics or sudden loud sounds around him. He was slender and small, with close-cropped greying hair, and hell, he made *me* nervous.

He was far, far better outside, as the first line of defense.

And there wasn't time to swap houses or teams.

"I'll be okay," I reiterated. "You go. Call me if another job comes up."

We were scattered throughout Santa Barbara, a ragtag, scruffy-looking group of bikers, a family held together by our bikes and the taint of faerie magic we just couldn't scrub off, no matter how many times we showered or surrounded ourselves with iron.

And by the resolve we held to protect, no matter what the cost.

~

I bumped fists with Parvo and went in.

Inside, the house smelled of coconut milk and Chinese five spice and lemongrass. Grace had always loved to cook; had fallen easily into the role of wife and mother. Maybe that's what started the decline of our friendship: she judged me for falling back on Easy Mac, for wanting to go back to work after Eva was a few months old. (Not that I'd had the chance...)

I shook myself—I really did, a head-to-toe shuddering release. Glamour had a way of making you feel inadequate. Bad about yourself. Susceptible to other forces. To being led away, led astray...

There are a few tales of adults being coerced into the Faerie realm. *Tam Lin*'s one of the most famous, but there are others involving faerie rings and standing stones and being in the wrong place at the wrong time and seeing the Wild Hunt ride by as a beautiful, glittering, magical spectacle rather than the dark despair it really is.

I would not get suckered in, not here, not now.

If I went back in blinded, I'd never find my way out again. Never find my daughter, never return to the real world.

People think Faerie must be breathtakingly lovely and perfect. In some ways, there's perfection, but it's cold. Not cold as in frigid, but cold in the sense of both temperature and emotion. You're never truly warm in Faerie; even the fires burn blue and give off no heat. The land is in perpetual twilight; if you even make it outside, you'll find no sun.

And the Fae themselves? Disaffected, distant. Immortality breeds ennui.

Ice can be breathtaking, but when you shatter it, there's nothing behind it.

The scent of fresh Thai food faded as I ascended the wooden staircase, remembering even now which riser creaked if you stepped in the center. There wasn't much need to avoid it; Grace and her husband would be glamoured, and if Noah were awake, that could make things even easier.

Children have a magic of their own, and with protection, they can help ward off the Fae.

By the time I got to the top of the stairs, the homey smells of cooking had been replaced by sweet cotton candy laced with the ashes of snowflakes.

I paused outside the master bedroom, the reddish-stained five-panel door open just a crack, but then I pressed on through the sickly webbing of glamour. I didn't need to see Grace and her husband. Didn't need to see the pale yellow of her bedroom walls, a paint color that soaked up the golden California sunshine and made the room bright and airy—a color I'd suggested, and helped roll onto those very walls.

Didn't want to gloat and think *See, see? It could happen to anyone.*

The bedrooms were arrayed around a central landing. Noah's was catty-corner from his parents'. His door was also cracked open, the faint blue-green glow of a nightlight leaking out.

I pushed the door the rest of the way open, pushed through the strongest glamour woven across the doorway, that disgusting, clinging cobwebby cotton-candy stickiness.

The last time I'd been here, it had been a baby's room. Now it was a little boy's room, and Noah apparently loved the ocean. The night-light was a dolphin, a bedside lamp was a smiling octopus holding up a bulb at the end of each of its legs, and one wall was a mural of sea creatures above and below the surface, some of which glowed in the dark.

The crib had been replaced by a bed, and there was Noah, dark hair rumpled, his face round and cherubic, his skin pale and smooth.

I had only the flash of a moment to admire him, to experience the regret of not seeing him grow from baby to preschooler, before the Fae arrived.

I'd known it would be soon, given the thickness of the glamour I'd fought through. I was more prepared for them than I'd been for seeing Noah.

They wove their doorway out of shadows, between one breath and the next. I'd noticed in the past, as I did now, that they tended to create them as close to a human doorway as possible; perhaps that made the magic easier.

It also explained the monsters-in-the-closet problem.

Two Fae stepped through. Tall, cold, slender, beautiful, terrible. They shone with their own luminosity, and it took me a moment to adjust my sight.

Still, I faced them, placing myself between them and Noah.

"This child is not for you to take," I said.

The one in front, with long, pale hair the color of moonlit tears, cocked his head. "On whose authority?"

"All humanity," I said. "Human children are not playthings to be stolen away for your amusement. You may not come into our world and kidnap at will."

"You think it is at will?" he said, and took one, achingly graceful step to the side, so I could see the second Fae who'd accompanied him.

For the briefest of moments, my brain scrambled to understand, to come up with the simplest solution, which was that there'd been a mirror on the closet door that I hadn't noticed.

But I'm not vain enough to think I could ever be so stunning.

Or so soulless.

She was my doppelgänger.

I remember my time in Faerie very, very well. I remember fighting to get out, every chance I got.

I don't remember getting out, or seeing my shadow, my other self, in this world.

"So," she said. "Finally, we meet."

Her hair was long and dark, a long, graceful braid down her back, where mine was haphazard and matted. Her eyes were an ocean of blue mine could never attain.

It didn't matter. I didn't want to be her, and I didn't want to be where she was from.

I felt as if I'd been punched in the stomach, had the wind knocked out of me, but I still took a step closer, wanting to see her more clearly.

Drawn, in hindsight, into the glamour of her own making. Of our own making.

"Are you...okay?" I had to ask. "Did my getting out, forcing you to return to Faerie...was that bad for you?"

She laughed, but it was the farthest thing from humor you or I or anyone could imagine.

"You humans and your concern, your care," she said. "Your *honor*." She said the word as if it tasted bad on her tongue. "It will always be your downfall."

And then, yes, she was right, I realized my mistake. I'd let her distract me.

While the other one grabbed Noah.

He was around me in a blink of an eye, a movement I could see only because of the time I'd spent in their world, the same way I could recognize their glamour. But I wasn't as fast as they were.

My twin smiled without any emotion except some hideous mix of triumph and pity.

"Good-bye, sister," she said. "Enjoy the life you have here." She stepped backwards through the doorway, vanished.

The Fae holding Noah stepped through as well.

I didn't have time to think, to process, to consider. I had time only to do what was right.

I dove after them. After Noah.

She was right. Our honor would be our downfall.

Thing was, ever since Eva was taken, I'd tried to find a way back into Faerie. A way to enter with my full faculties intact, not enchanted and dazed by glamour. Maybe I hadn't been looking in the right place —or maybe I'd never had the courage.

All I knew was that right now, I had to save Noah.

Faerie doorways are never simple; they're not a step between one world and the other. They're passageways. Dark, cold places full of disorienting magic, designed to get you lost forever.

I didn't even get fully inside. If I had, things might have gone differently. I might have made different choices.

I didn't realize right then that I had a choice. All I knew was the job I'd sworn to do...the child I'd promised to protect.

I got in just far enough to reach them, to feel the bone-chilling cold, and I snatched Noah out of the Fae's arms and backpedaled as fast as I could, and then I was falling to the wood floor, the breath knocked out of me as my back slammed down, and I through a haze of stars I saw the doorway close. The veil thickened. It was past midnight.

I didn't have much time.

Noah was still under the glamour, so I scrambled up and tucked him haphazardly under the covers. Then I was running down the stairs as the glamour faded behind me. They'd wake up any second now.

At least Grace and her husband would find Noah safe in his bed. If they even woke up at all, sensed anything had changed.

I flashed a thumbs-up at Parvo. Then I jammed my helmet on, buckled it with shaking fingers, twisted the key. Asfaloth answered with a rumbling purr only I could hear.

"We can get into Faerie," I told her, my voice small. Then I repeated, louder, "We can get into Faerie. We just have to find the door. I know you'll help me with that."

I knew I should tell Joe-Joe, Parvo, any one of the others, where I was going, what I was going to try to do. But I had to go, had to try, before I lost faith.

I had to cling to the madness to survive.

I'm given to understand that no matter where you cross, you end up in the mythology of your own people—your ancestral DNA, sort of. Doorways to Faerie can be accessed anywhere; you didn't have to be in Britain to find the portals to Celtic deities, or in Greece to find that pantheon's arches.

In the Southern California desert—and it's all desert, right down to the ocean's edge, no matter how hard people have tried to build Los Angeles into an oasis—you'd expect the doorways to open into a Native American dreamworld. But even the Coyote doesn't steal babies while he forces their parents to slumber.

Now I knew I could reach through, touch the Faerie lands.

Now I knew I could get back in and find Eva.

In Grace's house, the Fae had opened the doorway. I'd sacrificed my chance in exchange for saving Noah.

I didn't have the power to open a doorway, but doorways existed. And Asfaloth could help me find one.

I pulled out into the suburban street, headed for the freeway. The 101 South to the 33 North through the mountains, then beyond.

We were going out into the desert, my motorcycle steed and I. We were riding through the longest night of the year until we found the weak spot between the worlds.

We'd make that weak spot a doorway.

And we would go through, and I would find a way to bring Eva home.

ABOUT THE AUTHOR

Dayle A. Dermatis is the author or coauthor of many novels (including snarky urban fantasies *Ghosted*, *Shaded*, and *Spectered*) and more than a hundred short stories in multiple genres, appearing in such venues as *Fiction River*, *Alfred Hitchcock's Mystery Magazine*, and DAW Books.

Called the mastermind behind the Uncollected Anthology project, she also guest edits anthologies for *Fiction River*, and her own short fiction has been lauded in many year's best anthologies in erotica, mystery, and horror.

She lives in a book- and cat-filled historic English-style cottage in the wild greenscapes of the Pacific Northwest. In her spare time she follows Styx around the country and travels the world, which inspires her writing.

Find out more about Dayle at:
daylerdermatis.com

facebook.com/dayledermatis

twitter.com/dayledermatis

goodreads.com/DayleDermatis

bookbub.com/authors/dayle-a-dermatis

amazon.com/Dayle-A.-Dermatis/e/B004W5KAZY

SUMMERLAND'S PALADIN

DIANA BENEDICT

Todd crouched in the crotch of an ancient oak tree. Water dripped from the naked branches onto his pounding head, his clothing was soaked, and his fingers were cramped with the cold. The pouring rain had been miserable, but it kept the scents and the visibility down.

Now the drops were interspersed with flakes.

He wished he was in his bed on this night. But his brothers would likely murder him there the same as out here in the forest. He would take the possibility of freezing before morning over either of those alternatives. He reached to the back of his head and felt the jagged, bloody bump there.

Colin had tried to kill him. His *own brother*. And not even in a rage, like when Colin fell for one of Todd's pranks. No, it had been calculated. He'd waited until Todd turned to latch the sheep gate, and hit Todd square on the base of his head with a stout stick.

"Shoulda gone t'the Watch when Da died," his oldest brother had said, standing over Todd. Colin always gloated, and Todd always took advantage of it.

"Ye would have thought if ye were trying ta kill a man, ye'd leaved off the gloating until ye'd killed him," Todd said. But Colin could never pass up a chance to rub Todd's face in it.

Even if Colin ended up with his own face in the mud. Which he did, once Todd tangled his legs around Colin's, pulling him down and twisting out from underneath him. Todd picked up the cudgel and hit his brother on the head as he wobbled to his feet. Then he ran, unsteadily, straight for the forest.

Evidently Todd hadn't hit Colin hard enough, given the baying hound to the east of him. But then again, he hadn't wanted to kill his brother. Fratricide was nothing he wanted to live with.

Todd shook his head, which made him dizzy and threatened to make him sick. Again.

Joining the Watch wouldn't have been any good, and he knew it. The same as the priesthood. Besides, third sons never got anything. And first born of a second wife was worse. Worse yet, his Ma's blood ran strong in his veins.

It hadn't mattered to Da. He'd loved her dearly. His first sons, though, were another matter. They'd not loved her at all, and had not mourned when she passed.

The snow intensified and Todd wished for his fur. He'd used every trick he knew—double back, cross the river, run with the wind, climb steep hills and a dozen trees, shimmying out across branches in the hopes that he could leave a wide gap on his trail. He could only hope it would be good enough to fool Fergus, his other brother's hound.

The branch above him shook as the raven landed, showering him in a sudden avalanche of wet snow.

"Grawwwwk," it said, as Todd brushed snow off of his head and shoulders.

Damn thing had been following him since he'd entered the woods. It had to be the same one he'd been seeing for a fortnight—atop the barn, perching on the cairn along the trail he used to get the sheep to and from pasture, and sitting on the pasture wall.

It would cock its shiny black head and stare at him with one white-ringed beady eye, as if taking his measure. Then it would make the same caw and flap its wings.

Sometimes it would walk right up to him, or sidle close as Todd leaned against a wall to eat his lunch, daring him to—to what? He would never hit it with his crook, or throw a rock at it like his brothers would. His mother had taught him to respect the creatures of the world, even when they didn't like him. Like his brother's dog, or the chickens.

But it seemed no ordinary bird.

He couldn't blame the chickens, or the dog either, if he was honest. They knew him, knew what he was.

"Fleee, fleee," the raven croaked softly.

Todd looked up. Had he heard right?

"They come, they come." The bird flapped his wings, showering more snow down on him.

Todd lifted his head and listened. Yes, the soft but regular swish of wet branches and the panting of men working hard, not caring for their woodcraft.

The dog was a ruse to make him think he was safe. His brothers knew him well, damn them.

"Go, go," the raven squawked as it flew down into his face.

Todd scrambled away from the trunk to get away from the daft bird, losing his balance and falling off the branch. He caught another and swung out, landed in a snowy bush, and rolled. When he got to his feet, the raven flew low over him.

"This way, this way."

Birds did not talk. Was it the Morrigan? What had he done that a goddess would pay attention to him? No matter now; he was not about to pass up a bit of help. He could hear more rustling in the brush and a yelp, a human yelp, then a sharp curse. He recognized Fergus' voice.

The raven glided to a nearby branch and waited for Todd to catch up. The snow was sleeting down and the wind was picking up. He thought about changing, but it would take time and, if they caught up to him in the middle of it, he would be helpless.

No, best to stay two-legged.

The raven launched itself off the branch, sending an additional blanket of snow onto him. Was the damn thing trying to freeze him? He glanced at his surroundings as the bird led him deeper. There were still wolves here, and they would harass a man as soon as a fox.

"Here, here," the raven cawed. He perched on a branch over-looking a hill that was covered with a densely overgrown patch of brush, now blanketed in thick snow.

"Todd, ye worthless pile of shit, come out and stand like the man ye pretend t'be," Colin shouted from behind and to his left.

Todd was a man. Most of the time. He had stood up under his da's rearin' with a fear of God and the belt to make him know right from wrong. And his ma had taught him to be honorable. He was more honorable than his brothers, who stole and cheated whenever they could. He'd caught them cheating Old Seamus O'Sullivan. He'd told them it was wrong. He should have left then, but where would he have gone?

He should have known they would come for him after Da died and he got in their way. But, he'd reasoned, they were his brothers. That meant more to him than it did them. No, Colin and Fergus had put their heads together and Colin had clobbered Todd, hoping to kill him off and keep their dirty little secret.

But Todd was not going to lie down and die, so it had come to this. He wished that Colin had realized Todd could have killed him after he pulled him down. But no. His brothers only saw cowardice in him.

"Go through, go through," the raven croaked, flying down to make a pass at his head, urging him on. Todd ducked and threw up an arm. There was nowhere to go. The brush was woven so tightly only a mouse could pass.

The raven cawed with clear disgust and dived at him, pecking at his unprotected head, driving him forward.

Todd slipped on some ice, then tripped on a root. He crashed headlong down the small hillock, straight for the tangle. As he tried to gather his feet under him on the sheet of ice, he saw a slender opening, a narrow arch. The raven slipped through with a final, "Follow, follow."

He obeyed, and found himself in tunnel of branches and vines grown together tightly. The snow did not penetrate here, though the ground was moist, smelling of earth *and m*ulch, and fresh running water. How that could be in the freezing cold, he had no idea.

A faint pearly light shone ahead of him, and he followed it. It grew brighter as he went, which made no sense, as it had been dark of the night when he went in. Soon the air grew warm, warmer than a snowy night warranted. And how would that be when it had been pelting down snow on the eve of the winter solstice a moment ago?

The smells changed to summer smells: new grass, flowers blooming, and sun-warmed rocks. But he caught a hint of rot under all the smells, like hay gone bad or milk gone sour.

The tunnel ended abruptly, leaving Todd staring out at a soft summer day, with a gentle sun peeking through a thinning mist.

The raven sat in an ash tree spotted with leaves turning yellow. It fluttered its wings to shake off the now melted snow. He looked down at Todd, his head cocked, one beady black eye aimed at him.

Todd heard footsteps to his right. Two warriors dressed in bright armor marched out side by side between a pair of trees that were splotched with dying leaves. They halted, leaving an opening between them.

A beautiful woman with pearly white hair stepped gracefully out from under a grandfather ash tree, and walked between the two men-at-arms. Todd stared at her. He caught a whiff of something sweet and spicy. Not a human scent, no, something much more beautiful and dangerous, but with a hint of corruption like apples left too long in the dark.

A lithe, pale man with a haughty face, who wore a red and black shirt and trousers, followed and stood slightly behind her. He stared hard at Todd with dark eyes that glittered even in the shade.

Todd's head ached like to fall off. He almost wished it would, so the pain would stop. He watched as the woman walked toward him, her wispy orange and blue gown shimmering when she passed through a ray of sunlight.

"And this is the one you spoke of, Ri Fiach?" she asked, looking to the raven. "Looks like a ragamuffin to Me, more than any get of Renart."

Todd's ears perked. Ri Fiach, the Raven King? So the bird was a king then, not a goddess in disguise. He wasn't sure which was better. Or worse.

And who was she to know of his grandsire Renart, the king of foxes?

He made a leg the way his mother had taught him to do when speaking to his betters. "Mban, my lady, I don't know who ye are or why." He glanced at the raven. "His majesty has guided me to ye, but I be grateful for the succor of this place."

He looked around. The tunnel he had emerged from, speckled

with the same sickly leaves, let out into the center of this small grove of ash trees. By the height of the shadows, the sun was high. Fescue vied with acaena, mugwort, mouse-ear, and oxlip to carpet the ground, and was cropped quite closely, but also showed the same signs of sickliness as the trees and brush.

He felt like he would fall if he didn't sit. A log lay along the edge to his right, and he went to it, his boots squelching softly as he walked. His breeches were wet, his cloak soaked and torn. He took it off and hung it on a broken branch to dry before sitting in his shirt sleeves. He let his head down into his hands, and felt it throbbing to his heartbeat.

Wherever he was, he wasn't sure he was any safer. This Raven and the woman played some kind of game, with him as a mark. But his only choice was back through the tunnel, into winter and his brothers' unloving and deadly arms.

A breeze sprang up, and he smelled the forest and the creatures who made their living in it and more of the sweet, spicy scent the woman exuded. He could hear titters in the branches, not squirrels, nor birds—at least none he'd ever known.

Todd glanced around, looking for the others, and was rewarded with bits of color interspersed through the leaves. Ah, so more folk similar to the lady, who was still taking him in like he was a horse she was considering buying.

"He'll do, he'll do," the raven cawed.

"Do for what?" Todd asked.

"We'll see," the woman said to the raven as she walked toward Todd, ignoring his question. She leaned in so close he wanted to lean back, but felt he would fail a test if he did.

She was beautiful, with pale skin like milk, almond-shaped eyes that glittered like jet, an impish, upturned nose, the sharp, thin-lipped mouth below it lifting on one side to show her doubts about whatever the raven had brought him to do.

The rotting smell clung to her like a shroud. No mortal woman then. Was she a wraith?

"You're out of Renart?" she asked. "How do you come to smell of sheep, then?"

He smiled and shrugged. "The chickens and dogs dislike me somethin' awful."

She laughed then. "I imagine they do. Who is your dam?"

"My dam was Nia."

The little woman glanced sharply at the raven. "Nia, eh? She surfaced then. And you found her, Ri Fiach?"

This woman had known his mother? And the raven, too? His mother had never said anything about ravens, talking or otherwise.

"She's passed, she's passed," the raven cawed sadly.

The lady shrugged as if it were no matter, the same way his brothers had when his mother had died. Todd breathed deeply to calm the anger that rose in his breast.

"Well, hope that her whelp will do. We've little time to spare."

"He'll do, he'll do," the raven said, and preened his chest feathers, watching Todd with one bright, shiny eye, and then with the other.

"Who was his sire?"

He felt more like a horse being spoken of. Or was it that he was not worth acknowledging?

"My father was Patrick Bryne," Todd said.

"He may have raised you," she said, flipping her hands to dismiss his comment. "But he was not your sire." She sniffed delicately. "You have blood untainted by any mortal man. Nia left Renart's home after he tried to marry her to the Green Man himself. And then she found herself a mortal." Her face told Todd exactly how unsatisfactory that chain of events was.

His mother had run away? The only story his mother had ever told was that his father saw her at a dance and begged her to marry him. If his father had not sired him, who had?

As if the woman read his mind, she asked, "Did he know your blood?"

Todd shrugged. "He ne'er spoke of it, but he loved me mother with a powerful passion. His heart 'twas broken when the flux took her."

Todd remembered how his father took her body out and laid it to rest on a high hill overlooking the farm, refusing the priest's cajoling for a burial in the churchyard.

The woman laid a finger alongside her nose and took a breath as she thought. "Be that as it may, you are now adrift, offspring of Nia, raised by Master Bryne. Ri Fiach said your mortal brethren tried to kill you." She smiled, but it was not a pleasant smile. "We have a need for one such as you."

"And what need would that be?" Todd asked, and looked up toward the bird. That turned out to be a mistake, because his head suddenly swam, his stomach lurched, and he found himself on his hands and knees, sick and dizzy.

A pretty voice, like water on rocks, said, "Och, his head. They did verra nearly killed him."

Through his dizziness, he saw feet in front of him, lovely dirty, bare feet leading up to pale, shapely, narrow ankles, topped by a faded blue skirt.

He wanted to look up further, but his head would have none of it. He settled for rolling onto his side and curling up around his belly.

"Your highness," the pretty voice with the lovely bare feet said, "he'll be no help to anyone if he's not cared for. I'll see to it."

"Very well, Flanna, see to his hurts," her highness said.

And then the pretty voice, Flanna, said, "Well, do na jus' stand there, fools. Pick him up. Take him to my cottage that I can care for the poor, handsome fox dog."

She thought he was a handsome dog? His mother had always said he was a handsome fox, but mothers always thought their sons handsome.

Hands lifted him, none too gently, and carried him by the arms and legs, in a curious swinging gait that made him moan. He looked, but saw nothing but wide chests covered with filthy tunics and hands that seemed as large as shovels. He closed his eyes again.

"Fools," Flanna said, "he's not a bag of oats. Treat him like the gold he is, and bring him gently."

Gold, he was gold? He would trade any amount of gold to be in bed now.

A fair face with wide set red-gold eyes and red-gold hair blowing in the gentle breeze leaned over him. "There, there, my precious Todd," she said. It was the same pretty voice. Pretty face to go with the pretty voice and pretty ankles. And a fiery name to go with her fiery hair. "I'll get the ninnies to bring ye along fair, then we'll see to your head."

She smelled like grass and sun, and vaguely like his mother. The smell sparked memories of his mother running wild in the moonlight, the white tip of her bushy tail leading him deeper into the meadow on the other side of watery rill that was the boundary for their family farm.

He remembered her teaching him to jump high up over the grass and straight down onto a fat field mouse. Nothing had ever tasted as good as that blood and life when his sharp teeth crunched down into living flesh.

The woman laid a cool hand on his forehead, and for some reason, he thought of sun-warmed rocks under a blue sky, a breeze ruffling his fur and bringing all the news of the world to his black, twitching nose.

Before darkness took him, he wondered again what he was doing here, and what they wanted of him.

When he opened his eyes again he was in a snug room, mostly dark except for the glow of a peat fire across from him. The room smelled of sausage, herbs, porridge, the peat fire, and raw stone. He smelled only a hint of the pervasive corruption here.

He looked down and saw he was covered to the neck by a pale cream woolen quilt made up of puffy spirals. It smelled of the grass and sun, and of the woman with the red-gold eyes. He dozed again, dreaming of running after her through glorious moonlit nights, surrounded by a welter of smells and sounds.

When he awoke next, he realized that whatever the raven king and pale woman wanted, there was sure to be a price to pay, and likely in the coin of his blood as was ever the way with the mighty when it came to the lowly.

"Ah, you're awake then," the pretty voice that had succored him said. "Sit up, laddie, have some tea. If yer belly likes it well enough, I've porridge on the hearth ye can try next."

The fire-haired woman swept across the room, and Todd watched her while he managed to get himself up. Swinging his legs over the edge of the cot, he saw he wore a woolen night shirt that fell past his knees.

Had she undressed him? The thought mortified him.

She bustled about at the fire and brought him a warm mug. "Here then, have a wee bit o' that and see if ye don't feel better."

He took the mug and smelled deeply. Chamomile and rue figured prominently in the steam, and a bit of honey, which almost covered a hint of fustiness.

He sipped, felt it go all the way down his throat and settle in his belly with a sigh. "Thank ye, mban. My name is Todd Bryne, and I am at your service."

She laughed, a tinkle of merriment that he would do anything to hear again. "Ye're no much for service at the moment, Todd Bryne, but I'll remember." She stared down at him a moment, then blushed. "Och, where's me manners? My name is Flanna Maguire."

Red and dun-haired, her names meant. Todd sniffed again and she smiled at him, revealing white teeth with two sharp canines. "Aye, take a deep breath. We're cousins of a long sort, you and I. Renart is my great-grandfather's cousin."

So they were cousins, but far and away from consanguinity. That made a bit of warmth settle in along with the tea. He smiled and took another sip.

She didn't look old enough that Renart could be her great grand-father. Unless the old codger was busier than Todd knew. And he knew little but the name and his relationship to it.

"And so how do ye come to be here in this land? And just where is it?" he asked.

"Ye be in Faerie, young Todd. Summerland. And ye be here at the behest of Mab, queen of Faerie. She sent Ri Fiach to find a likely soul to save us, and he brought you."

Todd shook his head and immediately regretted it. It seemed a great bell had taken up residence there and was clanging, the clapper banging where Colin had hit him. He put one hand back to touch the ragged bump and felt instead cloth padding. A strip of cloth went round his head, tied in a knot on his brow.

"Yes, quite a goose egg on yer head. Did ye fall?"

He started to shake his head, then thought better of it. "My brother coshed me."

"Was it brotherly rage?"

"No. We've never had much love between us. He was trying to kill me. I caught my brothers cheating a neighbor."

Flanna's mouth twisted thoughtfully. "Hmm," she said. "Just as well ye be here then."

He finished the tea and she took the mug. "Ye feel like a bit o' porridge then?"

Todd thought about it for a moment. It had been since lunch yesterday that he'd eaten last. The nausea had faded and he could feel the gnaw of hunger. "A bit," he agreed.

"Come to the table. Do ye need help up?"

He started to stand and sat back, the bell gonging in his head so he couldn't catch his balance.

"Here," Flanna gave him an arm and hoisted him up. Her hands were strong and capable, but kind. She led him to the rough table and sat him down. He let his hands down into his lap, and squeezed his eyes shut against the thudding.

Todd heard a thunk as she set a bowl down in front of him. He opened his eyes and cupped his hands around it. The warmth on his skin was pleasant. He sniffed and smelled bits of venison and berries and greens with the same faint hint of rot. He lifted the spoon and tasted. The flavor filled his mouth and ran down into his belly as he swallowed. He'd eaten and drank much worse in the middle of winter, and beggars were never choosy.

The gnaw suddenly turned ravenous and he ate as fast as was

polite. She watched and filled it again when it was apparent he could keep it down. He set the spoon in the bowl at last, and leaned back in the chair.

"Better?"

He belched. It was only then that he remembered the tales of the unwary who ate in Faerie lands and came to regret it.

Ah, well. What did he have to look to on the other side of that tunnel?

His thoughts must have shown on his face because she nodded with a quick grin that made her look wicked. He wanted to make her grin like that again.

She must have seen that, too, because she flushed a deep red that raced down her face and across the top of her breasts.

Flustered, she said, "Queen Mab is eager to see you if you can clean up and face her."

Todd considered. The raven, a king, he remembered, had rescued him, and this queen of the faeries wanted him to save something. He wondered if it was related to the pervasive rot he smelled.

"And is she a young queen, this Mab?"

Flanna barked a laugh. "Och, nay, she's been the queen for centuries. She nay grows old, they none of them do."

Todd considered the trouble he now found himself in. Nothing for it, then, but to go forward through to the end.

"If you could get my clothes, I'd be grateful. Then I will meet this queen."

After a washup, a shave, and back in his newly cleaned and mended clothing, Todd felt ready to face the queen.

Flanna led him through a wide meadow filled with deer that fled at their approach, followed by young fawns kicking up their heels as they leaped away.

If it was always summer, did the fawns grow up? Did the stags rut and fight out of season? He shook his head. It was too much for the likes of him to understand.

At last, Flanna led him into the forest and a small clearing. She gestured him forward, hanging back at the edge of the trees. Queen Mab sat at the far edge of the circle, ensconced in an ornate woven throne made of living saplings. He saw none of the dying leaves, but could tell the creation was carefully tended, no doubt snipped of any offending imperfections. Squirrels and birds flitted amongst the branches.

Tall, lithe men flanked the chair. They had the same silver hair as their queen, but pulled back tightly into a club at the nape of their necks, and tied with leather thongs decorated with silver and gemstone beads. They wore boiled leather armor and stared at him, seeming to take his measure and find him lacking.

Todd stood a bit taller and held his head high against that judgment. Their queen knew what he was, and there was no shame or danger for it here.

He approached until one of the guards gestured him to stop. Bowing in what he hoped was a courtly manner, he stood waiting for the queen to say her piece.

Under the honest smell of woods, flowers, and the wine she sipped as she stared at him, he caught the ever-present hint of rot.

Her eyes seemed tired as she looked down at a goldfinch that had the temerity to land on the lip of her cup. Did her queenly manner slip just a bit as she flicked her fingers, startling it away?

The bird flew off, circling to dive near Todd's face. He stood, letting the little bird be, and kept his eyes on the queen. What would it be like to rule for centuries? Wouldn't it grow onerous? Would the cycle of life prick at her?

"So," she said, all hint of any weariness gone from her demeanor. "Ri Fiach has brought you to Us to be Our savior."

"And what would you be needin' savin' from?"

"The Robin King. He seeks to invade My lands, take summer from the Wren King."

The battle between robin and wren was ever fought at the solstices. It was a never-ending battle. But how could this fight to bring the light back figure in a land that was always summer?

"And what do I have to do with such an ancient fight?"

She regarded him for a long moment and the clearing seemed to go silent, still, as if all the world held the same breath.

Then she spoke. "I wish for the robin to not prevail. Have you not noticed, young Todd, that the winters in the mortal realms are harsher?" She shook her head. "No, you're just a kit still. Perhaps Renart would have told you had your mother not taken her own road."

She held a hand up to forestall his indignant defense. "Take My word, young fox. I watch what happens in the world of Man. The winters are overlong there lately, the summers too cool for crops to grow, the rivers stay frozen months too long."

What she said was true. His father had told of his youth, when the year turned as it should, the harvest had been bountiful, and they had stayed the hand of famine. Todd had never seen the year turn smoothly as his father told. Everything that grew or lived upon the land suffered from long winters and cool summers for as long as he had lived.

Famine had caught his family in an especially tight grip during the depths of last year's winter, taking his father before he had to face another spring that came too late to plant.

"The Robin King has held the seasons in the mortal world in his tight grip of late," the queen said. "And he seeks to extend his dominion into My land." Her voice became harsh, angry with indignation.

How could that be? Was she not a mighty queen? He could smell the magic on her. How could she allow the mortal world to creep through? Is that what caused the rot?

"And so, what would you have me do?"

"Be My Wren King and defeat the Robin King on the solstice in My name. Protect My land from his depredations." She gestured at the trees with their dying leaves.

Todd had never been much of a fighter. Foxes practiced stealth and wit over brawn and bluster. He looked about the clearing. Summer held sway here even with the subtle decay that seemed so pervasive. The sun was bright, the land was green, and the squirrels he could see were plump, the deer plentiful.

There was more to this than just the changing of seasons. He looked more closely at Mab. She appeared young, just a bit older than his twenty summers. But Flanna had said she was ancient.

"I be no wren or king," Todd said. "Nor be I much a fighter, yer majesty."

"But you're out of Renart and you've a canny wit. You managed to stay safe in the world of men. You can defeat one little robin."

"Aren't ye looking for a wren, in truth?"

She tapped one finger on the arm of her chair. The squirrels fled for the safety of the trees.

"I'm looking for someone who will protect and preserve my kingdom. The Wren King has failed me. It's time for something new. Ri Fiach thinks it's time for a fox, evidently. I think perhaps he chose poorly."

"Well, I never asked to be chosen."

She lifted her chin a bit, looked down at him from that angle. "Well, you can certainly go the way you came. I am sure your brothers have followed your tracks and will be ready to greet you when you return."

"Ah, but won't time have passed anon while I've tarried here?"

She smiled, but it held no warmth and less humor. "I am the queen of Summerland, and I control the keys to the doorways."

Todd thought about it. His choice was to suffer the bitter cold and a meeting with his brothers that would leave him rotting in the woods at their hands. Or meet the Wren King and have a death on his hands. Either way, it seemed there would be a death.

"It seems as though I'll be doin' some choosin' then. And if I prevail in this contest?"

"Then I give you a wife and a home befitting the savior of Summerland. Fail and you shall be buried as befits the fallen king."

Likely helped along by one of the warriors that flanked her. He could smell Flanna behind him. Would she be the wife? A snatch of the dream where he had chased her fire red and dun hair surfaced, and a smile flickered at his mouth.

"Then, yer majesty, it seems ye have found yer paladin." He made a bow and gave her a saucy folderol with his right hand.

"Now what?" he asked her.

"Now you swear fealty to me."

A warrior stepped out and bade him kneel and swear on his honor that he would obey her and honor his commitment to save the kingdom.

"Rise, fox dog, and go out to seek how best to fulfill My command. The Solstice is two days away. Be at the festival grounds in time for the battle. You must prevail by sunset." Mab nodded down at him regally, then flicked her fingers in dismissal.

Flanna came forward to take his hand, and led him from the audience.

Where would he search, and how would he prevail against a Robin King?

As they made their way back to Flanna's hut, she pointed east. "Leave your clothes at the base of the grandfather ash," she said.

Ah, so then he would not be searching as a man.

He turned to leave, but she caught his hand. It was hard and strong from work, but her touch was tender. Looking into her red gold eyes, he saw another hint of his dream, and he knew she saw it too.

"I wish ye luck, Todd."

Her words held an intensity that was more fervent than kindness.

What was this battle about then? What was at stake for Summerland? And what lay under that wish for fortune?

He smiled back at her and lifted the hand she didn't hold. "I'll take it," he said, making as if to grasp her offering from the air.

She nodded. "Wise ye are, Todd; 'tis the left hand that receives and the right that gives. Ri Fiach was true in his search."

With that she slipped her hand from his and headed for her home, skirts swishing and the sun playing in the fire of her hair.

He took a deep breath to capture her scent, and stepped off the path into the deep grass that bordered the lane. He made for the brush and slipped amongst the dark and cool thickets until he found the tree she meant. It was a huge tree, wider around than he could reach and taller than ten men, with great branches lifting to the sky. There was a notch at the bottom, enough for someone to claim for a den. He checked to see that no creature was in residence.

Then he stripped his clothes off, laying them neatly in the depression, and stood. Lifting his nose to the sky, he sniffed, breathing deeply, letting the day and all its possibilities embrace him.

He dropped to all fours and let the fox inside him rise up as his human self fell away. He felt the moist soil beneath his paws. Right here it smelled intensely of Flanna and that warned off the other small animals. He shook himself from the tip of his black nose to the fluffy end of his dun-tipped tail and set off, looking for what he needed to know.

He put his nose to the ground, smelling Summerland. This forest held the same leaf mulch, discarded feathers, owl pellets, deer scat, and horse dung as his forest at home, but with the spicy smell of fairies intermingled throughout.

And, underneath it all, a sense of age, of decay.

He realized, as he made his way through the trees and brush, there was no hint of winter's breath. Crossing out of the forest, he came upon a field. His ears pricked up as he took in the industrious mice that lived here. He smiled a foxy grin and then padded quietly into the grass. Standing in the sudden silence, he swiveled his ears as he listened for them to settle.

There. His head craned to his left. He hunched, gathered himself, and sprang up and over the grass coming down upon the hapless creature, which he bit and swallowed in two warm and crunchy gulps. But it had that same corruption, which ruined the flavor. He gave up hunting and sought a place to rest and think.

Settling under a bush, he reveled in the dappled sunlight, listening to the calls of the birds. At last he heard the "check, check, churrrrr," of a bull wren in the thicket off to his right. He rose and padded silently around the backside of the thicket, where he lay and groomed himself as the bird called to its jenny.

Watching from the corner of his eye, he saw the tiny bird. He smiled at the round brown puff ball, with his bright beady eyes and tiny beak.

And how would he know which was the king? And what would he say to him? Offer to fight the Robin King for him so that Summerland was saved?

His fur did not lie smoothly under that idea, nor did the idea smell right.

His thoughts were interrupted by a series of tweets and chirps.

Todd looked up and saw a cock robin staring down at him from the branch of an ash tree, head tipped so that one bright eye could take his measure.

"Fox," the bird chirped softly. "Come with me."

He flew off of the branch, around in a circle, and away toward the east, circling about to see if Todd followed.

Todd watched him for a long moment, then got up and trotted after him into a cluster of trees. The robin waited for him, perched on the jagged branch of a fallen tree.

"You watch for the Wren King," the bird said.

Todd sniffed at a flower. It smelled sweet, but with the same underlying scent of decay about it. He sneezed.

"I am the Robin King," the bird said. "I will defeat the Wren King."

Todd found a very interesting patch of grass. A mouse had been busy here this morning. Its droppings littered the ground, leading off through the tufts of grass. The trail called to him. Not so much to fill his belly. No, that was full. But more to avoid what he thought was becoming a conundrum.

He knew nothing of this land, the people, the nitty politics that drove their lives. He had been brought here, rescued, yes, but it seemed more and more that there was a morass of danger here, and he had not had enough time to sniff out the safe path.

"You are central to Mab's hopes," the robin said. "But her hopes are vain. You are no Wren King. You cannot play one, no matter her command."

The bird was right. Todd was a fox, not a bird. He had no role in this ancient cycle. "What are her hopes?" Todd lay down and worried the mud-caked fur between his pads.

"The Queen hopes to hold back time, to stop the world from turning, make the natural cycles grind to a halt. She hopes she can turn you to that purpose."

A cricket chirped to his left. One ear swiveled to home in on it. "Come to me, my love, come my love, accept my love," the insect called. Todd spat mud and switched to the other paw.

"What do you fear?" Todd asked. "Do you fear the Wren King can hold you back?"

"Chhak, chhak, chhak," the robin laughed. "Easier to hope I can stop time."

The bird flew down and landed on the ground, careful, Todd noticed, to stay out of range of his mouth.

"Then what, Robin King? What am I to do?"

"Play the part the Queen has brought you here for."

Todd leaned back, whiskers lifted in surprise.

"Me? I am no wren. And what part could I play in the ancient battle between light and dark?"

The robin hopped closer and tapped at Todd's paw with his beak, hopping back when Todd started and leaped to all fours, his bushy tail up in the air.

"You are not Renart's better blood. This is no battle between light and dark." The bird tchhed, his beak clicking in disgust, or perhaps sorrow. "How do the boys do it?"

Todd stared at the bird, who was now seemingly looking for worms in the moist earth.

The boys in the village below Todd's farm made straw wings and tails or put on a cape and a fancy hat for a crown. Then they had a mock battle in the pasture surrounding the town, shouting and lunging at each other until the Wren King was thrown down and the Robin King strutted victorious about the village square, leading everyone to a feast.

"Foxes don't make wings, and I don't think Ri Fiach brought me here as a man to pretend to be a bird." He scratched his ear and snapped at a fly that came too close. The breeze turned and he smelled deer in the woods, resting in the heat of the day, snugged down in the thick growth that crowded between the trees.

"You're right about foxes, but you're no man, nor mortal either."

Todd's ears pricked forward, and he stared at the robin, who pretended to be absorbed in the hunt for worms. He could tell the bird would fly away at the least twitch right now, so he stayed still.

"How do you know?" he asked casually.

"Nia was a kind one. She laid out bread every morning and turned the compost every day to lay bare the juicy worms. Word of her kindness spread, following her even after she left her father's house."

Some of Todd's earliest memories were of his mother feeding the wild birds.

"Where did she go when she left her father's house?" he asked. She had never spoken to Todd of her life before marrying, except to say his grandsire was Renart, Fox King. She had said working the farm and taking him into the forest as a fox kit to learn to hunt were all that mattered.

"She lived on the ragged edges of Summerland for a time," the Robin King said, "hunting mice and rabbits, lying on sun-warmed rocks, staring into the stars at night. That is where she met Pieleto."

The name was a pixie name. They were notorious for their trick-ster ways. They lied, stole, misled, prevaricated. Not out of malice. Just because.

"Ah, you begin to see. Your heritage is what Ri Fiach brought to bear. He sees the truth where Mab sees only her own comfort, which is a lie, and wounds the land and all who live here."

"And how is this my portion?"

"Chhhak, chhhak, chhhhack," the robin laughed, his wings flap-ping so that he hip-hopped in a little dance. "Renart would be ashamed and so would Pieleto. And your mother, well, she would only turn away from your ignorance and your oath breaking."

That was a sharp knife in his belly. In her human form, his mother never chided when she caught people in a lie or an obvious mistake. She just turned away. It had had no effect on his brothers, except to embolden them.

But now, if Todd could have flushed, he would have. He had promised to protect this land. And he was missing the path to keeping his word. His tail drooped and he shut his mouth with a clack.

"I am not like my grandfather or my father."

But that was a lie. Todd had played pranks on his brothers and the village children as long as he could remember. He loved jokes, and would sit and listen to the old men and the rare bards when they came, memorizing their stories, their riddles, their japes and puns, repeating them endlessly to the sheep.

"Evidently. Well, perhaps your brothers have given up and the storm has moved on." The robin's voice didn't sound hopeful.

With that he hopped twice and took wing.

Todd got up and stretched. He trotted through the trees, sniffing at the mulch, some deer scat, and followed a trail that smelt strongly of unshod horse and hounds. They had passed through last night, gauging from the scent.

He veered off on a deer trail and found himself on a ridge overlooking a broad, green plain cut through the middle by a mighty green river. In the very center of the plain, he saw a construct emerging from the grass, with people swarming over it like ants.

Summerland was a beautiful, bright land. Its inherent magic overlaid everything, sparkling like frost on a sunny morning. It hurt him to think of it wounded, suffering.

He pictured Flanna trotting across that green expanse, the tip of her tail beckoning him to follow. He imagined she must as beautiful a vixen as she was a woman. He could make a place with her. He would not need to hide who he was.

Turning uneasily to settle himself, he stretched out on the rocks and let the warmth sink into his bones as he pondered the robin's words.

He did not want to go back out through that tunnel into winter. He did not want to face his brothers. And the Watch, the Church, and the Mortal world would never be a comfortable fit for him. There would always be a danger of being discovered for what he was.

Here, he was accepted for who he was.

But would he be accepted if he did as the Robin King intimated? And how would he do it? He had no place in the ancient battle against the Wren King.

The smell of decay was on the breeze. It was in his fur, on his tongue.

He got up and left the way he came, ending up at the ash tree where he'd left his clothes. Standing, he stretched his front paws as high as he could against the tree trunk, and yawned widely, letting the human rise up and the fox fall away.

The cool breeze on the forest verge brought goose bumps to his naked skin, and he shivered. Quickly donning his clothes, he made his way back to Flanna's hut.

When he reached the door, he knocked softly.

"Come in, Todd, come in and sit. I've some venison stew on."

They ate quietly and she watched him from under her lashes, from the corner of her eye as she took the dishes, and in a quick glimpse as she tidied the table.

"Sit by the fire wi' me, will ye?" she asked, offering her hand. He took it and they settled in on the heavy wooden chairs. He could smell her and his mother, recognizing now that he smelled the vixen in Flanna, the same scent he had grown up with. He also smelled her warmth, her desire, as she turned her face to him. He met it, tasting her lips with his own, brushing his fingers over her cheeks, her throat, her breasts.

Later, he stroked her flanks, bare now in the glow of the dying fire. He wondered if she was giving him a hint of what his prize would be should he prove Ri Fiach's hopes.

And if she would share his fate should he fail.

As he rose over her again, and stared down at her milky skin and the fire in her eyes, he swore he would not fail.

〜

The morning of the solstice dawned bright. He left Flanna with a kiss and went to the meadow where he harvested grasses and several sticks. Sitting cross-legged, he twisted the long stems into bundles and tied them onto the twigs. When he was happy with his work, he found mud and covered them in a thick coat.

Afterward, he left them drying in the sun and went to a rill bubbling over rocks. Kneeling down, he drank his fill of cool water.

By the time the sun was high overhead, they were dry. He cut his hand across the palm and painted the blood over the breast piece. Washing his hand in the same rill, he wiped his hand on a twist of grass, and sought out the robin king. Todd found him sitting on a tree branch in the same clearing they had spoken before.

"Where do ye do battle then?" Todd asked the bird.

"Down on the meadow in the center of Summerland."

Ah, where he had seen the frenzied activity. "The queen will be there?"

The robin dipped his head in agreement. "It's quite the festival. They build a viewing stand, and mummers and dancers lead the queen's procession. Afterward, they set up planks for feasting as they welcome the new year."

"And you and the Wren King do battle there as she watches?"

"Yes, and her son, Oberon, and his wife, and all the courtiers."

"What happens to the wren?"

The bird hopped to a new branch. "The ancient circle turns. He goes to our castle to rule over the great wheel of the year, so that order is maintained until it is time for him to battle me again." He ruffled his feathers. "The king dies. Long live the king. The mortals understand that. They see the wheel of life because it turns their own lives. Faeries forget because they are ageless, outside that circle."

Todd digested that. "I wish ye well then, Robin King."

"And you, fox."

Todd nodded and left, his heart full of sadness and fear. He returned to gather up his bundles of grass and twigs, now light brown with their coat of dried mud and deep red with dried blood.

He set out on a trail that would lead him to the center of the plain. The sun was at its zenith and the path seemed to speed him on his way, as if it hurried him to meet his destiny.

When he arrived at the edge of the festival grounds, he stood off to the side, taking it all in. The land must have been used for a long time, because the grounds had been pounded flat and were devoid of any vegetation. Colorful tents and booths with pennants snapping in the breeze lined the edge of the great circle.

Even now, merchants hawked their wares—wines, punches, delicacies from faraway lands, fine garments, weapons, toys. The air was pungent with the smell of food and leather and spices, but soiled by the same scent of corruption.

As he gaped at the merchandise laid out, Todd realized he had no idea there was this much to be had in the world. It made him feel small and inconsequential. Who was he to champion anyone or anything?

He headed into the crush of arriving revelers. They called out to him, calling him their Wren King, and wishing him good fortune. Word spread as they pointed to him.

He tried to blend into the hustle and bustle, but he stood out from the tall and graceful people with their pale hair, paler skin, and bright clothing. He felt faintly ashamed of his clothing, which made him angry. He was a farmer, or had been a farmer, but he had led an honest life.

The faeries wouldn't let him keep to the verge. They made way for him, urging him through the center of the crush with bright laughter and much waving of beringed hands, creating a sparkling rainbow around him.

Making his way reluctantly through the festival, he found a pounded circle some fifty feet across, marked off with stakes and ribbons. This was the combat area. It was fronted by a tall stand of benches rising up at least three times his height.

The center of the viewing stand was carpeted with colorful rugs that spanned the first six rows. The first row held the queen's living throne, decked in gay flowers. Other stately carved wooden chairs took up the rows behind it. Pennants waved atop poles marking the royal seating area, and a handful of warriors stood in a loose square around it. He guessed the rest of the benches would fill with richly dressed courtiers, while more common folk stood around the perimeter.

He made his way around behind the stand. The shouts of the crowd seemed quieter, farther away, and he leaned against a post to think.

"You're here, you're here," he heard above him. Looking up, he saw Ri Fiach perched high up on a cross beam.

"I am. I am not sure what I be doin' though."

"You will, you will." The raven leaped off the beam and landed on one at Todd's eye level. "You see, you see."

Todd shook his head. "More I smell. There's decay here. That's what's wrong. Nothing to do with the Robin King or the Wren King."

The raven said nothing, but leaned out to tap his beak on the bundles of mud-covered twigs.

"She said she wanted a champion," Todd said in response to the unasked question. "So here I am."

"Caw, caw, caw," the raven laughed harshly, and flew off the beam and up into the sky.

A warrior came around the corner and spotted him. "You can't be here." Then he looked again. "Ah, the fox dog. The queen will want you out front." He spotted the bundles under Todd's arm. "What's that?"

"It's for the battle."

The warrior looked at him and sniffed at the apparent silliness of a fox. "Well," he said doubtfully, "come along then."

"I need to put this on."

The warrior considered. "Very well. Prepare and I will return. You'll make your entrance as part of her procession."

Todd set the bundle down, his hands shaking. He took off his cape and hung it over a cross beam. His throat was tight. He would rather take off his clothes, change, and flee into the forest, but the queen had dogs and huntsmen. They would find him, and then he would wish he had gone back through the tunnel.

It was not too late. He still could take his chances in the mortal world.

But his dream of the dun tip of Flanna's tail calling kept him here. He wanted her. He wanted to keep his word. And he wanted to right this wrong.

Quickly, he tied on the wings, the red chest piece, and knotted the cord for the tail around his waist. The brown woven cap with its eyeholes fit closely down over his head, sloping over his nose to end in a short beak.

He heard the flutes and drums and tinkling just as the same soldier came to retrieve him. The warrior shook his head as he took in the rough costume. "Come along then."

Mab frowned as she saw Todd on the side of the road. Todd flushed at her distaste, cocked his head, crossed one wing over his chest, and made what he hoped was a graceful leg.

Then he goggled at the line behind the her, headed by a stag with an immense antler rack, a huge rabbit, birds, and other animals, followed by faeries, satyrs, giants, and other creatures he had no names for.

He collected himself at a nudge from the guard, and eased himself into the place the guard pointed to behind the queen and her son, who walked with a beautiful woman that smelled of the spring flowers woven into the silver coil of her hair.

"Who's that," he whispered to the faerie guard.

"Titania, Oberon's wife," the guard whispered back, and signaled him to hush.

The queen wore an elaborate, rust-colored gown with cloth of gold trim. An immense silver crown studded with a rainbow of jewels rode atop her head. She held her head up, her eyes on the reviewing stand as she marched steadily, in time to the music, her hand on a warrior's arm. But from his vantage, Todd could see the muscles of her hand tensed in an effort to keep her poise and her balance.

He also noticed she danced none of the graceful steps everyone else performed as they jingled bells and beat drums and tootled on horns on their way up the road.

Summerland's inhabitants flanked the entrance, fronted by rows of warriors. The folk bowed and Queen Mab inclined her head slightly from side to side, acknowledging her subjects.

Todd expected the crown to slide, but it stayed in place. He smelled enchantment and wondered if it was helping the heavy headpiece remain secure.

Ri Fiach swooped and dove above them, cawing "Solstice approaches, Solstice approaches," counterpointing the joyous noise the revelers made.

Todd stood uncertainly as two warriors settled Mab on her throne. Her son and his wife stepped up to the next row on the carpet, seating themselves in a pair of magnificently carved chairs. Oberon's sported stag horns arching over the top, and Titania's held a bower hosting live birds that peeped and chirped as she sat and arranged her skirts.

Todd was mesmerized by her. Titania exuded life and energy, and her smile was soft as she caught Todd's glance. She inclined her head and Todd bowed back.

The crowd settled as a horn blew a long note, the sound curling around the grounds like a swallow riding an afternoon breeze. When the sound died away, the people turned expectantly to the Queen.

She stood. "We gather today to witness the battle between the Robin King and the Wren King. Although, I think Our Robin has found his wings in a ditch. If you had asked, We would have found you suitable raiment." She scowled at him.

Everyone tittered at her words. The raven perched atop one of the poles and stared down at him.

Todd swallowed, his mouth gone dry, his legs suddenly shaking. This was far and away from putting eggs in his brother's seat, or a frog down Mistress Martin's churn.

"No matter. Fox, take your place." She sat, smoothing her skirts before placing her hands on the throne arms.

He saw that they gripped firmly, as if she expected to fall.

He walked to the center of the beaten circle and turned to see everyone ranged about him. They looked at him, with eyes open wide for the battle they had come to see. He was afraid he would disappoint them.

"Chancellor," Mab cried imperiously. "Call out the Wren King."

"Aye," Todd said before the servant standing beside the queen could speak, his voice echoing about the circle. "I call ye out, Queen Mab. Ye be the Wren King, and I the Robin King come to battle for Summerland."

Everyone drew a breath and it seemed like the world paused. Then the crowd ringing the circle gasped at his words and a susurration of questions rose up.

The Queen looked confused and then furious. "Ri Fiach, I think your choice was foolish," she said. "This stupid fox does not know the story he acts in." She flicked her fingers. "Remove him from the field." Two warriors stepped out to do her bidding.

"Nay, Queen Mab," Todd said, his voice only faintly quivering. "I know the story and I ken my part. You asked for a champion to protect your kingdom." He pirouetted to scan the faeries and animals circling the field. They stared at him solemnly. He saw Flanna, her eyes trained on him like a hawk to a rabbit, and his heart thumped hard.

He returned to the head of the circle and said, "You said 'twas time for something new. Aye. Tis time for something new. I hae seen the state of your kingdom, Majesty. Tis rotting from the heart. Yer heart. Ye are the lifeblood of the kingdom and ye hae no strength anymore. I smell it on ye, I smell it in the land and those that live upon it. Everyone must know it and fear keeps them from speaking the truth.

"It is time for the wheel to turn. Ye are the Wren and I the Robin. I challenge ye for yer right to rule this fair land. Let us battle now before the solstice overtakes us."

Mab stared at him, fury in her eyes.

"Very well, then, fox. I choose a champion to battle you in this ridiculous claim. Then We shall get on with this gathering." She gestured to one of the warriors standing next to her. He drew a silver sword from an ornate leather scabbard and stepped forward.

Todd's heart leapt into his throat. The warrior's face was bland, but his eyes were sharp. He would have no trouble besting Todd, and he knew it.

Todd straightened as tall as he could go and took a breath, hoping his voice would remain strong. "Nay, your majesty," he said. "I am yer kingdom's chosen champion. I accepted in front of witnesses. Ye must do battle with me or decline the challenge, forfeiting yer throne."

The warrior halted uncertainly, looking back toward his queen. Mab's hands tightened on the arms of the woven chair and then she stood tall, brushing off the hands that hurried to help her.

"You've got pluck, little fox dog, I'll grant you that." Todd saw her sway. Did any of the others? He searched the viewing stands. Oberon, Mab's son, stared at his dam, as did the Raven King and all of the courtiers ranged behind her.

"But you'll not stand there and bandy words with Me," the queen said, gesturing to the knight again.

The faerie knight moved toward him, the sword weaving a circle around where he would plunge the tip into Todd's heart.

Todd's legs quivered and his belly went cold. He was a pawn in an ancient game. The queen cared nothing for him. Neither did the Raven King. The question now was whether she cared about her kingdom more than her throne.

But he would fight the best he could, because otherwise he was going to die, and his hopes for Flanna would be gone with his last breath.

"Hold," called the chancellor, his brilliant blue tunic and silver trousers shining in the afternoon sun.

The circle gasped again as one. Someone shouted, "The Robin King and the Wren King battle."

Everyone looked up, and Todd risked a glance to the west. The sun was falling toward the horizon. From the center of that brilliant ball came a small figure, hurtling toward the Wren King, who flitted over Mab's head. The figure resolved itself into the Robin King, his feathers gilded by the setting sun. The wren dodged, and the robin harried him, forcing him to fly erratically.

"What is this, Chancellor?" the queen demanded of the faerie who had countermanded her. "How dare you defy Me?"

"The paladin is in the right," he said. "You appointed him to protect and preserve your kingdom. He has found the enemy of the kingdom and rightfully challenged it. You, your majesty, must answer the challenge. You cannot order a champion to battle the champion you chose."

The queen stared at the faerie lord, who had stepped down from the stand to take a place beside Todd.

"But how can I answer this challenge? I am no warrior."

And I cannot kill a queen, Todd thought. The idea of laying hands on her made him sick to think of it, and ashamed to imagine her coming to such an end through his agency. And he would not subject the fox in him to serve as the agent for such a useless death. No, he had taken the job on two legs, and he would see it through the same.

The Robin King forced the Wren King to dodge down over the queen's head. She flicked her hand, hitting the tiny bird so that he half fell, half flew, away from her. The robin pursued, allowing him no chance to gather his wits or his breath.

The Robin King seemed to be everywhere, heading the wren off when he would strive for distance, diving at him from above, to force him to stay low. There was no tree, no shrub, no bush on the battle-ground to offer haven.

The Wren King seemed panicked, seeking a way out, swooping over the crowd, only to be chivvied back to the center of the circle again by the Robin King.

And the sun fell relentlessly to the horizon.

"But, your majesty," the chancellor said in a reasonable voice, "you are the might of Summerland. You are the protector we all look to. If you cannot best a fox dog dressed as a robin, how can you protect the land and your subjects? How can you claim the throne to Summerland?"

Queen Mab paused, realizing she had misstepped. "But who

would rule then?" she asked, her voice gaining a whining edge. "Sons cannot succeed the crown, and my son's wife is a spiteful brat."

Todd looked up to see Oberon lay a hand on his wife's arm to stifle her indignant outburst.

"That is the concern of the future," the chancellor said. "It is ever the bane of parents that they can only do the best for their children, then send them into the world to make their own way." He gestured at Todd, sweating in the muddy bird outfit, to come closer, and then glanced back to Mab. "Now you must choose. Battle for the prosperity of your kingdom or yield."

Mab glanced from her chancellor to the crowd circling her, and back to Todd. Her eyes blazed furiously as she stepped down from the stand, one hand on a warrior's shoulder. She walked into the circle and brought her hands up.

Todd leaped away just as bolts of blue power shot from her fists. The ground erupted in a spray of dirt. Small rocks pelted Todd as he danced out of range.

The crowd shouted, whether in glee or relief, Todd had no idea. Just as he had no idea what to do. Neither Todd the mortal nor Todd the fox fought; no, they only ran and hid, and doubled back, leading a merry chase.

Well, then, to each his own. He turned and waggled his muddy robin tail at her, looking back over his shoulder cheekily. His insolence was rewarded with laughter from the crowd and another blast that caught his twig and grass tail, pushing him off balance and onto his hands and knees.

The crowd jeered. He looked back to see the muddy branches smoking. If they hadn't been coated in mud, they would have gone up in flame.

"Stop running, fox dog," the queen shouted. "Fight Me if that is what you intend. This is not a hunt. It is a battle."

The wren swooped low, right over Todd's head, in his efforts to avoid the robin's attacks. He could hear the whir of the bird's tiny wings as he struggled to gain an advantage.

Todd ran full at the queen, who smiled cruelly and raised her hands. He could smell the enchantment grow like a pot ready to boil, and zagged just as she lobbed the enchantment at him. It almost struck its mark, but instead caught the heel of his boot and burned all the way through.

Todd stumbled and the crowd roared. He recovered and hopped as he pulled off his boot. The other followed and he taunted her with it, throwing the boot. It landed at her feet, and she kicked it away contemptuously.

As a Robin King, he was not very impressive. He circled around Mab, watching for any opening, anything that would give him an idea of what to do. She shot another bolt at him and his right wing smoldered. He tore it off and threw it at her. She batted it away.

Her face contorted into a rictus of cruelty and anger. Working her hands, she created a ball of blue energy that crackled and hissed with sparks. She shaped it lovingly, caressing it as she stared at Todd.

"You dare to challenge Me, fox dog? You think you are My champion, that you protect the land? I will show you." With one hand, she crooked a finger and Todd began to walk toward her.

What was he doing? He was walking to his doom. She was going to blast him dead. But he couldn't stop his feet. He tried dancing, backing, leaping, skipping, standing still, but nothing worked.

The crowd roared and laughed and shrieked. He could make out no words, only the raw emotions of hatred, horror, and glee.

As he was drawn inexorably toward the queen of Summerland, to his demise, he saw Flanna. Her eyes were beautiful, even far away. The setting sun caught her hair and set it gloriously on fire. She bared her teeth and they were white against her red lips.

He turned away, unable to bear the sight. Looking back to Queen Mab, he saw her face turned into an unrecognizable mask. And then he understood. He stopped fighting. He let her pull him toward her, his feet dragging over the hard-packed ground.

He had sworn an oath to protect the kingdom, but he had also sworn to obey her.

When he was in front of her, she gestured and he slumped to his knees.

"I am yer champion, sworn to protect yer land, yer majesty," Todd said softly. "And yet, I also swore to obey ye. 'Tis the same with the land. Summerland is yer subject as much as these folk gathered here. They must obey ye even as ye corrupt them with yer weakness, yer breach of the sacred trust ye swore as ruler."

Mab paused, the enchantment sparking in her hand. Todd could smell it thickly, like he was suffocating in a bed of heady rose petals. The sparks dripping off of it burned where they touched his skin, but he stayed impassive, waiting for his end.

The Queen looked at Todd and to her riotous subjects. Her eyes blazed with hatred and sadness by turns. The ball of power bounced lightly, ready to descend upon him.

Then she shook her head, and her shoulders sank.

"Perhaps Ri Fiach chose well after all," she said sadly. "I am tired. I want My land to be abundant, I want My subjects to prosper. They do neither now, nor have they for some time. And it is true; I am no longer a font of abundance. I am old and foolish to boot." She flicked her hand and the enchantment drifted away, shredding on the breeze, fading the same as the sunlight from the fiery ball dipping below the horizon.

The crowd stilled, confused. Mab lifted the crown from her head, and the crowd gasped as one when they realized what it meant.

At that moment, the robin drove the wren down to the ground on Mab's right. The poor Wren King lay on the hard-packed earth exhausted and panting, while the robin swooped victoriously overhead and the people cheered.

"The Robin King prevails, the new year is upon us, the light returns," the crowd chanted.

"But I still think My daughter-in-law is an insufferable child," she said to Todd as the chancellor approached. "And I shudder to think of what the kingdom will endure before she finds sense."

She looked to the wren on the ground and back to the chancellor as she handed him the crown.

"Oh, do get up, Robin King," she added, glancing down at Todd.

"Kings should never grovel on the ground. And take off that ridiculous costume."

Todd stood and untied the rest of the costume. He was covered in muddy sweat and itched abominably. His heel pained him, and he lifted it to find a scorched mark on it.

"Thank ye, yer majesty."

"I suppose I should thank you. But go on with you now. I promised you a wife and a home befitting your station should you prevail. Go on, see to the wife. The home will be arranged shortly."

The chancellor offered his arm, and she took it gratefully, moving slowly off the grounds as if she were an old crone, aching in every joint.

"Well, ye've done well enough, fox," he heard from behind him.

Turning he saw Flanna standing nonchalantly a few steps away, one foot scratching at the hard-packed earth.

"I did what she commanded."

She smiled then, and his heart swelled.

"And thanks to ye; we've a new year to look forward to and a return to more than the light. Come. Ye need a bath, and sumpin' to fill yer belly."

The look she gave him said there would be more than that waiting, and he bowed to her, sweeping his hand over his leg gallantly.

As he bowed, he saw the wren. Picking the tiny bird up gently, he cradled him to his breast. The wren's heart pounded as he lay limp in Todd's hands.

"Och, poor thing," Flanna said gathering his boots. "We'll find him a nest and get him some food. He'll be right as rain in no time and plotting his return."

~

They walked toward her hut, and she made a place for the wren in the crotch of the ash tree where Todd had left his clothes before his jaunt.

Flanna gestured to Todd to precede her through the door of the hut and bade him sit at the table while she bustled around, stoking the fire, lighting the lamps, putting stew in a kettle and setting it over the fire.

She poured two tankards of ale and offered him a toast. "To the wiliest Robin King I hae e'er seen."

He clanked his tankard to hers. "Aye, and the luckiest, too." He held up his left hand and kissed it. She blushed, remembering the luck she had given him.

He loved the way the color rose on her cheeks, and smiled broadly at her. They drank companionably for a moment, and he realized the fusty taste at the back of the ale was gone. So he had saved the land. He hoped this Titania would be a good queen.

Flanna refilled the tankards. "And so now, Todd. What do ye now?"

He shrugged and gazed up at her under his brows. "Queen Mab promised me a wife and a home befittin' a champion. What d' ye think o' that?"

She got up to stir the stew. She angled her head toward him as she said, "I'd think ye be a lucky man. And the lass that ye take to wife will be luckier yet." Her eyes caught the reflection of the peat fire, and her hair seemed like flames crowning her head.

"As for a house," Todd said, "I don't need much. Just a bit o' farmland, enough to keep a man busy."

She came back to the table and lifted her tankard. "And a woman happy?" She drank, but watched him over the rim. Her eyes crinkled with the smile the cup hid.

"Aye, that be most important," Todd said solemnly. "A man with a happy wife is content indeed. Or so my da always said." He lifted the tankard to his mouth, watching her.

"Well, yer da was a wise man."

He put the cup down and took her hand in his. "Will ye be my wife, Flanna Maguire?"

She smiled, her teeth brilliant in the lamplight, the light from the fire playing in her hair. "Aye, Todd Bryne, ye handsome fox dog. I'll be yer vixen wife." She cuffed him on the arm.

He caught her and pulled her to him for a kiss. Her mouth was soft and sweet, and he knew he would not want for contentment.

When he let her go, she said, "Now that's ciphered, it's time to eat." She brought bread to the table and slathered slices thickly with butter.

That, and the smell of the venison stew, made his belly grumble. Nothing like surviving to remind you of the basic things.

He stretched out his legs and watched as Flanna tended to the supper, imagining her in his house, his bed, his life. He realized he quite liked it.

The fox in him did, too, and as soon as they finished eating, Todd stared out the window, where the sickle moon had risen, shining into the room.

"I fancy a run. Do ye care to join me?"

She nodded and took his hand, following him out the door, which she carefully shut, and together they walked down the lane to the tree.

They shed their clothes without haste, without modesty, and folded them carefully before stretching up on the tree and dropping to all fours.

She was as beautiful a vixen as she was a woman, Todd thought, sleek of limb, fine of face, and with a thick, red bushy tail with a dun tip that beckoned him like a beacon as she trotted into the trees.

ABOUT THE AUTHOR

Diana lives in a small suburban Colorado city a mile away from where she grew up. She loves studying magic and history and will take any opportunity to combine them into a good story. She once tried to work a spell inspired by a tale her great aunt told her and has always felt lucky that it only turned her fingers green for a week.

Find out more about Diana at:
dianabenedict.com

a amazon.com/Diana-Benedict/e/B00ZDT6IIS
BB bookbub.com/authors/diana-benedict

THE ICE SKATING FAIRY

LEAH CUTTER

"Geez, this bites."

Cindy looked around. Who had just voiced the exact words going through her head? She hadn't heard anyone come up behind her. She looked down both sides the row of seats where she sat, as well as behind her. The empty seats of the arena stretched out in both directions until they curved away.

Cindy repositioned her earmuffs, careful not to get stray pieces of her brown hair caught in them and end up looking like a dork. She'd worn the neon-blue earmuffs today, the ones that matched the warm gloves she wore. Her bright-green down jacket kept out most of the cold, though Cindy was used to the frigid temperatures of the practice rink. More than once Cindy's coach had told Cindy that the chilled air gave her pale cheeks a nice, healthy, pink glow, as a way of derailing her grousing. Plus, the color hid her totally typical teenage acne. Black ski pants covered her legs, the kind that zipped at the bottom so she could wear them over her cast.

On the ice of the skating rink in front of her, Janice was *still* not picking up the choreography. It wasn't that difficult. Turn, turn, leap, camel. Cindy could do this simple of a routine in her sleep. She couldn't help but roll her eyes as Janice stumbled again. Cindy sighed. Wouldn't Janice *ever* figure this out?

Then Cindy turned to glare at the crutches resting against the seat beside her.

Could have done this sort of routine. Before her stupid sister and her stupid friends had agreed to drive Cindy to practice, only to slam into the back of a stopped pickup truck. At least no one had ended up permanently damaged. Cindy, though, had gotten the worst of the injuries: a fractured tibia.

Which meant she couldn't practice. Couldn't *perform*. Wasn't going to be going be part of the annual mid-winter jubilee celebration put on by the best teen figure skaters in the state of Washington.

Was stuck on the sidelines, kissing nationals goodbye. As well as any chance of qualifying for the Olympics this year...

Just beyond Cindy's metal crutches she saw something glowing with a clean, white light, as though a rogue spotlight had directed its beam there.

It took Cindy a moment to realize it wasn't something shining that way, but rather, some*one*.

A fairy.

The fairy looked like a regular fairy, with a sharp nose, thin lips, high cheekbones, and a pointed chin. Cindy instantly envied the fairy's clear, acne-free skin, the color somewhere between gold and bronze. The fairy's black hair had French braids along the sides of her head, then was all gathered together into an impressively thick braid that went halfway down her back, a dark black line between her yellow-and-white gossamer wings.

Cindy had missed the fairy the first time she'd looked around because the fairy barely came up past the handles of Cindy's crutches. Like all fairies, this one was diminutive, maybe eighteen inches tall when she stood. Of course, fairies could use magic to seem as big as a human, though she'd always have her wings, no matter what her appearance.

The fairy wasn't wearing a jacket, despite how cold the arena was kept. Instead, she had on a tight, white, sleeveless top that showed how bony her chest was, and a short, white-and-blue satin skirt. Blue-and-white striped stockings covered her legs, and she wore bright-blue ice skates that were so tiny they looked like blueberries.

The fairy gave a rather loud sigh and waved toward Janice, who'd fallen down (again!) and was slowing getting back up. "Just look at that."

"I know. Pitiful. Right?" Cindy said, working to maintain the appropriate level of teenager disgust in her voice and not excitement. She'd never talked with a fairy before, not personally like this. She'd seen them at school during the inter-species classes she'd been required to attend, and occasionally at Commodore Park when she'd been hanging out with her friends, but that was it.

Her family lived in an old rambler, built back in the early 70s, before the fairies, brownies, and pixies (FBP) started signing time-sharing agreements with humans. Mankind would get to use their outdoor spaces during daylight hours, while the FBP took them over at night, in exchange for keeping them pristine and lush.

No one Cindy knew had any fairy friends, not like those TV shows, such as "Frankie and the Fairy". Cindy's family lived north of Seattle where fairies weren't as common. Plus, it wasn't as if any of the FBP attended the same schools or went out to the same restaurants as humans. Though Cindy had heard about this one coffee shop that now had a fairy boy-band playing regularly...

"I could have done a much better job," the fairy grumbled, waving her hand toward Janice and the rink.

"You?" Cindy asked, astonished. "You skate?"

The fairy rolled her eyes at Cindy. "No, I just like the cosplay of dressing up like a figure skater. Of course, I skate."

Cindy blinked, still surprised. "I didn't know fairies skated. Do you compete?"

The fairy sighed and shook her head. "Not enough interest in the community to get a competitive circuit going."

"I'm sorry," Cindy said. If she couldn't compete...she didn't know what she would have done. Perfecting her routine and performing for the judges was as much a part of her life as breathing.

"I came here today to audition for your position," the fairy said. "But the officials claimed I would have an unfair advantage. You know. With the magic and flying and all."

"But couldn't you agree to not use your magic or your wings while performing?" Cindy asked. She felt flattered that the fairy had wanted to be in the mid-winter jubilee.

"That's what I said!" the fairy said, slapping her hand against the hard plastic of the seat, making a tiny sound despite how much emphasis she used. "But the officials didn't have a way to test for my magical ability, so they said no."

"Wouldn't your people have a way to verify that you'd kept your promise?" Cindy asked cautiously, fascinated by this glimpse into actual real fairies and not the crap they showed on TV.

"The officials didn't trust them either," the fairy groused. "They needed an 'impartial' panel."

"That's so unfair," Cindy said.

"I know, right?" the fairy said. "I'm Belinda, by the way."

"Cindy," she replied. She knew better than to stick her hand out or something. Fairies didn't shake hands, not like humans. Something about magic making it uncomfortable to touch mundanes.

"I'd love to see you skate, sometime," Cindy added shyly after a moment.

Belinda gave her a sharp grin. "I did convince the assholes that they had to give me practice time. Regular, human practice ends at 10 PM, and I can have the rink after that. Want to come watch?"

Cindy bit her lips together. Normally, that was way past her bedtime. However, she wasn't competing right now. She could cheat a little on her sleep. "I'd love to."

"Great. See you tonight," Belinda said. Then she flew off, a bright white streak running high along the rows of the arena.

For a moment, Cindy thought that Belinda might turn and fly over the ice, maybe do a strafing run over Janice, see if she could get the girl to fall again. However, Belinda merely disappeared at the far wall, where the arena curved.

Janice fell soon after anyway.

~

C indy waited by the end of the arena, her injured leg raised on the seat in front of her, her crutches to the side. Though sometimes practice did go until 10 PM, no one was actually out on the ice. She'd gotten to the rink a little early, but was disappointed when she didn't find anyone there.

Still, she was determined to wait. She shivered a little, despite being dressed for the cold with her black ski pants, bright red down jacket that night, and brilliant white gloves and earmuff covered in long fake fur.

Exactly at 10 PM, Belinda appeared.

Cindy couldn't help but jump. One moment, she was by herself, watching videos on her phone, the next, Belinda was hovering directly beside her.

"Good! You're here!" Belinda said. She sounded relieved.

Had Belinda thought that Cindy wouldn't show up?

"Of course," Cindy said. "I really wanted to see you skate." No one she knew had ever seen a fairy skate.

Belinda beamed at Cindy. She wore the same outfit she'd had on earlier, though now, it, too, seemed to have its own glow, the white sleeveless top covered in glittering rhinestones, the blue-and-white satin skirt lined in bright light, the tiny blue skates pulsing with neon. "Come out onto the ice with me," Belinda said. "Let me give you the best seat in the house."

Cindy bit her lips together, then nodded. She felt like a dork on the ice with crutches. But she'd figured out how to do it, moving very slowly so she wouldn't fall. She had a full walking cast and wouldn't graduate to a shorter one for a couple weeks.

And while Belinda didn't seem like the being with the most patience in the world, Cindy was still going to go slow. She stood up, grabbed her crutches, and made her way to the entrance, doing her best to ignore the impatient ball of light vibrating over her left shoulder.

The world opened up for Cindy as soon as she stepped onto the ice. *This* was her home. She felt alive on the white face of the rink, while everything else, all her troubles and cares, just faded away.

She wished with all her heart that she could glide away from this spot, taking sweeping steps and skate all around the rink. Instead, she planted her crutches, swung forward carefully, paused, balanced, then brought her crutches around.

Belinda hovered in the air beside Cindy, at head height. "I knew you were injured," the fairy said, her voice holding many questions.

Cindy nodded. "Car accident. Broken tibia. It'll heal and I'll compete again next year." She was keeping herself in shape with primarily upper body work. Coach had told her that stronger arms would help her with her lifts.

"Must suck losing a year," Belinda said.

"It does," Cindy admitted. Then she shrugged. "Can't do much about that, though. Unless the FBP have healing powers they've never shared?"

Belinda looked startled for a moment, as if she hadn't expected to be teased. Then she gave a snorting laugh. "As if." She grew serious. "My magic is mainly for illusions and glamours. Not much else."

"I still think it's cool," Cindy said.

Belinda rolled her eyes. "Yeah, whatever." She paused for a moment, before flying closer to Cindy. "Don't tell anyone, ever, but I think it's kind of cool as well."

Cindy nodded, understanding. Some days, controlling her enthusiasm was the only thing that made her feel like an adult.

When they were about one quarter of the way across the rink, Belinda stopped and asked, "Should I skate in this form? Or be bigger?"

Cindy thought for a moment. "I'd like to see both," she said. "First, human sized, then your natural size."

Belinda nodded.

Cindy jumped for a second time that night when suddenly, a full-sized figure skater stood beside her. The illusion body looked exactly like Belinda, with the white top fitting her well (and still showing more bones than muscles), the skirt hanging in lovely blue and white stripes, the muscles in her long legs outlined by the stripes in her tights, and her brilliantly blue ice skates shining with their own light.

Belinda did a slow turn, letting Cindy see all sides of her. Belinda's wings had grown as well. They seemed more like large dragonfly wings than butterfly wings. Cindy knew that different fairies had different types, and while there was speculation about what the different types signified, no one knew for certain and the fairies weren't telling. Belinda's wings sparkled with gold, as if sprinkled with radioactive glitter.

"You look gorgeous," Cindy said truthfully.

"Good enough for competition?" Belinda asked.

Cindy heard the catch in Belinda's voice, though the fairy was trying to play it cool. "I think so," Cindy said. She examined the fairy's skirt critically. "The satin isn't too heavy to lift when you twirl, is it?"

Belinda responded by suddenly spinning in place. The skirt lifted beautifully, just like it was supposed to.

However, no skater could just turn that way. They needed momentum to achieve a spin. The only way Belinda had managed it was by using magic.

"What?" Belinda asked when she stopped and faced Cindy again.

"The spin was great," Cindy said, feeling awkward.

"But, what?" Belinda asked. "Your face is all funny. Like you're trying to hold in a fart."

That made Cindy giggle. "Okay. I'll tell you. But you can't get mad at me for telling you the truth." That was one thing that her inter-species classes had all emphasized: while fairies might look mostly human, they weren't. Fairies could be spiteful, and many had a volatile temper.

"You used magic to go into that spin, right?" Cindy asked. She hurried on. "It's okay, it's cool, it's just us. But that spin was fueled by magic."

Belinda blinked at Cindy. "Yeah, I suppose. I didn't even think about it. That's just part of how I skate."

Was this what the officials had seen? That magic was so natural to Belinda that she couldn't skate without it?

"Do you want to show me the routine you did for the officials?" Cindy asked. "Or do you have a different performance piece?"

Belinda nodded, still deep in thought. "I have a couple pieces," she said slowly. "Do you want to see them?"

"Sure!" Cindy said. That was why she'd come here tonight, to watch a fairy skate.

Belinda stood where she was for a moment longer. "These pieces...I'm still using magic in them."

"That's cool," Cindy said. And it was. Her friends were going to be sooooo jealous that Cindy got to see a fairy not only skate, but do magic while performing.

"It just never occurred to me that I shouldn't use magic while I'm skating," Belinda said, her words rushed together.

Cindy nodded. She wasn't sure what was wrong, but before she could ask, the first few notes of "The Dance of the Sugar Plum Fairies" came tinkling over the PA system and Belinda took off.

It took Cindy all she had to not giggle at Belinda's musical choice.

Then the music changed subtly. Over the top of the lighter notes came an even higher melody. Cindy shivered. The music of the fae intermingled with the familiar human song. The effect was unsettling, as if it was the same tune being played on instruments slightly off key.

Cindy had heard before that fairy music couldn't be appreciated by humans. She'd scoffed at that, figuring that sort of opinion came only from people like her parents, you know, *old* people. Younger people, like herself, could learn to enjoy it.

Now, she wondered if maybe they were right, if the music of the FBP was just too unnerving.

Belinda had slowly skated away, doing a buildup for her first leap. Of course, she reached heights no human could match, shooting up ten feet into the air and landing gently. She immediately went into an arabesque, followed by an amazingly quick camel spin.

Cindy found herself getting dizzy watching Belinda. There were no long, slow buildups. It was all leap, jump, spin.

In addition, while it was technically accurate, it was just a series of tricks that weren't connected together. And more importantly, Belinda didn't have a good sense of musicality. None of her leaps were timed to the song.

Abruptly, the piece ended. Belinda appeared in front of Cindy, who tried not to be too startled, afraid she'd end up on her ass on the ice.

"What did you think?" Belinda asked.

Cindy noted with a touch of jealousy that Belinda wasn't even out of breath.

"It was technically impressive," Cindy said cautiously. And it had been.

"I can hear that big old 'but' hanging out just there," Belinda said. She sounded angry.

It took Cindy a moment to find the right words. "It *was* technically impressive. All those leaps and spins. But it wasn't an emotional performance. You just—did tricks."

Belinda blinked, looking surprised. "Isn't that what I'm supposed to do?" she asked.

Cindy smiled. She remembered one of her first coaches not letting her skate to the music he'd chosen, but instead, making Cindy dance on the ice to the tune. She'd felt so awkward and out of control. She much preferred skating, gliding across the rink.

About halfway through the song, though, something had changed. Cindy found herself moving *to* the music, feeling it with her arms in a way she hadn't been when she'd merely been performing the choreography. She'd stopped caring how she looked and instead, let the music move her.

Every time she had new music, she spent time just dancing and moving to it, to get a feel for the tune and perform beyond the choreography.

"You must *feel* the music," Cindy told Belinda. "You're telling a story with your dance. The judges want to see you dance your heart out, and leave it all on the ice."

Belinda shook her head. "I've heard people say that before. I don't understand what it means."

"Do you like the song you used for your performance?" Cindy asked. It was appropriate, but not the easiest piece to skate to.

Belinda shrugged. "It's got a good rhythm."

Cindy blinked, puzzled. It didn't have a good beat, at least as far as she was concerned. "But what does that song represent to you? How does it make you feel?"

Belinda tilted her head to one side. "Humans are all about the emotional side of things, aren't they?"

Cindy nodded.

"Fairies—our emotions run just as deep. But they're here, and gone. Like a rainbow," Belinda said. "It would be difficult to connect to a song, and not just perform."

"But that's what performance is," Cindy argued. "Not just the notes for a singer. Or the steps for a dancer. It's what you, the artist, can bring to a piece."

"I've never considered it that way," Belinda admitted.

Cindy nodded while Belinda thought for a few moments.

"Can you help me?" Belinda asked, her words all rushed together. "Not just figure out a performance without magic. But how to be a better figure skater? And maybe get a second chance with the officials, and still perform in the mid-winter jubilee?"

"I'd love to," Cindy said. She'd always known that would be her path: from artist and performer (and hopefully, gold medal winner) to professional coach. Working with Belinda would be good practice for her.

"Do you want to start tonight?" Belinda asked. Now she sounded breathless, as if she'd been performing hard.

Cindy thought for a moment, then shook her head. "What I want you to do is to find some music that *means* something to you. Music that breaks your heart, or makes you want to dance with joy. Something that moves you."

"I know just the thing," Belinda said. "It's fairy music," she warned.

"It doesn't matter if I like it or not," Cindy said firmly. "You need to feel it. Then I can help you express yourself more."

Belinda rocked her head from side to side, considering. "I'll figure out a few pieces. See if there's something less disturbing for humans."

"Good," Cindy said. "Then, meet here again tomorrow night?"

Belinda gave her a huge grin. "Thought you'd never ask," she teased. The fairy shrank back down to her regular, diminutive size. "Thank you," she said seriously. Then she took off like a glittery rocket.

Cindy shook her head. She knew that ice didn't really have a scent. Still, it smelled like sweet victory to her.

Then she slowly, carefully, turned and started making her way across the ice. Her mom would be thrilled that Cindy had found a student. She'd been urging her daughter to start training other skaters. It would be a way of keeping her own skills up.

But Cindy also knew that her mom, her stupid older sister, and all of their collective friends had *never* imagined that Cindy would find someone like Belinda.

~

Cindy frowned as Belinda did another flying sit-spin. She got good verticality. One leg was straight out in front of her and the other was bent correctly, as if she was sitting on a chair. However, she maintained the position for a good two and a half rotations.

Far too long for a skater without magic.

After yet another quadruple axel, Cindy held up her arm, the signal she and Belinda had worked out to get Belinda to stop her progression. At least Cindy no longer had to use her crutches. She'd finally graduated to the short walking cast and it was easier for her to balance.

Belinda skated slowly over to where Cindy stood at the mid-line, the fairy's shoulders drooping and her head down. She knew why Cindy had stopped her.

Cindy wasn't sure how much more she could help the fairy. Belinda was starting to finally feel the music she moved to. It had turned out to be a good thing that the fairy tunes were so disturbing: it made Cindy focus on the dance, because as a human, she couldn't feel anything but uneasy. It also meant Belinda had to work twice as hard to express emotion in her routine.

They'd quickly discovered that Belinda was most convincing when it came to sad songs rather than happy or playful pieces.

However, Belinda couldn't seem to let go of her magic. She always forgot herself, particularly once she started showing more feelings in her performance.

"Magic again, huh?" Belinda asked as she drew closer.

Cindy nodded. "I'm sorry," she said. "I wonder if it's just too much a part of you."

Belinda sighed. "That's what Mom said. That trying to give up my magic was like trying to cut off my wings. Can't do it, not and survive."

"I see," Cindy said. "I'm sorry," she said again. "I'm not sure what I can do to help."

"No, no!" Belinda said. "You've already helped me so much. I am a *much* better performer now. You can't be throwing in the towel on me."

"I'd love to keep working with you," Cindy said. "However, I'm not sure that we're ever going to have something to show the officials of the mid-winter jubilee." They'd scheduled another interview in just a few days.

"But I have to be able to perform there!" Belinda said.

"Why?" Cindy asked. She'd never understood why Belinda wanted to perform in a human spectacle. Though Cindy had asked before, she hadn't believed the story Belinda had made up about improving fairy-human relations.

Besides, didn't the fairies have their own great balls and parities at mid-winter? Wasn't it a special holiday for them? Why did Belinda want to miss it?

Belinda pressed her lips together as if debating whether or not to tell her coach. "My dad died earlier this year," the fairy said after a short while.

"That's horrible!" Cindy said. "I'm so sorry." She had no idea.

Belinda shrugged. "It's not like he was murdered or anything. It was a freak accident. The kind that aren't supposed to happen. He got caught in a plane engine turbine while he was flying. Tore his wings right off. Mom says he died instantly."

"Jeez," Cindy said. "I really am sorry."

Belinda nodded. "I *so* don't want to go to the mid-winter ball this year. Everyone will be staring at me, whispering about me and the *tragedy* of my life." She rolled her eyes so hard Cindy was surprised she didn't pull something. "It's sad, yes, that my dad is gone. I really loved him. But *he's* the one who died. Not me."

"Is that why you started figure skating?" Cindy asked. She knew that Belinda hadn't been performing for very long. She'd just watched videos of others skating. She'd never had a coach before. YouTube had been her teacher.

"Naw, I started last year. But Dad always encouraged me. Called me his icy glitter ball."

Cindy wasn't sure what that meant, but the endearment had appeared to be quite heartfelt, given the glint of tears in Belinda's eyes.

"I know you can't take my place in the jubilee," Cindy said slowly. Janice was finally starting to pick up the choreography. "But maybe you can perform on your own. Get a place as a special guest appearance, or something."

Belinda shook her head. "I'm a nobody. There isn't any draw to my name, you know? And none of the fairies would come to see me anyway. The jubilee is at the same time as the primary fairy ball."

"Then we'll have to come up with such an amazing performance that the officials will beg for you to be part of the jubilee anyway," Cindy said firmly.

Belinda nodded slowly. "Okay," she said. Her eyes had that far off look that she got when she was really concentrating. "I may have an idea. Meet me here tomorrow night."

"Same time, same channel?" Cindy asked, teasing. It had become a routine with them.

"You got it," Belinda said. "And bring your practice skates!" the fairy added just before she popped out of sight.

Her skates? Why would the fairy request that? Cindy hadn't touched her skates in weeks.

Sadness filled her. She *missed* skating so much. While the coaching was great, particularly with such an athletic (and magical) student, it wasn't the same.

Still, Cindy would do as Belinda had asked. The fairy had trusted Cindy's coaching all this time. Now it was time for Cindy to trust Belinda.

~

Cindy set both her favorite practice skates, as well as her performance skates, down on a seat in the ice skating arena. She'd arrived before Belinda, who was always surprisingly punctual, particularly for a fairy. The bus had been early, though.

The coolness of the rink helped Cindy center herself, the ice reminding her to be calm, focus on her routine. She'd worn all black and white that evening, black ski pants, white down jacket, black gloves and earmuffs. She'd considered wearing her bright red gloves, but that made her look too much like a TV serial killer.

Cindy looked down at the two pairs of skates: her practice set were made of bright white leather so her coach could watch her footwork better, the other, a deep plum color that would have matched her costume. She'd only worn them a couple of times to break them in. About a week after the accident she would have switched to them for all her rehearsals.

Maybe next year.

A soft white light appeared over her shoulder. Belinda had arrived.

"That's a pretty color," she said.

"Yes," Cindy agree, turning to look. "Sugarplum fairy colored," she said, teasing.

Belinda snorted at her. "Really?"

Cindy shrugged her shoulders. The costume had been dramatic, a rich, dark color that would have shown up especially well on the ice, particularly with Cindy's light skin. She'd been told that she'd wear a wig for the event, something long and white with an intricate braid going down the back.

"Take the guards off your practice pair and untie them," Belinda said after studying the skates for a moment.

After Cindy complied, she looked back at her friend. Belinda's eyes had narrowed. The intensity of her stare felt like a sunbeam striking Cindy, chasing away the cold.

"Can I touch them?" Belinda asked after a bit.

"Sure," Cindy said. Belinda sounded strangely stiff and formal.

"No, can I *touch* them?" Belinda said. "You know. With magic."

"Uh, sure?" Cindy said. She wasn't exactly sure what the fairy was asking.

"Okay. Here goes nothing," Belinda said. She stared hard at Cindy's practice skates.

Bright blue-white light suddenly outlined Cindy's practice skates. First the right skate, then the left, slowly rose up and stood on the blade. They wobbled there for a moment.

Cindy found herself holding her breath. While it was one thing to watch Belinda perform, and to use her magic with her jumps and spins, it was something completely different to watch her skates suddenly take on a life of their own.

"Pick them up and put them on the ice," Belinda said, her voice sounding strained.

Cindy finally tore her gaze away from her skates to look at the fairy. Her natural glow burned extra bright, but not hot. No, her magic burned cold.

Weird. Yet another thing the TV shows had all wrong.

Cindy slipped forward, trying not to block the fairy's view of her skates. The skates themselves felt covered in ice. Her fingers tingled as they slipped under the magic spell. She lifted the skates and held them to the side as she carefully made her way to the ice.

As soon as Cindy set her skates down on the ice, they glided away as if a ghost had possessed them.

Then she frowned. No, it was as if they were doing her most recent routine, the one she'd been working on before the accident.

What the hell?

She glanced over her shoulder at Belinda, who gave her a great grin, showing off her pointed, sharp teeth.

"The skates still have a little memory of what you were practicing," Belinda said. "Because you rehearse so often, your practice skates remember a lot."

"Cool," Cindy said, turning back to stare at the skates performing on their own.

"Now comes the hard part," Belinda said.

Cindy gasped as a ghostly figure coalesced above the skates. It looked something like Cindy, but a more stylized version, like a line drawing.

A bright light appeared beside the illusion on the ice. Suddenly, Belinda was there, full-human sized. The ghost figure and the fairy danced together as the music of the fae filled the air.

Cindy's heart beat hard, as if she was doing all the work. Her leg muscles trembled through the arabesque. She found her arms half lifting for the spin.

She felt connected to the figure on the ice, somehow.

She concentrated on her form, lengthening her lines making her hands softer. The figure responded, appearing more graceful.

It was a beautiful routine. Belinda mainly mimicked what the ghost figure did, except she added her own brilliant leaps and inhuman spins.

Cindy pressed her palms against her eyes to push out the tears that rested there as the routine came to an end. She wished she could hug Belinda, but all Cindy could say was, "Thank you. Thank you. Thank you."

Belinda nodded, then asked seriously, "Think that's brilliant enough for the officials?" She didn't look pale, exactly. Cindy could still tell that the routine had taken a lot out of Belinda.

"The officials would be idiots for not wanting to include that in the mid-winter jubilee," Cindy told her.

"They are adults," Belinda said sourly.

"True. I think they'll see how wonderfully magical it is," Cindy said. She paused, then said yet again, "Thank you. That was...I have no words to describe how beautiful that was."

"You felt it, didn't you?" Belinda said. "The magic. The routine. You were part of it, too."

"I did. But how? Humans don't have magic," Cindy said. While some humans were more sensitive than others, none had magic like the FBP.

"I think it's because you've been exposed to enough of my magic,"

Belinda said. "We've been working together and you know me. Better than some of my fairy friends."

Cindy bit her lip to keep it from trembling, then nodded. Skating had always been her primary focus. She had friends, sure, in school. She might, if tortured appropriately, even admit to her older sister being friend-like. But no one who shared her passion like Belinda, who worked as hard or strove so long. The other girls in the circuit were competitors, not friends.

"So let's do it again," Cindy said, her voice sounding harsh. "There's that triple lutz in the middle section that needs to be cleaned up."

"You got it, coach," Belinda said with a grin. The fae music started up again.

Cindy focused harder on the two figures this time, pouring all her pent up emotions and energy into the ghostly skater, perfecting the routine.

It wasn't the same as performing. She would take what she could get while her leg healed.

The routine seemed easier for Belinda this time. She actually smiled a few times and seemed more at ease.

Maybe her heart was healing as well.

"Stay still!" Cindy told Belinda as she tried to attach the last purple streamer to Belinda's wings.

"I can't!" Belinda whined. She vibrated in place.

Cindy had at first felt honored that Belinda had asked her to help with her costume. But the fairy was so nervous it had turned into a game of "pin the streamer on the fairy". Even in the small green room that had been assigned to just the pair of them it had been difficult to catch up with the darting fairy.

"Just one more," Cindy said, as calmly as she could, reaching up cautiously to touch the top part of Belinda's left wing. The wing was stronger than it looked. Despite how it sparkled as though it had been covered in gold glitter, it felt like smooth plastic under Cindy's fingers.

They'd tried (and rejected) a bunch of different adhesives, including boob tape, finally settling on old-fashioned spirit gum.

Cindy quickly wiped a last brushful of the smelly, sticky substance on Belinda's wing and attached the last streamer.

"There!" Cindy said, stepping back. "All done."

Belinda took off, darting to one corner of the green room then streaking across the ceiling to the other corner. The room was only big enough to hold two dressing tables, so it wasn't very wide.

"How do they look? How do they look?" Belinda asked, her voice squeaky with excitement.

"Great," Cindy told her truthfully. And Belinda did look wonderful. Her costume was a study in contrasts. One sleeve was white while the other was the same dark purple color as Cindy's performance skates. The skirt had purple and white stripes, and Belinda's tights were also one white, one colored, opposite to her arms. The plum color seemed richer than a human outfit, like it was actually made out of velvet, and the white parts sparkled with fairy magic.

Cindy wore black jeans (finally!) as her walking cast had just been removed the day before. Her blouse was also black, and she had a black scarf over her hair. She had darker makeup on as well, to help disguise the natural paleness of her skin.

She would appear as a shadow on the ice, a dark figure that everyone would ignore once Belinda started skating. It felt appropriate for their routine. Cindy's mom had teased her about being the power behind the throne. Cindy wasn't sure she liked being called that, however, she was also aware of how much power a coach had, now that she'd been coaching someone herself.

"Aren't you nervous?" Belinda asked, pausing for a moment in front of Cindy before taking off again.

"I'd run three laps around the arena if I could," Cindy admitted. She always had pre-performance jitters. She also knew that her physical therapist would *kill* her for straining her leg that way.

The door to the green room opened. "Two minutes," said the friendly stagehand.

Belinda froze in place. All the magic drained out of her. Cindy stared in fascination. Though the fairy still glowed, she appeared more angular and bony, as if she was made up out of sticks and twigs held together with the lightest coat of skin. Her costume grew plain and Cindy suddenly saw broad stitches along the side seams.

"You can do this," Cindy told Belinda. "Once the music starts, just let it flow over you. You've practiced enough it'll be easy. Trust me."

Belinda shook herself all over, like she was shaking off a sudden rain.

"And remember, this is just the first performance. You'll be great this time, and better next time, and the time after that," Cindy said.

Belinda gulped and nodded, all the magic flowing back into her, plumping her up (though she was still awfully skinny) and making her clothes look rich again. The fairy nodded again, then turned to Cindy. "You ready?"

Cindy couldn't help but smile at the impatient tone the fairy had adopted, as if Belinda had been the one waiting all along for Cindy.

"Ready," Cindy said.

She walked out of the room, a bright glowing ball of nervous energy at her side.

They walked down the darkened hallway to the side entrance of the ice as the crowd exploded with applause for the previous performers. Cindy felt the focused calm that always came immediately before a performance. She carried her practice skates instead of walking in them, which felt weird.

The previous performers streamed from the stage through the gate. The smell of their sweat and excitement mingled with the cold scent of the ice. Cindy nodded at them, relishing the shocked and surprised looks a couple of them threw at her.

In the program, only Belinda was listed. Cindy was just there as a coach. And she shouldn't be on the sidelines tonight.

They had no idea.

The lights stayed bright as Cindy cautiously stepped onto the ice.

She was *not* going to fall and look like a dork. She held her skates high, the white leather covered in purple cloth that matched Belinda's outfit.

They walked to the center of the rink, the audience growing silent. They had no idea what to expect. No one had ever done anything like this before, even though the FBP had been around for ages.

Cautiously, Cindy put her skates down and stepped back.

The arena went black. The audience stirred restlessly for a moment.

A single spotlight hit the skates lying forlorn in the center of the rink.

The audience gasped as first one, then the other skate picked itself up, then gasped again as Belinda's magic filled in the shadowy figure who skated in them.

Fae music came trickling over the loudspeakers.

The performance began.

Cindy concentrated on the ghostly figure, ignoring everything else. She was aware of the officials sitting directly to the side. They weren't there as judges, not really. Still, Cindy knew she performed best to an audience and still found herself directing the performance that way, giving them the best view.

The routine went beautifully, with the audience gasping at the height of Belinda's jumps as well as clapping at the right times. Wild applause erupted as they finished. The number of roses and flowers thrown onto the ice was huge, bigger than Belinda's natural form. Cindy picked up a couple after grabbing her skates.

"Oh my goodness that was exciting! Don't you think that was exciting! Wow! The audience means everything!" Belinda said, burbling over as they walked back to the green room. During rehearsal, Belinda had always seemed slightly drained afterward. The energy of the crowd had fueled her this time.

"I know! I know!" Cindy said, wishing she could bounce along as she walked, but she knew she still had to take it easy on her bum leg. "It was amazing. You're amazing!"

An older fairy with the same golden brown skin as Belinda waited for them in the greenroom. She wore a sparkling white outfit that hurt Cindy's eyes.

Cindy turned to look at Belinda. "I can come back later," she offered.

"No need," the woman said. She gave the pair of them a glittering smile that looked like it hurt. "Thank you for helping my daughter," she said, bowing her head to Cindy. "I owe you one favor. You may call on Mrs. Marblewood when you're ready."

Cindy caught her breath. A fairy favor? She could ask for just about anything, she knew. That part the TV shows actually got right.

"As for you," Mrs. Marblewood said, turning toward Belinda, "that was fabulous! So ingenious! Your father would be so proud of you!"

Cindy had thought that Belinda had been a nervous ball of energy before. Now, she physically shook. "Thanks, Mom," she said, her voice cracking.

They looked at each other expectantly, half a room of empty space separating them.

Cindy sighed. "Jeez," she said loudly, in her most bored teenage voice. "Go hug her already. I'll come back later."

Cindy was glad that she already had the greenroom door mostly shut before the blinding light of two fairies touching each other exploded.

No wonder the FBP didn't like touching mundanes. Not if when they touched each other it was, well, magical.

About a minute later, the door opened and Mrs. Marblewood flowed out of the room. "I'll be seeing you," she said.

Was that a promise? Or a threat? Or perhaps both? Cindy wasn't sure. It sure explained why Belinda made her uncomfortable sometimes, if she was emulating her mom.

"So what'd she say?" Cindy asked as soon as she came into the room. Belinda cruised from one corner to the next, not as nervous as she'd been before, but still flying high.

"She liked it! She really liked it!" Belinda crooned. "And she's going to help me find other fairies to compete against!"

"That's wonderful!" Cindy said, happy for her friend and yet at the same time, sad that Belinda would no longer need her as a coach.

Belinda came to hover just before Cindy. "She also said that our routine would be perfect for the next FBP-human alliance summit meeting. In Switzerland!"

Cindy gasped. She'd ever been to Europe, though she'd skated all over the US. "Really?"

Belinda nodded. "Really. And she really likes you. And she wants to be our manager, and arrange for us to perform all over!"

"Wow," Cindy said. She knew that she'd go from competing to performing someday. She just hadn't expected it to happen so soon. She would get back to competing, though. Maybe next year.

Shyly, the fairy held out her hands to Cindy.

Cindy told herself not to shake as she reached out and touched the fairy's cold fingers. Uncomfortable fairy magic raced up her arms, making her shiver. Her heart beat wildly and she found herself panting.

They mutually let go after just a few moments. Cindy understood that Belinda had just shared something deeply personal: how the fairy truly felt at that moment.

"You really are that calm," Belinda said, her head tilted to one side as she looked at Cindy. "Weird."

Cindy chuckled. Then she paused, considering. "Do you want to keep the routine exactly as it is?" she asked slowly.

Belinda looked confused for a moment. "Of course!"

Cindy nodded. It didn't surprise her. Belinda liked doing all that magic and illusions. She wouldn't want to actually skate with Cindy.

"Only you'd be the one in your skates next time," Belinda added. "Dork."

"Dufus," Cindy countered. She knew it was a different path than what she'd originally intended for her skating career, skating with a fairy partner instead of competing on her own.

And maybe she'd get back in the circuit after a while.

But for now, the gold found in fairy wings would be better than any gold medal she could win.

ABOUT THE AUTHOR

Leah Cutter writes page-turning fiction in exotic locations, such as a magical New Orleans, the ancient Orient, Hungary, the Oregon coast, rural Kentucky, Seattle, Minneapolis, and many others.

She writes literary, fantasy, mystery, science fiction, and horror fiction. Her short fiction has been published in magazines like *Alfred Hitchcock's Mystery Magazine* and *Talebones*, anthologies like *Fiction River*, and on the web. Her long fiction has been published both by New York publishers as well as small presses.

Find out more about Leah at:
leahcutter.com

facebook.com/leah.cutter
bookbub.com/authors/leah-cutter
amazon.com/Leah-R-Cutter/e/B00IH6WDEM

TREASURE

LESLIE CLAIRE WALKER

The blond girl in the faded green sweatshirt couldn't have been more than nineteen. She handed over her grandmother's mirror with the same desperation all Adeline Morgan's pawn customers brought into her kitchen.

Despair was Addie's particular magic, after all. She drew it to her. Held it close. She could smell desperation like dry rot wafting under the scent of the chocolate chip cookies baking in her oven.

Her magic had given her purpose. Once upon a time, she'd had nothing to call her own. Now, among her many treasures: A book of prophecy that only worked if you sacrificed a human heart. A glass eye that blinded everyone it regarded—in an opaque case, of course. The oldest written love spell in the US of A, on yellowed, brittle paper. It had caused a murder-suicide, last Addie knew.

All of these things were more precious to her than a whole bank full of hundred dollar bills. All of them evil.

This girl's mirror with the silver waves carved into the back, this prized possession? Evil. If the girl didn't pawn it here, it would destroy her life.

Addie gazed into the mirror by the dappled mid-winter sunlight that streamed through the window. Her reflection looked exactly fifty years younger than she actually was. Hmm. The Mirror of Memory Lane. Clever, clever. After all, who at her age wouldn't kill to look twenty-two again? Or to *be* twenty-two again? Some previous owner of the mirror had probably done just that.

"I'll give you fifty bucks," Addie said.

"But it's special."

To the kid, sure. Damned if Addie could remember her name. "I'm telling you what it's worth on the street."

The girl's eyebrows climbed all the way to her hairline. "You're gonna sell it?"

Not on a cold day in hell. She never sold the items her customers brought her. She kept them here. Safe from their owners, and their owners safe from them.

"You have a month to buy it back," Addie said. "Those are the rules. You knew 'em when you came here."

The girl nodded. Jennifer. That was her name.

Jennifer would pawn her precious, poisonous heirloom. Then she'd forget about it as soon as she walked out the door, like all the rest of them. She'd go on to live a happy life—or whatever life fate had in store for her.

"Seventy-five," Jennifer said.

"Fifty-five. Not a penny more." The timer on the counter buzzed. Addie grabbed a pot holder.

Jennifer glanced away, gaze moving over the small, homey room, its walls of shelves filled with previous acquisitions. "What you saw, that's not all it does."

Addie wouldn't be surprised. Still, she shook her head and pulled the sheet of chocolately, gooey goodness from the oven.

"I got rent to pay," the girl said.

How original. "So do I."

The girl rocked forward and craned her neck to take in the narrow hallway off the kitchen that led to the rest of the house. It was much bigger inside than out, deceptively so. In point of fact, the inside of the house went on for nearly a mile. An unwary stranger could (and had) easily become too lost to ever find her way out. Some of them, Addie had never found their gnawed bones.

Jennifer shivered, settled back on her heels, and frowned. "But you've lived here forever. That's what they say."

Addie'd been here so long this part of Houston had not only grown up but gentrified around her. From the outside, her little shotgun house on its small overgrown lot with its peeling brown paint was an eyesore. The city kept trying to tear it down. Bulldoze a house of magic? Good luck.

She put the tea kettle on to boil. "The devil doesn't care whether the mortgage on this place is paid off, missy. Fifty-five. Take it or leave it."

In the end, the girl walked out clutching her worthless claim receipt, with cash in hand and a complimentary cookie. And Addie spent her tea time sipping on Earl Grey, munching, and gazing at her younger self, dropping crumbs onto the looking glass.

Once upon a time, she'd had auburn hair that fell in thick waves to the shoulder, dusky olive skin, bright brown eyes that turned near to black when she got angry. She'd have been a beauty if not for the bruises, the too-hollow cheeks, the track marks she couldn't see in the mirror but knew were there on her twenty-two-year old arms nonetheless.

She'd wanted to save up money, back then. To get out of the neighborhood, find a nice apartment, have a little fun. She never got the chance. Instead, she got booted from home and every place she stayed after that until Hot Corner Fred became the only person she could turn to. She turned tricks for him, and she got high when he wanted, or he tuned her up.

He made her cringe. He made her feel like a coward.

She saw a ripple in the mirror and blinked. Her reflection had changed—it wasn't even hers anymore.

Fred's image filled the looking glass. Chin raised into the wind. Lips curved. Mean baby blues. Hadn't he been something? Yes, he had. The bastard.

What comes around goes around, even if it took a few lifetimes for fate to catch up. He'd got his, hadn't he? She'd made sure of it.

The reflection rippled again. Addie held her breath, waiting to see which face from her past would come clear next. Slowly, she picked out the new features.

Eyes: too shiny green, with the whitest whites she'd ever seen. Like a doll's. Nose: acorn. Mouth: a stitched, uneven line of black thread, cross-hatched with little black thread Xs. It had stick arms and legs and hands and feet. Fingers crafted of brown and black safety-pinned buttons. It wore a yellow baby bonnet, a yellow polka-dotted matching shirt and bloomers.

She'd made that thing. Created it on the worst night of her life. The night she fell into the pit of hell and clawed her way out. She'd made a deal with the Fae. She'd snatched a baby. Kidnapped a human child and replaced it with a changeling, that stick figure in the mirror, Fae-charmed to resemble the human child in every detail.

The Fae told her she wouldn't regret it. She'd never see the baby or the changeling again. None of it would come back to haunt her. And she believed him. After all, remorse had never been her strong suit.

What freaked her out the most? Not only could she see the poppet, the poppet saw her. It glared at her, in point of fact.

It couldn't be a coincidence that this mirror found its way to her. Coincidences didn't happen to people like her. No. Her past had come back to haunt her.

If so, she was in way over her head. She needed help. Asking for it could get her killed—or worse. Bargains with the Fae required absolute adherence to the letter of the agreement. Breaking the contract resulted in a fate worse than death. No mercy.

She'd vowed never to tell a soul. That she'd allow no one to find out what she'd done.

She trusted exactly one person enough to go to him with this. Michael. He had a strong, true gift for seeing into people and things. More, he could gauge patterns and motivations.

She'd known him since grade school, when they'd been best friends. Hell, they'd been *only* friends. They'd lost track of each other after high school. She'd always counted that a blessing. He never knew the things that'd happened to her. The things she'd done to survive. It was better that way.

That way, she'd always be the girl who lived around the way, the one who traded him bologna sandwiches at lunch, whose laugh made him smile.

He was the only person in the world to whom she'd ever come close to confessing what she'd done or why. In the end she hadn't because of what would happen to her if she broke her end of the Fae bargain—and because he just plain didn't need to know. He would've fallen out of love with her faster than she could blink.

Even so, when the Fae came calling again to ask for another "favor," Mike protected her. Although he didn't ask direct her questions, he asked plenty of indirect ones. The kind she could answer without breaking oaths.

He figured out too much. Put himself in danger. Her, too. She couldn't have that. If he wouldn't stay out of her business for their own good, she'd put him out. She married him because of his bravado—and divorced him for it, too.

They stayed close after they split. He brought her things. Half the treasures on her shelves, in fact. They did business together, too, sometimes. Traded information.

She needed information more than anything right now.

She wrapped the mirror in a handy black dishcloth to keep it safe from prying eyes and prying eyes safe from it for the time being. Slipped it into her coat pocket and let herself out into the cold, bright afternoon.

A loose corner of the yellow notice stapled to her door whipped in the wind, caught at her coat. Her blood pressure rose. She tore at the paper. Some of the peeling paint came with it. She crumbled the mass into a ball so small you couldn't see the brown streaks of color, or where the paper said Condemned.

Had the inspector messed with anything when he'd come to fix that godforsaken thing to her door? She scanned the short, wide porch meant for warm weather sitting, for catching a breeze and listening to the cicadas. All her shiny glass baubles still hung from the eaves. The windows on either side of the door looked like rheumy eyes. There was life in them still.

Grass grew tall and seedy against the sides of the house, the tips of the stems thick as fingers. One of them clutched a size ten brown work boot.

So much for the inspector.

She stepped lively down the walk to the gate, sparing some narrow-eyed contempt for the three-story town homes across the way with their manicured hedges and beds of red and purple pansies soaking up the late afternoon sun. The developers sold them for three hundred grand and up. Criminals, she called them.

But there was also the corner store she'd shopped at for years, its parking lot stained with grease and stinking of burnt motor oil, its windows still tacky with fake, sprayed-on snow and the gummy outlines of stick-on Christmas trees taken down two weeks past. Mr. Johnson waved at her from behind the counter.

And Rick, who hunkered down on the asphalt around the way and out of sight of Mr. Johnson, homeless for years and preferred it that way, eating out of a Styrofoam to-go container and sharing his meal with his two big, yellow dogs.

Cars, pick-ups, and buses roared past, racing the traffic lights. Everyone in a hurry. Headed north into downtown's glass, steel, and concrete canyons. Or out to the freeways and the suburbs.

Addie walked east, brisk at first and then more carefully as the cold seeped through to her old bones and her arthritic hip began to mouth off. Seven long blocks, into the shadow of the baseball stadium and the warehouses to the bar.

She knocked on the door. Seven-foot-tall Ingram the Bouncer tipped his ball cap to her as she went inside. She inclined her head, although he didn't much notice; he'd already returned his attention to the cavernous main room, where a few regulars clustered around tables drinking and doing business amid the low hum of conversation and the clink of glasses. The dry heat that pumped from the vents didn't quite chase away the chill, and it made her cough.

She took the winding staircase one ache at a time to the PI offices on the second floor. What the heat failed to do downstairs, it made up here in spades. She took her coat off.

Mike stood in the doorway of suite 201-B, his flat-top full and bristly as it had been when they'd met; he'd worn his hair like that all his life. He wore a plain tee-shirt, jeans, and sneakers. His neighbors dressed up in leather now, used it like a billboard to advertise how tough they were. Mike didn't need all that to look tough. The lines around his eyes and mouth said it all.

His office held a beat-up metal desk with a veneer top and chairs. Nothing on the walls. He liked to keep the important things out of sight.

He settled down in his chair and offered her one, but she perched on the desk. She felt too on edge to get comfortable.

One look at the mirror and he pronounced her screwed.

"It's a Faery glass," he said, careful not to gaze into it straight-on.

"I thought it was harmless. And rare."

He leaned back, turned the mirror face-down on his thigh. "Oh, they're rare all right. Anyone in the human world looks in one, they can see straight through to Faery. Anyone in the Faery realm can do the same thing—see all the way through to this world. These things are more windows than mirrors.

"And they don't just pass hand-to-hand around the city by accident," he said. "Once they're given to a person, they belong to that person and can't be taken away, only re-gifted. Addie, whoever gave you this, they did it on purpose."

"Jennifer." And she thought she'd put one over on the kid. Boy had she been wrong.

"What do you know about her?"

Addie shrugged. "What do I know about most of my customers?"

"That they're easy marks. Right." He ran a fingertip along the edge of the desk where the veneer had peeled. "What'd you see in the glass?"

"I saw my own reflection, but I looked like I did around the time we got married," she said.

"Something sweet. To get you to take the mirror off Jennifer's hands."

Aw, hell.

"What else?"

"I can't tell you, Mike."

He nodded. "This is about your contract with the Fae. Same stuff all over again."

"It is."

"I haven't asked you about that since we split up," he said. "But I'm going to have to ask you about it again. No direct questions."

She could handle that.

"I know the terms of your contract even if I don't know everything else. You've kept the terms never to tell a soul, no one else can know?"

"Yes. To the letter."

"Is the thing you saw in the mirror the Fae being you made the bargain with?" he asked.

"No."

He frowned. "Then the agreement's broken. Someone else knows."

Who? The poppet?

That changeling still ought to be indistinguishable from a human being in the human world, all grown up by now. Maybe married, popped out a baby or two of its own, along came the grandkids. As she understood it, the changeling would never discover it wasn't human. Never leave the human realm.

What had happened to change all that?

"You can tell me now," Mike said. "Tell me everything. It won't matter to the Fae if you do."

It mattered to her. "It's bad."

"For me to get you out of this, I need to know, Addie."

But there was no way out. Fae contracts had no loopholes. You couldn't run or hide from them. You couldn't outsmart them. This time she'd spent in Mike's office—every minute from here on out— would be the only time they had left together.

How could she tell him? She never wanted to see his expression broken and wary, for him to look at her like he couldn't decide if she was a monster. Or a stranger. She'd have no right to expect anything different.

More than that, though, she wasn't the same person who'd done that terrible thing to save herself. Time and experience had worked their own magic on her. She'd changed.

"I'm sorry, Mike," she said. And she meant it.

He twined his fingers with hers. Squeezed her hand. "I figured you'd say that."

She closed her eyes so she wouldn't have to look at the love in his. His determination filled every molecule of air in the room. She could all but hear the wheels turn in his mind.

"If we can find Jennifer, we can get to the bottom of this. I won't let you go without a fight," he said, his voice full of fierce and stupid hope. "We've gotta go now, and fast. Stay ahead of the Fae until we can get a bead on things. If we can't run from this problem, then we run at it."

He shoved her coat into her arms. Pulled her out of the office and down the hall.

Whatever he wanted, she'd try to do it. She tried to hope, too. No matter how alien it felt.

Or that it lasted all of ten seconds.

Ingram met them at the second floor landing. "Trouble," he said.

Red eyes. Black wings, difficult to camouflage under human clothes. At the bottom of the stairs.

She kissed Mike's cheek.

"Don't go," he said.

But of course she had to. She let go of his hand and walked down to meet the Fae with her head held high. She hadn't cringed since the last time Fred had struck her—all those fifty years ago—and she didn't intend to start again now.

She glanced back only once, to reassure Mike. But he'd vanished.

"The letter of the agreement has been broken," the Fae said, in a voice so deep it rattled her bones. "The changeling has discovered what it is, abandoned its human life and its family. It came back to us."

"How?"

"Politics," the Fae said. "It was the work of an enemy, exposing this secret. One of my enemies."

Addie closed her eyes. It was so unfair. This whole mess—the changeling had done nothing to cause it. And it wasn't Addie's or Jennifer's or even this Fae's fault.

She could rail against the unfairness of it, but she'd known the rules when she agreed to them all those years ago. The terms that bound all of them. "So what's my fate worse than death?"

"You'll come with me," the Fae said. That was all. That was enough.

She'd never see Mike again. Never go home again, never see all the treasures on their shelves in her sun-dappled kitchen. There'd be no more unwitting pawn customers to bake cookies for.

The life she'd built on the backs of that little girl she'd switched and her parents would be gone. It was the only life she had.

Well, at least she'd had one. Not everyone did.

The Fae being led her out into an afternoon laced with evening. The new sickle moon hung low on the horizon, the sky streaked with orange and pink. The wind tore at her. She shrugged her coat on and pulled it tight across her chest, breathing car exhaust and the salt scent of her own tears.

She saw Mike at the corner of the building. That alien hope flared in her again, and sputtered.

She memorized every angle of him, the rhythm of his gait as he strode over and spoke to the Fae.

"I won't try to stop you taking her. I came to ask you something." He didn't wait for the Fae being to respond. "I wanted to know who broke the contract between you and Addie since she sure as hell didn't. I'd have searched regardless, after you'd taken Addie away. And I'd have started with a young lady named Jennifer who brought Addie a looking glass today."

The Fae being looked pointedly at the mirror handle sticking up from Mike's back pocket.

"You know, I thought it'd take me hours," Mike said. "It's a big city. She could've been anywhere. But do you know where I found her? She was right here the whole time. Outside, out of view, sitting cross-legged on the sidewalk. She's still over there, matter of fact. Why is that?"

"Jennifer followed Addie," the Fae said. He turned to her. "You're the last human being she saw before she came to live with us. You're the reason her whole life changed."

Jennifer, the human child she'd stolen? She was so young—but then time moved much more slowly in the Fae realm.

Mike held Addie's gaze. "I want to know what happened, Addie. And I want to know why."

"No." She'd made up her mind about that upstairs, and it'd stay that way. She understood, too, that there was someone else she would have to tell. Someone else to whom she owed that story first.

They left Mike standing there on the walk, staring after them.

Jennifer joined them half-way down the block, keeping a fair distance as they walked into the sunset. She seemed to be gathering nerve to say something.

Addie braced herself for a tirade. For rage. For grief. But the girl didn't show her any of those.

"Did you know my mother?" she asked.

And, somehow, that was worse.

A ddie hated Faery. Everywhere green and in bloom, in colors so bright they hurt her eyes and sounds so sharp they hurt her ears. They gave her a room of her own, and she supposed she should be grateful.

They gave her new terms. Do what they told her. Obey the letter of their law. And there were so many laws to learn. It took up all her time. She had no treasures—other than her own company.

Until the day Jennifer knocked on her door, carrying a brown paper-wrapped package, and asked what had happened, and why.

Addie started slow, with Hot Corner Fred. Not that she expected Jennifer to understand or to forgive her, but because it felt important to say she hadn't done it for kicks. Or for any more power than power over her own life.

She told Jennifer about the smell of fresh paint in the living room of the dark, still house. Parents asleep in their bedroom with the door cracked wide enough to hear a crying child. The infant with the strawberry blond curls and pink-flowered pajama set, asleep in her crib.

The rhythm of the child's breath held her in thrall for what seemed like forever and couldn't have been more than a minute or two—until the little one scrunched up her face and waved her arms.

She had to move then.

Five long minutes to recite the spell she'd been given to hush the baby and the space around her so she wouldn't wake. To wrap her in a blanket and replace her with a homemade doll made of scraps and sticks. To do as she'd been ordered: keep from bolting long enough to witness the poppet come to life. She watched the doll assume the glamour the Fae had charmed into it. Take on every detailed characteristic of the baby who belonged in that crib.

She brought the baby to the Fae. God, but he looked like the devil. She expected him to smell like sulfur. But he smelled like green. Like crushed grass.

He took the child from her arms. *Never tell a soul,* he said. *No one may find out. Those are the terms. On pain of a fate worse than death.*

After, she went back to the place she shared with Fred. He'd been killed, just like the Fae promised her. She stepped over his body to get her things. She left and never looked back.

Addie finished the story, her last word echoing off the walls.

"Thank you," Jennifer said.

Addie took a deep breath and blew it out. "I never even knew what the Fae wanted you for. At the time, I didn't care."

"He told me he wanted to be a father."

But she'd had one. She'd had human parents.

The way the girl looked at her, Addie could tell she had so much more to say—all of that rage Addie expected and feared the night the Fae had come for her, it lurked below the surface. It would out eventually. And Addie would bear it.

Jennifer gave her the brown paper package.

The mirror inside looked the same as the one the girl had handed her a million years ago.

"I want you to have it," Jennifer said.

Addie waited until the girl had gone and then some, afraid to look and of what she might see.

In the wee hours that night, she took the chance.

In the looking glass, she saw her kitchen. The table set for tea. And Mike, gazing back at her. She couldn't hear his voice out loud, but she heard it in her heart.

"I'm working on a way out for you, Addie," he said.

She couldn't think of one that didn't involve making a deal with a heavy price, the kind she'd never want him to pay. Because she loved him. In whatever twisted way she was able, she loved him. She had nothing of her own here to hold onto, but she could hold onto that.

She wanted her life back.

If he was going to help her get it, she'd give him everything she had. That's what you did with high stakes, with people you loved. The people you treasured.

Mike would have to hope for both of them. It'd never been and would never be her strong suit, even now.

Despair was her particular magic, after all. She'd find a way to use it.

ABOUT THE AUTHOR

Since the age of seven, Leslie Claire Walker has wanted to be Princess Leia—wise and brave and never afraid of a fight, no matter the odds.

Leslie hails from the concrete and steel canyons and lush bayous of southeast Texas—a long way from Alderaan. Now, she lives in the rain-drenched Pacific Northwest with a cast of spectacular characters, including cats, harps, fantastic pieces of art that may or may not be doorways to other realms, and too many fantasy novels to count.

She is the author of the *Awakened Magic Saga*, a collected series of urban fantasy novels, novellas, and stories filled with magical assassins, fallen angels, faeries, demons, and complex, heroic humans. The primary series in the saga are the *Soul Forge*, set in Portland, Oregon, and the *Faery Chronicles*, set in Houston Texas. She has also authored stories for *The Uncollected Anthology* on a mission to redefine the boundaries of contemporary and urban fantasy.

Leslie takes her inspiration from the dark beauty of the city, the power of myth, strong coffee, whisky, and music ranging from Celtic harp to jazz to heavy metal. Rock on!

Find out more about Leslie at:
leslieclairewalker.com

facebook.com/leslieclairewalkerauthor
twitter.com/lesliewalker777
amazon.com/Leslie-Claire-Walker/e/B004LYBYLA
bookbub.com/authors/leslie-claire-walker

WINTERNIGHT

ERIC KENT EDSTROM

The body was little more than a chunk of ice half-buried by snow. It lay against the wall of the narrow alley running alongside the Cherry Bottom Inn. The way wasn't much traveled by honest folk, for it led to a dead-end right at the Starside city wall.

But thieves did sometimes use the alley, and two of them stood in the snow, bare feet wrapped in rags, holes in the elbows and knees of their ragged clothes exposing skin to the bite of the wintry air.

Kila had spotted the body first. Wen wasn't surprised. His little sister was very observant when she chose to be. What had drawn her attention was the muddy red stain of frozen blood in an already filthy snowbank.

"I s'pose that puts an end to our search," Kila said. She was trying to smooth over her upset, but she failed. Wen heard the quaver in her voice, saw her blinking a bit too hard.

The dead boy was Pons, a fellow Cheapsgate lad who sometimes teamed up with Wen and Kila to steal coin. He had been a wild thing, given to violence when the situation least called for it. Wen had never pulled his blade during a mugging, but Pons started with his.

Wen stooped and swiped the snow-cover off the body. Pons's face was blue, lips purple. His eyes were open, fixed.

"Blade's gone," he said. Pons always kept his short stabber tucked in a leather band at his ankle, concealed under his trousers.

Sniffling, Kila grabbed Pons shoulder and rolled him. "There it is."

The roughly carved wooden hilt was covered with frozen blood. Pons had been stabbed in the back with his own weapon. More than once.

The killer had left it there.

"He had loads of enemies," Wen said. That was known. Wen always tried to limit his words to facts. Father had charged him with keeping Kila safe and training her to survive. The first principle was to see the truth. The second, speak the truth. And nothing else. The truth would keep you alive if you could notice it and accept it.

He scanned the alley. The wind pressed through it, sweeping most of the snow away from the compacted dirt. But something was tickling his instincts, making him hunch his shoulders. He looked up to where the eves of the inn hung over the alley, the undersides jagged with icicle fangs.

The smells of the city were overpowered by the garbage heap at the end of the alley where the inn's kitchen refuse was tossed for the pigman to come to haul it away for his hogs. This was the lowest section of the merchant's quarter of Terriside, making it the poorest and meanest area inside the city walls.

"We should go," he said. "If we're going to pay Odok, we need—"

"We're gonna leave Pons?" Kila said.

"You going to carry him?"

"No. But some Kil-kisser killed our friend. We can't just let 'em get away with that."

Wen gently touched his sister's shoulder. She was fourteen, skinny, smudged, and scrappy as a cornered rat-hound. "We don't know who did it and there's nothing here that tells us. We must go."

The chill on the back of his neck was from more than the cold air.

"We should tell somebody," Kila said.

"We will. But first we have to take care of ourselves. Odok wants his rent. I want roast goose. You want your first sip of trezz. All must be earned this night."

Kila relented, though she didn't stop staring at Pons until they had turned the corner. She ran into Wen, who had stopped in his tracks. Barring the way were three men of the Watch. They stood shoulder to shoulder, their burnished breastplates and naked blades reflecting the mercus streetlights.

The commander of the squad stepped forward. "Murderers. On your knees, hands behind your backs. Smuddy, watch 'em."

Wen had learned young that the Watch was made up of ordinary men, which meant you might meet a friendly one or a mean one, an honest one in rags or a villain in the livery of the law. Father had taught him that most of the Watch were doing their best, earning coin for their families and hoping to keep the peace inside the walls. But even the most generous man of the Watch thought Cheapsgaters lower than rats, an infestation to be eradicated.

This was why Wen and Kila had come into the city through the sewers rather than through the Cheaps, the main gate from the docks. The Watch posted at the Cheaps would never have let them in without paying a toll or simply shouting them away and giving them hard cuffs on the back of their heads to beat sense into them.

But Wen's mind skittered over this strange situation with the deftness of a street juggler. The Watch obviously knew about the body in the alley. All they wanted was to find someone in close proximity to it, declare them the murderer...and return to the Westbunk headquarters where it was warm. Their commander would never send them all the way back to lower Terriside to finish their shift.

It was Winternight. The shortest day of the year.

Their commander would send them to their barracks, or perhaps, as a reward for ridding Starside of two Cheapsgate thieves, send them to their families to enjoy an evening of feasting and jollity.

Wen wore his blade, Cayne, on his thigh, just as Father had done. Having Cayne close usually gave him confidence, but here, now, faced with men ten years his senior, fit and hale, well-fed, trained, and motivated to end things quickly, he didn't dare draw his weapon.

"Kila, run," he said softly. He didn't shout such things. Father had taught him to remain calm, to let his body rush with the energy of danger, but to keep his mind a placid sea. "You know where to go."

"We can both outrun 'em," she whispered. "To the roofway."

He might have risked it, except the one on the left had a flickbow slung over his shoulder. If he and Kila both tried to reach the roofway, the man would have at least three shots at them.

"Go."

Kila obeyed, regaling the men with a litany of trezz-dive obscenities as she darted back the way they'd come.

One of the Watch men went after her, shouldering past Wen and driving him into the wall of the Cherry Bottom Inn. The sound of revelry inside was muted by the block walls. He was no more than two feet from a warm hall, abundant food, endless ale and trezz, and raucous music and dancing. But here under the bleak night sky, with two swords extended toward him, he felt as alone as a man stranded in a mountain pass, hungry wolves cornering him in a shallow cave.

Kila would be safe, though. One man in armor would never keep up with her. The man with the flickbow had not gone after her. A stroke of Pol's luck, that.

Kila could climb faster than Wen, and once she got to the roofs, she could jump gaps no Watch man would dare to attempt while wearing his gear.

Knowing that she was safe allowed Wen to relax. Slightly. Being stared down by men of the Watch was never easy to bear.

He dropped to his knees and held his hands up and away from Cayne. More than a few of Wen's acquaintances had died simply because the Watch believed they were about to draw a weapon.

"My sister didn't kill that boy," he said. "You can see she's no murderer. She's barely fourteen. And neither did I. Pons was my friend."

"Perhaps true," said the commander. He wore the sigil of Starside —a silver raven's head in profile, beak facing to his right. His cloak was thick, muddy at the bottom, but otherwise in good condition. "But why did she run if innocent?"

"She ran because I told her to. Our father is dead. She obeys me." Sometimes.

The commander tugged at the fingers of his lambskin gloves, then pull them off and tucked them in his belt. His boots clomped in the slush, his buckles jangling with every step. He stopped just short of Wen when the man sent after Kila returned, breath heaving.

They didn't speak, but clearly Kila had escaped.

"It only takes one lad to murder another lad," the commander said. Then, as casually as he might swat a fly, he backhanded Wen across the face. The blow was so hard, Wen spun and fell onto his side. The man's massive hand had caught his ear, and in the stinging cold, the pain felt like great pincers had gripped and twisted his ear off.

His cheek pressed to the frozen dirt and the taste of warm blood filled his throat.

"Get him on his feet. We've a long march ahead of us."

Rough hands pulled Wen up. His arms were yanked behind his back and a man cinched them at the wrists with leather cord. The rattle of chains followed, and Wen felt the hard, cold grip of shackles clamp around his ankles.

"Move!" the commander said, shoving Wen ahead.

He moved. He had to breathe through his mouth, for his nostrils were obstructed by blood that trickled over his lips. The pain of the blow bloomed again and again in slow throbs. Surely his nose was broken.

"What about the body?" the Watch man with the flickbow asked.

"The pigman'll see it, most like. That lad'll be fattening a sow soon. And he won't turn, frozen as he is."

"So we leave him?"

"Yes. We leave him. Unless you want to carry that ice block up to the Westbunk."

"No sir."

Motivated by their likely early release from duty, the men set a brisk pace. If his legs were free Wen could have kept up easily enough. But his leg chain was short, allowing him only to shuffle. His bare feet scraped on the frozen road, and once they got onto the Street of Sorrows, the stone abraded his soles until they bled.

"This is a fine blade," the commander said, holding Cayne to the white-hot mercus light shining from atop a pole. "Too fine for a Cheapsgate wretch like you. Who didya steal it from?"

"My father owned that blade," Wen said. "He said he got it as a gift."

"A gift, eh? Then I'll accept it as a gift from you."

Wen bit back the angry words that came to mind. Kila would never have kept them contained, but he could. It was one of the most important skills Father had taught him. A man must stand up for himself, yes. He must fight. But a wise man knew when to attack, when to defend, and when to wait.

This was time to wait. To endure.

Starside was alive with lights in every window, sounds of laughter, of lively Winternight songs strummed on nickleharpas, blown on flutes, and sung in half-drunken unison.

The Watch men herded him, offering blows to his spine when he slowed, curses when he stumbled, hard jerks on his bound wrists when he fell.

The commander shifted from cruelty to holiday spirit in less than a second. One moment he'd sing a snatch of "It Comes upon the Winternight Moon" with the melancholy notes at the end of each verse, and then shout for Wen to move his swine-ass faster, slapping the flat of his sword against Wen's shoulders.

The wind had increased here on the broad avenue called the Street of Sorrows. The shops and homes on either side formed a sort of canyon for the mountain air to flow through, a river of Kil's breath in which he had to shuffle upstream.

They stopped once, at the Yin Inn. The commander left two men to keep an eye on Wen and barged into the shouting and song of the inn. He returned ten minutes later, smelling of trezz and some harlot's perfume. He handed his men small flagons of warmed cinnamon spirits, for which they expressed genuine gratitude.

Wen received nothing but curses.

By the time they got through Dunne Medow Plaza and began the walk through Gristenside, Wen's feet were numb as Pons' frozen body was. The chill crept up his shins and he was sure he would lose his feet to it. The blood had long stopped flowing from his nose and split lip, the trickle now a crimson icicle on his flesh.

The chain made a percussive rasp and rattle with every step now. And no amount of prodding or swearing could push him to go faster. The strength was simply not available to summon.

He drifted into a daze of pain and confusion and hopelessness. The cobblestones looked soft now, inviting. He would love to lie down upon them, curl up and sleep. He would welcome any nightmare but this.

His thoughts drifted to Kila. His sister. The girl Father had brought home a few years back, half wild, sharp eyed and quick.

From that day on, Father's focus had been on her survival, her safety. And Wen did not begrudge her that affection. He had felt it, too, almost instantly upon seeing her that first time. It was impossible not to love her, despite her temper, her insensitivity to risk. For Kila could look at Wen and her expression, her elfin brow, her striking loveliness, would instantly charm him. His instinct, like Father's had been, was to protect her. Always.

At some point he had fallen. He didn't remember it. But when awareness of the world swirled back into his mind, he found himself in the corner of a barren stone cell.

The only light came from a whale oil lantern in the hall. It bled an orange glow beneath the ironbound door. There were no windows. No cot. No appointments at all save a vile bucket for a chamber pot.

His wrists had been loosed, but the shackles and chain remained on his legs. He struggled to his feet, fighting nausea and a renewal of the pain stemming from his nose and blasting through his head.

He had nothing in his stomach to bring up, so the spell of convulsions that bent him over produced nothing but spittle.

When the heaves finally passed, he shuffled to the door and pressed his forehead to it. And now he understood what alone meant. Father had tried to explain it once. He had tried to convey the peacefulness of solitude, which he had felt wandering the wilds of the Honor Mountains. Father had made it sound wonderful.

The difference was freedom, Wen realized. Alone and free and alone and trapped make for much different experiences.

"Make friends with discomfort," Father had advised. And he had put Wen and Kila in many very uncomfortable situations. Hunger, thirst, danger, cold, heat. Idleness.

If anyone was prepared to endure being locked in a cold cell on Winternight it should have been Wen. But he had allowed himself to look forward to the night's celebrations. He had planned to bring home a roast goose from Critt Sanglo's Cheapsgate tavern. He had looked forward to watching Kila drink her first swallow of trezz. He was going to be there when she threw it up, and he would calm her when she ranted from the trezz visions clouding her mind.

He returned to his corner and hugged his arms to his chest, knees curled as close as he could get them to his body. After the long walk to the Westbunk, he was frozen. And though there was no wind inside his cell, the walls seemed to radiate a death's chill.

He began the breathing exercise Father had taught him, the Breath of Inner Flame. Deep breaths, quickly exhaled, again and again until he became light-headed. Then he'd exhale and hold it until his body demanded he breathe again.

Twenty minutes of this warmed him. And he had to stop because he would soon start to sweat, and then he would get chilled further.

The Inner Flame had cleared some of the muddiness from his mind, and it had banished the chill even from his toes. But it had also awakened hunger.

Would the Watch bother to feed the prisoners? Perhaps the night's meal had already been served before Wen had arrived. No matter. Wen could survive hunger. He would survive and he would escape and he would return to Kila.

They would have their Winternight celebration tomorrow night. Or perhaps the next if the Watch and magistrate were too hungover to deal with Wen on the morrow.

But his spirit could not maintain the lie.

They would get to him when they got to him. Cheapsgaters who entered the Westbunk did not usually ever leave it. And those who did were transformed into something less than they had been upon entering.

Escape. That was the only way. He would escape.

He laughed ruefully, and the sound slapped back from the walls, mocking him. Escape from a stone cell with an ironbound door? And then pass through how many locked gates, manned by how many armed men? And then how would he slip through the great portcullises of the tunnel leading from the Westbunk fortress?

To entertain such a notion was folly. No, Wen had to see the truth. Only the truth. To attach his hopes to fancy was to give into death.

He knew no facts other than that he had not killed Pons. He did not know what his captors were doing, or what they *would* do, or when.

So. What could he do?

Preserve strength. Calm his mind.

He returned to his Inner Fire breathing, going more slowly, not seeking to make heat so much as to empty his mind. When faced with a problem with no solution, there was no point in frantically guessing at answers.

He must become like the stone of his wall. Still and chill of mind.

He didn't sleep. But as the night wore on, his mind drifted into a hazy somnolence, where images of Father and Kila and Pons and Critt Sanglo and Parlo Odok appeared before him, walked across his cell to either shake their heads or frown or squat and look at him with concern.

It was the image of Pons, lips purple, eyes whited over with frost that brought Wen out of his half-sleep. The horrific vision of his dead friend kneeling before him, wringing his hands and asking over and over, "Are you dying? Are you dying?"

Vision clearing, Wen shrank back into the frigid corner. This wasn't Pons before him, but a living man. A very short man, dressed in prisoner's rags, beard dangling from a narrow chin and nearly brushing the floor.

"Are ye dyin', laddie?" the man said. "Wouldna be so smart o' ya to keel o'er on Vinternekt. Why don't ya stand up and hop 'round to warm yer blood?"

The man had rough hands. And so tiny. But they gripped Wen's wrists and urged him onto his feet. Ah, his aching feet. He didn't think they would bear his weight.

But the man was insistent. And strong. Impossibly so for a man his height, no more than four feet. Probably less.

His trousers were rough spun, and in the dimness of the cell it was impossible to tell what color. His shirt—if it could be called that —looked like a burlap sack with armholes cut in.

"Who are ya? Am I dead? Are ya here ta lead me cross the river?" Wen said, his confusion getting the best of his tongue and letting a bit of the Cheaps-talk escape.

"Ha! Imagine that. Lumne wouldna let me inta her waters if I paid her in whiskers."

Wen was too frightened to comment on the oddness of the man's words. But he was on his feet now, and the man was so small, he no longer felt threatened. He straightened, tried to show strength he didn't have. "How did you get in?"

"Through yon door?"

"It's unlocked?"

"No. But I didna need it ta open to pass through."

Insane. The little man was beyond the reckoning of men. Surely the Watch had thrown them in while Wen had been in his daze.

"Yer chain'll be a hindrance," the man said. "Let me..."

He touched a shackle and it unclasped and clanked onto the floor. With another touch, the other fell away.

"Kil's thumb! How did ya do that?"

"Locks are my speciality, laddie. Didn't yer father ever tell ya 'bout me? No? Allow me t'introduce m'self." He bowed, very formally, flourishing one hand behind him, and taking up his beard in the other to keep it from touching the floor. "I am Sazeenie, Opener of Locked Things. In Reignini they called me the small god of keys and locks. In the south I am considered a demayne."

"*Are* you a demayne?" Wen asked. His shackles had surely been locked, and Sazeenie had not held a key. Surely he'd used some dark mercusine power to unlock them.

"I'm no demayne, laddie." The little man's features darkened and his nose wriggled in irritation. "Nor am I of yer sort, neither. But let's put that aside." He pointed a slim finger at Wen's chest. "You need to get back to yer sister. She's in it to her hips."

"Kila? What's happening? How do you know her?"

Sazeenie tapped his temple. "The one who sent me mentioned

that Kila has tracked down a murderer. Someone who killed a rascal named Pons. But...she got caught."

"Who is it? Where is she?"

"Dox Viller. She's somewhere inside his rambling fortress o' shacks in Cheapsgate."

Wen cursed, arms going slack. "I know of him." If she was truly in Dox Viller's mitts, she was in worse danger than he was.

"Then why are ya standin' here and gaping like a pike-gawper?" Sazeenie pointed at the door. "Go."

Wen stumbled across the cell, feet sending glassy stabs up his shins with every step. He pushed against the door. It was locked. There was no handle or latch on this side.

"Oh. I forgot," Sazeenie said. "Take my hand."

Wen took the small hand.

"Follow me." The little man walked into the door, body disappearing into the solid wood as if plunging into black liquid. The grip firmed on Wen's hand and dragged him after.

Passing through the door made Wen's stomach do flip-flops and his skin crawled with a hot oily feeling. But then he was in the corridor and the weird sensations vanished.

Sazeenie led him through a maze of prison passageways, keeping a tight grip on Wen's hand. They passed cell after cell, and the only sound aside from their footsteps was a distant clanking.

The sound grew louder the farther they went, ascending stairs and slipping through halls. They finally came outside, into a great courtyard. Men of the Watch would usually be posted atop the walls, but they were all inside for Winternight revelry. The sharp report of a hammer on iron resounded from the walls. The smoke from a smithy wafted through the chill air. Some poor apprentice was at work, missing out on the holiday festivities. A pang of pity shot through Wen and he stumbled toward the sound.

Sazeenie caught his hand. "Is yer blood made of sweet syrup, laddie? Ya canna ease all the pains of th' world. Not this night, nor any other." The little man's voice was firm but gentle.

It rankled Wen that the rest of the Westbunk was inside, cavorting and drinking while so many had so little.

But why shouldn't they be? There was no enemy force threatening the Westbunk or the Citadel. For the Watch, the world was as it should be. There were villains for them to hunt and arrest and kill, and a placid, law-abiding citizenry to pay their wages.

"Come!" Sazeenie didn't make any effort to stay quiet, he simply *was* quiet. And the one time a man of the Watch appeared from his barracks to unfasten his trousers and relieve himself against a wall, Sazeenie led Wen past as if they were supposed to be there. The man didn't notice.

And then Wen was upon the Street of the Diadem, high up in Gristenside. The sky had cleared, and Winternight stars shined like diamonds strewn upon a field of black velvet.

"This is where I leave you, Wenton Sigh," Sazeenie said.

"That was my father's name. I'm called Wen."

"Short fer Wenton, no? Never you mind. I have something for you." He reached inside the throat of his burlap shirt and extricated a sack, one much too large and bulky to have been concealed there. He fiddled with a ragged bit of twine that held the bag shut. Clenching the tie in his teeth, he rummaged in the sack, muttering to himself. "No, that's not the right one. Oops. Forgot about him. Aha. My itch cream. I've been lookin' fer that. Oh! Here it is." He pulled out Cayne, sheath and all. "Nicked it from the commander who dragged ya in. I didna like the smell o' his muffins, no I didna."

Awed and now truly frightened, Wen accepted Cayne. "Who are you? *What* are you?" he asked as he buckled the sheath to his thigh, just as Father had worn it.

But Sazeenie didn't answer. Wen looked up from his task, determined to get the facts out of the little man.

Sazeenie was gone.

The bell tower at the Baths of Ori rang eleven. Wen was shocked to hear the tolls ring that many. He had assumed it was nearing dawn. But it grew dark early on Winternight, and the Watch had taken him just as he'd come out of the sewers, the beginning of darkness in Starside. The time of thieves.

His worry drove him downslope, though his feet quickly grew numb from the cold. On a night like this, he and Kila would have hovered on the rooftops in lower Terriside, not needing to go far to find drunken marks to rob.

That was important, for without shoes, they simply couldn't travel far. But Wen had trudged all the way to the Westbunk, and now he had to get back to Cheapsgate. To Dox Viller's ramshackle lair of harlot dens, trezz counters, flop-bunks, and bawdy excesses of every kind. At this hour the fighting round would be full of roaring men and women, waging coppers on shirtless brutes with knuckled noses and few teeth as they bashed each other senseless.

If Kila had been taken by Dox's men, she very well could be dead by now. Or worse. Wen knew what men in Dox Viller's circle could do to a girl, a menu of perversions even Kil himself would rage as foul.

No. He mustn't let himself think such things. The truth. He must see only the truth, not speculate about what was likely. Nothing was certain until it was known.

The clear truth before him was that he would never get back to Cheapsgate on foot. He had no coin with which to hire an atlen hack even if a driver were willing to take a Cheapsgater as a fare. But there were few hacks out and about on Winternight anyway.

He stumbled down the Street of the Diadem, past the huge wrought iron gates of the Gristenside greathouses occupied by Radiant families, the poorest of whom could buy up every soul in Cheapsgate with the coin they spent housing their horses and atlen birds.

He didn't know how to ride a horse. People occasionally tried to ride on the backs of atlens, but the huge draft birds used by the Radiancies were not accustomed to such treatment.

What he needed was a Radiant's carriage to roll by. He might be able to cling to the back and ride it partway downslope. But why would any of the Radiant families go downhill on Winternight? They were all—

The sound of revelry pulled his eyes past an open gate to a brightly illuminated greathouse. A long row of carriages stood in the drive, atlen birds standing in harness, most perched on one leg, heads tucked under a wing for warmth.

Footmen and drivers stood by open fires, enjoying food and drink provided by the Radiant's staff as a consolation for missing the evening with their own families. The men tossed their red faces back and laughed, some sang Winternight carols, others stamped their feet and smoked on pipes as they told big lies to each other and gossiped about "their people," the families they served.

Wen stumbled down the drive, noting that the house armsman on duty was asleep by the tiny wood furnace in his shack.

Wen didn't know how to drive a carriage, but he understood the principle. He slipped along the driveway and climbed to the driver's bench of the first carriage he found. A Radiant's crest was emblazoned on the side, a fox head flanked by crossed swords and crossed blades of wheat on the other side.

He unwrapped the reins from the halt post next to the bench and clicked his tongue.

The birds in harness did not respond. He flapped the reins, sending a snap down the leather lines to where they draped across the birds' feather hindquarters. They startled and drew their heads into the open. One looked back to eye him, a great amber stare of such coldness Wen felt he knew how a pig looked to a bear.

He flicked the reins again and barked a "yah" like he'd heard atlen drivers call out his entire life.

The birds leaned into their harnesses, but the carriage didn't move. One bird squawked irritably.

Wen remembered the brake. He found the wooden lever and released it. Instantly the carriage began to roll. Pulling hard to the left, Wen carved a huge circle in the drive and urged the birds to run.

And run they did. He was through the gates and racing downhill by the time he heard the cry of outraged drivers and footmen rise behind him.

He abandoned the carriage well before he reached the Cheaps, sending it empty back up the Street of Sorrows. With no driver at the reins, the birds continued toward home by memory, surely longing for feed and a warm place out of the wind.

Feet aching, Wen descended to the sewers and passed under the city wall to Cheapsgate.

~

Dox Viller's realm was a sort of hell within a hell. Cheapsgate was not part of Starside so much as it was a barnacle attached to the exterior of the city. Set outside the city wall, it was a stretch of shacks that tumbled toward the old docks. At ground level it was a maze, since it had been built and rebuilt over the centuries with no plan.

Cheapsgaters moved about on the roofs. But few were up top at this hour, and the sounds of revelry below were muted and held a tinge of angry madness. That was just Cheapsgate.

Wen stood on a rooftop at the edge of Dox Viller's territory. Father had taught him and Kila to avoid the man and anyone associated with him. Though he had taught his children how to steal, Father had very clear notions about what crimes were allowed and what were forbidden. The distinctions were clear to Wen, less so to Kila.

But even she knew not to come here. Pons had not been a good friend, nor very trustworthy. Even so, it was very much like Kila to take his murder personally. As far as Wen could tell, her logic would go something like: if Pons deserved murdering then *she* should have been the one to do it. Otherwise, hands off.

After Wen had been taken prisoner, she must have gone off looking for Pons' murderer. Wen winced at the notion, realizing she had chosen to do that instead of come to the Westbunk for him.

A foolish thing to worry over, he thought, shamed by his feeling of hurt. He was good at reprimanding himself. *Of course* she wouldn't come to the Westbunk. What could she possibly do to help him there? The more likely outcome would be that she would find a home in a cell, too.

No. She would reason that finding the real murderer, and twisting a confession out of him, would be the way to get Wen out of prison. He felt better about that idea.

She should have robbed someone and gone back to the Warren, paid Parlo Odok, and bought dinner from Critt Sanglo. But Kila only did as told some of the time, and when Wen wasn't around, she did as she pleased.

Now Wen was standing where she had likely stood a few hours ago. She would have gone to Critt Sanglo's first and asked the old sailor if he'd heard anything about Pons. Critt knew almost everything that happened in Cheapsgate and he was more trustworthy than anyone else.

Had Critt pointed her here? Or had she gone to confront the murderer somewhere else only to be captured and dragged here?

Wen bounced on his numb toes. He had to get indoors now. No sense in speculating about how Kila had gotten captured. The only thing to do now was get her out. He'd promised Father he would look after her. Wen took promises seriously, for they were a form of truth. If you broke a promise, then you had lied.

He crossed to the closest rooftop and walked briskly to a central area clear of shacks. This was a sort of courtyard that led into various sections of Viller's disgusting hive of treachery.

There was no ladder, just a pole to slide down. Wen's feet touched the ground, and he immediately went to the door of the largest of the many trezz dives. A sign above the door read VILLER'S & KILLERS in red.

Wen passed from the stinky chill into a fetid and smoky hell.

All that was ugly about humans was on full display. Men of few teeth grinned in lurid whale oil light at bare-breasted women dancing on tabletops. Everyone held mugs of trezz, and the biting smell of it competed with overcooked meat, pipe-smoke, and the sick-up of a portly, half-clothed man lying facedown in the midst of the cavorting women.

At the fringes of the room, men ate huge slabs of meat with their hands, women and men sat on laps, naked and sweating.

The deeper into this realm Wen walked, the barer became the lascivious appetites of Viller's clientele. Merchantmen of Terriside sported with humans chained at the neck, whipping them with leather crops and glorying in their domination of another mortal.

Disgust and rage threatened to overpower Wen's focus. His hand rested on Cayne's hilt, and he dared not meet anyone's eyes lest he provoke a fight.

He was not here to murder random villains. He was here for Kila. Viller's kind would devour themselves, Father had always said. From the looks of it, they would debauch themselves into early graves.

Stepping over a couple in the midst of bedroom intimacies, Wen pushed through a curtained doorway and into a quieter hallway behind. Here the people were soft-eyed, dazed. The smoke of their pipes was the thick and blue mind-sweetening leaf from the south. Most would never again leave here, having become so dependent upon the leaf they would offer themselves to be chained and whipped to have it.

Dox had a private guard of sorts, a collection of strong mercenaries who enjoyed free trezz, free women, and absolute immunity for their crimes. They did not wear the livery of an organized guard, but were identifiable by the black tattoos on their arms and cheeks. The inking was crude, done quick, all in black. The shape of a curved blade, a "gutter", meant to plunge in the abdomen, twist, and yanked out with bowels attached.

The first gutter-tattooed man Wen saw looked at him with flat eyes. This man had not consumed so much as a drop of ale this night. That made him exceptionally dangerous.

"I heard my sister is here," Wen said. He kept his voice calm, businesslike. He wasn't here for a fight.

"Ya look like ya fell on yer face," the man said, amused. "Doubt yer sister'll be pop'lar here if she looks like you."

"She doesn't look like me. Her name is Kila. I was told she's here. Can I see Dox?"

"Kila? The young one, eh? Yer 'sister' my ass. D'ya think Dox'll pay you fer her services, lad? Shoulda kept her away from here, that you should have."

"It's not like that. She *is* my sister. I want her back."

"It's Winternight, lad. Why don't ya go home ta yer shack and leave Dox to 'is pleasures. If yer sister pleases him, she'll have no more ta show fer her night with him than a black eye and a babe in 'er belly." He winked and nudged Wen. "But who knows who the father'll be."

Finding this enormously funny, the man bent double and laughed until he coughed. Eyes glistening, he said, "Mayhap you'll have a little brother soon, and I'll be the father, eh? Dox is generous."

"I'm sorry," Wen said, not meaning it.

The man's laugh faded and his eyes squinted.

Wen pulled Cayne from his belly, jerking slightly upward to sever more of the man's guts. "You should have told me where she was."

Wen sheathed Cayne, unconcerned about the blood on the blade. The strange weapon would absorb it.

The man was the third Wen had ever stabbed. He thought it the first he'd ever killed.

He felt nothing.

He continued down the hall the man had been guarding, through a door, and into a private trezz hall. The same sort of debauchery was in process, though the light was dimmer and the people tireder and more ragged looking.

There were more blade tattoos here. Wen approached the calmest looking of the bunch. "Dox summoned me." He snapped his fingers. "Don't waste my time."

He'd learned this trick from Father. Act like you are in command and one in three men will simply obey. This one did not jump up, but merely eyed Wen's rags and his bloody face.

"Dox's enemies did this," Wen said, pointing to his broken nose. "Dox wants the details. Move."

The man was young, perhaps five years older than Wen. He pushed back from the table and motioned for Wen to follow. They exited the hall and went through a series of corridors until they reach a section where the construction was of much better quality. The materials were not typical of Cheapsgate, where everything was built from pieces of ruined ships and cast-off shipping crates. Here the woodwork was fine, the rugs luxurious, furniture detailed in gold. Dox was not a poor man.

The blade-marked man spoke to a guard in front of a set of double doors. After a bit of arguing the guard motioned Wen forward and opened one door.

"If you lied, you'll die. Dox likes to see pain."

Wen shuffled into darkness and was engulfed in warmth.

Kila sat on a chair in the middle of the room. Her hands were tied to the armrests. It was a fine chair, oak, polished to a shine. Her blond hair was loose and tumbled over her face.

Everything in Dox's lair shined. Gold leaf frames held mirrors and paintings covering the walls. The settees and armchairs were upholstered in thick fabrics of maroon, the legs gold. An enormous hearth occupied one side of the room, huge timbers ablaze and shedding enough heat to keep the two hounds curled in the far corner on the opposite side.

The hounds came to attention at Wen's entry. Shaggy, thickly built, they growled, lips curled back to show their fangs.

No, three hounds. Another had been under the bed.

Upon the bed lay a man so immensely fat that Wen wasn't sure exactly where his body ended and the spread of furs and blankets began.

Dox Viller raised a hand, each finger encumbered with a huge ring. The man's round head drooped at the sides where folds of flab hung from his perfectly bald scalp.

"I see your blade," Dox said. His voice was deep, but guttural, as if he had something stuck in his throat. "Draw it and you will die." He waggled a finger and clicked his tongue and his dogs leapt toward Wen, barking and gnashing their teeth. But at Dox's whistle, they froze, went utterly still and silent.

Kila was facing away from Wen. He saw now that her head had been braced by rope to keep her from turning it.

"I'm here," he said to her. It was all he could say. The truth, no more. No "You'll be well, I'll get you out." He could not say that. Not yet.

He could kill a dog. One dog. The others would be on him a second later, surely trained to bite his blade wrist. He might injure a second. And then he would die.

His eyes flashed to Kila. There was something odd in her posture, aside from the fact she was tied to her chair. She seemed too upright, too stiff. And why wasn't she saying anything? He'd never known Kila to keep her mouth shut when confronting people, even when she would be wiser staying silent.

Dox said, "I'll call my hounds back if you agree to leave your interesting blade sheathed. Deal?"

"Deal." The man made it sound like a negotiation. But when one side has no choice but to agree or die, has a bargain truly been struck? Wen didn't think so. He would strike if needed.

"I'm here for her," he said tilting his head at Kila.

"Oh, I know. Sargent Fyooks of the Watch sent word. The Watch always sends word to me when they throw someone in a cell. It's a matter of courtesy, in case the prisoner is one of mine."

"I'm not one of yours."

"No. Wen Sigh, isn't it? I knew your father."

"He hated you."

This struck the man as funny. His massive body jiggled and waggled as he giggled, emitting a high-pitched warble that made his dogs whine. "The feeling was mutual, believe me. Wenton Sigh did not like how I do business. But we were partners early on. Did he tell you that? I was the brains, he was the hands."

Father had never mentioned working with Dox Viller. Wen did

not know if it was a lie or not. Looking at the man now, it was hard to believe. His red face, the body so large Wen doubted he could leave the bed. What kind of thief could he have ever been?

"I was not always so grand," Dox said wryly, as if reading Wen's thoughts. "I've had every healer money can buy ushered into this room. I've gone months eating nothing but dates, weeks on water and cheese. All to no avail. I am cursed. Alas, I cannot even enjoy my collection of pretties anymore. I simply have them brought in so I can look at them."

"And why tie her to the chair?"

"I like them to struggle. But come join me over here. The view is much better. I was just telling this sweet thing how I would command my dogs and men to—well why spoil the fun?" He waved a ham-sized paw for Wen to come approach his bed.

Wen obeyed, happy to get within dagger's reach of the man's eyes. But with two sharp whistles, Dox also instructed the dogs to join him. One leapt onto the bed, and stood at the ready, eyes fixed on Wen.

"Look at the girl, lad."

Wen turned to face his sister, fearing what he would discover. Had they beaten her? Had they cut her?

His eyes drifted from her bare feet to her face. He blinked. Those were Kila's clothes, but that was not Kila.

The filthy blond hair was the same length, but the girl's face could not have been more different. She was plumper, features more delicate. And her hands were clean, fingernails smooth and much too long. Kila always chewed hers to the tips.

The truth. See the truth.

This was not Kila, but she wore Kila's clothes. Did Dox know this wasn't his sister? Did Dox even know who this was?

"Lovely isn't she? But tell me how she acquired the blond locks? Your father looked like you, reddish hair. And your mother...ah, what a lovely lass was Evvie."

Hearing Mother's name come from these repugnant and glistening lips enraged him. His jaw throbbed, teeth aching from the pressure of his anger. He said nothing.

The girl was staring at him, glassy-eyed. She did not appear to be at home inside her head. "Is she drunk?"

"It'll wear off soon. Just a special brew I concocted a long while a go, a bit of something to make women more compliant." He clicked his tongue and the remaining dog approached the girl. It snarled and barked.

The girl's head swung toward the dog, eyes seeking to focus on the source of the noise. She smiled wanly. "Hello, puppy." Her words slurred out of her, like the incoherent things Kila said when Wen woke her from a deep sleep.

The dog continued to snarl, taking slow steps. Its head hung low, spine and tail level. It was stalking her.

"Stay back, pup," she said. "You're mean."

Dox's lips twisted in dissatisfaction. "This is no good at all." He eyed Wen, and his expression compressed into suspicion. With the petulant look of an angry child he clicked his tongue three times in short succession.

The dog lunged, clamped its jaws on the girl's leg and started to shake and pull, using the full weight of its body.

The girl screamed, the pain and terror burning the remainder of Dox's concoction from her mind. Her eyes were scrunched with agony and she flailed against the restraints.

Dox laughed.

Wen's hand was on Cayne's hilt. He gripped it.

The dog on the bed growled, the one behind him answered.

This wasn't Kila. That was the truth. But she had Kila's clothes. She screamed and begged as the dog snarled and jerked its head, gnawing on her shin. Blood flowed to the floor, dripping from the beast's jaws.

"That's your sister, man!" Dox said, laughing. "You're watching her be eaten alive! But let us savor this dish a while longer, eh?" He called off the dog. It obeyed instantly, releasing the girl and backing three steps. "Wondrous animals, these hounds. Trained by the best. Spared no expense."

The girl sobbed and continued to pull at her restraints, but the strength was out of her. Tears and snot traced down her face.

"You are not very observant, Dox Viller," Wen said quietly.

"Eh? What do you mean? Speak up, boy."

"Her fingernails are too fine, too clean. Her hair is all of a length, groomed and tended by someone with skill. And listen to her cries. Not a curse for you among them."

The man's flaccid lips came together and pursed in a thoughtful pout. "Hmm." He snorted and hocked a glob of phlegm toward a spittoon on the side table behind Wen. "Hmmm. Targle! Targle, get in here!"

A bit of wall paneling immediately opened. A concealed door. The room beyond was dim. A lean man with the gutter tattoo on both forearms came in. His blade was in his hands. "Shall I do him or her?" he asked.

"Neither, Targle, you fool. Fasten your trousers, man. I don't want to see your lolly and pollies! Besides, we have company."

Targle set his dagger on a table and laced up his breeches. "Sorry, Dox. What d'ya need?"

"Where'd you find this girl?"

"She was asking 'bout yer son at Sanglo's. I asked a man I knew about her. He looked her up and down and said she was Kila Sigh, the one you wanted."

"This isn't Kila Sigh," Dox said. He looked to Wen for confirmation. Wen nodded. The girl was very alert now. She shook her head in frantic fractions, more hair spilling across her face.

"I'm not her. I swear it."

"Where did you get those clothes?" Wen demanded. He wanted to approach her, get to where she could see his face while the other men could not. But the dogs held fast, ready to lunge at Dox's command.

"I—I traded a girl for them. My clothes were too fine for Cheapsgate and she wanted to go into Terriside. I thought Pol had smiled so kindly on me when I found her. Now I know she wanted me to suffer for her."

Kila would never knowingly put someone else into this chair. The idea that Kila would trade clothes for any reason was very strange. But then Wen understood. She was looking for Commander Fyooks, the man who had arrested him. And now that he thought more about it, he was sure she had trailed them on the way to the Westbunk. She had heard Fyooks call back his intention to return to the Yin Inn.

She had found more suitable clothes and gone there to wait for him. Clever girl. But to accomplish what?

"Your son," Wen said, mind catching on something Targle had said. A new connection snapped in his mind. "Pons was your boy?"

"One of a hundred. But yes." Dox's laced his fingers across his chest. "Your sister killed him."

"She didn't."

"Then you did."

"No. We found his body in the alley alongside the Cherry Bottom Inn. Frozen. His own stabber in his back."

"O' course he'll deny it," Targle said. He had his dagger in his fist again. His eyebrows lowered and a sly grin grew on one side of his mouth. He was a man who liked his killing.

"Pons loved that stabber," Wen said. "I trained him how to use it. He just wanted to know which spots produced the most pain."

This made Dox chuckle approvingly.

"Let me go," the girl pleaded. "Please. My father will pay. Anything. I swear it."

"Who's your father?" Dox asked. The idea of being paid a ransom clearly appealed to him.

"Hackworth Keel. I'm his middle daughter, Binni."

Dox was already a pasty-looking man, like a huge lump of white dough rested and ready for kneading. But at the mention of Hackworth Keel's name, his face went white.

"You lie," he said, the warbling giggle rising from his mouth even as his eyes seemed to sink into his skull. It was false laughter, nervous laughter. And it sounded just like Pons. Poor, crazy Pons.

"Kila found out who killed your son," Wen said, proposing what he hoped was the truth. "She had proof. She needed to approach Commander Fyooks at the Yin Inn, where she knew he would go for

Winternight revelries. She traded clothes with this rich merchant girl."

"Release this girl at once," Dox ordered Targle. He whistled to his dogs and the two on the floor retreated to the corner. The one on the bed remained.

"If your sister has discovered who killed Pons, I want to know. I *will* have revenge. Targle, go collect the girl from the Yin Inn.

"Kila will smell your man coming," Wen said. "You'll never catch her, and never hear what she's learned."

"You said yourself she went to confront Fyooks with what she's learned. I'll have her tale straight from him. I don't need you or your sister."

The outer door swung in. The guard poked his head in. "One of the new men got it in the gut, Dox. Just down the hall." His eyes shifted to Wen.

Dox pursed his lips and nodded. "Dispose of him. If a lad of fifteen can get the best of him, he was no good to me anyway."

The guard nodded and closed the door.

Dox eyed his prisoner, who Targle had finally cut loose. "Girl, I'm going to have to make amends with your father if he is who you say he is. If not, I'm going to double the agony I had planned to deal you. Do you understand?"

She nodded vigorously. She stood like a chastened child, face down, shivering, shoulders bobbing with sobs. The wound on her leg bled freely.

Wen saw a deal in the offing.

"She was never here," he said, even before the whole plan had formed. He looked at her. "Were you?"

She didn't understand. Kila would have gotten it instantly.

"Binni, you were never here. The dog that bit you was a stray in Terriside."

"That sounds right to me," Dox said, giving Wen a look of grudging respect. "Strays all over. Commander Fyooks knows of my concerns on that front."

"I don't understand," Binni said. "That beast right over there bit me. You made him."

"Do you want your father to know you were in Cheapsgate on Winternight?" Wen said.

"No." Her voice was small as a voice could be.

"Then the bite happened in Terriside. By a vicious stray." And now to secure his own safety. "And I was there to witness it. I'll tell your father how I fought the dog off and escorted you home."

She understood then. She didn't smile. She was in too much pain to smile. And her eyes were broken. Not injured, but something behind them was shattered. She had left her greathouse bound for a bit of adventure in Cheapsgate. Probably to meet a young man. But she had been drugged and tortured and now the world was not a safe place, but a realm of terror.

"Your father need only be angry that feral dogs roam the streets. And Dox here..." Wen didn't know how to finish the sentence. The man was reprehensible. Evil.

But he wasn't Her Enlightened's hand; it wasn't for him to deliver justice when she could so easily do so if she chose. No. Dox would go on doing what he did. Disgusting. Terrible.

But Wen saw the truth. He could not protect Kila if he was dead or locked up in the Westbunk. This was the pragmatic answer. The only answer. Kila had to live. She was special. Yes. She mattered more than Dox, or Targle, or even Binni Hackworth.

Dox finished Wen's incomplete thought. "I will put Pons's murderer in that chair. You and your sister go on your way and have a good Winternight. Targle, go. Fetch Kila Sigh."

"She'll never go with him. And I would never allow her to come here. Not without grave assurances of her safety."

Dox raised his hands and clapped. The door guard popped his head in. "Yep?"

"Clear it out. Clear it all out."

"Viller's Killers?"

"No. All of it. Not a man or whore under these roofs. Wake up your men and clear the place."

"Where will they go?"

"They can jump in the Sourwater for all I care. Send them to Sanglo's. That bastard's desperate for business, I hear."

That was not true at all.

The noise of the forced evacuation was not merely shouts and drunken complaint. There were shrieks, the sound of shattering glass, and great thump as a portion of the structure collapsed.

In the end, all fell to silence. Two hounds snored in the corner, one back under the bed.

"Targle, take this to Kila. Give it to her." Wen handed over Cayne in its sheath. "It is the only thing I know for sure that will convince her to come here."

Dox flicked his fingers at Wen, shooing him away. He stroked his dog and sipped at a goblet of wine. Wen went to Binni and moved her to a settee in the corner. He cleaned her bite with trezz, which made her suck air through her teeth. But the liquor would do well to clean it. He bound it best he could with a cloth from the basin and a piece of the rope that had once secured her to the torture chair.

She accepted his assistance with sniffles, but no gratitude. "Why are you helping him?"

"Binni," he said quietly. "I'm helping you."

"But what he did to me. It was horrible."

"Yes."

Kila was wearing a dress. A blue velvet frock with fur trim at the sleeves. Her face had been scrubbed clean and her hair—well, not much had been done about the tangles in her hair. She'd pulled up the hood of the Binni's fine woolen cloak to mask that mess.

Her eyes caught Wen's and her brow instantly softened as a wave of relief passed through her. Wen knew that seeing Cayne would have led her to one conclusion, no matter what Targle said. That he was dead.

And that would've been enough to get her to come here.

"Who killed my son?" Dox asked without so much as a nod of greeting.

"Pons was yer son?" she said, voice even.

"Sister," Wen said, warning her with the word that she was walking a narrow ledge. "Answer the question."

"Hewlit Sorge. Pons lent him a silver skillet a ten-day ago. He gambled it, lost it. Rather'n pay it back, he killed Pons."

"And how do you know this?" Dox said.

"He told me. He was proud of it. Said Pons was rich an' didn't need a copper plug." I thought the man was pickled. I never knew Pons to *have* a copper plug.

"And why would this Sorge fellow tell you?"

"I went to Sanglo's and started talking ta folk. I kept sayin' how I was glad somebody did Pons and I'd buy 'em a Winternight swallow of trezz." She held up her right hand, fingers spread. "Five people confessed. But only Sorge knew that Pons died by his own stabber, six times in the back."

Targle said, "Our boys are grabbin' Sorge now, Dox."

Dox turned his heavy gaze on Wen. "Get out of here. Take the Hackworth girl home. If she points her finger at me, I'm sending my boys to the Warren to hunt a rat."

"I understand. You'll send word to Fyooks to leave me be?"

He heaved in a great breath, making his nostrils whistle. "I think I will. This time. I understand a deal. Keeping Hackworth's eyes off me has value. I appreciate value."

Since the place was empty, it was easy to find an empty room for the girls to exchange clothes. Kila complained about her torn and bloody pants until she realized how small-minded it made her look, especially since Binni was standing there with matching holes in her flesh.

The man Wen had killed still lay in the hallway. Wen took his shoes and his cloak. Someone had already lifted his purse.

They left Dox Viller's and went to the roofs of Cheapsgate. It was hard for poor Binni, he knees paining her so that she sucked pained breaths through her teeth with every step. Wen sent Kila home to the den and accompanied Binni back to Terriside.

The bells were ringing twelve. The taverns and inns roared as Wen took her through the Cheaps where the guards were drunk and waved them through and wished them good cheer.

With shoes on his feet—though a bit too large—and a cloak on his back, the chill wasn't too bad. Binni clung to his arm, and alternated thanking him for saving her and swearing she would personally kill Dox Viller. Wen thought this all foolishness, but he said nothing to dissuade her from her fantasy of vengeance.

The Keel greathouse was not far upslope as they were trezz traders with many ships to manage and being close to the docks was smart business. There was a dance underway in the greathouse. When the servants saw Binni hobbling in, they immediately called for their master. Hackworth Keel came out to the foyer, mug in hand. His youngest boy, Raginalt peered from behind him, hair pale and falling over his eyes.

Hackworth face reddened with rage as he heard Wen's story. Binni cried on cue and lifted her skirt to show her dog bite. In moments she was ushered away by worry-browed maids.

Hackworth Keel patted Wen's shoulder and asked his family name. Wen said he was just an orphan apprenticed to Master Olliv the locksmith.

"That's an honorable and valuable trade. Well done, my boy. You have my thanks. Stay a while. Enjoy a sip of fine trezz and a bite or two."

"Apologies, sir. My sister is home alone and we have not yet had our own Winternight dinner. I fear it will be a lean one."

The man cleared his throat and snapped his fingers, manner going cold. "I see how it is." His butler produced a lambskin purse.

"No, no, sir. I did not mean to hint at any expectation of payment. I'm not refined like yourself, so I talk a bit plain sometimes."

Hearing that he need not pay out any of his precious coin, the man regained his magnanimity and again snapped his fingers. "Accept a Winternight feast, then. My man will send you off with a grand platter for you and your sister. Just return the plate in the morn."

"That would be very welcome, sir." Wen sketched a ridiculous bow, which made some of the curious onlookers chuckle. Word spread of his heroism chasing off the vicious cur that dared to lay tooth to a daughter of Hackworth Keel. And then coins were pressed into his hands by others. "Good Winternight to you, lad." "Winternight blessings for you and your sister." "Til smile upon you, laddie."

And so Wen returned to Cheapsgate, bearing a platter of goose, and turkey, and potatoes, and cinnon cakes and pumpkin biscuits, and gravy, and carrots, and green beans. A basket hung over his arm, stuffed full of bread and butter. And inside his stolen cloak, two bottles of trezz and two of beer.

In another pocket, no less than five gold skillets of coin.

When he entered the den in the Warren, Kila was asleep on her pallet of rags. Their fish oil lantern glowed softly, sending up a black tendril of stinky smoke.

The smell of food roused her. Her eyes widened as he revealed the food, now gone cold. It didn't matter. They ate and ate, their fingers delightfully slick and glistening with grease.

He poured a little trezz into Kila's cup and watched with amusement as she sputtered and coughed as the stinging liquor went down her throat. Her eyes watered, but there was nothing in them but joy.

Wen felt a bit of it, too. But in this he was his father's son. Knowing the truth of what was out there in the world, he could not commit fully to happiness.

It was well enough that he could enjoy Kila's happiness, for she could *feel* it. Truly. She didn't have to think about whether she *should*. He hoped she could hold onto that for a while longer.

"Do you know a little man named Sazeenie," he asked as they lay on their backs in darkness, bellies overstuffed. His blood glowed from the beer and a bit of trezz. Not too much, for he had to remain vigilant.

"Did he have a long, reddish beard and wear a burlap sack?" she asked.

"Yes."

"No. I don't know him."

Wen sat up, Cayne already in his hand. A finger pressed his lips and a spark of mercus light appeared. Kila lay on her pallet, curled into a ball, still asleep.

Sazeenie stood before him. "Let's keep our friendship a secret," he said, perfectly mimicking Kila's voice.

"Who are you? Why did you lie and say Kila was at Dox Viller's?"

"Which question would you like me to answer?" His own voice now, but none of the Cheaps-talk accent he'd used earlier.

"The second," Wen said.

"There are many pieces on the board, lad. Some are expendable. Binni was not. Her part is small, but crucial." He turned to eye Kila. "Does she know who *she* is?"

"No."

"That is well. Now I must go. You will not see me again. Already the force of destiny gathers to engulf what we have wrought today. It will not bear my interference again. Not in this age. Good-bye!"

The mercus light winked out and Wen was left in darkness, mouth open to speak, but with no one to speak to.

He lay back, remembering father's story of how he'd found Kila. It was a wide world, full of illusion and lies. But Wen knew one thing for sure as he huddled in his blankets that Winternight.

Kila was true.

ABOUT THE AUTHOR

Eric is the author of the epic fantasy series Starside Saga, the YA dystopian series The Scion Chronicles, and numerous short stories. He lives in Wisconsin with his wife, daughter, and two silly Brittany dogs.

Find out more about Eric at:
ericedstrom.com

BB bookbub.com/authors/eric-kent-edstrom

FIRST RAYS OF NEW SUN

RON COLLINS

"Katazarra," Hadroc said as he came into the library, "I need you to take care of James."

I set my book on the stand beside my upholstered chair, noting the golden glow the soft daylight gave as if fell over the exposed skin of my shoulder. The cold remains of my tea had long ago filled the crevasses of the room with its flavor. From outside the window came muted voices and the clatterings of preparation for tonight's festival.

Hadroc came to a halt, his silk-lined cape swirling to a rest.

He was a beautiful man—angular and tall in the way of all fae, but even more fair and more angular than the rest. The musk of soil and harsh-cut wood surged at his entrance, scents that were mixed with the unmistakable odor of recent sex. His cheekbones were flush. The gaze of his eyes—which could be beautiful one moment, then freeze to daggers the next—was crystalline and watery now. As always occurred, I shuddered with memories of his body as soon as I laid eyes on him: the strength of his arms, the hardness of the muscles along his back. I remembered the feeling of his fingers pressing into the low slope of my backbone.

Even now, after everything, I felt pulled to him.

That is the nature of fairy magic. Hadroc's hold is as bold and wonderful as it is terrifying and everlasting.

"I assume, then, that this must be James," I replied, examining the man who followed Hadroc.

I might have considered him to be stunning also if it weren't for the nearness of Hadroc. The human was the flipside of the fae lord, dark complexioned with a shock of black hair falling over his forehead. His sharp-edged cheekbones underscored eyes so dark that irises melted seamlessly into black pupils. James was as thin as Hadroc, too, but where the fae's movements were smooth and pure, James's were awkward and abrupt, made as if his mortal brain continually interrupted them to consider some other action. He wore human clothes as well as a human aura—hiking apparel, mostly, denim dungarees and a flannel shirt, both of which had certainly been removed earlier, but now had been returned to cover James's toned body.

141

His fear was palpable under a forced stoicism.

His bootsteps were heavy on the hardwood floor.

"I am needed at the construction," Hadroc said. "And I need James to have a partner for lunch."

"I see," I replied.

Those words, combined with the undercurrent of annoyance in the fae's gaze, were enough to tell the tale. James had fallen for the fae, as will most humans Hadroc desires. But unlike most, James was conversant with lore. He understood that to take food in the Fairyland would bind him to Hadroc forever, and that wasn't on his agenda. Hadroc was in command of the preparations for Alban Arthan, the forthcoming Winterfest celebration that would draw the old year to its end and see the birth of the new. There would be dancing and music, much wine and, of course, much of all the other frivolities that came with dance, music, and wine. It was the highlight of the fae year.

Hadroc's position meant he had a built-in excuse for his departure, but the years had been long for me and I knew he was more inconvenienced in this matter than he was overworked. Rather than do the dirty work himself, the fae lord wanted me to find a way to get the young man to eat. The edge to his watery gaze also said that the punishment for failing him would be severe.

Severe for Hadroc, as I already understood, was not a trifling thing.

I stood and ran my hand down the velour side-panels on my dress, mostly to remove wrinkles that had come from my time seated though I cannot lie about my desire to see a moment of hunger on Hadroc's gaze. The garment was well fitted, and the fae are nothing if not transparent in their admiration of beauty over certain other qualities.

"I'm sure I can keep James entertained," I said, drawing the approval from Hadroc I craved.

"That's wonderful, love," he said.

My heart clenched as Hadroc breezed out of the room.

The silence he left behind was as if the entire place took a collective sigh, then, thankfully, the distant crash of an axe cleaving wood broke the moment.

I drew a breath and glanced to James.

His eyes drew half-closed as he appraised me in ways he hadn't while Hadroc was here. Without thinking, I found myself presenting an angle that would let the dress do its work. A moment later I lifted my hand toward James, palm-down.

"Come, come," I said, beckoning with a glint to my eye that I knew would convince any who were not fae.

"I'm not hungry," James said, clearly in control of himself now.

"You may not desire food," I said. "But I have my orders, and you can save me no little trouble by at least accompanying me while I partake."

His smile was as abrupt as if I had interrupted him.

"I can understand that," he said.

I turned my hand over, still extending it. This time he took it.

His grip was smoother than I would have guessed from his outdoorsy attire. His fingers were as strong as Hadroc's. His hand was firm and warm.

I understand what Hadroc saw in him, I thought as I led him from the library, through the hall, and toward the kitchen.

The building was a huge network of chambers and passages built under and around the canopy of the great expanse of Fairyland forest over the years. Wings of the manor serve both as Hadroc's living quarters and the place where he conducts his business, whatever that is at the moment. Like most fae, his interests shift like tides along the oceanfront.

James spent the trip looking at the place as if he was seeing it for the first time, which I suppose is true enough. I was certain that he'd not been out of Hadroc's, uh, sight since coming to Fairy, until now, and as long as Hadroc is in a room the glamour he emits will absorb all attentions.

Seeing wonder on the face of new arrivals is the only part of my role that I liked, so I watched as we progressed past the arched gold-enwood of the central hallway, and traversed the simple passage of stairways that led to the working areas of the center. His gaze was like a squirrel in a tree, skittering from limb to limb in short bursts, landing, hesitating with nervous anticipation, then moving again.

The kitchen and dining centers are on the third level of a backhouse. The sweet smells of cold meats and fresh fruits stirred my stomach as we approached.

I took a plate and filled it with more than I could eat.

James remained emptyhanded, which I allowed.

"This is an amazing place," James said.

"Yes," I replied. "I call it the Tree Castle."

He gave the desired chuckle. "I see why."

We took a seat at an ornate table of carved oak that sat on the open patio. It gave us a view that looked over the forest to the north and the open grounds where the dancing would be held later tonight to the east. The manor yard's magicked grass was vivid green against the dead of winter around it.

At this height the forest felt like a tapestry of leafless branches.

The dry air was cold, and blowing hard enough that it threw James's dark hair back from his head, but fires at each corner of the space kept the table warm enough.

Below, fae folk worked on the grounds, without, of course, any help from or even sighting of Hadroc. A set of three podiums had been constructed at equidistant points around the open glade, each large enough to hold a band of musicians when the event began. Evergreen and holy-spruce ringed the area as if it were a protective fence against the press of oak and birch that filled the forest around us. Every door in sight was adorned with arrangements of holly or mistletoe. Unfurled banners rolled from the sills of every window, adorned with the fertility symbols of goats and lions.

"I like it outside," I said, taking in the sky as we sat. "It makes me feel like the world is limitless."

I slid my plate to the space between us, hoping the pure nearness of faeland nourishment would sway his senses, but he was resolute. Undaunted, I selected an apricot. Its flesh was coarse and tasted sweet on my tongue.

"How long have you been here?" James asked.

"Time is hard to track in Fairy," I replied, knowing I could tell him the exact passage, but that he would find the answer annoying. "Besides, clocks move differently here."

"When were you taken?"

"The year I last remember was 2026."

James's lips curled upward and a crease came to the corner of his eyes. He nodded with a motion that was hard to interpret. He looked at me with an unnerving calm.

"Do you like apricots?" I said to deflect my anxiety.

"No."

"Then maybe you should try the turkey. It's fresh and straight from the heart of Fairyland. Beyond belief."

"I'm sure it is."

My suggestions did nothing to bring food closer to his lips, nor did it dampen the inquisitive edge to his expression.

"I'm sure it's been ages since you last ate," I said, thinking pragmatism might win out. "And given your recent activities you've got to be starving-hungry by now. You might as well eat something. You won't be allowed to leave either way."

"We'll see."

I ate in silence for several moments, absorbing the nature of James's temperament.

He examined the area with the eye of a surveyor.

I put myself in James's position and assessed the Tree Castle as if I were not enthralled, looking for paths to escape if such a thing had been possible, but finding the drop to the forest floor too far, the nettled branches of the treescape too dense, and the guarded perimeters too well staffed.

The food was suddenly less flavorful.

Gently, James reached across the table and ran a finger down my jawbone.

I let him.

The caress was light, just the tip of one finger. I thought about where that finger had been earlier this morning, imagined it

145

caressing Hadroc's jaw, tracing a path down the fae lord's neck to his chest and then the soft hairs that lined the smooth skin on Hadroc's belly.

Then the sensation was gone and I was left with nothing but an empty form of jealousy.

"You're an artificial life," he said, pulling his hand back. "A robot."

"You can tell?"

"It's not hard when you know exactly what you're looking for. You're an older model."

My face must have darkened.

"I'm sorry if that hurt you."

"It's all right."

"How did you wind up here?"

"Same way you did," I said with a sharpness that gave me back the sense of self I had temporarily fumbled. "I gave in to Hadroc."

He frowned.

"That doesn't make sense."

"You'd best get used to it," I replied with a wry chuckle at the quaint sense of betrayal he showed. "When it comes to beautiful creatures and sex, you'll find Hadroc isn't particularly discerning when it comes to gender."

He blushed. "That's not what I meant."

"Then what did you mean?"

"I meant you're not human."

I glared at him, fighting an automatic response to an old prejudice. "If you're trying to be less offensive, you're failing miserably."

"I mean..."

"We have to eat, too, you know?"

"Yeah, I get it. Eat the food here, and you're caught. But while you eat to be more humanlike, you're still not human."

"I convert food energy to fill my batteries, or I die."

"Of course you do," he snapped.

I peered at him. If form held, then Hadroc had picked him up in a hard-pounding bar someplace in the middle of a metropolis. But his questions made me wonder about him. Was there something more here than the usual? Something in James's appearance here beyond a random hookup with a deliriously beautiful fae lord?

Where was he from? What was he doing here?

"So I'm not human," I said, pushing the idea away for now. I had a job to complete, and I intended to do it. "What of it?"

"How does fae magic work on a robot?" he said.

"How does it work on a human?"

"That's not the point."

"Yes it is," I said, an old, more familiar anger rising. "That is *exactly* the point. It's always been *exactly* the point." I stood up and the chair juddered over the slats of the patio floor as I felt heat surge through my spine to crash over the rest of my body. Other fae in the area stared. "I may be out of my time phase, James, but even when I was in your realm I understood the fact that I had my autonomy. And I understood that people like you would do whatever you could to take it away."

I stomped off, then, feeling the glorious release of pent-up frustration tingling all the way to my fingertips.

Let him starve, I thought as I stomped through the Tree Castle and out into the chill of winter.

Hadroc would be upset if he found out, but I had had enough.

It was several minutes later before that feeling faded.

The woods were empty on this, the shortest, coldest day of the year.

I had chosen my boots for their fashion with my dress, but they were comfortable, too, as most fae footwork will be. They crushed dry leaves and crinkled peat moss as I rushed through the evergreen barrier and entered the wooded expanse. I ran further, wanting to be away. The conversation with James had brought up sour thoughts that laid across my already sour sensations about being alone for so long.

The call of a solitary owl echoed in the space between my steps.

Though the air was crystalline sharp, it smelled of barren soil and future snow.

I adjusted my inner works to raise my temperature, expelling bursts of breath in cloudy plumes as I went, knowing those breaths brought me oxygen I craved just as surely as they brought humans the oxygen they needed, oxygen that helped the fleshy portions of my body grow and that made me who I was as much as the code and networks that ran the core of my body's operations did.

As I ran, elements of anger gave way to the feeling of a certain joy that I hadn't felt for too long.

Too long cooped up in the Tree Castle.

Too long reading and sleeping, talking to the staff, and, occasionally, far too rarely, accepting the visitations of the fae lord who had enthralled me so many years ago.

How long had it been?

I stopped my running and leaned on an ancient oak. Its bark was thick and corky to my fingers. I put my forehead against it, remembering the first time.

Hadroc had captured Alonzo, a human who was technically my sponsor—the man who, by the new human laws, agreed to vouch for my behavior, effectively cosigning a loan on my freedom and giving me the autonomy so many humans take for granted. Alonzo and I were together that night, dancing at the Car-a-Go nightclub, a place like others I now know Hadroc patrols. Alonzo saw him. Hadroc did his fae thing, and things led to things.

It was fun.

We woke up in the place I came to know as the Tree Castle.

Alonzo was famished. How was he to know? Hadroc left him a plate on the nightstand, and he ate it before anyone could suggest otherwise.

I remember Alonzo begging, grasping Hadroc's hand.

"Please," he said. "I have so much to do."

Hadroc's lips curled in the sympathetic manner he has, his eyes softening in a way that makes you think he's going to give you what you need. "I love you too much to give you back," he said.

I remembered Alonzo turning to me, perplexion on his face.

Heavy footsteps behind me broke the spell of my ruminations.

James crashed through the forest, panting, the cold air bringing a ruddy glow to his skin that served to heighten his ruggedness. I was not without my urges, and it had been a while since Hadroc's last visit. I am not of a mind to hide myself from the truth, no matter how painful it might be. At that moment, James carried a sense of hero with him that made me stir. I remembered the firmness of his grip while we were in the library, paired with the softness of his hands. My distaste for the image brought me confusion. Where did this desire come from? Was it lust of the heart, or a piece of code dropped somewhere in a register of my memories and processors?

Did I really want to know?

He stopped several arm distances away.

The forest seemed to shrink to the span of this tiny clearing, and the breeze settled to stillness. The chill was still strong enough, though, that I worried that the thin flannel of his shirt would not keep away the pneumonia. Humans have weaknesses that artificial life forms do not.

"Don't run," he said, already gathering his composure from the exertion.

"Who are you?" I said.

"I'm just a guy."

"Don't lie to me."

His self-congratulatory smile gave him away.

"Your meeting with Hadroc was no accident, was it?" I asked.

"I heard stories."

"And you were intrigued?"

His next smile confirmed the deduction.

"I'm a student," James said. "Studying culture and anthropology."

His earnestness made me laugh.

"So this was all just an experiment for a term paper?"

"I wanted to know."

I sighed and arched my eyebrow as I leaned my back against the tree. Its bark was sharp against my shoulders. I looked up to the sky, letting the bark bite further into the back of my skull, my vision taking in the tangle of barren branches that etched their black, spiderwebbed patterns into the gray overcast.

"You should be careful with your research," I said resolutely. "Unless you want to be enspelled and captured here forever."

"How would you know?"

"It happened to me."

"I don't think so," he replied.

"It's true. I volunteered to stay so my sponsor could be free."

"I can pretty much promise you've not been magicked in any way of the fae."

"What do you mean?"

James came near enough that I could see him shivering. I turned my gaze out to the woods.

"Your name is Katazarra, right?" he said, waiting.

After several moments of silence, I turned to look at him. "Yes," I said. "I am Katazarra."

"You're not magicked, Katazarra," he replied. "You're programmed."

"Is there a difference."

"I assure you there is."

I stared at him, anger returning.

"You have flesh and emotions, like a human. And I'm not saying you shouldn't have rights. But your physiology is different. You're a machine."

"A machine can do anything a human can do."

"Yes, but only if it's been programmed to do it. Or at least has learned how to program itself."

His unspoken question hung in the air.

Have you programmed yourself?

He was right in a way. I was a learning being. In that way, I could program myself. My automated routines were highly advanced for their day, built from deep thought robotics and augmented with self-learning technologies. I taught myself by reading, storing, and indexing information, and constantly watching the fae lead their lives

—I had taught myself the subtle differences in the Alban Arthan dances and the Alban Hefin jigs. I understood their meanings, perhaps even more so than the fae themselves. I understood the way each of the fae had as they dipped and curtsied, and held their hands to one another.

I understood now that there was a difference between lust and curiosity, and between interest and love.

Perhaps this was no different than a human, either, except my readings and watchings were cross-indexed with every piece of information I had ever come across, and my conclusions were made with lightning speed.

James's expression was a mixture of patience and pain from the cold.

Could this man be right?

"No," I said. Then I described the day Hadroc had enthralled me. "I remember Alonzo's expression," I said as I finished. "I remember needing to help him."

"Do you remember Hadroc's enspellment?"

"I remember the taste of breakfast cake as I ate it."

That didn't answer the question, and we both knew it.

I remained silent.

"Your sponsor gave you up," James said, his voice carrying the tone of a new learning. "That's what I think."

I shook my head. "No."

"He made a deal with the fae. Offered you as a gift for his own freedom, programmed you to love Hadroc, and left you to build your own memories from that core."

The memory played again, and I tried to ignore the warps I knew to be missing information. That happened sometimes. Memory fades in the best of constructs.

James's voice came through the murky distance. "You know it's true."

And it was. Or at least it could be.

It would be just the kind of thing Hadroc would enjoy, too. I knew the fae's sense of sardonic sarcasm well enough by now. They all loved this kind of irony, but Hadroc was a connoisseur of it. He would take sadistic enjoyment at this kind of situation.

"Alonzo wouldn't have done that," I said, but even as the words processed, I knew that wasn't right. Alonzo was human, and humans are flexible in the way they go about their lives. It was possible he had swapped a program that pushed me to love Hadroc, possible he had erased a memory and left me here in his place. It was possible that my learning processes had added the rest, creating who I was as much from how they'd discovered this environment as they did by pulling from my base coding.

Yes, it was all possible.

James took a step that brought him close enough I could smell his musk. Or was it Hadroc's? It was all very confusing.

He put one hand on the tree bark over my head.

I raised a hand to his cheek, tilting my face up to his.

I wanted him to kiss me. I wanted to feel his lips, wanted to warm his body with mine.

Was it his scent? His closeness? Was it Alonzo's programming that made my cravings match that of the fae? Was it my own layers of complexity that brought desire to the forefront of my being, or was it something else completely?

James bent his head. I felt his breath on my cheek.

At the last moment, I turned away.

He straightened, obviously hurt. "I'm sorry," he said. "I misread the situation."

I cleared my throat, not sure what to say but then finding my voice. "How long have I been gone?" I asked.

"Long enough."

I nodded absently as information gathered and formed.

"I see," I said, extracting myself from his embrace and moving toward the Tree Castle. "We need to get back to the castle. The festivities will be starting soon, and Hadroc will be looking for us."

~

H adroc was not pleased to find James still fasting, so rather than join the festivity and chance suffering his wrath further, I decided to watch the festival from the same patio I had shared with James during lunch. I sat in the same seat, and as the sun set and the darkness drew itself over the shell of the sky I stared down at the same areas of land.

As fitting the theme of rebirth and renewal, the overcast of daytime had cleared to reveal a nighttime sky that was as deep as the universe, and scattered with the gleaming points of a thousand more.

Out with the old, in with the new.

There is little in either realm that can match a Winterfest.

A huge cauldron had earlier been settled at the center of the manor yard. Now it blazed with fire so strong that it cast an orange and yellow glow over the whole gathering of the fae creatures here. The feasting tables were lined with rich clothes, and stacked high with every delicacy known to Fairyland. Music began early, and the fae folk arrived as if called en masse—one moment the grassy patch was barren and fresh, the next the entire manor was overflowing with creatures, each more perfect and more beautiful than the next.

Torches and candles burned bright like stars in the sky.

Wine and sweet beers flowed.

Outside reach of the light, the forest writhed with energy.

And that was just the pre-festival.

Hadroc's arrival rang in the festival's true beginning.

He was resplendent in a gold-threaded suit, his chariot pulled by a procession of white horses and flanked by dancers and flautists. He raised his hands to the fae to signal the festival was now open. A moment later, a goblet of wine appeared in that hand, and a smile crossed his face. The gathering cheered.

At the back of the chariot, I saw James, covered in a warm cloak lined with wolf fur now.

The sight of him brought me to another brief memory.

Me, less than an hour ago, slipping past the guards who sentry the hilltop that served as the closest portal to the other realm. Me, putting my hand forward, testing, trying to make myself free to step through and return to the timeline I had left so long ago. I had not been able to, but what did that prove? It could be Hadroc's magic, or it could be my own programming on top of Alonzo's.

Either way, for now, I was here.

I thought about that as I raised a glass to my lips.

Mead.

Honey wine, sweet and delicate. I licked my lips, and focused on James and Hadroc.

The fae lord draped his arm over James's shoulder and played with James's hair. The human did not appear to be partaking in the party—which told me he had not yet touched the forbidden fruit, so to speak.

To some, perhaps it seems strange for a god to label one fruit forbidden while leaving the rest unencumbered of such constraint. It is certainly strange from the point of view of the fae, for whom the world is mostly a simple binary set of rules. But I understand.

James will be Hadroc's new toy, but for how long?

Things change.

The cauldron at the center of the manor will burn through the night, illuminating drunken debauchery through the darkest part of the night and fading to embers only just as the light of the New Year's sun breaks the horizon.

Except for me, of course.

All things change, except for me.

Perhaps.

I waited, sipping mead and watching the party. As I waited I saw Hadroc kiss his new toy, and drink. He ate of the feast tables and pushed James to do the same, laughing as the human fought back.

I waited while Hadroc drank more, and while his anger built.

Which I have always known makes him drink more.

The music built and the firelight rose in the darkest depths of night.

Finally, when I could wait no more, I stood and drank the last of my own mead.

This night of all nights is the one night that such a bold move could be made by one of Hadroc's discarded toys, and the one night of all nights when that discarded toy could walk with such wanton disregard for the past down to the manor yard and into the pageantry of the party-goers, the music that pulsed across the land, to bring the sense of change and freshness and new birth. This is the one night of all nights where the pure force of life energy released in the dance and the drink combined to hide my intention.

I found James just as Hadroc left to find more of his drink.

His hand was as soft as I remember it, though his resolve had faded with his strength.

"Come," I said as I led him back through the crowd and into the darkness.

Once, when Hadroc's butler wandered past, I wrapped James in my arms and kissed the human hard, pulling his cloak up over his head to cover his identity, though I knew it would give me nothing but the spare bit of time that I needed.

"What was that?" James said when I was done.

But I shushed him, and led him further away, letting the drums of the festival music fade in the distance as I crossed into the dark forest, letting the light of the cauldron fire become blocked by the thick trunks of oak and elm as we climbed the rise that led back to the top of the hill where the portal lay.

"Go to the crest," I explained. "Step through the two stones there, and you'll be back in your world."

He nodded, but his gaze was filled with doubt.

I slapped him across the cheek.

"Top of the crest. Walk between the stones," I said. "Do you understand?"

"Yes," he said. "I understand."

"Good."

Two sentries monitored the gate this evening.

I may not be able to cross over myself yet, but I knew how to distract these guards so that another could.

I stepped into the light of their sentry fire.

"It's a shame to miss the festival," I said to them, lowering my own cloak.

They both smiled.

~

The eastern horizon was growing light when I stepped down the hill. I was tired and hungry. Sore, but in a good enough way.

At least the sex had been good.

Perhaps that was programming, or maybe it was the satisfaction of doing something on my own for the first time. Taking from the fae whatever small piece of control the fae had taken from me. Or that I had allowed the fae to take from me. That was the right attitude, I thought as I adjusted my temperature up.

That was what I needed to think like from here on.

There was work to do, maybe years' worth.

But I could change. I felt that somewhere deep inside, somewhere that perhaps a human would call a soul.

My boots crushed dead leaves, but in the nook of a thick oak, I saw a green shoot. As I stepped into the manor yard, I saw the cauldron had burnt down, leaving behind the smoky residue of an exhausted husk.

On the horizon, the first rays of the new sun painted the sky.

ABOUT THE AUTHOR

Ron Collins has contributed stories to many premier science fiction and fantasy publications, including *Analog*, *Asimov's*, and several issues of the Fiction River series. He is the award-winning author of *Stealing the Sun*, a series of space-based SF books, and the fantasy serial, *Saga of the God-Touched Mage*, which sat at the top of Amazon's Dark Fantasy best seller lists for several months. His work has garnered a *Writers of the Future* prize, and a CompuServe HOMer award. His short story "The White Game" was nominated for the Short Mystery Fiction Society's 2016 Derringer Award.

Find out more about Ron at:
typosphere.com

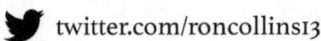

twitter.com/roncollins13
facebook.com/roncollinssfwriter
bookbub.com/authors/ron-collins
amazon.com/Ron-Collins/e/B00AP2IYEW

AT THE HEART OF TRICKERY

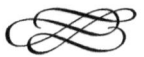

REI ROSENQUIST

Outside the snow-covered window of a small lonely cottage, brightly colored streamers flap in a freezing breeze. From street pole to weatherworn street pole, strings of frost-peppered fairy lights make the city positively glow. Streetlamps have all donned pale, confetti-colored shades, and their speckled light casts magical shadows on the gray, snow-dotted cobblestone paths. These meandering roads duck and spin through ancient-style arches and modern-style doorways leading to the heart of Stratford, North Carolina.

There, on an old wooden stage, huge brilliant triangle flags wave to the potential visitors.

Good morning! Hello! Come for the Show!

From tired-out rafters above the stage, a banner alerts passersby of the coming celebration: Midwinter's Coming of The Bard.

An elaborate but poorly timed yearly festival put on by the Shakespeare society to try and urge the city's 54,000 inhabitants into cheerful engagements to make for a happy, if not long and hard, winter. As if yet another repetition of the old, tired Midsummer's Night Dream painfully set in a winter wonderland could do that.

Most people buy into it. The pricey "rare" tickets. The outdoor standing room only arena. Every year, a packed audience stands shivering to the bone in their "summer clothes"—cleverly disguised shawls of thick wool and nude-colored long underwear.

Chandra alone isn't thrilled.

Elbows lean against the wooden sill as she stares out the cottage window at the coming festivities. Several slow and steady breaths fog up the recently cleaned pane. A hand pressing over a frowning mouth reveals Chandra's deeply rooted dread.

She takes a tentative glance in the direction of the city's main square. A finger automatically raises and runs nervously against an aged necklace. The pendant is a small family crest. An heirloom passed down for generations. The last thing from Chandra's family that she kept.

Outside the window, at just the right angle, Chandra can see the stage. Complete with red curtains pulled back with tattered gold twine. Same stage, every year. The floorboards, covered now in flurries of snow, are well-worn by the same actors playing the same exhausting roles.

Chandra sighs and gets up, starts pacing.

It's not just the cheesiness of the Midwinter festival that's unsettling. It's not the denial of the cold—standing out there talking as if the trees were all in full bloom, and the summer solstice were around the corner, while snow sprinkles down on clever hats full of felted flowers. And it's certainly not the town's merriment that gets Chandra up in arms. Hell, it's not even the sheer bore of it—the same events each winter solstice.

It's this: that every year on the longest night, at least one unexplainable occurrence happens.

Three years ago, a forest appeared out of nowhere, and faeries hosted delightful tea parties everyone was too afraid to join. Two years ago, a field in full harvest offered pick-your-own delights. Again, nobody tried them. And last year? Well, last year was a different story altogether.

Chandra shakes her head, trying to forget all the weirdness.

"This year'll be different," Chandra says aloud to Orville, a big feral orange and yellow tabby who's just wandered in from napping. Sweet cat, Orville is. If not a strange and sudden roommate.

The poor dear showed up one day, raggedy and all bones, looking for scraps. Not being a monster, Chandra obliged. After that, the cat just stayed. Chandra inquired around town and posted posters, but no frantic owner turned up. So, the two became fast friends.

Orville purrs and rubs against Chandra's leg. Chandra reaches down to give Orville a scratch behind the ears.

"We'll see. Things will be normal this year. Won't they?"

Orville stretches high into a typical cat-like pose: claws extended, spine arched, tail dusting the ground. The cry that comes out sounds too much like "No."

"Hmph," Chandra play-scolds with hands on hips, pretending to be moody, and failing because these goddamn hips are nothing to focus on. Flat cliffs, that's what they are. Of all the things the hormones fix, that's apparently not one. Not for Chandra, at any rate.

Orville looks up and yawns wide, as if laughing silently at Chandra's hippy plight. Chandra drops to a knee and reaches out to pick Orville up. "That's not nice."

"Nyaw?" Orville cries, and hops into Chandra's arms.

A flicker of something deep inside stirs like a snake uncoiling, right where the soft furry body curls against her chest. Chandra jumps and accidentally lets the cat drop.

"Oh! Vil, I'm sorry!"

"Merr," Orville says, and pads away.

"I'm losing my nerve," Chandra complains, stands, and shivers despite thick wool stocking feet and thick woolly gray-green sweater.

A grumble rises from Chandra's gut, followed by a stab of hunger. She charges from the bedroom to a nondescript kitchen and pulls out two small cast iron pans. Three eggs, cracked straight atop a thin layer of flavorless cooking oil. Two yellow potatoes, grated with a standard box grater, washed in simple tap water, splashed with the same flavorless oil. A dash of salt—no more flair than that.

Chandra breathes in the smells of breakfast sizzling in the pans. A frown tempts the edges of a tired mouth, ever so slightly. The faint pain of loss bubbles up like vapor over a roiling pot of herbs.

Chandra used to love to cook. Really cook.

Mixing flavors and ingredients with panache. Constantly expanding into new creative endeavors. Back then, the kitchen had been stocked with pretty, hand-carved spatulas, ornate pans, lovely dishware to rival art museums.

The cupboards, too, had been stocked to the brim with unique ingredients: spices from around the world, herbs grown in local window boxes, fruits and vegetables lovingly produced by local farmers. Rare spiced meats lovingly made and aged by crafts folk. Preserves decorated wide shelves lining every wall. Vegetables marinated in hand-crafted olive oil flavored with herbs, unusual fruits stewed with unexpected sweeteners, various pickles floating in colorful menageries of clever brines.

It was a festival all its own, this kitchen—once.

Then, the magic came and everything went haywire.

Water floating as it boiled. Sparks flying across the ceiling like fireworks. Imaginary birds perching on Chandra's shoulders whistling tunes that somehow complimented the aromas of stews and soups. Butterflies dancing in twisting patterns, leaving glitter everywhere.

Beautiful as it was, the neighbors grew concerned. And before too long, the city council got involved. Petitions were signed. Law enforcement came. Police in riot gear told Chandra to cool it or else.

Then, Chandra made the biggest mistake of her life.

She took the magic to be a sign. A chance to alter the face of her life. And, seeing the townsfolk's concern as a chance to prove herself —she went public about the transition. Came out in a big press conference as trans. Made a statement about being a "good lady witch with a big heart."

Big mistake.

The town grew even more terrified. In small town America, a transwoman witch might as well be the devil himself. Preachers accosted Chandra nonstop to repent. Only she couldn't see going back into the closet now. And so, finally Chandra made the lesser of two hard choices and went into hiding physically.

This small cabin near the edge of town, well hidden behind ample shubbery, was a lonely if not effective hiding place. A place to root out the magic and bury it fast and deep. That meant keeping the most mundane of homes. The most lackluster of existences. The plainest of lives—so as not to draw the tricksy spirits' eyes.

Chandra picks up an average wooden spatula and carefully flips the eggs, trying to enjoy this moment of private quietude despite its blandness. The rest of today was going to be hell.

"What if I just don't go?" Chandra thinks aloud, stirring the potatoes.

Only, that won't do.

That's what instigated the disaster last year.

Chandra thought to avoid the whole magical swelling around the winter solstice by staying indoors. But the strange occurrences came knocking on the walls. Literally. Eventually, riled up swirls of color and glitter forced Chandra out the door around midnight.

The peak of the festival.

In a matter of minutes, a colorful cloud rushed Chandra into the middle of the festivities. Spirits swirled through the air like streamers. The ground undulated like a liquid wave. And as for Chandra? Well. She was completely overwhelmed.

Her lips opened without her consent, and in a single heartbeat, sounds strange and broken flew out. Then a giant blue-green sky dragon burst forth from the sky, encircled the downtown's central park blocks, and roared so loudly it shook the windows. Sparkling dust rained down everywhere.

Muttering some kind of apology, Chandra collapsed and blacked out.

The next day, law enforcement found Chandra in the middle of a green patch of grass with a string of brightly colored magical flags wrapped around wrists, middle, legs, neck. The heirloom necklace was where it ought to be, but it had burned a scar into Chandra's chest.

Chandra inadvertently touches the scar now. The lines are familiar and well-defined. If not for the necklace hiding it, the emblem of a wand would be perfectly visible.

After that, Chandra decided that facing Midwinter head-on was the better approach.

The potatoes hiss with steam as if to agree.

Chandra eyes the golden edges, deems breakfast complete, turns off the pans, and scoops a healthy amount out onto a flat white plate. A sudden longing for rosemary, marjoram, thyme. Chandra shakes it off, heading for the small rectangle of wood that serves as a table. Pulling up a pale wood stool, Chandra digs in with a sense of acceptance.

This year will be better. Chandra will go out there and head off questions with lots of smiles. And when anyone mentions Chandra's identity or magical ability, she'll distract them with discussion of the familiar and well-known Puck. The master trickster of the town's favored play. And oddly enough—a distant relative of Chandra's. A cousin three times removed? Something like that. Dad would know, only they no longer talk.

Chandra finishes the plate, washes up, and goes to face the closet.

What to wear? How to dress? How to behave?

Chandra sees a flash of the townsfolk giving that nasty stink eye while magic uncontrollably rises in Chandra's chest. A few sparks in the form of moths or butterflies might sputter off. Someone will scream. Then, there will be the court order, and a hefty fine that'll add to the stack of other fines Chandra can't pay working a measly writing-internet-info-articles job. Not to mention the cost of hormones has only gone up and insurance is shit.

In the doorway, Orville plops down and cries.

Right, focus. Clothes.

Grabbing a pair of blue jeans without shape, Chandra selects a black t-shirt and gray hoodie, then heads to the shower. Toweling off afterward, Chandra's heart begins to hammer. One step closer to the festival. One step closer to the cold, not of winter, but of the population of Stratford, North Carolina.

Padding to the bedroom, Chandra steps into jeans and pulls on the black shirt. An acceptable gender-neutral look. Nothing too masc. but definitely not very femme. If Mom were here, she'd be not proud but...satisfied.

Chandra's hand finds the necklace, adjusts it, falls. A nervous tick. Need to stop doing it. But then, the crest is a symbol for something more than familial. A connection to a rebel—that's what Chandra really clings to. The idea of someone who goes against that grain. For that's what the family crest stands for after all—being a free thinker. Daring and willing to take chances.

And what happens to bold free thinkers? They are often used for others' good. Manipulated and made to look like liars and fools. The infinitely misunderstood. Chandra gets that, too.

A loud knock shakes Chandra back to reality.

"How now, spirit!" Chandra inadvertently blurts out the greeting of Puck from A Midsummer's Night Dream. Being related to a fictional character can be strange.

"Not spirit, I. By name of Apple do I go," someone answers through a crack in the window. "Open up, willst thou?"

"No one's home," Chandra calls back, hoping making a joke will make wanting to be left alone sound less awkward.

A heavy sigh comes through the cracks like a stormy wind. "Oh, come on now...ahem. Hold there, lofty creature! Come you not to the festivities this Midwinter eve?"

Not quite authentic Shakespeare, that.

But this Apple person is trying and that's kind of...endearing and outrageous. Unheard of. Nobody seeks the trans-devil out. Nobody. Chandra silently ponders who this visitor could be, and even debates opening the window. But then...think of the rest of the town and—

The knock comes again.

Hobbling with one foot into a boot, Chandra loses balance and falls flat on her bony ass.

"Ow," slips out accidentally.

"See! You are in there!" Apple cries, playing the joke. Which, again, is nice. Chandra can't remember the last time she bantered with...well, anyone. Mostly, it's been arrangements with Mom and Dad, fights with neighbors, court orders.

"You must be going to the festival," Apple calls again, persistent.

"I'm going to the festival, yes, fine," Chandra calls back, mouth pressed to the window's crack.

"Can I go along with you?"

"You—" Chandra starts before realizing what the end of that sentence is. "—want to be seen with me?" Not worth saying. So instead, Chandra says nothing.

"Please?"

So sweet, so gentle, so sincere that one word is, as it sneaks through the cold crack in Chandra's bedroom window and reaches down further than words ought to do. And, despite every fear and misgiving, Chandra is instantly convinced.

"Hang on," Chandra calls, and claws at the window.

Only, it hasn't been thrown open in years. Paint and mold and ages of wood warp hold it solidly in place. Yanking does nothing. And then—utterly without thinking—Chandra's lips are moving. Colors are flying out of her mouth in full rainbow. Sparks burst along the seams of the window. A brilliant rosemary-scented wind puffs from the seams of wood. And, with a pop like a firecracker going off—the window flies open. Chandra sees it happen a split second before it comes, and ducks just in time to miss the swinging glass.

"You did it!" Apple cheers and claps while stumbling back against a trampled bush.

Chandra takes in the stranger. Freckled cheeks brightly rouged. A sheet of blazing red hair, curling naturally in big fat turns. Maroon-lined, mauve-painted lips smile wide revealing a mouthful of slightly crooked, imperfectly off-white teeth. Evergreen eyes sparkle with a fire Chandra has never seen.

"Hi," Chandra mutters, stunned.

"Hi! I'm new in town. You sound cool!"

Chandra, yet again, is at a complete loss of words.

Across the street, the neighbors with their hawk eyes come out of the woodwork, gather in their yards, and glare at the scene. Chandra makes the mistake of making eye contact, and then the jeers start coming.

"The freak's at it again!"

"Get that sicko out of town!"

"Pervert! You are what's wrong with this place!"

Among others—unrepeatable.

Chandra sags under the weight. All the old shame and the familiar burden of social anxiety crowd out the joy of the brief and small success of opening a goddamn stuck window. Chandra stands inside the small cottage on shaky legs, hunting for excuses. Reasons. A hiding place now the old one has been blown open. Literally.

But before Chandra comes up with anything, the neighbors start to gather. To advance.

Apple's voice rises above the din, ferocious and terrible. "Off with you and your bigoted traps! You wouldn't know the lord Jesus Christ if he bit you in your ass. Now feck off you horrid lot!"

The neighbors start and scatter like paper in the wind.

When Apple turns back to Chandra, it is with a flushed face.

"Why?" tumbles out of Chandra's gaping maw instead of "thank you."

Apple has the grace to chuckle and not look wounded.

Chandra blanches and rambles, "I'm sorry. That was stupid. I'm sorry. Thank you...I just...I don't...why did you do that?"

"Because I've had it with that lot of losers. Up to my ears. They can go stuff one. Now, are you coming?"

"What?"

"First show's in ten minutes." Apple sticks a hand through the window. "Coming?"

Yes, Chandra planned to go to the festival. No, not like this. But then, wouldn't having a white knight by her side make the stink eyes and jeers easier to face? Wouldn't company dull the flaming darts of panic and fear in everyone else's eyes? Even just one friend in the midst of the enemy would alleviate something.

Chandra reaches out for Apple's hand, and just before grasping it, has a realization. Climbing through the window makes no sense when there's a perfectly good doorway. Only the idea strikes too late and their hands touch.

In a flash—the world evaporates.

Winter snaps away like a white sheet. And hiding behind it—a tumble into free fall. The wall, gone. The sky, poof! Everything, undone. Chandra swirls in a limbo of gray nothing for a moment. And all there is in the world is...

"Orville?"

"Meow," the cat replies and floats away into the grayness. In Orville's place, an apple forms out of the strange nothingness.

Chandra does a double take, reaching to touch it. The fruit has its typical weight. A cool round, smooth surface the same color as Apple's hair. The stem matches Apple's eyes in an eerie way, almost hyper-real. And then, there is the mouth. A smiling red stripe that looks exactly like those thin smiling lips.

"What in the—?"

"You have to choose," comes a voice that sounds...British. Definitely British.

"Choose? Between what?" Chandra asks.

"Between summer and winter. Between home and this."

~

Chandra comes to in a meadow wearing a lovely old-world country dress. Sandaled feet stand open-toed in soft green grass. In the distance, soft brown grain wavers in between massive leafed maple trees. Rolling hills rise and fall, leading the eye across this soft summertime distance to a small, thatched-roofed village.

Thin white smoke trickles from a few chimneys despite the day's pleasant warmth, indicating that perhaps it is mealtime. The smells of savory and thyme, grilling onions, and baking bread waft on the breeze, confirming Chandra's suspicion. Pulling Chandra toward whatever village that is.

From overhead, a blazing bright red apple falls into a clump of mottled green moss. Picking it up, Chandra rolls the fruit between her hands. No way this fruit is a person, trapped. Right? That makes no sense. But...best take it along. Just in case.

As if conjured purely from need, a bag appears at Chandra's feet. A nice leather satchel with Chandra's heirloom crest scarred and burned into the front flap. Chandra's hand reaches for the familiar necklace automatically and finds it in place.

Whew.

Trying on the bag, Chandra finds it fits perfectly over her shoulder. The apple fits nicely in the bottom, with ample room to not get damaged. Tucking the front flap through the strap and buckling it, Chandra ambles down the hill toward the village, following the tantalizing smells of food.

The walk to the village takes much less time than Chandra imagined. Down in town, a fair is going on. Over the main thoroughfare, a banner hangs. [Midsummer's coming of Trickery!] Well, that's a different approach from home.

In the streets, actors of varying skin tones and gender identities stand gathered reciting lines in traditional Shakespearean English. Booths full of unique handmade crafts. Smiling patrons picking out their heart's delights from towers of gourds and mounds of fresh purple carrots, red onions, golden potatoes. In wide alleyways, people dressed in traditional Shakespearean clothes drift past one another, carrying all manner of satchels, bags, and baskets full of goodies. Smiles on every face. Laughter in every mouth. Chandra can feel in big warm waves how full of life, harvest, and the sun these people are.

"How now, spirit?" comes a whispering in Chandra's ear. "Wither wander you?"

Chandra whips around, but there is no one there. Then, she sees it! A smear of tabby colored fur! The big fluffy cat bolts around the corner and down an alleyway. Chandra gives chase, calling Orville by name. But then after several turns down unknown alleyways, Chandra can't even be sure she really saw the cat. Maybe it was a shadow or a glint of sunlight hitting a puddle just right.

Passing through a portal into another world probably does funny things to your eyes.

Besides, what would Orville be doing here? It had been weird enough to see the familiar feline face in the grayness. Projection, clearly. Any well-known images for the mind to grasp at.

Chandra gives up and wanders closer to the main street. On a huge stage, a loud voice bellows at a crowd of people.

"Come one, come all. Hear the mighty Puck! Poetry from another world!"

Puck? As in...master trickster of Midsummer Night's Dream? Puck as in distant cousin? It can't be...

Chandra edges toward the stage, along with everyone else in the crowd. It's positively packed, elbow to elbow and shoulder to shoulder. And after a couple more steps, no one can move an inch.

A tap comes to Chandra's left shoulder.

"This way," comes that same quiet whisper from before.

Chandra cranes to the left half-expecting to see the smear of tabby fur again. But no, there's nothing but a narrow path. Chandra follows this despite ill-givings. The cobbled stones echo with the clacking of her hard-soled sandals. Around a bend, the alley opens into a square. And that square empties into another series of alleys—all traveling in the direction of the main stage and the booming voice of the announcer who is still laboriously introducing Puck.

As if stalling. Waiting for something. Or someone.

Chandra turns down what feels like the final alley, darker and closer to the sounds of cheering. A few meters down, the alley ends abruptly in a curtained archway. Chandra walks over and tentatively pulls it back. There is the stage. The announcer turns discreetly, makes eye contact, and nods.

What? Where is Puck? And...why is the announcer nodding like... they want Chandra to come out?

Chandra's heart skips a beat. Dropping the curtain, Chandra steps back uncertainly.

"And now, here for your delight—ladies, gentlemen, and magnificent creatures of the in-between. I give you, the great and mighty —Puck!"

The curtain flies back to reveal Chandra inadvertently waiting in the wings.

The announcer—a young, bright-faced fellow—waves a hairy arm dramatically in the air. A black coat snaps against the air as the announcer twirls, tabby yellow petticoats fanning out from pink and blue striped stockings. Knee-high brown leather boots look almost the exact pattern of Orville's tail. Which is a weird thing to think, but Chandra can't help but see a cattiness in the announcer as they slink closer and closer.

And finally, the announcer strikes a pose right next to the archway. One lace-gloved hand in the air, the other—holding an ornate wooden wand? No, a cane, pointing to the ground. A brown top hat miraculously stays put atop their head. The announcer grins huge.

"Our darling Puck!"

The crowd cheers.

Chandra makes eye contact. Yellow cat-like eyes flash. Chandra takes a tentative step back, away from the archway and into the safety of shadows and cloistered alleyways. The announcer returns to a normal stance and gives Chandra a frown of confusion. Chandra steps back again.

The announcer snarls, small pointy teeth flashing. A lace-gloved hand reaches into the darkness and grabs Chandra firmly by the wrist. In a single effortless motion, the announcer flings her out onto the stage. The crowd goes ballistic. The announcer gracefully bows, a mixture of a gentlemanly bend from the hip and a feminine courtesy from the knees. Then, twirling toward the archway, the announcer disappears in a flutter of coattails and tabby-colored curls.

"Puck! Puck! Puck!" the crowd chants.

"Recite us some merriment!" a kid in the front row with gangly arms propped up on the stage bellows.

"A poem! A song!" another calls from deep in the standing-room-only masses.

Chandra panics, frozen, staring at the crowd.

"Magic," whispers a voice from Chandra's satchel.

The apple? Impossible. But then, what isn't possible in this bizarre dream?

So, Chandra decides that—yes, magic is the best way to appease this crowd.

However, one problem stands in the way of this plan. Chandra's never willfully conjured anything. It's always been an accident. Something unwanted, terrifying, and bad. Never once has a spell risen to mind—in word or image, or otherwise. No. Magic is a thing that happens *to* Chandra. Not a thing she controls.

Like this body, she thinks, remembering the male bits she wishes were gone. And then, suddenly the thought occurs. Chandra looks down.

And there it all is—the dream come true. The roundest of chests. The fullest of hips. The most curvaceous of curvy bods a gal could wish for. At least, this gal. Always Chandra had longed to have hips like rolling hills. A chest like two mountain peaks. Legs that swell and narrow into ample thighs, defined and strong calves. And here it all is. As if this world somehow asked Chandra exactly what body she would want—and provided in full.

Can it be that magic will be the same?

"Try," whispers the apple's voice.

Chandra gives it a whirl, strikes what feels like a very femme pose —left hand on hip, right knee bent, shoulder thrust forward, chin high, lips curled in a tantalizing grin.

"What, a play toward! I'll be an auditor; An actor too, perhaps, if I see cause."

The crowd laughs merrily.

Chandra reaches into the satchel, thinking of a wand to conjure more actors on the stage. And, yes. There it is! A nice applewood wand with a well-worn soft leather grip and fluttering pink and gold tassels, just as Chandra would wish for. From the wand's narrow tip come sparks, glittering white, neon blue and hot pink, all snapping and crackling into the air. The crowd oohs and ahhs. And from the glitter blows silver and gold dust, and from the dust comes a shape. Another actor on the stage.

"All the world's a stage, and all the men, women, and in-between merely players; they have their exits and their entrances, And one human in their time plays many parts," says an apparition of Jaques from *As You Like It*.

A wild tousle of long, midnight-black curls pours down Jaques' slender body and frames a high-cheeked, deep desert red-brown face. Black eyes covered in heavy eyeliner flash at Chandra, dark lips painted with blood red lipstick smile, revealing rows of white tombstone teeth. Long lush lashes flutter and bat.

Chandra blushes and turns to the audience.

"A play you shall have," she says.

The crowd waits with bated breath. They seem to have no preference. Old Shakespearean quotes or not. Real humans or conjured-up magic. They seem pleased as punch to be entertained at all.

"More, more!" they cheer when Chandra conjures up a dragon

with shimmering iridescent scales and has a female Macbeth battle it to the end, all the while a non-binary Juliette dressed in a pageboy costume scrubs at the brim of a brown hat, muttering "out damn spot."

As the sun sinks toward the tops of the thatched roofs and the sky colors red and orange, Chandra takes center stage and swoops into a low curtsy.

The crowd holds its collective breath, awaiting the final word of the evening.

Chandra waves her wand and gathers about her a collection of fluffy minions of a full rainbow of colors. Rabbits and raccoons, birds and squirrels. The fairies who have been flitting about sprinkling confetti across the streets gather themselves to the center, fluttering and chittering happily, if somewhat drowsily.

Both arms raised toward the crowd, chest raised high, back ramrod straight. Chandra takes in a heavy breath and begins Puck's final lines by rote. No magic needed. These are from heart.

"If we shadows have offended,
Think but this, and all is mended,
That you have but slumber'd here
While these visions did appear.
And this weak and idle theme,
No more yielding but a dream,
Friends, do not reprehend:
if you pardon, we will mend:
And, as I am an honest Puck,
If we have unearned luck
Now to 'scape the serpent's tongue,
We will make amends ere long;
Else the Puck a liar call;
So, good night unto you all.
Give me your hands, if we be friends,
And Robin shall restore amends."

The crowd reaches their hands forward at the critical moment. Chandra flicks the wand, and a flurry of red robins burst forth filling the dusky sky. With a sudden green flash, the last crest of the sun disappears below the horizon. Evening falls warm and still as the crowd's cheers slowly taper off and people wander, exhausted, toward their homes.

Chandra waits until the whole street has emptied to sit cross-legged on the stage. Her right hand absently turns the wand over and over while the left drifts upward to the familiar scar. Chandra gasps when her fingers find smooth, unmarred flesh. Eyes drift to the wand. An embodiment of the magic that has always been trying to escape.

And here it is, now. In the real.

How could Chandra say no to this world? Choose? Was it even a question? The answer is obviously yes.

Are you sure? a still small voice says that sounds almost like the announcer in that tabby-colored coat.

Chandra thinks, remembering the apple, and reaches into the satchel to draw it out. The last rays of sunlight speckle across the glistening red skin and remind Chandra of Apple's freckles—but also, of the announcer's. Setting the apple back into the satchel, Chandra rubs her tired eyes.

What a funny day.

Soft footsteps echo across the stage behind Chandra's back. Startled, Chandra jumps up and whips around, wand out. In the shadows, a body looms.

"Chandra," comes a voice that is at once familiar and strange.

Chandra can't help but think: Puck?

The body steps from shadows, small in stature, only rising to Chandra's elbows. A youthful face framed by a messy crop of dusty blonde hair holds brown simple eyes that make direct contact.

Chandra stumbles back. "Who approaches?"

"It is I. Your distant cousin. The honest Puck. How now, wayward spirit?"

Chandra blinks in disbelief. "Greetings. Where am I?"

"Haven't you guessed?" Puck winks slyly.

Chandra shakes her head, frowning.

A chuckle comes from Puck's quirked mouth. "Ah ha. This here, the land of your Midsummer dream."

"What am I doing here?"

"You are here to be happy!" Puck grins.

Chandra looks at the wand, recalling the festival. The stage, the cheering, magic freely made. So very different from the Midwinter festivals back home. Here, the townspeople are in love with magic. With merriment. With Chandra just as she is.

No. Not quite.

"The townsfolk all think I'm you."

"That will pass once you have made your choice. Either you take up this life here or you return to Stratford. What'll it be?"

Chandra stares, stunned. Choose? Now? But..."I need more time."

Puck frowns. "Time is up. I and the town await your answer true."

"I..." Chandra feels trapped. Why didn't Puck explain there would only be this one day? Because Puck is a trickster, that's why. Not the rebel or free-thinker Chandra would like to believe the real Puck was. No. Just a liar, stealer, and cheat.

But, that didn't mean the whole world here was bad, did it? Certainly not. And, regardless of Puck's approach to this deal—this dream world was infinitely better than Stratford and its bigoted assholes.

"I'll stay."

"So be it."

There is a green flash, and with that, Puck disappears in a spin and a puff of black smoke.

Chandra stands and finds she's exhausted.

Now, if this place is truly her land of dreams, there is a warm cottage with dinner already going and a warm bed awaiting her. She stands and lets her mind take her down the streets, around corners, across the main square, and to the door of what her heart knows is her home.

A banner waves overhead and on it big bright pink, white, and blue lettering reads [Home of the good and true.]

Chandra reaches into the satchel, withdraws a decorative key, and fits it into the doorknob. The door opens, and like comforting arms, the warm spicy smells of dinner beckon her in.

A small den of a place with the wood-burning stove right smack in the middle. Above it hangs a suspended loft on thick heavy chains. A drop-down, handmade wooden rope ladder dangles against the far left wall. A row of cushions provide seating along the opposite wall. A plain unstained oak door with the word "Clean" carved into it in curling letters indicates the washroom and toilet.

Just like Puck's cottage—there is no kitchen. But the air is full of aromas. Rosemary, clary sage, lavender, and lemon balm accenting the brightness of the cedar-y wood fire. Chandra breathes in deeply, feeling at once at ease and let down.

All this and no kitchen? No way to cook even in Chandra's own "dream home?"

Still, the place is nice. Everything else is just right.

Chandra climbs the ladder to the loft. A large feather bed tossed with furry down comforter takes up the center space. A few small chests of drawers in a deep red-brown cedar, complete with wood grain that looks like rivers flowing into oceans. A glass-topped armoire with a tea cozy in a delicate purple and green floral print awaits. Beside it sits a fine bone china teacup with matching saucer and dessert plate, all patterned with little pink hearts and pale lavender buds painted neatly around the rim. On the plate sits a variety of shortbreads. Simple, lavender, brown sugar, peppermint.

Most alluring of all, however, is the fluffy bed full of delightful-looking pillows in the corner. Chandra scarfs down the food, feels full and satisfied, and lays on the bed and instantly falls into warm, soft dreams.

~

"Open up, willst thou!" Apple's voice rings clear as a bell.

Chandra bolts upright from the soft, voluptuous bed. Tossing pillows smelling of flowers this way and that. Frantically staring around the small unfamiliar cottage room. A wide bar of golden summer sunlight catches Chandra in the face.

The voice does not come again. A dream, then?

Chandra stretches and slips out of bed. On the table, Chandra finds a delicious breakfast already prepared. Eggs with fresh herbs de Provence, real shavings of rich coastal cheddar, brightly colorful mixed greens tossed in a light aromatic vinaigrette, peppered bacon grilled just the way Chandra likes it—a little charcoal around the edges and dripping in grease.

Chandra tucks in, savoring the flavors with delight. For a moment. Then slowly, the questions come. Who made this? And why isn't there a kitchen here? Or, is there, and Chandra missed it somehow? Also, where did Puck—the rightful owner of this cottage—sleep last night?

Also. Wouldn't it have been nice to make this meal? Even just once—to cook again. To really, actually cook with lavish ingredients like this? What a dream that would be. Better, by far, than eating. Maybe even better than performing magic on stage for a giddy audience. To have cooking back would be as good as having this perfectly femme body.

Knock! Knock! On the cottage door.

"Calling on Chandra, the magnificent, for the morning festivities!" comes a booming voice that sounds like Jaques from the day before.

Chandra freezes, suddenly questioning how magic works here. Has Chandra, in conjuring Jaques, created a new person? And if so, does that make Chandra responsible? Like a parent?

"Come now, open up!" the voice calls.

Chandra goes over and cracks the door open tentatively.

And sure enough! There is Jaques, dressed in yet another fantastically non-binary pants and skirt outfit complete with a lacy blouse and top hat. A black waxed mustache adorns red painted lips, and long, hot pink bangs fall aside heavily lined eyes. A blue-and-pink-striped beanie with a white heart hand-sewn on the side hides the rest of Jaques' hair. Chandra can't help but see the trans flag in those colors. Chandra instantly feels both excited to find another trans person and also certain that Jaques is a fine adult with no need of magical parenting.

"I like your hat," Chandra says. "Is it...?"

"The trans flag, yes," Jaques grins. "And I like your necklace, maestro. A fantastical piece of identity, it is too!"

Chandra blushes, touching the crest and feeling its smooth edges. The wearing down of generations and much love. The connection to Puck being one of the few familial connections Chandra can cherish. Mom and Dad, after all, have decided to be less than supportive.

Jaques reaches out a hand, gloved in black leather this time. "Come now, bright sprite! Midsummer's Fair awaits!"

"I was just eating," Chandra replies. "Are you hungry?"

"Plenty of easy food about," Jaques says with a wink.

That wink. Mischievous...or friendly?

"I'll just be one more minute."

"Best hurry. Everyone's waiting for your opening monologue. Meet me on the stage."

Chandra agrees, shuts the door, and goes back to the table to find breakfast gone. The table cleared. A cup of tea in a travel mug already prepared with milk. Picking it up, the smell is a wonderful complex blend of assam and ceylon. A nice malty Irish breakfast. Perfect for the morning.

Chanda takes a sip and savors the subtle honey notes, wishing to have seen the golden nectar before it went in—but hey, transplants to a new magical realm can't be too choosy. Better by far than getting shouted out of the local brunch establishment for ordering a "woman's drink" of cream tea. Right?

Outside, the town is gathered all over again. Chandra feels right at home. Openly adorned cross-dressers on epic heels strut down the street, avoiding treacherous potholes. A gaggle of genderfluid youth lean against a low wall, ribbing one another about crushes. Chandra listens and is delighted to realize she can't guess the gender or sex of someone's crush purely by a name or the identity of the person being teased. A poly triad holding hands, fingers interlaced with matching rings, sit on a porch swing. The furthest one waves long, painted fingernails, blushes deep rouge, and then runs a hand shyly through dark blue stubble at the back of a zigzag-shaved head.

In fact, Chandra doesn't see a single person who fits in with the old dominate cis-hetero-white culture of Strafford. Here, everyone seems free to express themselves in whatever manner they please. Also, there's a wide range of skin tones and varying cultural sensibilities. It's refreshing.

"This place is a dream," Chandra says to a dark ebony skinned passerby with a shaved head and a big gold badge that reads: [Please use they/them pronouns. I am agender.]

"Top of the morning," the stranger says, smiling.

The stage is just where it was. And the cat-like announcer beckons Chandra back onto the stage in the same manner. Only this time, Chandra boldly strides up to center stage with confidence and flourishes. The wand appears on command in Chandra's waiting hand.

"Recite us some merriment!" two cuddling, hairy, burly, manly-looking lovers shout in unison.

"A poem! A song!" a short non-binary kid with long black braids calls.

"A merrier hour was never wasted here," Chandra says and draws out the wand with a flick.

The crowd cheers.

Chandra easily works a few spells. Flowers grow from the stage. Colorful sparks fly into the air. A gaggle of big balloons float out over the people's heads for them to bop playfully around. Chandra takes a risk and plays around with some new ideas. A pumpkin turning into a lantern. A mouse becoming a tiny dragon. Wings sprouting from twigs. The crowd eats it up.

After what feels like no time at all, Chandra chances another glance overhead. The sun is angling toward the horizon—nearing dusk. Chandra goes to spin another spell and feels the magic sputter out. A few sparkles crackle and fizzle.

The crowd doesn't gasp, though. Instead, they slowly begin to clap.

"The time is done!" one calls when Chandra tries to announce the next spell.

"The night falls!" another bellows.

And as if on a cue Chandra doesn't know, the town quickly disperses.

"Too all adieu, then" Chandra mutters and frowns. What was that all about?

Footsteps on the stage, echoing dully, startle Chandra into turning. "Who goes?" Chandra asks, half expecting Puck to reappear for some reason.

"It is I, Jaques."

Chandra deflates, relieved but also...disappointed? "What are you doing here?"

Jaques approaches with a glaring snarl. "You shouldn't be here."

"I...I'm sorry, what?" Chandra balks.

Jaques, the actor conjured from Chandra's own wand, thinks she shouldn't be here?

For a flicker of a second, Chandra almost knows what Mom and Dad feel like—a creation turning against you. But then, that was only the lie they told themselves. Because being trans isn't "turning against anyone."

Jaques, however, is a spell, and is also looking dangerous, with black eyes narrowed into angry slits.

"You should have gone home by now," Jaques growls.

Chandra holds the wand out, scared by this sudden turn of events. "Off with you now, or I'll put you back where you came from."

Jaques doesn't stop, teeth flashing sharper than ever. "No, you won't."

Chandra thinks of erasing Jaques and waggles the wand. Nothing happens. Not a single sparkle. Zero.

"What the—"

Jaques reaches out, takes the wand easily from Chandra's hand, snaps it in half, and tosses it aside. They step aside politely and let it hit the ground with a clack. When Jaques speaks, it is with a voice deep and strange. Almost alien.

"Go hide you somewhere dark."

And then, in a puff of white smoke, Jaques is gone.

Chandra slaps back the curtain only to see night has descended, fully. Another trick—the working of Puck—no doubt. The streets and square are completely empty. Coming down from the stage, Chandra looks around for the broken wand. It's gone. And in its place...

...is an apple.

No longer perfectly round and glittering, but bruised, with one side banged in where it landed on the corner of a cobblestone. The luster is gone too, the whole fruit turning a slightly brownish yellow. When Chandra picks it up, the skin is dry and the meat inside, mushy. And the faint smile that was there yesterday has turned to a thin dark line of a frown.

Chandra takes the same route off the stage and through tangled town alleyways to end up coming out at the cottage. Like magic. Without even really trying, Chandra doesn't get lost. And doesn't that feel right? Safe? Nice?

In the doorway, Chandra's hand closes around the knob.

It's locked. Chandra gasps from shock, tries again, rattling the metal in case it got jammed. Definitely locked. Chandra can feel the metal in the latch catch on the door jamb.

"What's the meaning of this?" Chandra says aloud, stepping back and looking up.

The name plate overhanging the door is gone. Not ripped off, but missing entirely. As if it had never been there. And the yard is different too. Slightly smaller, dried out. As if Chandra has neglected it for a whole season in the hot sun.

But...it was lovely only moments ago, wasn't it?

There's only one explanation.

"Puck! Come and explain yourself!"

There is a clap like thunder and suddenly, Puck is there standing beside Chandra in a staunch suit, complete with tails and top hat.

"There you are. I have questions for you."

"They can wait," Puck snaps, eyes flashing wild and terrible.

"What?" Chandra balks and staggers back. Why is everyone so nasty suddenly?

"I come calling for Her Majesty, the Queen of Dreams."

Chandra blinks. "The who? What's going on?"

"You have been summoned. As the new heart of Dream Land."

"I..." Chandra's at a loss for words. 'You could have told me' is far too accusatory. So, instead of saying anything, Chandra points inside the cottage. "I need a..." What? What excuse to let Chandra get inside the cottage again? "Let me grab a jacket."

It's not cold out, being Midsummer and all. Honestly, Chandra just wants to grab the satchel that should be inside. Also, have a second to collect a few thoughts. Come up with a plan of some sort. Try to sort this nonsense out.

"Fine," Puck huffs and flicks a wrist. At the end of it is a well-worn, scarred applewood wand. Apple never falls far from the tree, huh? Of course cousin Puck would have a similar wand. Although Puck's looks like it's battle-torn.

"Unlock," Puck commands the door, and twitches a few black flecks from the wand tip.

The door to the cottage creaks open. Chandra quickly ducks in, looking for the bag from the first day. Magically, it appears hanging on a coat rack that wasn't in the entry way before. Beside the coat hangs a nice heavy-looking light purple cloak. Chandra grabs it and can't help but notice how soft and soothing it is. As if it were somehow woven together out of the essence of lavender.

Chandra desperately reaches for a plan. Go with Puck for now. Try to get the wand out of Puck's hands. Run. Cast a spell to do...what?

Puck pokes a head back in, lips downturned. "Come now. We must hurry."

Flustered, Chandra makes a show of draping the small satchel over a shoulder. It still fits like a glove. Only now that seems inconvenient for cramming anything so large as the cloak into it. And yet, Chandra tries, half-folding and half-rolling the cloak and lifting the seal-emblazoned flap. Despite the mismatched sizes, the lavender cloak somehow fits inside perfectly. Neat and tight.

And, Puck doesn't seem the wiser that this wasn't what Chandra had in mind. That delaying was simply for delaying's sake.

"Now you're done, come!" Puck snaps—patience gone—and reaches into the cottage with a hand like a snake and grabs hold of Chandra by the wrist. Fighting Puck on this feels instantly foolish, but Chandra can't help it. It's not the first time someone grabbed her, tried to shove her around, told her what to do. It seemed like here—maybe—those moments were past. And yet, violence and aggression seem universals in the human experience—Dream Land or not.

Chandra snaps out of Puck's grip. "Don't touch me," is supposed to come out hard, but it comes out as a squeak.

"Don't be foolish, woman. In order to stay here, you must face the Queen with your heart."

"You didn't tell me that!" Chandra cries.

"Don't slay me. I am merely the messenger of foul news," Puck says bluntly.

Chandra thinks now of the amazing food, the festivities, the celebration of her magical abilities, the wonderful food—with ne'er a kitchen to be had! The queer people who never felt more than cut-outs of reality. Slices of perfection. Props for Puck's illusion.

"You tricked me!"

"Perhaps," Puck says, changing tone to a quiet whisper. One that sounds exactly like the one Chandra first heard here. The one that led to the announcer and the stage.

"Why?" Chandra asks, hoping Puck has suddenly come into an explanatory mood.

Puck merely winks. "I cannot say. We each must face our own trickery."

"What does that even mean?"

"No time to waste on answers. We must away. No time to waste."

Puck waves the torn-up wand proudly. More black sparks fly and gather together into an impressive black carriage complete with two massive shimmery ebony steeds.

"Up and in," Puck motions with the wand like it's a sword or a gun.

Chandra obliges because if she doesn't, she'll have to physically fight Puck. And busted wand or not, Puck has decades of experience on Chandra. Plus, there's no guarantee that fight can even be won in Dream Land.

As Chandra follows Puck to the carriage, the horses stamp their thick black hooves and huff nervously through massive nostrils. Chandra looks into their eyes and sees nothing but fear.

Some Midsummer's dream this is turning out to be. More like a fever nightmare.

~

The carriage arrives as soon as it leaves. Apparition magic, no doubt. Puck's assuredly a much more powerful magician than Chandra can ever hope to be. There isn't even the illusion of hooves clacking against cobblestones. Just a faint whoosh in the air and Puck stands at the carriage door with a hand held out.

"Down you come."

Chandra obeys out of fear, stepping carefully down the thin metal rungs of the ancient style carriage and stepping into black sand. The heels of her shoes sink down, making it difficult but not impossible to walk. Slow, that's how the going is. All the while Puck prances on ahead as if the sand takes no effect. Up ahead looms a castle rising from a collar of dark, ominous clouds. Flames shoot up from the mouth of a massive oily-scaled green and black dragon, coiled around the entrance to a bridge that arches high over a black bottomless mote. The air smells of cinders and smoke. Ash and brimstone.

"Don't look the dragon in the eyes," Puck warns, flourishing that busted wand again.

And Chandra can't help but stare. The dragon huffs and flaps scaly wings—huge and ridiculously scary. The dragon snorts black smoke and rises, barrel of a chest up on stout armored legs.

Chandra blinks and realizes she's looking the dragon dead in the face.

The dragon blinks back. Then, its giant maw of a mouth opens and a blaze of fire shoots forth. The flame licks the air, popping and snapping. Chandra and Puck's hair crackles. The smell of burning fills the air.

Puck gasps and casts a bubble of shimmery protection around them. "What in the name of the seven hells do you think you're doing?"

"I'm sorry, I didn't mean to!"

"You fool!" Puck rises up to meet the looming dragon, who is huffing smoke now. Puck's chest puffs up, eyes narrow, nose flares. The broken wand sparks yellow and green—proving that it still works.

The dragon shrieks and puffs a blast of fire over their heads. It's hot and blustery and terrifying. Chandra ducks under a licking flame that curls from the angry dragon's mouth. It lashes overhead, but then bounces off Puck's shield.

"Testing your luck, I see," calls a sudden booming voice from somewhere within the castle ahead, amplified unnaturally.

Chandra jumps and looks to see Puck cowering from this sudden voice. Even the dragon shrinks back against the walls of the castle, like plastic wrap under heat.

"Come," the voice commands darkly.

In front of them, another black and aggressively decorated wrought iron gate clunks and shrieks, raising into the roof of the archway. Puck turns up behind Chandra suddenly, urging her on with a hiss.

Chandra plunges into darkness lit only by thin wavering candles that throw clingy, uneven shadows onto huge gray flagstones. Stairs rise up out of nowhere and lead up in a wide curve. As Chandra moves upward, the stairs grow narrower and narrower until a door no wider than one person appears out of the darkness, lit by two red-flamed candles. Chandra notes the handle looks like a withered, shriveled up, old and ugly apple.

Chandra hesitates, horrified by the withered skin.

The doorknob twists on its own, glowing red, accentuating the ugliness of all those lines. The door swings inward with a grating whine to reveal a massive octagonal room with a black marble floor that stretches to high stone walls. On the walls hang a variety of flags in no comprehensible order. A messy rainbow of spewed-up colors and geometric shapes. The one purpose the flags serve is to draw the eye toward the black center of a room, where a pure bleached bone throne glows as if lit from above. On the thrown sits a humanoid body with a massive bulbous head, giant beady black eyes, and a crown atop a withered scalp peppered with wiry straggles of gray hair.

A dark line of a mouth opens. A gaping maw from which a rattling vibration tumbles out. A breath? Chandra doesn't want to think too much about it. The shape raises a withered limb, at the end of which is a long, vein-strewn hand with long, curling fingernails.

"Puck, you bring me yet another heart to devour?"

Puck appears beside Chandra as if out of thin air, bowing low over shaking knees.

"Oh Queen, my Queen. I bring you Chandra, my dearest of cousins. The could-be ace magician of Stratford, North Carolina," Puck bellows. The voice echoes against the polished floor and the stony walls.

"Come, my delicious meaty heart," the Queen calls, a single long, yellow fingernail beckoning.

Chandra doesn't move.

"Come now. You cannot think your dream is without a price," the Queen mocks, quirking a bushy black eyebrow.

Still, Chandra holds her ground.

"Silly fool. Oh folly of the young. Everything has its cost. If you wish to keep your heart, I will consume another's in your stead."

A burst of ultraviolet light. A blast of ice-cold air. A crackling tear zips through the air. Chandra blinks and beside the Queen's throne sits a cage. And inside the cage, a human shape sits shivering and clutching exposed knees to naked chest. Long strands of dirty, rust-colored hair cover the face. And muted as the color is in this dark place, Chandra would know those long locks anywhere. Only, it can't be!

"Apple?"

"Your sacrifice!" the Queen bellows.

The red hair tumbles back to reveal a blanched face, freckles standing out like stars on a moonless night.

"Apple! No!"

The Queen's laugh cracks like thunder rolling through the room.

Chandra looks to Puck for help, only to find the trickster in a ridiculous bow.

The Queen's laughter turns to blazing red hot rage. A disgusting hand raises over the Queen's hideous head. The fingernails curl in on themselves as the fingers tighten into a ball. A tightness grows in Chandra's chest. Not the old constrictions of fear. No, this is something tangible and unarguably real.

The Queen's mouth smokes. The palm raised high opens, and a spark of blue bursts from the center of the Queen's closing palm.

Chandra feels the tightness burst into a thousand aching shards. Coughing and doubling over, Chandra's knees crack against the hard ground. "No!" comes out as a sob.

"You will be silent and obey me!" the Queen shouts.

Chandra's whole body goes down, slammed to the ground. An invisible boulder presses Chandra down, crushing her spine. Bones crackle as they realign. The old familiar necklace now becomes a hundred tiny daggers, digging into Chandra's clavicle. The pressure keeps coming. Chandra's nose is smashed flat against the marble. Inside her head, blood squeezes and throbs against the bones of her skull. Chandra's smashed mouth tries to scream, but to no avail. Sucking in a tiny breath makes the pressure worse. Chandra's ribs pop and shift, clacking like hard heels against hollow wood.

"Now. Say please, and I will eat this human being's heart instead of yours."

Chandra can't say "please"—even if she wanted to. Can't move.

Can't do a damned thing. And yet, Chandra's heart hammers out: "No! Stop! It's not right! Let Apple go!"

"Ah, such a waste," the Queen feigns regret. "You humans and your emotions. Pity. You could have been as great as me."

There is another sudden snap against the ground right by Chandra's head. And for a horrifying moment, Chandra's certain it's the sound of her neck breaking in half. But when the world doesn't go dark and there's no new stab of excruciating pain, Chandra has to rethink.

The cage opening, Chandra's inner quiet whisper confirms. And next will come the gruesome, unbearable sounds of Apple being devoured.

Instead, a flood of silver light so bright Chandra can feel the rays radiating everything, filling the hall and bathing Chandra's oppressed body in the pale flood. Suddenly, Chandra feels less weighted down. Lighter somehow.

And then, whose voice should fill the hall but the damned trickster Puck's.

"Ill met by bright moonlight, proud Queen of Midsummer's Dream. I give thee warning now. The time for your reign is passing. Surely, cousin, you will not stand for these games much longer."

A clacking sound right by Chandra's ear. Puck's heels, moving away.

"Puck! You lying trickster! Get you back here this instant!" the Queen seethes.

More clacking recedes from Chandra's side and moves quickly across the room. The sound disappears against the distant flagstones. Coward and liar, indeed. If it weren't for Puck, none of this would be happening. If it weren't for magic, trickery, and people being willing to use their power to hurt others.

Heartless, that's what it is. Completely heartless.

Chandra can't help but think of the conjured-up Jaques, of the stage, of the crowded-around town, gasping in pleasure at all the silly things Chandra made on the spot purely to be praised. Can't help but think of all the magnificent food here, without any of the hard work laboring in a cramped and sweaty kitchen. Can't help but think of Apple, and how it's all over for someone just because Chandra chose to live in this dream instead of going back home where she belonged. Where, yes, life was hard. But it meant something.

Chandra sees Apple standing at her window, hand held out. She hears Apple's voice shouting down the neighbors. It's people like Apple who have real heart. The ones willing to risk everything for someone else.

And in that case, what is Chandra then? A coward and cheat like lying Puck, or someone with heart?

"No!" Chandra's whole body says in response to the idea of Apple dying here.

It's not right.

Chandra thinks of the snapped wand and Puck gone. There must be some way out of this smashing force. The Queen controls everything. The pressure, the castle, and that nasty dragon outside. The one pressed flat against the castle walls.

Pressed flat...

The image comes to Chandra again because it's so familiar. That image of being melted onto a surface, of shrinking like thin plastic wrap in a blast of heat. Chandra knew what that felt like, now!

And if that's the case—is the Queen controlling the dragon in the same way?

In that case, all Chandra needs to do is get a hand in the bag, pull out a new wand, and set the dragon free.

Easier said than done. Chandra struggles to move, to see what's going on. And in the process of struggling, something thin and pointy knocks into Chandra's elbow.

The wand!

The one Puck had waved in Chandra's face in front of the carriage, and again on the bridge! And those lines—the feint scars of breaks magically healed in the place where Puck had snapped it the day before.

That wand wasn't Puck's, after all. It belonged to Chandra all along!

She'd called it from the magic within her. Just...just like the dragon she'd called into existence back in Stratford that one festival winter. Which—come to think of it—looked almost exactly like the dragon currently shrink-wrapped against the side of the Queen's castle!

Chandra tries to visualize the two dragons. The rippling blue-green scales. The long glittery body. The bright, kind, golden eyes. No, not almost alike. One and the same. Just like the wand.

That's it! Chandra doesn't need the bag. The magic, the trickery—it's here, lodged deep in her blood pumping through her heart. She focuses on the thumps. One, two. One, two. And as she tries to pull the magic up from her chest, she feels a swelling sensation. Like a snake uncoiling. Like that one moment right before the portal opened up—when she held Orville.

Orville, the stray and sudden friend.

Is it possible Orville is...Chandra's familiar? The heart's protector for free thinkers?

Chandra's not convinced, though, that Puck should be included. After all, the damned fool just ran off. But left the wand.

Right. Focus. Get the wand.

Chandra just has to move a couple of centimeters. Grab the wand. Call the dragon. And let the magic devour this withered, outdated old ruler of this nightmarish dream world. Then, all can be restored!

It takes everything inside Chandra to concentrate on moving even just a smidge. Everything aches, burns, stings. Gritting and clamping down on the pain, listening to its call like a motivating coach, Chandra musters up the courage to edge toward the wand. The pressure lets up ever so slightly. Closer, closer, closer Chandra's trembling fingertips get. And right as two fingers finally close on the warm wood, Apple's sharp shriek shatters the air.

"Stop!" Chandra belts out, whisking up the wand and leaping up into a standing position without even thinking if it's possible. It just happens and there stands Chandra, wand aimed like a weapon, tip bursting in a shower of white sparks.

The Queen gasps. Apple cries out.

"Dragon!" Chandra bellows. The sound is a blaring war horn blowing through an echo chamber. "Dragon, come!"

A shower of black glass shards burst from the window over the Queen's throne. The dragon snakes into the chamber, forelegs plucking Apple from the Queen's grip with ease. Gently setting Apple down in front of Chandra, the dragon turns on the Queen. Fire hisses from between a massive mountain range of pearly white razor-sharp teeth.

The Queen screams. The castle walls shake. The throne behind the hunched and lumpy body ignites. Blue and orange flames jump about as the dragon's maw opens and a loud roar rushes out. The queen freezes, caught in terror. The dragon lands right beside her.

"Now, snap the queen right up like a biddy snack," Chandra commands.

The dragon hesitates.

Chandra feels the glowing of the necklace against her skin. The burning that put the scar there once before. It glows hotter and hotter. Chandra gasps, grasping the necklace. Her fingers burn and she drops it.

What in the seven hells?

Then, light bursts forth from the necklace in the shape of a heart. A real anatomical human heart. The bloody thing beats, its cells rhythmically squeezing against each other, pumping blood to the rest of the body. One, two. One, two. Chandra stares at the dragon through the projection of her own core powerhouse.

Before Chandra figures out a response, clapping fills the hall.

"You broke the spell," Puck's voice echoes from the far end of the hall. "Well done, cousin."

Chandra turns. "What are you doing back here?'

"You can't believe I actually left you to a monster like that, can you?" Puck points at the frozen queen. She looks more like a projection than a person, now. And Apple, too. Chandra's heart outglows them all.

"This...this is all an illusion?"

"Not quite. More of a trick, you might say. A play of your future."

"Wait, you mean...that queen...is me?!" Chandra gasps, the truth feeling like a punch in the gut.

Because Puck doesn't need to answer. It's clear. The dragon, Apple trapped, the lack of heart.

"That's what I'd become if I stay here," Chandra says without question.

"Indeed," Puck says and bows.

Chandra looks the queen in the eyes. The shriveled, stone cold eyes. "No. I want to go home."

"I know. But you have some work yet to do."

"I do?"

"The heart must be returned."

"My heart?"

Puck nods.

"How?"

Puck motions behind Chandra, to the front of the hall.

To Apple.

Chandra turns back. Through the projection of her heart, Apple lays cowering, shivering, and naked on the ground. The queen stands over her with a nasty glare, frozen like a figurine. Without thinking, Chandra follows her gut and rushes over. She bolts right through the glowing image of her heart, feels a momentary hiccup of time, but keeps going, keeping Apple in her sights. Passing through the heart, she crouches down by Apple's side.

"I'm so sorry."

Apple looks up, no longer terrified, but sad and exhausted.

Chandra pulls from her bag the soft coat she grabbed before getting in the carriage. At the time, it had been an excuse. A way to get more time. But now, it had a perfect use. Chandra drapes it over Apple, puts a supporting arm around her shoulders, and turns to the dragon.

"Dragon, take us both home."

The dragon puffs a tuft of warm smoke and nods its long serpentine head, winking. And for a brief second, Chandra seeks something catlike in the dragon's eyes. Something familiar and feline.

Before Chandra can ask the dragon's name, a voice interrupts.

"I can help you lot."

Chandra turns, expecting to see Puck, and stands ready for a fight. Wand out. But instead, there is the sweet-faced, conjured-up creation: Jaques.

"Jaques? What are you doing here?"

"Doing my service for the ace magician of Stratford, what else?"

"You want to do my bidding, Jaques?"

An earnest nod. Chandra wonders if that's not heartless—asking Jaques to help after all this—but then, they are a conjured actor from Chandra's heart...so probably not. More like, an extension of Chandra's will here. But, to be safe, best to ask Puck.

Chandra turns looking for the familiar face and finds nothing.

"Where's Puck gone this time?"

"Back to the heart of magic, I suppose," Jaques shrugs.

Chandra nods though that makes no sense. "You can help us get home?"

"Indeed. You have the wish-maker. It is all you need."

Jaques helps Apple, who still looks pale and weak, while Chandra figures out what to do with the satchel. A wild idea strikes her. Reaching in, Chandra hopes desperately for a pillow. Fingers curl around soft tassels and drawing her arm out, there is an exact replica of the kind of pillow Apple needs. Better than Chandra's own vision. Thinking of a dragon saddle, Chandra reaches in and pulls out a thick blanket.

"How is this working?" Chandra marvels aloud while draping the blanket over the obliging dragon.

Jaques stands, helping Apple hold the blanket and balance. When they near the side of the dragon, Jaques points at the satchel.

"That bag holds the heart of magic. Your heart, now. Decades ago, it was lost. The ace magician of Stratford, refusing to be a part of the magic, tried burying it. When it came back, the magician burned it. When it came back again, the magician used a spell and cast it into the ether."

Chandra gasps, about to ask who the magician who lost the bag was. But, it's clear, isn't it?

"Dad," Chandra says.

Jaques nods. "Your parent, yes. But not Alexander. The could-have-been great Feria."

"Mom?"

Jaques nods again.

Now Chanda thinks of it, that makes even more sense. When Dad stopped talking to Chandra, it wasn't just because of the transition—truth be told. Dad had said Chandra needed to "grow up," to "stop hurting others with this silliness." Chandra had thought it *was* all about the transition, but what Dad meant was magic. And this "hurting other people" was because Chandra's magic reminded Mom of what she'd tried to bury, to cast off. The whole situation was a blunt reminder to Mom of how she'd failed herself, failed magic, failed the test to be genuine and true.

"Sometimes," Jaques continues, "accepting who we are forces others to realize what they've tried to hide, and they don't like us for it."

Chandra thinks of the terrified, hiding, stink-eye-giving towns-folk. Yes, that rings true, too. What's the point of helping people then —if they'll just dislike you for being strong?

Chandra glances across at Apple, who has fallen into a napping position against the dragon. Because there are people like Apple who reach out instead. Chandra turns back to Jaques.

"What happened after my mom tried to cast the bag into a void?"

"Being the ace magician, it worked. The bag vanished and left the people of Dream Land to slowly fade into non-existence. When you were born, Puck prophesied to the remaining scraps of us that the days of fading were gone. Those days living in fear of the dark, waiting to see if you might be the next one snapped up by the night. And now you are—the wish maker returned to you because of your heart."

"My heart?"

Jaques nods. "You are true to yourself. That's what it takes to be the true ace of Stratford. Honesty, bravery, and a willingness to face our own heartless future queens." Jaques bows at Chandra. "Well done, maestro."

"And what about mom? What happened to her? Is she fading too?"

"No. Magicians don't fade, Chandra. They lose their hearts," Jaques says darkly.

Chandra nods, knowing that's true, too. No wonder they can't even be in the same room together. No wonder Dad has become Mom's stalwart guardian, always standing in the way of Chandra even trying to approach.

Chandra's heart burns and aches. The projection, still cast into the air, glows blue. Then, Chandra gets another wild idea.

"Is there a way for the old magician to get it back?"

Jaques frowns. "Only Master Puck would know the answer to that. I am merely a historian, not a trickster."

Chandra thinks of Puck's short stature, those gentle brown eyes, that tousle of dirty blonde hair, and reaches into the wish-maker.

"How now, spirit!" Puck's voice calls from within the bag.

Chandra yanks at the trickster's arm.

"My dearest of cousins," Puck says smiling, climbing out of the bag like it's the top of a well. "What do you call on me for?"

"I want to know if I can help Mom get her heart back."

Puck's smile falls away. "I...I'm sorry Chandra. What's done is done. There is only forward on our chosen road, not backward."

Chandra's face turns gray. It can't be. It's not fair. "But what if I... give Mom my heart? The satchel—"

"Must stay here," Puck says.

Chandra turns to her dragon and their eyes meet. "Fine. But I think I have an idea. I'll have to trick her into talking to me!"

Puck winks. "Now you sound like me."

"The apple never falls far from the tree."

"Then, off you go. Back to Stratford, hm?"

"Yes. Help us up, Jaques, will you?"

"Of course, maestro. Up you go."

Jaques helps both Chandra and Apple load up on the patiently waiting dragon's back. The dragon's massive shimmering wings begin to beat the air into a great swooshing roar. Up and up they go, toward the sky. The dragon's body slices the air like a highly sharpened blade, smooth and effortless. The air offers no resistance. It rushes high overhead, barely touching even the top of Chandra's head—protected as they are in their little nook.

The dragon's shoulders flex and ripple. Higher, the three of them fly. Toward, not the small village or the river or even Puck's cottage, but directly toward the sun. And as they draw ever nearer to the brilliant light, a shining golden gateway opens up in the middle of the sky. Chandra feels the edges of the familiar crest glowing against the old scar on her skin. The new edges where the necklace had been crushed by her heartless queen against her bone feels warm and strange.

Suddenly, the gateway turns bright blue and a white line appears in the middle. The white line cracks in half, and two massive gates swing open. One bears a glowing wand behind Chandra's family crest, and the other bears a ripe apple behind its own unique crest. One Chandra has never seen. Very odd, indeed.

It's almost as if this gateway changed to accommodate not just Chandra, but Apple too.

My own stalwart guardian? Chandra recalls Apple shouting down the gathering townsfolk and thinks—yes, indeed.

The dragon slips effortlessly through the portal. On the other side is none other than the blue sky hanging over Stratford, North Carolina. Chandra knows those woods crowded in by those cookie-cutter houses, that city center and its massive ugly parking lot off on the south end.

"We're almost home," Apple says, raising a head up, bolstered by being back in the real world.

Chandra eases back into the riding blanket and rests beside Apple as the dragon descends. Chandra bolts up as the dragon turns away from Chandra's lonely cottage toward another ridiculous flapping banner. It hangs over the town's city hall. Mom and

Dad's place of employment. The banner like so many others reads: [Celebration of Shakespeare! Remember the Midsummer in Midwinter!].

The dragon roars still high in the air, breathes a puff of white steam and lands with a thud on a clump of fresh snow.

Already the townspeople are gathering, their expressions honed and ready. The city hall doors fly open like castle gates and out charges—who else?

Dad—stalwart guardian—in a blazing fury of rage. Eyes flashing, dangerously locked on Chandra. A hand like a wand waves sharply in the air.

"Get you down from there this instant, Peter!"

Oh, here we go.

"We will not," Apple barks before Chandra can even open her mouth.

Bolstered by Apple's boldness, Chandra puts one hand firmly on a hip. Does it feel slightly curvier? The remnant effects of magic? Her other hand reaches for the satchel and grabs at thin air.

Shit. That's right. Puck said the wish-maker must stay in Dream Land. And that means the wand too is gone. What now?

"Your necklace," Apple whispers.

Chandra's hand comes up automatically and fingers the family crest. Behind it, the lines of the new scar run like a circle around the old wand-shaped one. Yes. That's it! Chandra's lips move without thinking and a bright melodic sound pours out.

In her hand is a smooth applewood wand. The scars of the fighting in Dream Land—all gone. Chandra flourishes the wand and blue, white, and pink sparks fly.

"Dad. Stand down. I want to talk to Mom!"

Dad frowns, shaking a fist in the air at Chandra. "Your mother has no interest in seeing an abomination like you!"

Chandra feels the blow resonating deep inside where all her parents' hateful words go. Right down to the core. But then, a hand on Chandra's elbow rallies her. Apple's gentle touch—a reminder of the truth.

"That's not true. Mom is scared of me. She's scared of magic. And she's scared I'll find out what she did and be angry."

Dad's eyes go wide in disbelief. Chandra's never stood up to him. Not once. Chandra waggles the wand and a host of robins fly out and flutter down. The gathered townsfolk gasp. Dad stumbles back away from the spell, eyes full of a mixture of terror and surprise. Almost awe, but not quite. Still so far to go. How can Chandra even hope to convince Dad to stand down?

A tap on Chandra's shoulder, warm and gentle. "Look."

Chandra follows Apple's gesture to the left, where a side door of city hall has been cracked open. And in the crack, Chandra sees a pair of eyes. Purple and glowing, like the great Puck's. Like Chandra's, if she looks close enough. The sign of a trickster. A free thinker. A rebel of her time.

"Mom!" Chandra calls. "It's okay. I won't hurt you."

The door starts to close.

"Please," Chandra says, not bold and loud—but small and quiet. Like that first "please" of Apple's back at the cottage window. "I want to help you," Chandra adds, hoping these words will mean something.

The door cracks back open ever so slightly.

"I know why you did it. Why you tried to throw the heart of trickery away. I tried too because it's scary, all this magic we don't know what to do with. All this...power. I'm scared too, even now, Mom. Can't you see that?"

The door opens even further.

"Let me help you."

The door swings open fully and there, standing with a wet face and red eyes, is Mom. Small as a child, she looks, cowering and hugging her arms to her chest. Chandra puts a hand on the dragon, who extends a leg. The big blue-green scales are like a shimmering staircase that Chandra descends. The robins gather from all around and follow her toward Mom, a train of protection and the mending of errant actions.

"I'm so scared," Mom whispers when Chandra gets close.

"Of me?"

Mom's head shakes ever so slightly, a finger points not at the wand —but at Chandra's chest. And for a sick, stabbing moment, Chandra thinks this really *is* about the transition. About seeing these round hills of breasts on a child who you still want to call "Peter" and think should love sports and going to the bar with bros. And Chandra is about to lose her nerve. To throw out a spell that sends Mom away. To do the unspeakable, if only in protection of herself.

But then, a hand on the small of Chandra's back makes her turn. There is Apple, with those brilliant green eyes, and those wild tumbling curls flaming like a lick of fire from the dragon's mouth.

Apple smiles warmly and touches Chandra's crest. "I think your Mom would like an explanation, perhaps."

"Yes!" Chandra bursts out, realizing that Apple's right. Mom's not pointing at Chandra's breasts, but at the crest. The symbol of their magical lineage.

"Puck, honest and true, told me you lost your heart. And that there's no way to get it back. But I think that's wrong. I think you just have to want it. That's all."

Mom's face falls, gray and stricken. "Oh, that can't be. That's too easy. Don't you see?"

Chandra shakes her head, long femme hair tickling her shoulders. Longer than it was, isn't it? "See what?"

"Things don't change. Once you mess your life up, that's it."

Chandra looks down and thinks—no way. And then realizes, that might just be it! Chandra holds her small hands out. The narrow wrists are so femme, so dainty, so pretty. Even back in the days of being Peter. They were always her reminder. You're a girl, not a boy, these hands and wrists say.

"Look at me, Mom. I'm proof that's wrong."

Mom does look up and, for the first time in years, they make eye contact. Dark heavy circles under each eye. Red-rimmed almost permanently. And in those trembling irises, deep down at Mom's core, Chandra can see just how hurt, how scared, how sorry Mom is for everything. Not a monster with a stone instead of a heart. No.

What's standing in the way is a wall, a stalwart protector of the wrong sort. Chandra's sure.

"You just have to want your heart back, Mom. Really want it. Here, take my hand."

Mom hesitates.

"Chandra's right," Apple jumps in. "I watched her beat a nasty, heartless queen with these sunken eyes and a shriveled head and a heart of stone. You are not she. You are brave, right?"

Mom nods and tentatively reaches out.

Chandra takes her hand in the empty one, holds it high for all the town to see, and walks with Mom to the steps of city hall. Dad, seeing the two of them come, shuffles out of the way. Once in the middle of the gathering crowd, Chandra raises the wand high and calls her magic heart of wish-making to herself. Sparks of blue, white, gold gather around their heads. The dragon takes wing and circles them. The robins chirp and join in. The crowd begins—for the first time ever—to clap. It's a slow build, but within minutes they are cheering and hooting for Chandra's spell.

Chandra knows just what to say. Right from the heart.

"Watch now as we rehearse our song by rote
To each word a warbling note:
Hand in hand, with fairy grace,
Will we sing, and bless this place."

The sparks turn into fireworks, popping and sending brilliant colors into the sky. Clouds coloring with dust sparkle and glint with magical birds, moths and butterflies of all sorts. Smells of baking and sweets and aromatic herbs fill the air with a gentle warm summery breeze. The last rays of sun break through the gray and light the snow at Chandra's feet like a spotlight.

Chandra curtsies low, then stands erect. Back ramrod straight.

"If we shadows have offended,
Think but this, and all is mended,
That you have but slumber'd here
While these visions did appear.
And this weak and idle theme,

No more yielding but a dream,
Friends, do not reprehend:
if you pardon, we will mend:
And, as I am an honest Puck,
If we have unearned luck
Now to 'scape the serpent's tongue,
We will make amends ere long;
Else the Puck a liar call;
So, good night unto you all.
Give me your hands, if we be friends,
And Robin shall restore amends."

The robins and dragon swoop low, gathering not around Chandra —but Mom. The faintest of voices whispers Mom's name: Feria, Feria, Feria. Chandra listens underneath their whispers for the beating of her own heart. One, two. One, two. Chandra closes her eyes, reaches down deep with the magic, and casts a projection of her own beating heart. It flows out from the family crest and fills the air with a blue glow. Chandra pulls it up and from the crest coils a long serpent of light. It winks two yellow cat-like eyes at Chandra. A flash of a tabby-colored tail brushes against Chandra's cheek as the light snakes its way from the crest to Mom's chest.

"Orville? Where's my little Jaques?" Chandra calls, recalling the conjured friend of Dream Land and thinking it a fitting play-name for the cat.

Mom's eyes go wide. "How do you know that name?"

"Jaques was my friend in Dream Land."

Mom colors visibly, blushing and turning away.

"Wait. You know Jaques?"

"My imaginary friend as a child, yes. Jaques kept me company when I was too weird for friends."

Chandra nods. "Same as Orville. Came to me when I had nobody."

"You share the same familiar!" Apple exclaims.

Which then gives Chandra an idea of how to help fix things.

"Mom, put your hand on my heart."

Mom balks, blushing again.

Chandra points at the blue light. "There. Touch it."

Mom looks uncertain but nods and reaches out to touch the light. As Mom's finger reaches the edge of Chandra's heart, a bright flash fills the sky.

And deep in Chandra's chest, something unravels. A snake, uncoiling. That feeling of holding Orville. That feeling of taking command of magic. And yet, that coiled thing feels like something else. Not Chandra's own heart, but someone else's. Mom's!

The snake descends on Mom's shoulders and wraps around her like a warm coat. And then, the image evaporates. And around Mom's neck is a matching necklace, family crest glowing ever so slightly. Mom picks it up and holds it in her hand, amazed. And underneath the crest, Chandra can see the distinct and bright new lines of a wand-shaped scar. Not like Chandra's, but unique. A twisting ornate wand, possibly made of deep red cedar, mahogany, or even ebony. Something sleek, deeply rich, and beautiful.

"You did it!" Apple cheers from Chandra's other side, rushing up the steps and wrapping Chandra in a sudden hug.

Chandra embraces Apple and feels the strength radiating all the way down to her exhausted bones. When the two let go, Chandra glances worriedly at Mom. What will she think of this new development? Her "Peter" with a white knight all her own? And a female knight, at that.

Mom looks up, their eyes meet, and in their depths Chandra sees a new thing. Light.

"Thank you, Chandra."

"I only did what I felt was right."

Apple lays a hand on Chandra's arm, protective and soft. "That's because you have a golden heart."

Chandra shrugs. "Just a trickster's heart, really."

Mom nods, suddenly looking nostalgic. "Just like your distant cousin Puck."

"Speaking of Puck," Apple says, "Shall we go to the festivities? I hear there is a new ace magician in town, and things are going to be amazing!"

Mom nods and eyes Chandra. "First show in ten minutes?"

"Yes, indeed. Come one, come all. Ladies, gentlemen, and magnificent creatures of the in-between! A magic show to delight the senses. On the main stage in ten minutes!"

Chandra flicks the wand and sparks rain down around, pattering on the snow and leaving little gemstones instead of holes.

The gathered crowd cheers loudly, disperses, and regathers instantly at the main stage. Apple and Mom rush to the front row. Dad hangs behind, walking slowly and looking lost. At first Chandra's chest tightens worried that even now, they'll have conflict. But then, a quiet whisper bubbles up in Chandra's mind.

"Give him time," it says, in the soft voice of Orville, the gentle familiar.

Chandra dabbles behind on the steps of city hall, pondering this. It's true. Being someone's guardian for all those years and then suddenly having the need for you whisked away must be a difficult roadblock to get through. Because Dad never made a decision about how he felt. He never faced his own emotions surrounding losing a son and gaining a daughter. He only did what was best in his mind for mom. And now, he has to work through all that junk. It'll take time, but Chandra's hopeful. And how can she not be, what with magic on her side.

Which reminds her! Time calls!

Chandra goes to make her way through the crowds lined up for the show, and there is standing room only. Elbow to elbow and shoulder to shoulder. Among them, Chandra sees a small collection of visibly gender-bending youth waving several banners. Asexual flags, pansexual flags, bisexual flags, rainbow flags, genderqueer flags —among others. The group is small—sure—but they feel bolstered enough by Chandra and all this to-do to come out on a big day like today. And that alone is huge.

As Chandra tries to make her way through the crowd, she instantly picks out the blue, white, and pink banner that reads [Make magic happen! Take a stand for Trans today!] Chandra feels a warmth glowing. Being a big bold trans-lady as Stratford's ace magician might work out after all. If not without some struggles. For curious as they all are, the crowd Chandra picks though certainly isn't devoid of stink eye and judging sneers.

But, like Dad—give it time.

A few more meters of struggling against the bodies, though, and Chandra realizes it's futile. There's nowhere left to move. No way to get to the front of the stage. Up near the front of the masses, the voice of an announcer rings like a bell from center stage. Chandra gapes. Not just any announcer. It's Apple, who has somehow managed to ascend front and center on the stage.

"Come one, come all to the fantastic Midwinter Showcase of Stratford's very own ace magician!"

The crowd loses it cheering. Party poppers go off. Hands clap. It's madness. And Chandra can't move an inch one way or another. Then, a subtle tap on Chandra's shoulder calls her attention to a one of those old faux antique archways off to the left.

"This way," a quiet whisper says from down the narrow and dark alleyway. Chandra turns to follow it and, sure enough, there is the big tabby Orville, ready to lead the way.

ABOUT THE AUTHOR

Rei Rosenquist is a queer agender (they/them) speculative fiction and romance writer who depicts a wide variety of identities struggling to find a place in a wide variety of worlds. They are also a barista, baker, musician, and lifelong semi-nomad.

Rei has traveled to many countries, engaged many peoples, picked up new habits, and learned new languages. Across lands, they find constant inspiration in the stories we tell each other, the food we share with one another, the music we make together, and the world we can build when we allow ourselves to dream.

Find out more about Rei at:
reirosenquist.com

facebook.com/reirosenquist
twitter.com/rylrosenquist
instagram.com/rylrosenquist
goodreads.com/reirosenquist

A SQUALOR OF CHICKENS

KAREN L. ABRAHAMSON

"There is something to be said for wretchedness. Let it rust away that backbone of yours."

Those were the unSeelie queen's last words before she banished me from the summerlands. Wretchedness can transform your blood and bones. It can sink into your soul and turn everything to bitter foulness, like this village.

And its chickens.

~

"Well that's it then," Da said as he ducked through the doorway, shushing the village's hens away from the door and stomping snow all over my clean-swept floor and beaten rushes. I'd cleaned them to greet the new year, just like Ma would expect. Behind him, the open door let in the cold midwinter dawn, the smell of rotting leaves, the creak of ice on ponds as well as the clucking of the chickens that always gathered at our door as part of my penance. Though I might be able to forget my plight most of the time, those birds were a constant reminder of where I was and what I'd lost.

"Milch cow and goats are fed and the pig's on roasting," he said. "All's to do is get the beast turning. I'll get John's son to give me a hand after breakfast. It looks like the bonfire will be a big one." Da was a big man, all broad shoulders and thick neck that came from being a miller. Joseph Miller his name was, and my mother was Posy and I was the bramble Rose of the family, though once I had another name.

He glanced over at me, his gaze a warm hazel. His eyes always reminded me of the flickering shadows and light under the spring leaves down by the river. The same light filled my bitter dreams with yearning for the summerlands.

But forgetting was a gift denied me—part of the infernal geas that bound me here and bound my magic in all except one thing.

Our house was a solid one my Da received from the manor-bound lord of these lands in exchange for Da's labors in the mill and

Ma's husbandry of goats. In return they got a share of the mill's wheat and the safety of the lord's protection.

Unlike the many airy halls of the palaces of the summerlands, this house was one room only, but a stoutly built one with a hearth on one wall and thick beams running beneath the thatch ceiling. Foot-thick walls of white-washed clay kept us warm against all but the worse of the winter—like that of midwinter's eve when the curtains separating the worlds were thin. Instead of down beds, blankets rolled against the walls were where we lay our heads on the dusty rushes to sleep, but the crackling apple wood fire filled the air with sweet scent and gave us light. It was the best place Da had brought us to in a long time and I knew he wanted to stay more than one winter this time.

If I could make my peace with the chickens.

I had chased them from the house and scrubbed the place free of their remains—unlike the other villagers who let the blasted things live with them.

From the thick bed of rushes by the fire came a rough, hacking cough and Da's gaze sharpened, travelling from me to the thick woolen blanket over the huddled figure. "How's your Ma?"

"The same, I think." My throat tightened. "It's as if the river pools in her chest. I brought her water, but she won't drink." My voice sank to barely a whisper, so I motioned to the untouched wooden cup on the floor.

"If her chest's full, she won't need more of the stuff, now will she, Rosy?" He lightly touched his knuckles to my forehead. "Got to use your head, girl."

As if I truly was a girl—I had seen more years than him by far. And water—water was life for all things, except if it filled the lungs.

"My head alone is not going to get your breakfast ready." I hauled up onto my crutches to give one last stir to the thick oat porridge in the fire-blackened pot hung in the hearth, and then ladled a bowl for him and fumbled it with the almost ease of old practice to the rough oak table that filled the center of the house.

I filled a second bowl and, too conscious of my awkwardness, joined him on another stool at the table. The good thing was he never watched me stumble with my twisted spine on my stick-thin limbs and never said a word like the other villagers. He just settled into eating while I tried to ease the old ache of my spine and shoulders. At this time of year it was always worse, digging through my flesh from inside.

"So you going out with your friends tonight to celebrate?" he asked. "Wash the old year away and welcome in the new?"

I tensed and looked over my sweet-smoky porridge at him and thought of midwinter in another place—the music, the lights, the warmth and laughter. I set down my wooden spoon and set away the longing, for that way lay madness and that was the unSeelie queen's intention.

"Ma needs tending. And I have my own way of celebrating." And though I might know the villagers, I had none that I'd call friends among them.

He shook his head. "Not good, Rosy, an' you know it. We haven't been here that long. You've got to try to fit in or the tale-telling will start up again. You've got to know it."

He was right of course. All of my paltry human existence the tales had followed us like some patient cur no matter where we'd lived. My parents with their first born babe, healthy and whole one day and the next with warped back and withered legs—or so the tales went. The fact they were true was evidenced in the bend in my back and the withered limbs beneath the table and the way the chickens pecked at me whenever they got close. The whispers said it was a sign of the unclean, but truly it was a last taunting curse of the queen's—cast to torment me for attempting to rescue the Seelie king's son. As if being here wasn't enough.

Changeling the villagers called me, fairy droppings. In their whispers and in truth, the miller's true child was lost to the summerlands, the unSeelie queen her heartless host.

Some parents would have drowned me and mourned the loss of their babe until another more natural child filled their hearts. Mine didn't. Instead they loved me with all their hearts, which eased the wretchedness of my situation. Which was why their milch cow gave milk almost all winter and why their gardens always grew lush even in poor ground when other folks' fields might falter. That fact was part of the tale-telling, too.

And the curse.

Da looked at me thoughtfully as he chewed his porridge. "Young Seamus—now there's a good lad. He was asking after ya. Change your plans and attend the celebrations tonight." He reached across the table and caught my hand. "Yer seventeen, Rosy. I want to see you happy, child. It's my greatest wish to see you wed with babes of your own."

For a moment, I felt—lost. To wed a human—that would mean I was well and truly condemned to this place, this borrowed life amidst the chickens. And yet a part of me yearned for that belonging. In this life Seamus was... well, Seamus. There was no one else like him in this village, nor had there been anyone like him anywhere else we'd been. Like a knight of the summerlands, he was tall and strong and with piercing blue eyes that had the other girls sighing. But not me. Never me. A man like Seamus could have anyone.

And I did not want him anyway. I was not of here, though I might fool myself from time to time. I pulled my hand away and hobbled up, then turned and let myself down to the floor at Ma's side. The dirt floor was cool beneath my withered knees, the rushes rustled as I caught Ma's hand.

She was usually a pale woman with hair like spun gold and pale lashes that caught the light and brought a twinkle to her deep blue eyes—unlike the silver of my hair and my almost invisible lashes. But now her eyes were closed and her cheeks carried a ruddy, overblown glow. Her hand was heated as if she'd stirred the pot too long over the fire and she smelled of infernal iron. She coughed and gasped and I could feel her soul loosening, just as the earth's soul broke free every cold midwinter. This year I had to tend her, just as I tended the earth each year. That was part of the geas, too. From time immemorial my people have ensured that the earth receives the bounty of the sun's rays. Each midwinter as the old year's strength fades, it is my kind who keep the earth alive until the newborn year has the vigor to succor the earth to spring waking. In the past, this magic has been maintained by a changeling who would only remain for a year, before returning to our homeland. But with my banishment, no others have needed to come these past seventeen years and this year was no different.

"I'm better here with Ma. Tell Seamus that I've no interest in him or merry-making."

Da shook his head. "Ya can't hide here forever. There's a world out there and somewhere a husband waiting. Why not here?" When I stayed silent he bowed his head and I watched his mouth set in a line. "Have it your way then, but I'll not discourage the boy."

His spoon scraped on the bottom of his bowl, wood on wood, and then he stood and once more shook his head. "I love ya for trying, Rosy, but your Ma's been fading these past three moons..."

I looked sharply up at him for I heard what he'd left unsaid. She was dying with the year and there was nothing a crippled daughter could do. "I *will* be here for her!"

His sigh was heavy as he put his stocking cap on and went out the door. His passage let in the fingers of the cold north wind and a hiss of snow across the floor.

And the cackling of the chickens.

There were certain matters that I had known since I was a babe. Beyond the glamour that made me lame, others felt the cold more than I did; Ma and Da could be shivering in all their clothes while, laughing, I would drag myself in my clout out into the snow— much to Ma's horror.

Neither Ma nor Da, nor anyone else that I had met could see the cords of light that bind the world's soul to the earth and give it the power for life. I saw them shimmer in the wind and saw how the sun's light traveled down them into the soil. I could watch that same light travel up snow-bound trunks to wake the slumbering trees and unfurl into the burnished leaf shields of shady groves and the rich waves of grain fields.

As a babe, I would clumsily grasp the cords that break at midwinter and coo them down to the earth again so my parents' garden would be reborn. As a child I would sit in my ma's garden and whisper them down for the village. As a young woman with an old goat bell and a song the entire vale and beyond would come to greening again.

That was my sole magic and my one contact with my people's blessed powers—and always it was my family's undoing. Over the years my song and the bell grew as repellent to the villagers we lived among as the chickens were to me. Each town had driven us out and on until we were here in this vale in the mountains. And though I knew it would bring down our departure again, I could not withhold the singing for the life of the earth depended upon it. If the cords of the sun were not kept joined to the earth, there would be no way for the new year to bring spring.

The morning spun away and from outside our thick door came the music of the midwinter celebration. Pipes and drums and a lonely harp that was owned by the lord of the manor all struck up a merry tune and there was laughter. There would be dancing around a bonfire in the village center and a feast upon the green. There would be prayers led by the local priest and late at night the lord would open his gates to his people and then would come the stout and mulled wine. It had been the same at every village we had lived in and each time we left the village soon after, trailing shoals of stone-throwing children on our way.

Da said this time would be different—that the lord and villagers liked our family. Besides, surely they would take pity on such an ill woman. But I knew better, didn't I. Man is always the same to those who are different.

All morning I nursed Ma by the fire. Beyond the door a shout went up and fiddles began to play. The music would become wilder as the day progressed in hopes of aiding the new born year to overcome the old one. Only then could the people be sure that the lean winter months ahead would end in spring.

Ma's flesh smelled of iron. Her cough increased, and the lines of light that bound her soul to the earth were fading. She stirred in her blankets and moaned as I used snow and ice water on her brow and trickled liquid between cracked lips into her parched mouth. This was worse than being banished from the only home I ever knew to this land of—of chickens and squalor. How could these people stand their loved ones tortured so?

"Ma, you've got to live. You've got to. We can't leave you here and like as not we'll have to leave this village." I whispered it into her ear and her watered blue eyes flickered open.

"Rose. My lovely Rose." Her voice was as faint as snowflakes on winter boughs. "You'll go with your Da. There's naught to be done for me." She swallowed and grimaced and I brought her water in a wooden cup. I fought her head and shoulders into my lap against the restrictions of my back, but she spilled more liquid than she drank.

Then her eyes closed and she went limp in my grasp, her breath a rough rattle in her chest. When she coughed, bloody spittle spilled down her chin. I wiped it off, and then laid her down before scrambling up. I balanced on my crutches above her. The mother I loved was drowning.

There had to be something more that I could do. Perhaps with Da's help I could help her sit up a little and help her breathe. If she could breathe she might sleep more easily and then regain her strength. It was a hope. It was something I could do for her.

Pulling my shawl around my crooked shoulders I went to the door. "Ma, I'll be quick as I can be. You just stay well, you hear?" I would be back to her soon and with the falling of the light I would perform the ceremony with the song and the bell and replenish the land and, hopefully, my mother with it. If I could only keep her alive that long.

She murmured something unintelligible and I shoved out the door.

After the warmth of the cottage there was a tang on the December air. It bit at my cheeks and nose and ears and pinched at my nose with each inhale of the smoky, pine scent. Even though it was only early afternoon, already the sun lay low on the white mountain peaks and cast long shadows that wavered weakly in the gathering dusk. At this time of year, darkness waited like wolves in the shadows and under the eaves of the trees that flowed down the mountainsides toward the village. I pulled my shawl tighter around me as I had seen the village women do and scuttled awkwardly on my wooden crutches toward the center of the village where flickering light on the house walls said the bonfire was ablaze. Bright sparks rose up on gusts of chill wind off the mountains.

There were people singing amid the thatch-roofed houses. The angled sunlight lit the snow-covered thatch golden. Figures muffled by cloaks and shawls huddled in doorways out of the wind and feasted on pig cracklings and bread, then drank deep of honey mead and cider that filled the air with a sweet-sour tang. Around their feet cringed brown-coated curs snapping up bounty fallen to the frozen ground and ragged hens peck-pecked at the crumbs and last bit of seed before they found their way into the village pots. The earth was rough where feet had churned the soil before it froze.

The scent of roast pig sent my mouth watering more than the feasts of my youth ever had and I followed the smell through the fading sunlit lines of midwinter that trailed through the air. These were the cords that brought the sun's power to earth, but now many shivered, ends loose in the wind, awaiting the new year's return and their new binding, but for now they drifted and while they did the earth starved for sunlight and the hope of spring.

Ahead the cluster of timber and wattle houses parted onto the green in the center of town. Across the green stood the three-story massive face of the lord's timber and stone manor, and before its gates a huge fire burned, while to either side over smaller flames great spits turned, one for a pig, the other a cow. Around the frozen green, in the shadows of the naked oaks where the village elders stood, danced the village youngsters, intent on drawing in the new year. Even the village priest stood by, his arms crossed in disapproval though his fist held a chalice of mead.

That was when the chickens found me. They flocked across the ground, wings half-spread and clucking madly to dart in at my crutches and peck my withered ankles. Sharp beaks found tender flesh and struck again and again as I tried to wave them off with my crutches and nearly fell.

A hand on my arm nearly finished the job until it steadied me.

"Here! Go on wifya!" Seamus yelled and scattered the birds with a boot to their tails.

My shoulders throbbed and I went to tug away, but his hand on my arm was firm as he turned me to him.

"Rose. I was asking your Da about you. He said as you were not coming out of yer house. I was about to come looking."

Seamus's blazing blue gaze pinned me as well as any fae sword.

He came with a scent of warm wool and rich spiced mead on his breath. Instead of fae silks, his tunic and leggings were of well-worn homespun, brown with wear and age, but his cheeks were ruddy in the cold above his beard, and his smile was white and full of teeth and I wanted to believe him.

"I'm looking for me Da," I said, shoving my unnatural attraction away. For all my years in this land, I was fae, unhuman. I would not sink so low as this. "Ma's taken a bad turn and I need his help."

The brilliance dimmed momentarily in Seamus's gaze. "Poor woman. We'll have t' get her help, won't we?"

We?

His grip tightened on my arm and he dragged me with him—not toward the firepits that I was sure Da would be tending, but toward the elders huddled under the trees.

We threaded through the dancers and Seamus grabbed my waist and swung me around once, my crutches flying out to the sides. I demanded to be put down, but Seamus only laughed, his head thrown back and the belling sound could almost make me love him. His fair hair flew around his face, as pale and golden as the color of the cords of the sun and I could hear the music of the summerlands in his laughter.

Then he set me down and it was a dusky winter day again and the shadows were forming. A shiver ran through me as he half-dragged, half-carried me through the dancers to the line of trees and the waiting elders.

"Look who I found," he announced, as if they'd been waiting. "I don't believe you've met Father Michael." He almost dropped me in front of the black-clad priest.

Father Michael I had only seen from a distance because there was little love of his kind for mine. I bowed my head briefly, but then straightened as best I could, before him. If I could face an unSeelie queen, I could face this man. Better, I've learned, to know your enemy.

He was a black-eyed man with hard lips that limited themselves to a line. Gaunt cheeks and a narrow chin completed the look of a weasel, though weasels were perhaps a purer creature. The gaze of this man made me sure of my assessment. There was a sharpness to his gaze and little kindness.

"I was talking to Rose, here. She says her mother is desperate ill and needs tending."

That knife-blade gaze nicked back to me. "I've not seen you all day. Is that where you've been—caring for your mother?"

"Yes, sir," I met his gaze proudly.

"A child shouldn't be left to care for someone gravely ill." He turned to the woman next to him—the headman's wife in a shawl of plaid with her gray hair pulled up in a twist upon her head all covered by a sky-blue scarf. "Come, Good Wife Greeves, we must see to this girl's mother. She needs our care. It is not proper for her to be left untended."

As if I was of no worth at all.

He turned back to Seamus, the westering sun catching in Father Michael's gaze masking whatever lay inside them. "See you care for this young woman."

Then he left, dragging the village headman's wife behind him. A flock of clucking chickens pecked the earth just beyond the remaining elders. I started after the priest, but Seamus tightened his grip on my arm.

"I need to go with them. Ma will think I've deserted her!"

"They'll care for her fine. What could you do that they couldn't?" He stepped up beside me and I wanted to brush away the light strands that tangled in his hair, wanted to touch that cheek and stand so close that I could once more scent his damp wool scent. His hand was a brand on my arm.

"Dance again?" Seamus asked with a grin.

"I—I—I think not." Though I would recall that breathless spin the rest of my life.

"Then what? Some food?" he asked.

I looked past the swirling dancers toward home and then toward the sizzling fires and the slowly turning spits. For a moment it seemed I saw through the veils between the worlds to the macabre dance of the unSeelie courts where I'd been held prisoner with only hope of torture before me. I shook my head to clear the dizziness. "My Da will be there. I should tell him..."

Seamus tugged me back from the elders before I could finish, leading me, against my protests, into the darkness of the forest around the village. The air turned warmer almost as if we approached the summerlands and the ends of my crutches sank deep into the loam. I struggled to keep up the pace he was setting, but his scent of mead and warm wool set me off balance.

"Where are we going?" Unused to his touch, I struggled to free my arm.

Seamus tugged me into him, and pressed me back against a hoary oak tree. His body was warm, his woolen shirt tickled my cheek. His sweet-sour breath of mead flooded my face as he pressed in against me. "What's the problem, Rose? Don't you trust me? Is it because you're still a child as Father Michael named you?"

A child? I was a child when green first crept into the world, and yet I felt a child in this grim world of men. I swallowed and looked up at his blue gaze gone black in the darkness. "I'm not a child. I'd like to go back to the others now. To my house and my mother. She needs me."

Seamus gently shook his head and grabbed my shoulders. "But that's where you're wrong, Rose. You're the last thing she needs, being what you are an' all. Not a child at all, are you?"

My fae flesh suddenly turned cold as the night. I shouldered him away and squared off to face him.

"Just what is that supposed to mean, sir?"

"What do you think?"

In the almost dark the light streamers shifted like a golden veil. They would shift aimlessly until I sang them down and told them where to go. When I did, morning would come and spring would follow as the days grew longer. I would plait hope back into the world.

But now?

Now hope was replaced by fear and anger as I glared up at Seamus' smug face in the darkness of midwinter. Was this what the unSeelie queen had wanted? Was this what she had planned all along?

I turned on my crutches and headed back to the village.

Only to be yanked around so hard my crutches were wrenched from my hands and I teetered for a moment and went down, my wide skirts twisting around my useless legs. Where once I was known as fearsome with a sword, I went down hard in a heap of cloth and useless human bone and flesh. The earth was cold and damp through my skirts.

"Seamus, what is this?" I demanded. I was no meek child for him to do with as he pleased.

I glared up at him and wondered who was this stranger in the darkness. Surely not the blue-eyed young man who'd spun me around, his voice belling with laughter.

But his face was masked by the darkness and he said nothing, simply dragged me up by my armpits and hauled me into his arms. He turned and started walking deeper into the forest. Behind him through the snow trailed a flock of squawking chickens.

"Put me down."

He shook his head and the sweet scent of mead turned sour.

"My crutches. I need my crutches and I can walk on my own."

Another shake of head. "Not where we're going."

"Put me down, or I'll scream." I struggled in his arms, and battered his face with my fists. I'd fought with my hands in the summerlands.

He turned his face away and then used one fist to catch me in the chin. My head rocked back and the night went black. His chuckle sounded like a demon. "Scream all ya want. You think anyone's coming?"

His arms were a prison as I realized this was no game, no courtship. This was everything the unSeelie queen could hope for. She might not kill me for I was under the Seelie king's protection, but in this guise others could. I fell back on the role I was supposed to play.

"Seamus, please. I want to go back. My mother and father need me." And he and the village did, too, though they could not, would not see it.

Another shake of head and he shouldered into deeper brush. Tree boughs smacked against my face as the forest thickened and so did my fear.

The night deepened and the old year faded and weakened. The new year waited in the wings to be called to fill the breach and it was my voice that did the calling, but dread stole the words.

The sounds of the village revels faded and the forest was silent in the cold. There was the puff and sigh of Seamus' white breath in the air, the snap of branches breaking under his leather-clad feet and the pound of my heartbeat. Overhead, where the treetops parted, clouds scuttled across an almost full moon and stars glared back with the same distant twinkle I'd mistaken for friendship in Seamus' gaze.

My withered legs ached. My shoulders and back throbbed from the abuse of being carried. Finally, the forest parted and Seamus carried me out into a frost-bound clearing bounded by tree-sentries on all sides. Through the skiff of snow, grass stood tall and silver under the moon, the streamers containing the last of the old year's fading sunlight sifting through the grass with a sound like water. It would take so little to knit the streamers back in place.

In the center of the clearing lay a low, humped mound of snow that had smoke coming from its peak and a low wooden door.

"Hallo!" Seamus called. The door swung open a bare six inches.

"Seamus?" A girl's voice.

"The same. Is Robert here?"

"Father Michael sent him earlier. You brought her?" The girl's voice again and the door swung wider. "We've been waiting."

It was the village headman's daughter, Rachel. She was slim as a reed with dark hair that ran down her back like a flow of water from under-mountain. She had red lips and rosy cheeks and long dark lashes that fluttered in the light of a small fire within the mound.

She stepped out into the night to greet us and was followed by the manor lord's son, Robert, in doeskin breeches and high black boots. While Rachel wore a shawl much like mine, Robert wore a thick woolen cloak worth more than Da might earn in a year.

"Grab her feet. The door's too narrow and low to carry her in like this," Seamus said.

"What is this place?" I asked. It was too silent and far from the village, given I could barely crawl with these legs of mine. There was a scent of old filth that rose from the mound and from behind Seamus came the clucking of the infernal chickens, peck-peck-pecking at the ground.

"It's the home of a woman you would have had much in common with. A witch she was, and we got rid of her," Rachel said with a smile.

"We should be back with the others, feasting in the village," I tried again. If they would not listen to me, let me appeal to their stomachs. There were still months of poor fare ahead.

Instead Robert caught my feet and no matter how I twisted, and clawed and bit and their hands, between him and Seamus they carried me through that low door.

The room was warmer than the outside from a small, sooty fire in the center of the floor. It leaked smoke up towards a ceiling so low neither young man could stand upright. Stained walls were built of stout timbers that carried the green slick of old smoke, moisture and cold. The room reeked of chickens as if this had once been their home. They dropped me in a filthy, feather-strewn corner, my left leg twisting awkwardly under me.

The three of them studied me as if I was an injured dog.

"Will this hold her then?" Rachel asked.

"It held the old woman, didn't it?" Robert said.

Seamus crouched down beside me. "You asked why. You aren't one of us and Father Michael says the chickens are telling us that you don't belong. Only a witch draws such ire from the beasts and birds, and this village will not suffer one. We'll be rid of you before you cause harm with your wickedness." He stood up, his scent of warm wool fading from my nose. He shook his head. "It's the way it's got to be. The old ways are dead and dying. Your Ma might not be ill if she'd only drowned you!"

I recoiled and he and Robert stomped out the fire. Then the three of them left. In the dark, through old feathers and ancient chicken droppings, I crawled to the door. It would be hard, but I was fae and untroubled by cold. I could crawl my way back to the village. Seamus, Robert and Rachel's laughter and voices beyond the barrier told me what I would find when I pushed at the door.

They'd braced it shut.

There was no way out.

No way for a crippled human girl, perhaps. But I was fae. I always would be, no matter that the unSeelie queen had stripped me of most of my power. There had to be a way to triumph over these children—these fools. These *men.*

The dark hut's warmth quickly faded to a biting cold that seeped in from the earth as Seamus, Rachel and Robert's voices faded. Night deepened and the old year faded. The earth needed replaiting with the sunlight cords or the spring would not come again and the green hills would be lost. The plaiting had to be done before the new day dawned, so I had to be free by then unless I intended to let the world come undone.

Let the bastards freeze to death? My Da and Ma?

The place reeked of old chicken dust and rotten rushes and something else. Something had crawled in here to die a long time ago. I pulled my skirts in around me and my shawl around my shoulders. Surely someone would come looking. My Da at least.

I tried the door once more, but it gave not a whit and there was no sound from beyond. Seamus and his two helpers had left, and left me alone, gone to enjoy their revels.

An unnatural cold ate into my useless legs and up my twisted spine to my arms and breast. Cold, beyond that of winter. So cold and though I stirred the remains of the fire, Seamus and Robert had done too fine a job of stomping. There was no help there as the hours ticked past.

I searched the hut for something to work with, but the walls were stout with only the door and no windows. In one corner I found an old wood peg hung with an older leather pouch that released the fragrance of long-dried vervaine and chamomile. Herbs that would have helped my Ma, but herbs I could not get in winter. Whoever had lived here before had known their worth.

And died for it.

I found her body in the last corner, bones bound in rags of clothing, her hands bound behind her back as her killers had left her. Seamus's words told me the worst: they had bound her and left her, just as they had left me in this squalor of chickens.

I looked to the door and knew that though Da might go looking, he would never find me. They would send him in other directions while they offered their help to search for me here. They would tell him they saw me leaving, perhaps that I said I was tired of caring for Ma.

And with the coming of the new day and the lack of the ceremony, my mother would fade away and hope would die in my father's breast as the hillsides failed to green in the spring.

It was—a travesty. It was my failure—a last clean spell of reviving magic stolen from me and the world. The unSeelie queen would be laughing, toasting me with her chalice of blood. Long ago she had tried to bargain—my loyalty to her in exchange for my freedom. I would be her spy in the Seelie court. I would help bring the Seelie king to his knees. When I'd refused, I'd paid the price of my banishment amongst these fools and priests and heartless bastards.

After seventeen years I had had enough.

Using the rough timber walls, I pulled myself upright on legs more akin to twigs and peered into the darkness.

"It is done!" I cried. "Enough. You have your wretched servant!"

In the summerlands my cry must have been heard, and I could imagine the unSeelie queen's smile, for to turn a true heart wretched was her pleasure. There came a rustling in the small hole in the sod roof where the fire smoke escaped.

A single sun streamer wound its way like a withy down through the earth and bough roof to curl in the air, seeking. It brought with it a scent of clean air and sweet summer sunshine and hope.

The streamer's golden sides pulsed with the sun's sweetness and power. A single streamer meant for me. With it, could throw off this glamour. I could be whole and fierce in my own body.

My shoulders pulsed with wings demanding flight. My spine and legs throbbed for the strength that could soon return to their length.

I balanced on my withered limbs and reached, caught the streamer's end...

And stopped.

Its sweet promise bloomed in my fingers. Its power pulsed through my wrist. In my shoulders gossamer wings beat with new blood. I would flit through the chimney hole and wing my way westward to the summerlands where the sun never set and the air was sweet and there were no chickens squalling at my feet. Straight-backed I would dance with the bonnie knights of the Seelie court as I worked the unSeelie queen's black-hearted magic and there would be music and light forever.

Until I brought the dark queen's darkness.

I jerked my hand back into shadows.

No.

No to that half-freedom. No to that twisted life. There was

another whose need was purer than mine. Who deserved this streamer and its gift of life far more than I ever would. She had borne a child only to have it stolen away. She had been left me as a replacement and had, in turn, loved me and given me life far longer than most changelings ever had.

I bowed my head. If I accepted the unSeelie queen's bargain for the gift of my freedom, my befouled magic would no longer be capable of joining the sun to the earth. And in my sullied form I would forget my mother; my sole thought would be to return to my new liege in the distant summerlands.

I could not return to such a half-life existence and leave Ma to die.

My legs gave under me and I thumped down to the feather-strewn floor.

Do this before I could change my mind. Do this before my anger at the humans could lure me to take the unSeelie queen's offer. My hands at my breast, I bowed my head.

It started as a low melody barely heard beyond my lips, but the streamer heard. It trembled in the darkness as if in a wind. The song increased, a song of youth and health and hearts beating love for one another. A song of long life and strong limbs and always enough food to eat for oneself and those you loved for surely that would ensure at least a partial spring. Then I blew toward the streamer.

"Posy," I cried and the streamer shuddered and blew away, up through the chimney hole and was gone, seeking the one I had named.

The throbbing in my shoulders stopped. The bright pulse in my hand and wrist became the painful tingle of limbs asleep and my legs went leaden and cold as I laid myself down beside the rag-clad body. Beyond the blocked door I could hear the cackling and through the thinned veils between the world came the unSeelie queen's screams of wretched rage and anger.

Smiling, I exhaled what remained of my soul into the earth's sweet soil. And regained my iron backbone amidst the squalor of chickens.

ABOUT THE AUTHOR

Karen L. Abrahamson is a well-traveled writer who has explored cultures and countries around the world but British Columbia, Canada is her favorite place to come back to. She is the author of literary, mystery, romantic and fantasy fiction including the highly regarded Cartographer fantasy series. She lives on the west coast of Canada with two Bengal cats that aren't quite as well traveled as she is.

When she isn't writing she can be found with a camera and backpack in fabulous locations around the world.

Find out more about Karen at:
karenlabrahamson.com

facebook.com/karenlabrahamson

goodreads.com/karenabrahamson

bookbub.com/authors/karen-l-abrahamson

amazon.com/Karen-L.-Abrahamson/e/B004MACF98

BY WINTER'S FORBIDDEN RITE

DEANNA KNIPPLING

PROLOGUE

An isolated farmstead in the Midwest—December 9, 1889

No devil will fright thee then so much as she.

— WILLIAM SHAKESPEARE, LOVE'S LABOUR'S
LOST

The house had only recently gone quiet. The wind moaned around it, casting flakes of snow at it too fast for the eye to see—only white trails where the snow had once been. White snow clung to the rose-colored paint on the walls of the house and the red paint on the fences and the barn and the outbuildings.

Nothing living remained. Inside the barns, the milk cows were beginning to freeze to the straw on the dirt floor. Two horses, likewise. The white chickens had escaped from their coop before their slaughter, for the most part, and had been sucked away by the snow. A few of them might live until springtime. But most of them would lie trapped within the snowbanks until spring. Then they would sink into the dark earth and rot.

The farm cats had fled at the first sign of trouble, of course, but then so had the mice.

Human bodies lay in the house, the barn, and around the farmyard, cooling in pools of their own blood.

Crystals of ice formed in the red footsteps.

The babe in the Lady's arms shivered, but not from the cold. He was inoculated now with her genetic material, from a gentle kiss on the forehead.

As a mother, she understood what terrible hopes lay upon something so lovely and defenseless. As a scientist, she was far more aware of the mistakes she had made with other humans, over an immense amount of time. She was learning, though, what she needed in order to found a cross-breed race.

As a queen, she was running out of time.

She held the child tighter, and lay her cheek against his. "My son," she said. "You are now my son."

His face was hideously, terrifyingly pale. She kissed him again, this time only to comfort him.

It was time to go.

PART 1—BEFORE THE SÉANCE

When icicles hang by the wall,
   And Dick the shepherd blows his nail

— WILLIAM SHAKESPEARE, LOVE'S LABOUR'S
LOST

The table did not seat thirteen, nor would the parlor have seated thirteen if that many seats had been available. In fact there weren't thirteen women that the lady of the house could trust in a situation like this. Instead, there were five: Marda Stolte, the lady of the house; the medium, Madame Josephe Benoit, of Montreal; Stephanie Schiffman-Marushia, Marda's nearest neighbor at five miles' distance, a childless widow; and two spinster sisters, Lavinia and Leontine Arnel, who were Marda's cousins from town. A girl named Vella King waited on them, tromping indelicately back and forth between parlor and kitchen with teapots and trays. The baby, Edward, was in a bassinette in the kitchen, near but not too near the stove.

The day was bright and sunny, although chill. A steady wind drew a line of clouds from the west.

Marda's husband had driven into town to pick up some supplies for repairing a few things around the house, leaving their farmhand Timothy to hang around and take care of things; Martin would be home either late that night or early the next morning, depending on whether or not he cared for a drink.

Marda wore a heavy, rust-colored wool dress of a simple cut with gold-colored embroidery. She wasn't much of a seamstress, but she liked to embroider while tucked up under a heavy quilt. Madame Benoit wore a heavy black skirt and a plain white blouse. A knitted kerchief in black Shetland wool lay across her shoulders, almost but not quite as delicate as French lace. Stephanie wore a high-collared black dress that brightened her neck and wrists with tiny bits of white lace. One cuff's lace had come askew and was threatening to dip into her tea. She was the youngest of the group, already a widow and lame as well. She could walk with painstaking slowness from one room to the next, and on her worst days needed to be carried or pushed in a wicker wheelchair. She had a broad smile, golden hair, and a sharp tongue.

The two sisters, Leontine and Lavinia, wore two slightly different shades of beige cotton twill. What their dresses lacked in color, they made up for in detail—ruffles, flounces, pleats, piping, and fabric-covered buttons. With their glossy, raven-black hair pinned up in long coils on their heads, their dresses had a surprisingly striking effect. Their skin was pale as snow, their lips as red as blood—and their cheeks carefully pinched pink when their backs were turned to the table.

"The séance must occur after full dark," Madame Benoit warned them. "The spirits cannot pass the veil in daylight."

"What about the full moon?" Leontine asked. She was the younger and bolder of the two sisters.

"That will have no effect on the matter," Madame Benoit said. "Just as when a ray of sun strikes a surface, it gives up its heat, when sunlight strikes the moon, it gives up its power of maintaining the veil, so we will not need to contend with its light. The darker the night the better, of course, for the light of the stars, no matter how distant, still affects the spirits."

"Isn't it generally said that the light of the stars is beneficial to summoning spirits?" Stephanie asked with a straight face.

"It is generally said," Madame Benoit stated with an elegant assumption of queenlike dignity, "even though it isn't the slightest bit true."

"I appreciate your candor."

Marda cleared her throat slightly. "Are there any preparations that need to be made before this evening?"

"First, we must be uninterrupted," Madame Benoit said. "Your husband?"

"Is not expected to return from town until after midnight or early tomorrow morning," Marda said. "Although Timothy is still here to see to the livestock."

"I must ask that you speak to him, to ensure that he does not interrupt the ritual while it is taking place."

"I shall."

~

The four of them played whist until dinner, with Madame Benoit doing some knitting in silk in front of the fire. Vella King waited on them and cared for the baby, keeping him quiet and out of sight. He was a little one, not yet able to crawl or even hold his head up steadily. In fact he seemed weak, pale, and bloodless, and Miss King was always at his side, making sure he hadn't stopped breathing. She had had a baby brother pass that way, and she had nightmares about it still. She might have saved him, if only she had been in time.

Between hands the women talked about the baby, their homes, Marda's husband, the dead.

"Who is it that you're trying to contact, Marda?" Stephanie asked.

"My mother," Marda said firmly.

"Whatever for?"

"Advice about Edward. He's a sickly boy."

"Has the doctor seen him?"

"Yes, for all the good that it does. Something is wrong with his blood—that's all that the doctor will say."

"He isn't haemopheliac, is he?"

"It doesn't run in the family."

"Why your mother? It wasn't as though she were any great doctor or wise-woman."

"She can see past the veil…she will know his fate. I want to know whether my son will be all right, or that if worse comes to worst, that he will be cared for in the other spheres."

"The other spheres?"

"Spiritualism holds a great deal of wisdom, my dear."

The sisters tittered, more at Stephanie's ignorance than at Marda's comment. Leontine shuffled the cards awkwardly, as she always did.

The only reason Stephanie had come to the séance was out of sympathy with her friend; as a Catholic she personally found the idea of interfering with the dead repugnant. Of the two of them, Marda had always seemed the more stolid—but it was she who ran from belief to belief, searching for "answers" to the world's suffering.

The only answer in this life is that we must bear whatever comes of it, Stephanie thought. *Although I would just as soon bear this farce with some hot tea.*

The tea *had* gone cold.

Leontine began to deal. Stephanie pushed her chair back. "I'm going to see what that girl is up to."

"Have her put the kettle on," Marda said.

Stephanie entered the kitchen. Miss King held the baby at her shoulder, a frightened look on her face, patting the baby's back.

"Is everything all right?"

Miss King bit her lip. Suddenly Edward gasped and threw his head back. The girl put her hand on the back of his head to keep him from flopping about. His pale skin had taken on a bluish cast, Stephanie noticed, that quickly brightened to a rosy pink.

Stephanie crossed herself.

"Hot tea in a jiffy," Stephanie said brightly as she entered the room and seated herself, noisily scooting the chair forward. "She was dealing with Edward, that was all. I've helped her a bit. She's a good girl."

The others agreed that this was the case. Stephanie picked up her cards and looked at them. Her partner was Lavinia. It was simply the undeniable fact that when the two sisters were partners, they were unbeatable. Whether this was due to some sort of mental sympathy or to a sophisticated signaling system could not be determined.

That might be a question to ask the "spirits" in the séance. If anyone in the room were likely to be an expert on signaling systems and other trickery, it was Madame Benoit—if that was her *real* name anyhow.

Stephanie caught Madame Benoit glancing up at her and held her eyes for a moment.

The woman had worn smoked glasses most of the day; as the afternoon light began to fade (it being an early sunset in December), she had removed them in order to see to knit. They were gray eyes that seemed almost powder blue around the edges, but that turned slate gray, then faded to back at the centers of the pupils. They were the most naturally hypnotic eyes that Stephanie had ever seen. If the woman hadn't become a medium, she would have had a happy career as a seductress.

She appeared to be making a delicate shawl, in appearance somewhat resembling the one she was wearing, although this one was in a dark rose color, not quite scarlet.

Stephanie was prepared to accept that the woman might be possessed of certain supernatural gifts; it would have been foolish to assert that nothing beyond the material existed, given her own faith. But the woman was a liar of some sort, that much was obvious.

L avinia looked at Leontine; Leontine looked at Lavinia. And they both nodded.

The feeling that they had discussed upon arriving at the farm had intensified. A presence had come to the farm, one that, as budding Spiritualists themselves (as well as possible mediums), they found it difficult to ignore. The presence was not a new one, exactly; it had been present across several visits. They had, during a series of lovely autumnal days earlier in the year, covered the entire Stolte farm on long walks. The presence had not remained motionless; one week it had been in the barn; the next, near the well; on a third visit, it had seemed to linger near one of the fields, just out of sight—they had both startled when they had been trying to peer through the high corn stalks, only to face a scarecrow.

Now, it had settled inside the house.

It was not a beneficent presence, nor even a neutral one. Wherever they found it strongest, they also found the most evidence of rot and ruin: peeling paint, dead chickens, mold. And now, if only for a moment, precious little Edward had stopped breathing. They had felt it.

Whatever presence lurks on the Stolte farm, it's too close to the baby. It wants him.

That was the thought.

But what would be the action?

❧

T he world inside Marda Stolte was all a-flutter, a thousand moths in the darkness, bestirred by the grim light of one last hope. The first two babies she had lost were girls; this one was a son. Martin—*Martin and Marda, how droll*—had already hinted darkly and repeatedly that if Edward died, he would know that the farm was cursed.

At any rate he looked at her differently now. She was running out of time.

Madame Benoit felt the tensions running around her; she wouldn't have been half so good at her profession if she had not. She tried not to dip into the atmosphere too deeply. At some point, sensitivity became vulnerability, and she intended to give herself a margin of error. She anticipated an evening where the work would be easy—she wouldn't have to call for long to summon the spirits, and she *certainly* wouldn't have to use her little tricks of knocking and rapping in order to provide signs of their presence. Presences seemed to follow her from room to room, eager to catch her attention.

The spirits were practically already scratching at the door, like farm cats waiting for their daily dish of milk.

Timothy, sitting in the barn with the cattle, turned the page of his book. He was careful not to waste the dim afternoon light. Soon the milk cows would complain of their milking and so on—his round of chores would begin anew. But for these last few moments, he would read. The book was Wilkie Collins's *The Woman in White*. It was full of madness and swindling and people who were the spitting image of each other. Timothy had never seen anyone who was the spitting image of anyone else but the misses Arnel, although he had to wonder about one of the traveling salesmen that came past the farm every year or so, with all kinds of household goods. He went around to the farms, selling his wares to the lady of the house, every year the same man.

Except it hadn't been, that last time near a month ago. Not quite.

He had asked Mr. Stolte about the salesman, and Mr. Stolte had said, "Strong drink changes a man, and invites evil into his heart."

The salesman had given Mrs. Stolte a pamphlet on spiritualism, and sure enough, right after he left, she had written away for Mrs. Benoit to please come.

Foolishness, although he'd never say so. It was right after that, that baby Edward started to sicken and everything started to break anyhow.

~

Vella shivered. The babe against her breast had been so near to death as to have crossed the threshold and come back again, like a beetle wandering stupidly underneath a door.

If she didn't *do* something, he would die. That much was clear to her. She couldn't be with him every second of the day, and who knew if she'd be able to call him back every time he crossed? She knew that she wasn't supposed to talk about it, about pulling the threads of the dying back to the side of the living; both Mother and the priest had told her so. Only it was going to start looking suspicious, that she had brought him back from death's door time and time again.

She licked her lips. It was bad luck that Mrs. Schiffman-Marushia had caught her at it, but it couldn't be helped.

If she was going to save Edward, she was going to have to do *it*.

The one thing that both Mother and the priest had absolutely forbidden her to ever, ever do. It was evil, they told her. It was an invitation to an evil worse than all the devils combined.

But it might save Edward.

Still shivering, and still holding the babe against her shoulder, she poured some milk into a dish, and added some of the fine summer honey, stirring it with a pricked finger so that the fairies would smell who was trying to call them. She also added a drop of Edward's blood. She almost burst into tears when she pricked his finger with the needle, for he didn't cry at all, only stirred a little on her shoulder. And then she had to squeeze his finger so terribly in order to make it drip a single drop of blood. Sniffling, she set the dish outside the kitchen door, on the wood step that kept the worst of the mud from being tracked in when Timothy brought in wood for the iron oven.

Inside the kitchen, she began dancing with little Edward on her shoulder as she minded supper. She took his stiff, cold little hand and began to waltz with him. One two three, one two three. Softly, she began to hum.

It was almost sunset.

~

The monster rose from the steaming horseflesh from the barn, where it had finally, terribly, begun to eat. Distantly, it heard the sound of harnesses jingling. Someone was approaching the farmstead with a horse and wagon.

The night was cold and thick, and it had recently begun to snow, but the white flecks had not covered the red trails of blood so thoroughly as all that.

The monster had to make a decision: to stay, and face whatever challenges the arrival brought, or to flee. The fields around the house were wide and flat; to try to escape through them would be to risk the end of its existence at the end of a rifle. About a quarter-mile away from the house, the land rose up in a slow hillside, while a stream in the gully ran its course, cutting a deep, tree-lined swatch through the ground.

It might be able to hide there.

Or it could kill. Kill again, and turn the deaths into a lingering mystery.

But then again, those who approached might carry weapons. Knives, guns, clubs. Its enhanced flesh could absorb many blows of feet or fists, but there were limits.

Kill or run?

It climbed to the top of the barn, staying low against the darkness. On such a night as this, it had trouble picking out the shadow of the horse and wagon. But at least that meant that it, too, was protected by cover of darkness.

The wind shifted and caught something in the center of the farmyard.

A figure stood there.

It was taller than any human, with curling, almost swirling horns at its brow. It had claws on its hands and feet and wore a long black cloak that managed to fade into the snow. The figure was watching the monster...and holding the missing baby.

The baby that it had wanted...such tender flesh.

So that's where it had gone.

The monster bared its teeth.

PART 2—THE SÉANCE

And Tom bears logs into the hall,
   And milk comes frozen home in pail

— WILLIAM SHAKESPEARE, LOVE'S LABOUR'S
LOST

The sunset had flared red through the clouds, lingering all across the farm, turning the snow to the color of burnished gold, then to flame, then to blood, and finally to darkness.

The séance would begin in the dark.

The five women sat around the parlor table, having just retired from the dining room. The parlor was a fine room, kept apart from the concerns of everyday life, the mud and the feeding and the washing and everything else. It was a delicate room, deliberately so—just as there was a day set aside for concerns of the spirit, so too was there a room in the house set aside for concerns higher than mere survival. But it was also a chill room that rested along the northwest side of the house, devoid of sunlight and facing the ever-present wind, which had risen up since sunset. A bank of clouds was moving across the sky, roiling with trouble and making the open prairie feel smothered and close.

What books belonged to the farm were placed on a bookshelf along the north wall. One book was absent, and Stephanie's eye returned to the empty spot like it was a missing tooth. Marda had said that the new hired man, Timothy, was a reader.

The cards for whist had been put away and the mirrors covered with black cloths, as if there had been a death in the house. The little table was bare, exposed down to the well-tended wood. A cluster of beeswax candles rested directly on the wood in the center of the table, their flames stuttering in the wind that had begun to rattle the house and make the branches clatter.

They sat in a circle. In front of Madame Benoit was a dyed silk handkerchief of deep blue, with silver threads stitched into the patterns of moons and stars upon it. On it rested a silver dish that had been filled with—and this struck them all as somewhat odd—milk, honey, and a drop of blood from each of the four women, Madame Benoit herself abstaining.

"Don't you use that odd card deck that fortune-tellers use, or a crystal?" Stephanie asked.

"Or a dish with water with ink?" Leontine said.

"Or salt?" added Lavinia. She and Leontine nodded at each other from across the table.

"It's an old ritual," Madame Benoit said.

"It seems more like an old Irish superstition, for summoning fairies," Stephanie said.

Madame Benoit said, "I doubt the fae of Ireland will find us here, my dear. It's a world away. I've been, you know, although that was back when I was a wee one." She held her hand a suitably low distance from the floor. "And there were no fae there then, only the sad barrows of the ancient dead."

The four women made understanding noises in the backs of their throats. Superstitions abounded in the new territories; a wild mingling of new settlers from all across Europe and other parts of the world had brought a confusing panoply of beliefs. New legends were as quick to spring up as rumors.

"Or Homer," Marda said thoughtfully. "When Odysseus summons the hungry spirits from the underworld, that's what he uses, isn't it? Milk, honey, and blood."

Madame Benoit gave her a smile. "Good! I always enjoy it when someone knows the older legends. And that is one the oldest to have survived, although not one of the earliest to have been invented! Homer also adds wine, water, and barley, but I've never found them necessary."

She looked around the table. The four women watched her intently, studying her black hair, which had been pulled back into a bun; her jewelry, which was silver and abundant; her red lips, pale skin, and long, painted fingernails.

She said, "Take hands with each other 'round the table where you can. Mrs. Stolte, Mrs. Schiffman-Marushia, please leave your free hands palm-up on the table. When I have completed the rite, I will take your hands in mine and complete the circle."

The women shifted, stretching forth their hands.

On days when it was more difficult to summon the spirits, Madame Benoit would have used clackers and other tricks strapped to her knees and ankles, so that the celebrants would have "proof" that she hadn't done anything while her hands were being held. But she had removed such things earlier that afternoon. The air was practically crackling on its own.

When their faces were turned toward her once again, Madame Benoit said, "We shall now begin."

She lifted her hands above the bowl of milk and began murmuring syllables that had been last spoken so long ago that she hardly remembered what the meaning of them was supposed to be. A song for children, a counting song involving oxen and sheaves of wheat? She couldn't remember. Seven thousand years tends to erode the memory.

The important thing was to release the hold she had upon her

247

mind *slowly*. It was an ancient trick that would have worked for anyone, although she had practiced it more than most. Every living thing puts certain limitations upon itself. Those limitations are necessary, in a way—the hunted need to be aware of the hunters; the hunters need to be aware of the prey, both so that they can find their next meal and so they know the prey haven't turned against them en masse. And always there are acts of nature and other dangers. One's mind can never truly relax, if one intends to survive.

But Madame Benoit was reasonably safe in the parlor; she had taken all the steps necessary to ensure it.

The mirrors were covered, and the servants had been instructed not to interrupt them. The doors throughout the house were all closed. The husband was away and the farmhand told to stay out, and the women had all removed their jewelry, so as not to raise any conflicting "vibrations" from the spirit world. The books were all put away on their shelves. The spirit world was agitated, but the other dimensions all seemed to be at rest.

The five of them would not be disturbed.

Madame Benoit began the work of dismantling the limitations around her mind as she repeated the ancient words again and again, letting her hands make passes over the heavy silver bowl filled with milk. The magic was in putting to sleep the parts of her mind focused on purely animal dangers, nothing more.

She felt her voice deepen, her eyes soften deeper into her skull, her breath slow. That cursed knot of a headache that always seemed to linger around the base of her skull slowly began to loosen. It felt like a silken cord that bound around her skull so tightly that it had worn a channel into the bone underneath. It had to be picked apart patiently with the words she was speaking. To attack it head on, as it were, would be to snarl the knots even further.

Soon she felt wonderful, all the way from the crown of her head to the bottoms of her feet. She wanted to take her narrow, buttoned boots off and stretch her toes out, but the women would have wondered at it. With the door closed, even though a fire burned low and dim in the fireplace on the south wall, the room had become decidedly chill.

The surface of the milk had begun to darken already. She took a deep breath, felt her lungs filling with the breath of the spirits around them, and exhaled a swirling, glowing green mist onto the surface.

~

S tephanie said, "Good God."

The mist that had begun to come out of the medium's body had formed into a shape above the silver dish. Stephanie had heard of such occurrences, called *ectoplasm*, but had never seen anything like it herself—she had not even known anyone who had.

If it was a trick, it was a most convincing one. Every mirror in the room had been covered, and the only light in the room were from the candles—which flickered with a golden, rather than greenish, glow. The mist glowed steadily as well, not jumping about with the candle flames as the wind grasped at them through the walls.

A trick of smoke and mirrors? She thought not.

The mist formed up into a swirling column above the dish, as though the silver edges served as some sort of boundary.

Stephanie was tempted to raise a hand and touch the mist, but was also hesitant. If this *was* a trick and the medium could only perform it once, then she did not like to spoil the illusion, for Marda's sake. Stephanie didn't believe the séance for a moment—but she also could not make herself to stand up and push away from the table, either. The least questioning now might lead to a broken friendship, when they might easily laugh over it later.

After Edward was gone, and the mourning for him was done.

Stephanie shook her head. She must not think such things.

Madame Benoit's hands fell onto the table. Marda reached out with her spare hand and clasped the medium's; Stephanie, after a moment's hesitation, did the same.

The woman's hand was like ice. No, not ice. Like a potato just brought up from the cellar and peeled. Waxy, stiff, almost inhuman.

The poor woman was freezing! Stephanie felt a moment of sympathy welling up for Madame Benoit, who had been so patient with them all afternoon, listening to them play bridge and having nothing to amuse herself with, not even a walk!

But they had all been worried about Edward, and playing cards had been the best way to pass the time.

Besides, the best place for the babe was around Vella King. The Kings had long been known for their, well, not simply their *good* luck, but their preternatural luck. They had left their home just before the fire in Chicago in 1871 to come here. And then, in 1873, just before little Vella was born, they had arrived in town with little more than the clothes they were wearing.

When asked what had happened, they apologized and said that it hadn't happened yet. The next night, the natives had burned down the farm and killed the livestock.

There were little things, too. If anyone in the county were a bona fide medium, it was one of the King girls. Not that they'd ever admit to it. The Arnel sisters sometimes put on a show as if they had mediumistic powers, but no one believed a word of it; it was all just an act to get attention. Two spinster sisters of modest fortune sometimes had need to rely upon such tricks, however, and Stephanie forgave them for it out of hand.

The glowing green shape was slimming around the top, becoming more sharply delineated, until it had formed into the shape of a woman, a foot high or thereabouts, in an old-fashioned dress. Her hair was pulled back severely into a bun, although little curls of it were obstinately coming loose. She had a broad smile, a heavy brow, and two mother-of-pearl earrings clipped to her ears, the kind where the old buttonholes could still be seen. She wore a man's pocket-watch over her left breast, like a brooch.

Suddenly Stephanie could hear the clock ticking from the other room.

Or was it the watch?

~

L avinia smelled it immediately: a distinctly soapy, iron-laden smell, sour and sharp. She wrinkled her nose and squeezed Leontine's hand. Leontine squeezed back, and Lavinia knew that she smelled it, too.

The smell of the spirit world. It could not be smelled by those who were not born to it.

Talents had need of development, but it was only blood that could that could open the veil.

The two of them watched Madame Benoit like a pair of Siamese cats at listen for their prey. Was it she? Was it she who had brought the evil presence to the farm? Or was she ignorant of it, a mere pawn in a game?

The evil had arrived before Madame Benoit. And yet it seemed to center around her, lingering.

Spying.

Waiting...

M arda Stolte's heart leapt in her breast. The figure that had formed out of the green mist before her was unquestionably of the form and manner of her mother.

A question formed on her lips.

"Mama," she said. "Is that you?"

The figure turned in her direction. Her hands twitched where they rested on her skirt, as though the figure were about to raise its hands—then remembered the boundaries of its freedom above the silver dish. She clasped them together around her waist.

"Marda," the figure said. "Is everything well about the farm?"

It was a faint, half-whispered voice, as if her mother had had laryngitis. It didn't sound like her mother, but it didn't sound not-like her mother, either.

"It's the babies, Mama," Marda said. "I've lost two of them in a row, before their second birthday. And now little Edward is sickening like the girls. And he's a boy. And Martin..." She felt her heart swelling up, and knew that if she did not take a breath, she would begin to wail.

"Hm," her mother said in a practical tone. "You've been giving them the tonic that I always have made up for them?"

The tonic was a mixture of spring water, sugar, several herbs, and some seaweed that had to be shipped in from the East once a year. On the farm, they gave it to anything that was sick, from cattle to babies to puppies, and it seemed to do just fine. It was only the babies that failed them.

"I have."

"And you've called in a doctor? And had yourself checked as well?"

"Yes," Marda said. "He's, I suppose you might say he's our last hope, and I thought..."

"You hoped that I would have some sort of say in the matter from the other side of the veil," her mother said briskly. "I'm afraid that is nonsense, my dear."

"Not that," Marda said quickly. "Only if you knew of some curse, or some spirit, that was harming the babies."

"There's a thought," her mother said. "Stay right there, I'll be back in a moment."

And the green figure sank down over the silver bowl. Underneath, the white milk had turned black as ink.

V ella King stood in the doorway, looking over the séance. It wasn't nothing she hadn't seen a hundred times before, usually with her older brother at the head of the table, but she didn't like that they weren't using clean water with ink in it for the scrying. She didn't like the way the milk turned dark—that was always a bad sign, her father said, when something changed into something it wasn't. They'd had milk turn dark a few times in the past, and it had always made Papa and her brothers order them all out of the house and on the run. Another thing not to talk about. When she had read the Bible for Sunday school the first time, she had stopped to ask whether the Lord Jesus would be murdered at the wedding by demons. "Whatever for, child?" the teacher had asked. "Don't you know your Bible stories?" She admitted that her parents tried to teach them to her, but that she kept getting them mixed up sometimes. She only remembered that the Lord Jesus had been killed, and that he had been attacked by demons that were possessing pigs. She was told that those were two other stories entirely, and that changing the water into wine was a blessing upon the wedding, not a sign of demons.

Vella King had nodded seriously and agreed that must be the case, then talked to her father about it later. He'd said, "You see a good many things that other people don't, little Vella," and ruffled her hair. And then her other brother had laid down the rules afterward for what not to speak of, ever: Papa liked to think the best of people, but her older brother Tom was far more practical.

She turned back to the crib, then checked Edward again, safely asleep.

She had been using the tonic on the babe, but only because she knew it to be harmless. He *would* wrinkle his nose up every time she gave it to him, too, from the pungency of the herbs, and it made her laugh.

"Sweet babe," she whispered, and adjusted his blanket. Then she opened the back door of the kitchen a crack and checked the dish outside the door.

It was freezing over, long, delicate feathers of ice in the milk, and a few snowflakes clung to the edges of the bowl, collapsing into slush.

The side of the bowl toward the parlor had turned gray.

She squatted down by the bowl and picked up a piece of dead grass from beside the door, to stir the milk a little.

The milk swirled and she knocked off the fragile feathers of ice, but the gray haze did not move.

She stood up again and looked out over the farmyard. From a gap between the buildings, she could see to the southwest.

"Please come," she whispered. "Please come and take the babe away from this."

After a moment she closed the door, but she hadn't finished yet. "Please hurry."

~

On top of the barn, the monster twitched as it spotted her.

The two of them stared at each other, and the Lady realized with disgust that she recognized it. A test subject. One of her own, that had been lost in this dimension so long ago, one of her first attempts to bridge the genetic gaps between humanity and her own kind.

In a way, the babe's older sibling.

Millennia had passed since then. Long enough for the thing to have moved from its original escape across the globe. It was only one planet, after all, and the humans hadn't solved the riddle of getting off it yet. Unless the test subject died—and why should it?—she would have run into it sooner or later. It was only logical. And yet she thought she had neutralized it, removing the more violent tendencies of its spirit so that it would not harm or be harmed by those around it. Obviously something about the process had failed.

She bared her teeth.

The test subject shifted its weight and began to turn toward her, its nails clicking on the shingles atop the barn. Then the Lady heard it—the jingle of a horse's harness. One of the men was returning to the farm.

In a moment, he would be killed by the test subject.

The Lady made up her mind swiftly, and sprang away across the farmyard toward the road.

The man heard a sound like the flapping of wings. Then he was dragged off the wagon and into the fields. Backward he flew, heels dragging across the snow. Then he was in the shadow of the trees next to the stream.

"Silence," a voice hissed. "The baby must be quieted."

He was wrapped in a hot black cloak that immediately made him sweat. It sealed around him, leaving only his eyes open to the white storm picking up outside, the flying snowflakes that erased his vision.

In front of him was a demon, eight feet tall if it was an inch, with horns, claws, and a lizard-like tail. And yet still a woman.

"Keep him safe."

She sprang away across the fields. In the middle of one enormous bound, she struck something dark, hairy, awful.

Worse than a demon.

Under the cloak Edward, snuffled and whimpered. On his skin was something sticky...something that smelled like blood.

"Shh," the man said. "It's all right. Shhhh."

PART 3—AFTER THE SÉANCE

When blood is nipp'd and ways be foul,
Then nightly sings the staring owl

— WILLIAM SHAKESPEARE, LOVE'S LABOUR'S
LOST

Stephanie waited for the green mist to reform itself into the shape of Elaine Wolbert, who had been Marda's mother. Stephanie tried to keep her mind clear on the matter, but the fact was that she *believed* the image was Elaine Wolbert's very spirit, come back from the dead to give her daughter one last piece of advice.

The mist roiled over the silver bowl; the milk underneath it had gone quite dark. Madame Benoit's hand had finally begun to warm a little underneath Stephanie's hand. Stephanie's hand was still the more solid and less potato-like of the two, however.

Suddenly Madame Benoit removed her hands from Stephanie's and Marda's, and began to pass them over the bowl again.

The green mist seemed to be fighting with her, struggling. To do what? It was still trapped above the bowl; it could not escape.

As long as the dark milk remains in the bowl, Stephanie caught herself thinking. And then, even worse, she saw her hand twitch toward the bowl, as if she were tempted beyond all reason to tip it over.

End this, she caught herself thinking. *You have to end this before it's too late.*

Caught between the twin traps of not wanting to annoy Marda and the idea that all of this was some kind of trick, she struggled, and her hand twitched again, almost as though it were being controlled from beyond herself.

From across the table, Marda glanced upward and caught Stephanie's eyes. She looked startled.

They both glanced toward the Arnel sisters.

Both of them had thrown their heads back, their eyes rolled back until only the whites were showing. Lavinia, who clung to Stephanie's right hand, clutched her fiercely, as if expecting Stephanie to pull her out of the depths and keep her from drowning. The tips of her fingernails dug into Stephanie's skin.

"The Queen is coming," she moaned.

"The Queen of the Fairies," Leontine added.

"But she will be too late to save us," Lavinia continued. "Because the darkness was already here, waiting for this!"

"The darkness!"

It was theatrical and attention-grabbing, same as always. The two of them must have been planning this from the start. Stephanie let a sigh escape from her nose. It felt as though everything had been suddenly spoiled.

But it hadn't.

The green mist in the bowl was starting to move again. Madame Benoit's hands flickered over it in arcane gestures, and her murmured words grew faster and louder, her voice higher pitched.

"The spirits are pushing," she said. "I am sorry. They're pushing."

"Are they trying to break through to reach us?" Marda asked eagerly. "My mother is trying to come through so she can help."

The figure in the dish had formed once again into the shape of a woman—the same dress, the same hair pulled back in an unruly bun, the same stolid expression, the same watch upon her breast.

But as the eidolon turned from side to side, Stephanie could see that it was *not* Elaine Wolbert, but something else.

Under its skin—the skin of green mist, that was, which was so finely detailed that it was easy to see what was occurring—were moving shapes of some sort, thrashing about quite violently, like snakes with their heads cut off. The eidolon's mouth opened and it began to scream.

"No!" Madame Benoit cried. She stood up, pushing the chair away from her so suddenly that it tipped over with a crash. "You must not! You must *not!*"

Stephanie leaned forward and grabbed the edge of the silver dish. Thinking that she didn't want to spill cold milk all over Marda's dress and have her catch cold, she tipped the dish toward the center of the table, where the lit candles flickered in the darkness.

They hissed and went out.

For a moment, the green mist lingered. The figure of Elaine Wolbert twisted in agony, clawing at her skin. Tears had opened up in the bodice of her dress, and something hairy and terrible crawled out of it, leaving an empty vessel behind—the eidolon of Marda's mother went limp, collapsing onto the table like a piece of discarded clothing.

"Mother!" Marda cried.

The creature that had crawled out of the misty green eidolon was slender and small, almost diminutive, but twisted, and of such a foul nature that Stephanie shuddered to look at it.

It was free of the dish now.

Madame Benoit had backed away from the table with her arms held in front of her. "*It* has come through," she said in a dead voice. "You must all go, and go now."

The only light came from the glowing green mist, the creature on the table. It was, Stephanie realized, beginning to melt.

"If we can distract it long enough?" she asked, picking up something from the floor—a footstool, she realized, once she had it in hand.

"It is too dangerous. Go now." Madame Benoit's voice shook. "Go!" she both ordered and begged.

Stephanie grabbed Lavinia and shoved her toward the door, then limped around the table to collect both Marda and Leontine. Everyone else seemed to be frozen in place, unable to make the slightest movement than to gape in horror. Her leg felt shaky and weak.

The green mist-monster turned toward Madame Benoit, grinning furiously.

Madame Benoit clapped both hands over her face. Stephanie shoved the other two toward the door, where the now-alert Lavinia helped catch at their clothes and pull them through. Then Stephanie grabbed her cane from its place along the table.

Stephanie turned to Madame Benoit. "Hurry!"

"Go!" The woman's voice had gone rough and raspy, and a shadow seemed to be creeping up all over her skin, as if the black milk had slithered up her legs and were coving her skin.

The mist-creature on the table barked, its jaws snapping loudly in the stillness of the room.

Madame Benoit's teeth clicked shut at the same moment.

Stephanie backed out of the room, tripping over her cane, stumbling and hanging onto the door, suddenly realizing that it was not darkness, but fur, that had crept over Madame Benoit's skin—and that the woman was grinning in the most unholy fashion, teeth bulging out of jaws that tore and stretched.

The mist-monster leapt from the table, clung to Madame Benoit's face, then began forcing its way down her throat.

∾

Vella King shouted, "This way, Miss!"

Lavinia pulled the other two women toward the kitchen. "We must find a way to block the door," she announced. "Does it lock?"

"It does."

"Then lock it."

"What about Miss Schiffman-Marushia and Madame Benoit?"

"Madame Benoit is a monster, or has called up a monster, or has otherwise allowed it to come through," Lavinia said. Now it seemed clear, so terribly clear. They had all seen it. The presence that had been lingering on the farm had been present on the other side of the veil, waiting for someone to thin the way through it so that it could emerge on this side. It had been *waiting* for the séance. "And Miss Schiffman-Marushia is almost certainly dead, or will be in a moment. We must lock the door now, before the monster comes."

When Vella King didn't make the least movement, Lavinia added, "The babe, girl, think! We spinsters and widows would gladly throw ourselves in the way of such a thing, if it meant that the babe might survive."

Vella King dashed forward with a key in her hand and locked the door, leaving the key in the lock so that it couldn't be opened from the other side, an irrelevant trick given that the monster most likely wouldn't bother with one.

Vella ran back to the bassinette and picked up the babe, cradling him in his arms.

"Swaddle him for the cold," Lavinia instructed. "We must flee."

"But it's five miles to Miss Schiffman-Marushia's farm, and the horses aren't ready."

"We must flee, or hide. Or we will be slaughtered."

Lavinia did not question her knowledge of this. A door slammed.

"The barn," Vella said. "We can go out to the barn. Tim's out there with the horses."

"Does he have a gun?"

"There's the rifle in the tack room, miss."

Marda seemed to have sunk into a stupor. She had gone useless. Leontine bent over, leaning her hands against her skirt, and coughed as though she were trying to push something out of her chest. Finally she straightened and explained. "I breathed some of it, Lavinia."

The wind must have pushed the mist in the direction of her sister and Marda Stolte. Lavinia said, "You sense what I do."

"That it will try to murder us all? Yes."

Lavinia nodded. That had been her thought as well. Out in the hallway came a terrific crash, which made Marda shudder. "My china," she moaned. The sisters hushed her. It was for the best.

"Can we hide?"

"It may smell us."

"The barn," they both said.

They turned toward the door, then hesitated.

Lavinia said, "I'll do it."

Leontine tried to protest, but it was useless. She was still wheezing and gasping. "What if I can't stay quiet?" she said finally.

"Then scream and run," Lavinia said ruthlessly. "Draw it after you."

"For the babe," Leontine agreed.

They held each other for a moment. It was not quite a farewell.

Outside the door, splintering wood and a gasp.

Lavinia picked up a wool rug from the floor by the outer door. It was filthy and scattered dust and clods of dirt from its itchy, packed fibers as she lifted it.

She turned toward the babe. Already Leontine had taken the babe from Vella and unwound its swaddling blankets. She thrust the blankets at Lavinia, taking the horrible rug at the same time. Lavinia quickly wrapped a log from the fire up with the blankets. The babe went into the dirty, itching, *stinking* rug.

The two sisters looked at each other. Then, with Vella once again holding the babe, they opened the back door.

S tephanie scrabbled with the door to the parlor. It had a lock, but she had no key and no way to lock it. Behind her, she heard the door of the kitchen slam shut and a brief, hissed argument.

Against the wall next to her was the large mahogany china cabinet, filled with Marda's favorite china pattern, inherited not just from her mother but from her great-grandmother. The inside of the parlor was filled with growling, tearing noises.

Still, she hesitated.

The key to the kitchen door turned in its lock. Stephanie heard it and thought, *At least they're behaving sensibly, even if they are leaving me out here to die.* She considered, as if she had all the time in the world to do so, screaming and begging to be let inside, where it was safe.

But it was impossible. If what was inside the parlor was a monster, then it was *not* safe, would *not* be safe even if she huddled in the kitchen with the others, or descended into the cellar. If it was all a hoax and Madame Benoit were *not* being possessed by some foul spirit, all the better, and they could laugh upon it tomorrow.

She tugged on the doors of the china cabinet. They were locked shut. Marda was a great one for locking things up.

Stephanie leaned the cane against the far wall, turned back to the cabinet, and jumped. The top of the cabinet wasn't far out of her reach, but it was enough that she *must* jump, and she must not fall.

Her fingers grasped the top of the cabinet and caught the edge of the decorative trim.

Her weight carried the heavy cabinet toward her, and she kicked backward out of the way as the cabinet fell, the precious china smashing into countless shards. She fell to the floor, her leg stinging with pain and her ears ringing. She felt dizzy. But the door was now blocked. It fortunately opened outward into the hallway. And the heavy cabinet was in front of it.

Stephanie crawled back to the cabinet and wedged herself into the space behind it. She tucked her skirts around her and shoved. The cabinet slid along the wood floor until it was against the wall, bracing the door closed even more tightly.

Now all she had to do was keep the monster on the other side of the door. Until...dawn. Or at least until Marda's husband returned home, or Timothy became too cold to stay outside and slunk back into the house...

The wood of the door over the cabinet splintered, and a claw reached through.

Stephanie gasped, then pushed harder. The monster had begun to shove against the cabinet, and it was stronger than she was.

The cane.

She hadn't been planning to flee, at any rate—coldly speaking, she knew she wouldn't make it far.

She took the cane, shoved it between the cabinet and the wall, and leaned on it.

The cabinet slopped scraping along the floor back toward her. She could feel the tension in the wood of the cane as the monster's weight strained against the door.

Then it stopped, and that was almost worse.

The air in the house changed for a moment. Colder. Then she heard the soft sound of the kitchen door closing.

They were going to run and hide, thank God.

The wood of the door began to splinter again. The monster had punched through the wood with a long, delicate-looking claw. It pulled on a piece of splintered door wood and pulled it free, the wood groaning loudly.

Stephanie leaned against the cabinet. She would hold it as long as she could. On the floor around her were pieces of smashed china and shattered glass. She picked a piece of glass off the floor and used it to cut off part of her skirt, which she wrapped around the glass to make a frail-looking dagger.

She touched the end of it to one finger. Fragile, yes.

But sharp.

Stephanie held the glass knife in one hand and her cane in the other. There was nothing she could do to trap the monster in the parlor. It was climbing out of the hole in the upper part of the door now.

It glanced at her, then bared its teeth and turned away, climbing over the china cabinet toward the hallway.

As if it intended to let her live, as long as she let it pass.

Stephanie snorted. An animal might try to flee and let bygones be bygones, but not this creature. It had started out as human enough; if it ever wished to return to humanity, it would have to kill each and every last one of them.

If it had meant only to escape, it would have smashed its way out one of the drape-covered windows. Far easier than ripping up an oak door.

Stephanie side-stepped to the end of the china cabinet with the monster looking over her head, getting ready to jump.

"Stay back," she said.

The pretense of being ignored ended and the monster's eyes snapped onto her. It growled.

"Stay back or it's blood," Stephanie said. It *would* be blood, one way or another.

The monster leapt at her.

The cane was bracing her from being knocked backward and the knife was pointed in front of her throat. But the monster arced over-head, thumping down on the hall floor.

They both turned toward each other. Stephanie braced herself again.

She had faced down coyotes, badgers, skunks, and rabid dogs. She had outlived her husband and her unborn baby.

She would not falter.

The monster leapt at her again, and Stephanie planted the shard of glass in its chest, gripping the cloth-bound glass as tightly as possible but still feeling the hilt slide and the glass slice into her hand.

The cane skidded and she went down. The monster's jaws were at her face. She ignored the pain and shoved the glass blade deeper, bucking underneath the monster as she felt the butt end of the glass dig into her stays.

~

L avinia ran into the snow, carrying the blanket wrapped around the log, clutching it to her chest. She had deliberately cut herself with her nail-scissors and was dripping blood as she ran. Some of it dripped onto her dress; the rest found its way onto the snow.

Her lungs burned but she forced herself to breathe silently. She was listening for something.

Behind her in the house, all was silent. Leontine and Vella and Marda and the baby had run toward the barn. *Let them be safe. Let them somehow be safe.* She couldn't imagine how that might happen. That she and Leontine were making more of this than there was, she could not imagine. They had both felt the evil awakening at the house.

Footsteps crunched through a thin layer of ice on top of the snow. Her own footsteps, echoing back at her.

Then she passed the far edge of the outbuildings, and the sound became muffled, silent.

Behind her, the door of the house slammed open.

She looked over her shoulder, screamed, and fell into the snow, then clambered up again, picking up the log and clutching it to her chest again.

It was like dangling a goose feather on a string in front of a farm cat.

The monster howled at her, then began its pursuit.

Lavinia ran faster. If she could make it to the bluff and slide down, then hide among the trees by the stream...

...then she could delay the monster a little longer.

She cursed her spindly legs for their weakness. The bluff was coming closer.

So was the sound of feet running through snow.

Panting.

She screamed as the claws caught her from behind, throwing the bundle forward as she fell. It slid down the bluff, miraculously staying wrapped as it came to rest at the bottom of the steep embankment.

A few moments later, the monster paced the top of the bluff, sniffing the air. It had wet blood dripping from its jaws as well as a nasty cut on its chest. In the dark it was impossible to tell, even for its eyes, whether the bundle was moving.

It picked its way down the bluff carefully, taking deep breaths of the air and trying not to stumble. Once it reached the bottom, it nosed the bundle of blankets until the log rolled out, shedding bark onto the snow.

Then it barked once, as if laughing.

~

The smell of blood, milk, and honey reached the Lady's nostrils. She wrinkled her snout. It was a grotesque sort of signal, but it was unique, and humans only mixed up such a disgusting, spoiled mixture when they wished to call to her. It was some sort of ritual from the islands across the ocean, for summoning the spirits of the dead. The ritual had somehow become associated with her people.

The spirits of the dead lingered thick that winter night, moving in the direction of the scent. A death was drawing them like swarming insects. She followed them.

Sometimes the humans asked her people for a favor. Sometimes they just wanted them to take a baby off their hands, one of the surplus ones they knew they couldn't feed, or that was sick with illnesses that their primitive medicine could not treat.

The dead rushed along the snow, a shadowy tide of men, cattle, coyotes, rodents, and birds. If she were the kind of scientist who worked with the energies of the dead, it would have been a spectacular testing day. But she was not; she worked only with the living.

She dropped to her forelimbs and began to trot. The behavior of the dead had begun to bother her. This was no mere death of a pig or a horse or a cow on which they hoped to feed, but a full-scale slaughter.

She hoped she would not be too late.

~

M arda huddled in the space behind the hay bales in the loft, with Vella and the babe behind her. In front of her, by the ladder, was Leontine, both hands clapped over her mouth to stifle the sound of her coughing.

The three of them listened.

The wind had brought them the slam of the kitchen door, which now banged back and forth in the breeze. Then—too close—the sound of Lavinia's screaming.

It had been silent for a time, the kind of silence that made them all twitch every time the wood of the barn groaned.

Timothy stood guard below them with the rifle. He had not believed them at first, but had done what Marda had ordered him to do. When the kitchen door banged open, he had taken a quick breath, then held it until the crunch of the monster's footsteps had passed.

In the dark, what could he have seen? A dark shape moving too smoothly and quickly?

It all seemed like a dream. Marda's heart still called out for her mother, even just the glowing, misty image of her floating above Madame Benoit's silver bowl. *Mother, mother...help me!*

She wished to have the world undone, picked apart thread by thread, and rewoven again. She would have done it all differently.

The footsteps began to crunch across the snow. The horses snorted and stamped, pushing against their stall doors. *Let them out, let them out!* she wanted to shriek at Timothy. They might serve as a distraction. Oh, why hadn't they tried to saddle up Stephanie's two horses and ride away? Even bareback, they would have a better chance than this. But it was her own fault. She had ordered the other women into the loft and told them to be silent.

Suddenly the door of the loft burst inward.

The monster skidded across the hay bales, scrabbling for purchase, then fell off the loft and onto the barn floor.

The horses screamed and began to kick their stalls. Even the placid milk-cows bellowed.

Timothy fired the shotgun. Once, twice.

Then screamed.

Marda and Leontine looked at each other. The fear was ready to burst out of Marda's throat.

In the dark below them, the horses were still screaming. They were at the back of the barn. Directly underneath them were the stalls for the milk cows. The whole barn was shaking from the way they shoved against the boards and support posts. One of the cows moaned, then went silent. Not that the barn was quiet. It was filled with a hideous tearing sound.

Behind them, the baby suddenly began to cry.

The sound muffled as Vella put her hand over the baby's face, but he would not *stop.*

The monster hissed. Then the loft began to shake again, as the monster found the ladder and began to climb up it.

Edward was going to die *anyway.*

Marda waited until the monster's claws rustled upon the hay. Then she climbed over the hay bales to the side of the loft and lowered herself onto one of the stalls below. In the dark, she walked along the tops of the stall, praying that the other milk cow wouldn't butt the door while she was trying to cross it.

She had done this a thousand times, to save the hems of her dresses. The smell of blood and other substances made her want to retch.

Behind her, Leontine screamed. "Get away from them, you monster!"

Then screamed again.

$\sim$

O ne moment Marda was there, the next she was gone. Fallen? Or killed before she could make a sound?

Vella struggled to keep Edward in her arms. He was afraid, and he wanted *down*. It was like holding onto a snake. But she had held babies before, and she had brothers. She had learned how to wrestle snakes.

Keeping him quiet at the same time, however, was beyond her.

Edward wailed as Leontine screamed in agony, right in front of her. Vella was trapped in the corner of the loft. The monster and Leontine were right in front of her. Around her was nothing but a wall of hay bales.

She laid Edward on top of the stack, pinned him with one hand, and climbed up after him, shoving her pointed boots in the cracks between the solid, square bales. Dust coated her throat.

Dragging Edward with her by his clothing, she crawled along the tops of the bales. They were packed in tight, as close to the eaves as possible. But the steep eaves always left a crack to crawl through. She felt hollows in the hay where the mice had nested. They were long gone now.

Marda shouted from the other end of the barn. Not in fear.

"Hiyaaa, hiyaaa!"

The slap of leather against flesh. Horse hooves.

The barn door, under the loft, was closed. Was it latched?

Vella crawled faster, to the edge of the hay. She held Edward tighter now. If he got away from her, he'd fall twenty feet or more to the barn floor. Break his neck.

The horse whinnied in terror. Then the crack of wood splintering. A rush of chill air swarmed through the barn.

"Marda! The babe! You'll have to catch him!"

He was screaming now.

More horse hooves. And the sound of something scrambling across the hay behind her.

She leaned over the hay bales, then swung Edward out over the empty space. She could see a little below her, a large shadow moving.

Then something rushed past her, dropped to the floor, and caught the horse.

It was terrible. She pulled Edward back into her arms and curled up on the bales, shivering. He had gone silent.

His mother had not.

Vella had to listen and wait even longer, as the monster killed the other horse, then the other milk cow. Then it left the barn to noisily chase the chickens around the yard.

Vella sobbed. It wasn't hungry. It hadn't *missed* her. It knew exactly where she was.

It was saving her and the baby for last.

After a moment, she wiped her eyes, grabbed Edward, and started to climb out of the loft.

The was only one hope left.

The Queen of the Fae.

~

The Lady reached the farm just as the girl's voice, a hoarse whisper, began to die. She lay in the center of the farmyard, after dragging herself forward on her elbows and leaving a swath of blood behind her.

The girl looked up at her. "Lady, Lady," she begged. "Take him, save him, the baby, oh Lady, Queen of the Fairies, Queen of the Fair Folk, the Good Folk..."

She sank forward in the bloody snow.

The Lady looked around her. No babe was to be seen or heard, nor any sign of the monster who had performed the slaughter. A wolf? A madman? She could investigate later, if the babe for whom she had been summoned was not soon found.

She looked through the house, then worked her way around the farmyard, checking each shed and outbuilding as she went. The barn was a slaughterhouse.

Finally, she reached the waste disposal shed, a small wooden hut with a thin door shaking in the wind.

Inside, wrapped in a torn piece of cloth and hidden by the stench and the sound of the storm, was the babe.

She picked him up. One fat human fist reached for her face, touching part of her jaw. His eyes widened with delight.

EPILOGUE

Love is a familiar; Love is a devil:

there is no evil angel but Love.

— WILLIAM SHAKESPEARE, LOVE'S LABOUR'S
LOST

T he man heard a roar of challenge that echoed across the prairie.
Then an answering shout, as the two figures circled each other in
the snowy field.

He huddled deeper inside the cloak with little Edward, covering his face
and lying as flat on the ground as possible. The cloak almost seemed to
move around the two of them like a living thing, pressing them downward
into the ruts of the field.

The fight continued, until finally it ended with a scream and a splintering sound.

Soon footsteps crunched on the snow, approaching him.

Were the footsteps death?

Or life?

The cloak fell away from his back and shoulders. In front of him was what he could only think of as a fairy queen, not some two-foot high imp, but a warrior. She stood on goat's legs with a lizard-like tail behind her. Her hands ended in claws, and on her brow were strange, delicate-looking white horns, now covered in blood. Her face was a goat-like snout.

She stretched her hand, and the cloak slithered up it, wrapping itself around her. The hood covered her face for a moment, then fell back.

Now she looked human, and beautiful, like a woman that could be made to laugh, and to love.

"Give the child to me," she said, holding her arm out again.

For a moment the man thought of protesting. It was his child, after all.

But the babe had already begun to change. On its heads were the nubs of horns, and the pupils of its eyes had turned to goat-like slits.

A demon child.

No, a fairy child, with a new mother now. The man held his child tight, whispered a brief, old blessing, then let him go—to cross over into the Summerlands, or wherever it was that the fairies lived, without fear or pain, without age or time, forever.

"Please keep him safe," the man said.

The Lady did not answer.

He said, "What about me?"

"Your life is your own," she said. Like a curse.

She tossed a book in the snow in front of him, a few flecks of blood on the cover. The Woman in White.

"The test subject tried to steal this," she said. "But it belongs to you."

Then she turned and walked back across the snow, returning to the lands from whence she came.

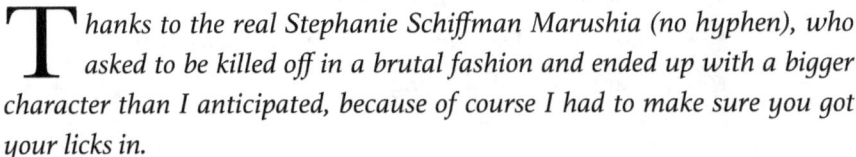

Thanks to the real Stephanie Schiffman Marushia (no hyphen), who asked to be killed off in a brutal fashion and ended up with a bigger character than I anticipated, because of course I had to make sure you got your licks in.

ABOUT THE AUTHOR

DeAnna Knippling is always tempted to lie on her bios. Her favorite musician is Tom Waits, and her favorite author is Lewis Carroll. Her favorite monster is zombies. Her life goal is to remake her house in the image of the House on the Rock, or at least Ripley's Believe It Or Not. You should buy her books. She promises that she'll use the money wisely on bookshelves and secret doors. She lives in Colorado and is the author of the A Fairy's Tale horror series which starts with *By Dawn's Bloody Light*, and other books like *The Clockwork Alice, A Murder of Crows: Seventeen Tales of Monsters & the Macabre*, and more.

As always, this story is dedicated to Lee and Ray,
without whose love none of this would be possible.

Find out more about DeAnna at:
wonderlandpress.com

facebook.com/deanna.knippling

twitter.com/dknippling

goodreads.com/goodreadscomdeannaknippling

bookbub.com/authors/deanna-knippling

amazon.com/DeAnna-Knippling/e/B0049HF320

pinterest.com/dknippling

PASSAGE

ANTHEA SHARP

The girl sat upon a stone, dangling one leg into the water. Fish nibbled at her toes, heedless of the runes marking the rock. Her gossamer-spun dress reflected the sunset hues suspended between sky and wave.

The cool touch of the waves soothed her, though her mind was full of confusion. One moment her world had been full of splash and glimmer and then, mid-leap, something had changed. She had changed.

She'd had a name, once. It slipped, elusive as a minnow, into the shadowed corners of her mind, but she was determined to lure it out.

Tangled memory made her frown as she stared down into the waters. She was certain she had not always had legs. The lazy movements of the fish were as familiar to her—more familiar, in fact—than the sight of her own two hands. She held them up and stared at the long, unwebbed fingers. Who *was* she? What was she, and how had she come here?

A soft wind brushed strands of her dark hair across her face, and with the touch came remembrance.

Brea.

She was Brea Cairgead, fisherman's daughter. And daughter of a sea-wild woman who carried magic in her blood. Magic she'd given to her daughter, though it had come nearly too late.

Memory returned in a hot, painful rush, and Brea bent, arms wrapped across her stomach.

Her father was dead, her village had banished her, and she had barely managed to escape the brigands who had robbed her, and wished to do worse. The ache of remembrance washed over her in a heavy wave, but in its wake came gentler memories: the healing silver current, the sibilant songs of the sea, the cool touch of water cradling her.

Brea drew in a deep breath and straightened. Surely her life had held sorrow, but also peace. Now, though, what did the future hold? It was a very human thought, one that her finned self would never consider.

"Ah, she has awoken," a merry voice said. "Welcome to the Realm, sometime-girl."

Startled, Brea looked up to see a small fellow dressed in tatters and leaves sitting cross-legged upon the nearby bank. She opened her mouth, but the taste of words was foreign on her tongue, and the air rushed in, making her cough.

"Steady now," the figure said. "You're new enough into this form that you must go slowly. Allow me to introduce myself. I am the sprite called Puck."

He rose, then kept rising until he floated several hand spans above the grassy bank. Eyes twinkling, he bowed, turning the movement into a somersault in midair. Then he conjured a bright green hat with a jaunty plume. Jamming it over his tangled hair, he strode across the empty air between them until he was close enough to touch.

Brea shrank back on her rock and considered plunging back below the surface. But this little fellow was, although a bit startling, not terribly frightening. Carefully, she rolled words out of her mouth.

"Where... am I?"

"As I said, you're in the Realm. The Realm of Faerie. Don't be afraid. You belong here, Mistress Brea Cairgead, silver fish girl, breather of both air and water."

She still wondered if she ought to slip off her rocky perch and into the cool, familiar safety of the water. It was home to her, more recently than the thatched cottage she'd once inhabited. She did not know how many turnings of the moon she'd spent in her other form, but she suspected the time could be measured in years. Perhaps decades. Yet something had prompted her transformation back to a human-seeming girl.

Magic, or fate, or even loneliness—she did not know which. Perhaps all three.

"Am I a faerie now?" she asked, afraid to hear the answer.

Puck tilted his head and regarded her a long moment, eyes bright. The wind riffled the surface of the water, and she smelled mint and thyme on the breeze.

"You are a curious creature," the sprite said. "You were never fully human, but you are human enough that you cannot entirely be one of the fey folk. As I said before, you are a girl of two parts—water and land, fey and mortal. As such, you have a part to play in things to come."

She did not like the sound of that. Brea hugged her knees close to her chest. "What if I do *not* want this fate?"

"What do you want?"

The answer was lodged in her heart, but she hesitated to speak it aloud. Still, Puck regarded her with kindness in his wild and merry eyes, and despite her wariness, she answered.

"To belong." It was what she'd always wanted, and what she'd never had.

Even as a village lass, she'd been too different. And now she realized there were none of her own kind. The selkies might tolerate her presence, but the merfolk would laugh at her ungainly human legs, and if she transformed she would not be able to speak with them.

"You have to make your own belonging," Puck said, a deep melancholy in his voice, as if he, too, were the only one of his kind.

Brea tasted salt in the back of her throat. She had no notion of how to fit herself into a world—whether human or faerie—that did not hold the shape of who she was.

"Do not despair." Puck shook himself, and she saw his sorrow fly off his shoulders and fade into the sunset sky. "If you are true of heart, you will find the way. Deep inside you, the path awaits."

"How will I know where to find it?"

"Follow the taste of the rowan berry," he said. "It will lead you to your fate. And now, Mistress Brea, I must bid you farewell."

"Don't go." She reached one pale hand toward him. Before he'd come, she had not known she was so lonely.

He did not reply—only spun himself about three times in a whirl of tatters and feathers and was gone.

Shore birds cried into the dusk, and the water lapped the bank. There was no one to talk to, except the school of silver fish swimming about the stone. And they did not speak in conversation, but in flashes of image and color.

Still, it was better than the silence of her own human thoughts. Letting out all her breath, Brea pushed herself off the rock and let the water surround her. Three heartbeats later there was no dark-haired girl pining upon a half-submerged stone, but only a new fish weaving through the current.

It was an unquiet current though, with an amber-gold thread of loam and smoke and shadows running through. It brushed along her sides, beckoning, and she found she could not resist its call.

Despite her efforts, she was not able to interest the other fish in following to see where it led. They desired only pale wave and lavender ripple, bright dart and flashing turn.

Alone, Brea-within-the-fish circled about her companions in farewell, and then left them to play in the light-filled shallows.

The taste of mystery pulled her on, past a rocky outcropping to a place where a stream poured into the larger water. Amber diluted with turquoise as the waters mixed and flowed, but it was that warmer taste within the rivulet that she must follow.

She dashed herself into the mouth of the stream and was pushed back. Once, twice, thrice—and then she discovered the trick of swimming against the current. First to one side and then the other she swam, stitching her way from bank to bank.

When she wearied she found a quiet eddy behind an algae-covered rock, and rested there until she regained her strength. The sky above the stream darkened as she followed the golden strand within the water, until at last she reached a small side-pool that tasted of contentment.

Flicking her tail, she dived in and out of the stream, but the golden thread had curled in on itself and gone to rest in the silty bottom. The undercut bank held peaceful shadows, and the tangled roots of trees wove a screen she might shelter behind. It was as good enough a place as any to bide.

Overhead, the evergreens nodded, their branches waving softly like a mother hushing her child. Above their dark heads the first sprinkling of stars shone, flecks of light springing up before the sickle moon could scythe them down.

~

There was no passage of days in the waters where Brea now dwelt. The sky dimmed and brightened from dusk to night and back again, skipping sunlight altogether. She discovered the rocks upstream where the current frothed and raced, and the quiet eddies where tadpoles fluttered. When the moon shone full, dew-winged sprites danced above the silver-lit stream, their footsteps light as rain over the water.

Brea felt no urge to move on. The golden strand that had brought her here did not reappear to beckon her forth to new rivers and depths. She splashed and darted, waiting without urgency for whatever might come. Some deep sense of knowing told her she was where she ought to be.

That peaceful contentment changed one dusky evening. The evergreens shivered, and she felt their roots stirring in the water.

Something was coming.

She darted beneath the bank and held herself there, suspended. Watching.

Brightness approached—a ball of flame hovering and bobbing through the forest. It halted on the opposite side of the stream, licking the surface with streaks of red and gold. She was too afraid to rise and see if it were a wisp, or a fallen star, or a light held aloft by some strange creature.

Sound filtered through the water, syllables with edges, full of question and danger. Brea back-finned into the shadows. She would hide until the forest became quiet and safe once more.

As if sensing her movement, the ball of flame floated out to the middle of the stream. Brea whirled and darted deeper beneath the bank, though she feared it was already too late.

After a dozen of her frightened heartbeats, the fiery sphere withdrew. It moved along the bank a short distance, but she knew the danger was not over. Indeed, the light returned soon enough, and the soil vibrated with the sound of footsteps. More than one creature roamed there beside the stream. They seemed to be seeking something.

A berry floated past, carried gently on top of the water. Brea ignored it and practiced blending with the roots she sheltered behind.

Another came past, and another, each *one leaving a trace of flavor behind*—something wild and tangy. Freedom. Adventure. Come, bite. The berries bobbed on the surface, red and full of magic.

She must not taste of them. Brea forced herself to stay in the deeps, her body quivering with effort.

A dozen floated slowly by, one by one. At the thirteenth, she could remain still no longer. Despairing, she flipped her body upward, capturing the berry in her mouth.

The taste trembled through her, urgent and immediate. Without letting it go, she fled downstream. Something pulled taut, then let her run, then wound up again. The far bank drew nearer, but she could not release the fruit. It was stuck fast in her mouth, and so she darted and ran, seeking vainly to escape.

The flame bobbed directly overhead, a tiny sun. She broke the surface in a panic of air and silver, twisting desperately. The light suffocated her and she thrashed, trying to break free.

Then darkness closed about her, but it was not the comforting liquid of the shadows. This was rough and dry, scraping her skin, smelling of something horrible. *Harsh* air surrounded her, and Brea gasped, drowning in the dryness...

Change. She must shift her form, or die.

Summoning all her streng*th, she bid her body to transform*. Hard earth beneath her. Not water. No longer fish, but girl. She clung to the thought, and at last her scales fell away. Pain rippled through her as she became heavy and slow, trapped by air and gravity, now elongated into her human form.

It was done—but she was still in darkness. Drawing in shallow, rapid breaths, she realized she was caught in folds of cloth. She clawed at the fabric until she was free.

Trees above her, and the orb of the moon. Beyond lay the safety of the stream—but two creatures stood between her and the water. Not monsters. Humans, but so strangely garbed.

One of them stepped forward, hair an odd, bright color, and said something that might have been a greeting.

Or a threat.

The other set one hand to his belt, where a knife hung.

Brea glanced down at *her* own form. She was naked, her long dark hair woven with white blossoms. Run!

A heartbeat later she was on her feet, leaping surefooted through the forest. If she could loop back around to the stream, or even find a pond, she could dive for safety.

Behind her the humans crashed and called.

Brea lifted her face, scenting the wind for water. Something golden and sweet tugged at her senses and she veered, leaping lightly over bracken fern. Despite her nakedness, the forest was kind. The moss cushioned her steps, and no sharp twigs scraped her pale unprotected skin.

The forest thinned, the scent drawing her on. A half-remembered taste, tart and lovely. Apples.

She broke out of the trees into silvery grasses dancing in the starlight. Before her rose a long hill, and at the top a tree grew, branches heavy with both blossom and fruit. She cast a glance behind her, to see her pursuers closer than she had guessed.

With a last burst of speed, Brea raced up the hill. The apple tree bowed and bent, a golden fruit caught high in its branches, but she dared not pause.

Onward, past the tree, past a faerie ring studded with mushrooms, past a low stone wall. At last, breath scraping in her lungs, limbs burning with effort, she could run no more.

There was no lake, no stream, no rivulet nearby to offer her shelter. Wearily, Brea dropped to the ground, the grasses rising around her. At least the human creatures no longer chased her. The silence of the night was broken only by the chirp of an insect, the rustle of the wind through the grass.

And then came a sound to freeze her newly-warmed blood: the wail of a hunting horn echoing across the sky.

The Wild Hunt was riding.

Even safe in her waterborne form, she knew to dive deep when the unearthly riders and spectral hounds galloped through the night. Once, she had seen the wavering shadow of the Huntsman silhouetted against the moon, his fearsome shape crowned with mighty antlers.

Shivering, Brea stood and scanned the silvery meadows surrounding her. Far ahead a dark smudge rose on the horizon; perhaps a sheltering forest, perhaps a low rise of hills. She lifted her face and scented deeply of the air, but there was no smell of water nearby. No safety she could plunge into and disappear.

She prayed there was still some cover she might find, a hazel copse or small tarn. Turning her steps toward the horizon, she began to run once more.

The horn did not sound again, but far too soon she heard the shrill yipping of hounds and the thunder of hooves. Brea glanced over her shoulder and gasped at the sight of the Wild Hunt galloping across the sky, bearing down on her in all their glory.

Glowing, gossamer-maned horses with fiery eyes bore stern and beautiful elfin knights, their hair whipping in the wind. Hounds raced before them, sinuous as smoke, red eyes burning like coals. And in the midst, the horned figure of the Huntsman, a midnight cloak billowing behind him.

Heart beating fast as a bird's, Brea raced over the meadows. Above the sharpness of her breaths and the drumming hooves, she heard the high keening of bagpipes.

There was no escape. She was too slow, and the hunt surrounded her.

The riders landed, hemming her in a circle, and Brea halted. Chin high, she faced the Huntsman, though her legs felt weak as water.

"What do you want of me?" she asked.

"The Dark Queen demands your presence," the Huntsman said, his voice deep and low. "You have aided the enemy."

"What enemy?" She cast her mind back, trying to understand, but his words had no meaning. Did this concern the humans who had chased her? "I have done nothing."

"That is for the queen to decide."

The horned figure gestured to one of his riders. Before Brea could utter a protest she was scooped up and set in front of a black-haired rider with cold green eyes. His arm was a vise about her waist, and she did not bother to struggle. She would conserve her strength for a fight that she might win.

Although how she could possibly win anything from the Dark Queen of the Realm, Brea had no notion. She knew very little about the queen, having never strayed far into the midnight side of the Realm. Neither had she forayed into the sunlit reaches ruled by the Bright King. The dusk-lit sky had been enough for her, the sunset-tipped waves and still pools lit silver by the rising moon.

All she knew was that the queen ruled the Dark Realm, and that even in the gloaming far from the midnight heart of her court, creatures spoke of her with fear and awe.

The eldritch horn sounded, and the Wild Hunt leaped into the sky. The air cooled and the wind of their passing blew Brea's dark hair back from her face. Around them, the stars hovered close as the fiery-footed steeds climbed into the sky. She felt as though she might lift her hand and cut her fingers against the sickle blade of the moon.

Night wove thickly about the hunt as they rode into the heart of the Dark Realm, until at last they reached the stillness of midnight. Gnarled oaks grew in the shadowed forest below, and she glimpsed a clearing lit with dozens of faerie-fire candles and a bonfire flickering with purple light.

Fey folk thronged there, some dancing wildly about the violet flames, others gathered at the long feasting tables set at one side of the clearing. She blinked to see so many creatures: dream-winged faerie maids and sharp-toothed nixies, a bone-white shadow inside a dark cloak, the wide-eyed stare of the banshee.

Music drifted above the tangled treetops—harp and drum and guitar twining together, sorrowful and joyous in equal measure. The Wild Hunt followed the melody down and landed in the center of the clearing.

At the far end stood a throne of vines and thorns, and upon it sat the Dark Queen. Her hair was smoke and obsidian, her gown starlight and cobwebs, and her eyes held the memory of countless centuries.

Brea swallowed, her throat dry with fear as the elfin knight set her on the mossy ground. Her legs trembled, and she looked down to see she was clad once more in a shimmer of a gown that clung to her like mist.

"Huntsman," the queen said. "Have you brought me the betrayer?"

"I have, your majesty." He made her a sweeping bow. "This maid is the one we scented, who led the humans directly to the tree of the golden apple."

Brea's skin prickled with fear, and she sucked in a painful breath. "I did not—"

"You." The queen's voice cut like frost. She leaned forward and pointed at Brea with one long, pale finger. "I should strike you down where you stand for aiding my enemies."

Brea had never meant to lead the humans anywhere, but only to escape. Had she done something terrible, all unwitting?

"Forgive me, your majesty," she whispered.

A bright-eyed, tangle-haired sprite tumbled into the clearing before the Dark Queen's throne. Brea recognized him—Puck, who spoke in riddles and runes. Standing before the queen, he made his ruler a flourishing bow, one foot pointed on the velvet green mosses.

"Your majesty," he said. "Might I speak?"

The queen let out a sigh, the sound like a wind stirring the empty branches of winter oaks.

"Puck," she said. "You have the freedom of the courts, much as it may displease my mood. Say your piece."

"Yon maid, all unwitting, played but a part in a quest. She does not deserve death—and there are few enough fey folk that her loss, though a small thing, would be felt within the realm."

Brea sent him a grateful glance. She did not know why Puck was defending her. Perhaps it had to do with their prior meeting and his cryptic words of fate and future.

"Banishment, then, shall be her punishment," the queen declared. "To the Shadowlands."

The denizens of the court shivered, and Brea felt her heart catch. Even hiding within her watery dwelling, she'd heard of that dire place where souls wandered, lost and alone, into eternity.

Though the words might stumble on her tongue, she must plead her case.

"My queen." She bowed as best she could on her unsteady legs. "I beg you, do not banish me. Surely there is some way to mend the harm I might have done?"

The gathered fey folk whispered, and Brea was glad she could not hear what they said. No doubt they suggested dire and dreadful remedies.

"Perchance there might be." The queen narrowed her eyes and gestured. "Bard Thomas, attend."

A man stepped from the shadows and Brea stared at him in surprise. Another half-magical human like herself, perhaps? But no —there was something ghostly about him. If he'd been human once, he was no longer. Silver strands ran through his brown hair, and his eyes were wise and weary beyond measure.

"Yes, my queen?"

"How best might I use this youngling in service to the court?"

The man turned, his gaze brushing past Puck and then resting upon Brea for a long moment. Sparks and promises flashed in his eyes, and she did not know whether to be hopeful or afraid.

"Send her into the human world," he said at last. "There, she might sway mortals to stray into the Realm. She can repay her debt by helping ensure that humans will cross over to the Dark Court when they enter the game of Feyland."

The queen gave a single shake of her head. "I mislike having to sacrifice yet another of my handmaidens simply to send a near-useless creature into the mortal realm. Your counsel pleases me not, bard."

"Milady." Puck sprang into the air and hovered there. "Though centuries have passed, the girl is part human, and still connected with the mortal world. I may be able to slip her through the gateway without further bloodshed. And if not"—he gave an elaborate shrug —"then do with her as you please."

"Your magic is fickle," the queen said.

"Yet you know it cannot be forced to do your bidding." Puck laughed and flipped in the air, landing once again on the soft ground. "I will attempt to send the maid through."

The queen leaned back, the pale moonlight illuminating her beauty. Overhead, stars sprinkled the edges of the sky, and a night wind stirred the oak leaves into whispering. Brea's nerves hummed as she awaited her fate. Her heartbeat pounded within her chest until she was nearly dizzy from the rhythm, yet she remained quiet and still, as she had learned to do in her watery form. Speaking on her own behalf would do little good, and she did not want to tip the balance of the queen's decision unfavorably.

At length the queen beckoned to Brea, who found she could not ignore the summons. She came forward, then sank to her knees on the velvety mosses before the throne.

"I lay a geas upon you, youngling," the Dark Queen said. "From now until the summer wanes, you are charged with marking and leading as many humans as you might toward the magic of the Dark Court so that the Realm may be replenished. Should you return without success, the Shadowlands will be your new home."

Brea bowed her head. There was no arguing, and no agreement. When the queen spoke, her word was law. Still, this sentence was a reprieve. If she carried out the queen's bidding well enough, she might escape dire banishment to the Shadowlands.

Behind the tangled throne, gossamer-winged faerie maidens cast Brea pitying glances. A nearby band of goblins cackled, clearly pleased by her plight. The queen held up one hand and called forth her magic. In a burst of violet light, a silver medallion appeared. It swung, dangling on a bright chain from the queen's fingers.

"Take this," she said, thrusting the medallion at Brea. "It is your passage back to the realm—but do not call upon it until Lughnasa is nigh."

Brea took the medallion. It was cool against her fingers, the silver disc inset with a pale moonstone, the edges inscribed with runes. She folded it into her palm, proof of the journey she must now undertake.

"Away with her," the queen said to Puck.

Without a further glance at Brea, she signaled for elderberry wine and music. The creatures of her court bestirred themselves, returning to their dancing and feasting.

"Come, maid," Puck said.

Brea rose and followed him. She did not look behind her as they left the clearing of the Dark Court, though the strains of a plaintive jig followed her into the shimmering darkness beneath the trees.

"I am afraid," she said, once the sounds of the court had faded.

"You are wise to be so," Puck said. "Yet who knows what doors will open to you in the human world, or what fate might hold in store?"

She did not want fate or a queen's commands to rule her—but she had no choice.

Puck led her along mossy paths faintly illuminated with starshine. Overhead, the dark oaks wove their tangled branches across the star-dappled sky.

"Quickly," the sprite urged. "We must slip you through before the battle commences. I have folded time, but we must make haste."

Brea gulped back her questions. She doubted she wanted to know the answers. Battle? Folded time? Instead she quickened her pace, until she and Puck were nearly flying through the forest. Or perhaps they truly were airborne. Her feet did not seem to touch the ground, and she would not be surprised if the sprite's magic propelled them forward. Overhead, the sky lightened to a pearly grey.

"Here." Puck halted before a strange clearing, still floating in the air. "We are in time."

Brea's feet landed on the cool moss, and she blinked at the clearing. It was not a single glade, but three, lined up like a triple reflection. The one nearest them held a faerie ring of moon-pale mushrooms, the far one was lit by morning sun and its circle made of white-speckled red mushrooms, and the one in the middle was a mixture of both—sun and shadow, pale mushrooms and red growing together to make the faerie ring.

Puck strode to the middle clearing and flourished his fingers in a strange gesture. Colored mist began forming in the center of the faerie ring—golden and violet and emerald swirling together.

"Keep the medallion safe," the sprite said, nodding to the silver pendant still clutched in her hand. "Step into the mist, and be brave."

She was not brave, nor had she ever been. She'd merely done what had to be done—which seemed to take her only from one trouble to the next.

"What must I do, once I reach the human world?" she asked, slowly walking toward the bright eddies of mist.

"Mark humans with a touch of faerie magic, so that they are called into the Realm," Puck said. "But most of all, trust your heart."

The sprite ever spoke in riddles, with few answers. She let out a low sigh.

Beside them, the clearing holding the moon-pale ring began to glow. Puck gave it a wary glance, then gestured at her to hurry.

"Farewell, Maid Brea," he said. "Luck be upon you."

She hoped the fates heard his words.

"Farewell, Puck."

Gathering the shreds of her courage, she stepped into the swirling mist of the center clearing. The world tipped, dizziness pouring over her until she fell to her knees. She could feel the sweet magic of the Realm of Faerie ripping away, and she cried out from the pain of it.

It was not the first time she'd been pulled from one world to another, though, and she vowed that whatever happened, she would survive this transformation.

Human or faerie, she would stay true to her word. And perhaps, one day, she would find her way home. Wherever that might be.

ABOUT THE AUTHOR

Growing up on fairy tales and computer games, Anthea Sharp has melded the two in her award-winning, bestselling Feyland series, which has sold over 150k copies worldwide. In addition to the fae fantasy/cyberpunk mashup of Feyland, she also writes Victorian Spacepunk, and fantasy romance. Her books have won awards and topped bestseller lists, and garnered over a million reads at Wattpad. Her short fiction has appeared in Fiction River, DAW anthologies, *The Future Chronicles*, and *Beyond The Stars: At Galaxy's Edge*, as well as many other publications.

Anthea lives in sunny Southern California, where she writes, hangs out in virtual worlds, plays Celtic fiddle, and spends time with her small-but-good family.

Find out more about Anthea at:
antheasharp.com

facebook.com/AntheaSharp

twitter.com/antheasharp

bookbub.com/authors/anthea-sharp

amazon.com/Anthea-Sharp/e/B006HQ2IFQ

MIDWINTER RUN

MARCELLE DUBÉ

T he pixie was dead.

It lay draped on jumbled slabs of ice as if it had fallen onto the frozen river from the northern lights swirling above Annalise's head. Perhaps it had—she could see no footprints in the fresh snow covering the ice. Even a creature as small as the pixie would have left marks in the snow.

Behind her, the dogs barked frantically and strained at their harnesses, shredding the silence with their eagerness to see and sniff this unfamiliar being.

She had never seen a pixie before—nor any of the Fey—but she knew what it was the moment she set eyes on it.

Five years ago, when Annalise was eleven, Father and Mother had traveled to Montreal for the opening of the Victoria Bridge. There they had seen the Prince of Wales, who had come to officially open the bridge on behalf of his mother, Queen Victoria. And yet, it was the Fey Mother could not stop talking about. She had been enthralled but Annalise had seen how Father's lips had set in a thin line of disapproval.

When she first saw the pixie, Annalise set the brake on the dog sled, and then tethered the lead dog, Rufus, to a picket she hammered into the ice. Even so, she had to decide quickly what to do before the dogs broke free and tangled their harnesses in an effort to reach the tiny thing.

In life, the pixie might have stood as tall as her knees. A round, felted green hat lay next to it, as if the hat had been knocked off the little one's head. It wore a green woolen jacket with a button torn off, and heavy black pants tucked into knee-high deerskin moccasins such as those worn by the *coureurs des bois*. No scarf, no mittens. It had probably died of the cold.

The small face had fine cheekbones, a pointed chin and a small, snub nose. Even closed, its eyes looked much too large. In the faint starlight, its hair was dark and stood out all over its head, as if it had never seen a comb.

Poor little thing. No one deserved to die all alone in the middle of a frozen wilderness. Not even a Fey.

"What is it, Annalise?" croaked Father from the bed of the dog sled.

She hurried over to him, pleased that he was conscious again. She pushed back his wolverine fur hood, the better to examine him. In the uncertain light of the stars and the dancing curtain shimmering above their heads, his face was drawn in lines of pain, his eyes narrowed, his lips compressed. His ghostly breath plumed against the darkness of the spruce and pine trees lining the banks of the river.

"Nothing," she said firmly. She set her rifle down on the furs covering him and replaced the hood around his head before turning to look down the river. Two hours they had been travelling and still another three before they reached home in Ste. Eulalie and the doctor who could mend Father.

"Nothing," she said again. There was no time to waste on a tiny, dead Fey creature.

Nevertheless, she picked it up and placed it on top of the sled, in between two ermine pelts, then tied it down. She had no idea what she would do with the body, but it felt wrong to just leave it there.

Father had fainted for the third time hours ago, when the dogsled first bumped over the bank and onto the frozen river. Starlight had reflected off the snow and ice, barely enough to light her way but it had to do—she dared not wait until morning.

She had tried to immobilize his broken leg as best she could, but it was a bad break, with the bone almost poking out of the skin of his lower leg. The second time he had fainted was when she had tried to pull the leg straight. She finally left it as it was, praying the doctor in Ste. Eulalie would be able to reset it.

It was the seeping wound in Father's side that finally decided her to chance the journey by dog sled. A branch had impaled him when he'd fallen down an embankment to land against a boulder. She had found him hours later, after she strapped on her snowshoes and followed the dog sled tracks along their trap line. She had no idea how long he'd lain in the snow before she found him but the dogs had been tangled up in their harness, hopelessly immobilized by their own confusion.

In the end, she'd had to tie a rope around his chest and use the dogs to haul him out of the gully. That was the first time he had fainted.

∽

The dogs were growing frantic with their awareness of the pixie, whining and barking their demands to be free. It was time to go.

Before they'd left their home in Ste. Eulalie, she and Father had discussed whether to bring all seven dogs or only five. In the end, they decided on five, as it was still early in the trapping season. The more dogs they brought, the more food they would have to haul. After Christmas, they would bring all seven dogs, as they expected their load of pelts to be heavier on the journey back.

It had pleased her that he considered her opinion. This was her first year on the trap line. With no sons to help him, Father had finally allowed her to persuade him, much to Mother's dismay. But Annalise was sixteen now, old enough and strong enough to be of help to him. And she suspected Mother was secretly relieved that Father would no longer travel alone into the winter wilderness.

When he hurt himself, Father had been on the last run of the trap line before they were to set out for home and the Christmas celebrations. They both longed to be with the rest of the family at this darkest time of the year, when the cold descended on them like a foe bent on their destruction.

He would not be returning to the trap line this year, but she would. The pelts they were bringing back now would not be enough to keep them in food and supplies all year.

She hurried back to Rufus to free him from the stake, her moccasined feet squeaking in the snow. Her hands were clumsy in their beaver mitts and she finally removed the mitts and tucked them between her knees to finish the job.

"Stop it," she warned Rufus as he strained to look backward at the sled and the pixie. A movement caught her attention and she glanced up at the sky. The northern lights were no longer green, but a faint pink, as though diluted with blood.

She shivered, despite her beaver hat and ancient, thigh-length marten coat that had once belonged to her grandmother. Even the dogs seemed cowed by the sight, crouching low and falling silent.

Only then did she hear the pixie moaning.

~

"What is it?" asked Father. His voice was weaker.

Annalise glanced up from her crouched position by Rufus, where she thumped the stake back into the ice.

"I'm not sure," she said. She hurried back to the pixie on top of the sled and bent over it. It looked exactly as it had moments ago. Dead. It must have been her imagination.

Just to be sure, she removed one heavy mitten and placed a hand on the little one's exposed neck. Its eyes fluttered open and her hand flew off as if scalded.

The tiny creature stared back at her, its eyes wide and dark.

"Annalise?"

"A pixie," she called to Father. "I thought it was dead."

It had to be very close to death. It might be a Fey creature but surely they were as vulnerable to the freezing cold as humans were. It looked up at her, blinking slowly, as if sluggish from the cold.

"It was only a matter of time," said Father.

She sighed, unable to hide her dismay. He was right. Once the Victoria Bridge spanned the St. Lawrence, the Fey were finally free to leave their island prison. Annalise was surprised it had taken them this long to make it into the interior.

No one she knew in Ste. Eulalie had ever seen a Fey, save for Mother and Father. And no one she knew wanted to. Life was hard enough without having to share the hunting grounds and fishing with newcomers—newcomers who could easily destroy them with their magic, according to the old stories.

The little one's hand lifted, then fell back weightlessly to the marten pelt and Annalise realized suddenly that this one was young. Even by Fey standards, this one was a child.

Impulsively, she unbuttoned her marten coat and scooped the pixie up.

"What are you doing?" asked Father. She heard him moan as he tried to sit up to see better.

"I'm taking it with us," she said, straightening with her light burden clutched to the warm sweater Mother had knit her. She used her scarf to tie the pixie against her body before closing the coat over it, covering its head and hoping she wouldn't smother it. But the coat was roomy. Grandmother had been a large woman.

It was probably too late—she had no idea how long it had been lying on the frozen river, barely dressed for the weather, but it felt like a lump of ice against her chest and belly. She would surely arrive in Ste. Eulalie to find it had died.

She removed the stake and returned the rifle to its leather sleeve strapped to the handle of the sled.

"Ready?" she asked her father.

"Ready," he replied from his fur shroud.

Then she cried, "Hike!" and Rufus sprang forward.

❧

An hour later, her face, hands and feet had grown numb with the cold. The pixie still lived, strapped against her, slowly leaching the warmth from her. Every time she checked on it, it had its eyes closed, whether asleep or unconscious, she couldn't tell. But she could feel the slight rise and fall of its tiny chest against hers.

Every few miles, she had to step off the sled's runners to run on the packed snow, hanging on to the handles, to heat up her blood. Still, she was growing sluggish with the cold. Exhausted.

The last time she had checked on Father, he hadn't woken to her voice, or her touch. Only the slow fog of his breaths told her he still lived. She didn't check inside the furs covering him to see if the bleeding had started again. Exposing him to the cold would steal too much of his remaining strength. She was losing him—she felt it as if it were her own life ebbing away. Her only hope was to make it to Ste. Eulalie as quickly as she could.

Even as she thought it, she feared she would be too late.

The dogs still ran well, but they, too, were growing tired. They hadn't had a proper rest since Father took them out onto the trap line the previous morning, and now they had been running steadily for three hours, with only a brief rest when she found the pixie. But if she gave them the rest they needed, Father would not live to see the doctor.

The only sounds in this cold, frozen hell were those of her harsh breathing, and the shushing of the sled's runners over the snow and ice. Even the dogs ran silently. Or perhaps she couldn't hear their panting with the fur flaps covering her ears.

At times, she thought the dark trees on either bank fled at her approach, but it was an illusion brought on by her exhaustion. The occasional white birch sprang out of the dark wall like a sudden torch as the dogs ate up mile after mile of frozen river. Once or twice, she felt herself nodding off from the hypnotic motion of the sled only to jerk awake when the dogs swerved to avoid a jutting ice shelf.

Then she felt the sled slow and focused her eyes on the dogs. All five of them were slowing to a stop, their lowered heads turned toward the right bank.

"Rufus!" she called. "Hike!"

Her lead dog ignored her and she looked around to see what had spooked him. All she could see were trees and more trees. Finally the dogs slowed so much that she stepped on the brake and ran to the front of the sled. All the dogs stood with their heads lowered but their hackles up, even Rufus.

"What is it, boy?" she asked as she came abreast of him. He looked up at her, his pale blue eyes glittering in the strange lights above. Removing her mittens, she ran her hands over the dog's body but found no injuries.

None of them seemed hurt, yet they all stood with their heads lowered and their hackles up, something she had never seen before. Their eerie silence unnerved her, but not as much as their focused attention on the right bank of the river.

As she held her breath, the small creature strapped to her chest shifted. She grew aware of its warm breath penetrating the layers of clothing she was wearing. It might yet live.

She realized suddenly that she was hearing something, something muffled. She pulled off her hat to hear better and the cold immediately attacked her forehead and ears. The dogs were whining.

What were they afraid of? Not afraid, she finally understood. Confused.

The dark woods remained silent and still, without even a breeze to lift the boughs.

She glanced back at the sled, torn between getting her father to Ste. Eulalie as quickly as possible and seeing what had spooked the dogs. It was probably a pack of wolves attracted by their passage. There was no real danger—wolves wouldn't attack this many dogs, not with her there. And if they did, she had the rifle.

"Rufus." She replaced the hat on her head, shivering, and knelt by the dog's side. She rubbed her mittened hands over his face and head. "We don't have time for the vapors, old friend," she whispered in his ear. "Father—"

A roar tore through the frozen air and Annalise sprang up, her heart almost stopping in her fright. The pixie stirred against her, jostled, but she didn't have time to check the bindings to make sure it remained safely fastened.

She ran to the back of the sled and kicked the brake off before she even turned to look in the direction of the trees. A dark shape had detached itself from the night-shrouded trees and now ran straight for the sled.

She blinked, wasting a precious second, even as her mind took in the dark fur, the rounded body and powerful shoulders, the claws flashing in the weird light.

Grizzly.

There was no time to wonder at the incongruity of a bear awake at this time of year. All she had time for was to grab onto the handles and shout, "Hike! Hike! Hike!"

The sled surged forward so quickly that she barely managed to leap onto the runners before it could escape her.

Shaken out of their paralysis, the dogs ran as fast as they could on the uneven ice. The ear flaps on her beaver hat flipped up in the wind of their passage, exposing her earlobes to the killing cold. She glanced over her shoulder only to see that the bear was keeping pace with them.

How was that even possible? No bear could run as fast as a team of sled dogs—especially frightened sled dogs.

She faced forward again, her frozen face bearing the brunt of the cold. Releasing the right handle, she fumbled for the rifle, grasping it firmly in a hand made clumsy by the thick mittens. She knew she risked dropping the rifle, but she needed to be ready, should the bear catch up to them.

Another glance over her shoulder showed the bear no closer, perhaps even farther back than it had been. Before she could breathe out her relief, another sound reached her. She looked over her shoulder again, but only the bear followed, the distance between them growing larger with every moment.

She needed her hands, both of them. She carefully replaced the rifle in its leather sheath before gripping the handles with both hands. Then, braced, she twisted to take a good look behind and on either side. Nothing but the bear, falling farther and farther behind but still not stopping.

What was that sound?

The pixie shifted against her chest and she patted it comfortingly a few times before gripping the handle again.

It sounded like the baying of hounds. And hunting horns. And wild ululations.

And it was coming from above.

Finally, Annalise looked up. There in the night sky, riding the northern lights as if it were a shimmering road, a horde of riders on horses, accompanied by red-eyed hounds, descended toward her.

A thrill of fear ran through her and her gasp was lost to the cold night as Rufus and the other dogs put on a burst of speed.

The Fey.

Mother had always said that the Fey were magical, but Father had only scowled. He wanted nothing to do with the Fey and their magic. Neither did she.

And now here they were, riding the night sky.

What did they want with her? In her one frightened glance, she had seen what looked like bows held aloft.

Were they *hunting*?

The dogs stretched their pace even more, striving to stay ahead of the horde descending upon them.

Annalise risked a glance over her shoulder. The forerunners were gaining on her. A movement on the ice reminded her that the bear was still behind them.

A small part of her found herself amazed. They had traveled at least three miles since she had first seen the bear. No bear she had even heard of would run that far, that fast, after prey.

Shouts overhead startled her and she looked up. Some of the riders had circled ahead and now bore down on her. On Father.

Releasing the right handle, she pulled her mitten off with her teeth and reached for the rifle. The wood stock felt cold to the touch, but not as cold as the metal trigger guard. She pulled the rifle out and struggled to aim it one-handed at the nearest figure bearing down on her. A glowing Fey man with flowing silver hair and a white fur cloak floating behind him leaned forward over the shoulder of a beautiful white stallion whose saddle and bridle were adorned with silver. Behind the horse, two red-eyed, black hounds bounded in mid-air as if on a solid road, clearly subordinate to the Fey man.

Rufus yelped a sudden warning and the sled caught the edge of an ice shelf. For a moment, the sled flew in the air like the Fey. Then it and Annalise parted ways as the handle jerked out of her hand and her feet lost their purchase on the runners. She landed hard, instinctively twisting to land on her side to protect the pixie still strapped to her chest. Her head slammed against the icy river and the world went away for a brief time.

When she came to, she was still lying on the ice. Her head throbbed and she moaned.

Father!

Her eyes flew open and she sat up, only to place a mittened hand on the uneven surface of the ice to keep from toppling back. She swayed where she sat, trying to focus.

Arrayed around her in an uneven circle, the Fey sat their horses, staring down at her, their faces closed and unfriendly.

She tried to peer between the legs of the horses but there were too many and she couldn't see the sled. If her dogs were there, they made no sound.

Where was Father? Had they taken him? Harmed him?

She scrambled awkwardly to her feet, only then realizing that she still held the rifle in her frozen hand. Would she even be able to shoot, if she needed to?

"What do you want?" she demanded. To her shame, her voice carried more fear than determination. She glanced around the circle. At least twenty riders, mostly male, all with the height and thinness Mother had described. All of them beautiful, despite the hostility on their faces.

They glowed, as if moonlight seeped from under their cloaks, so that the night was lit with incandescence. This, even more than seeing them descend from the sky, filled her with wonder.

They remained silent, all of them, studying her as she studied them. Their horses stamped impatiently on the frozen surface of the river and snorted steam out of their nostrils. For a fleeting moment, she wondered if the river ice would hold all that weight. Then she wondered if they weighed anything at all, since they could fly.

All the horses were white and richly harnessed, their bridles decorated with filigreed silver, their chests covered with fine tapestries, their manes threaded with ribbons of silver and gold. They were almost as beautiful as their Fey riders.

One of the riders urged his horse forward, stopping a few feet from her. She controlled an urge to step back in the face of the monstrous horse towering over her. She'd never seen such a fine horse, never seen so many white horses in one spot.

The thought triggered a suspicion in her but before it could fully form, the Fey man spoke.

"What have you done with our comrade?"

Annalise blinked up at him. The pixie. It had to be.

She almost reached for the buttons on her coat, almost relinquished the small Fey creature, but some instinct stopped her. She looked at the one who had addressed her.

"I don't have time to deal with this now," she said firmly. "I must get to Ste. Eulalie."

She had almost said she had to get her father to Ste. Eulalie, but she did not know these people, did not know what they would do to her. To Father. She peered around the stamping horses and finally spied the dogs. They were hopelessly tangled and lay on the frozen river, waiting patiently for someone to untangle them. The sled had landed on its side with the runners facing her.

Her heart squeezed with the need to go to her father. Did he still live? Was he dying as she stood there talking to these strangers?

Suddenly the circle surrounding her parted to reveal the grizzly padding up to them, its claws clicking on the ice. The breath caught in Annalise's throat as the bear stopped within a few feet.

"She killed him," it said in a woman's voice. "I don't know what she did with his body."

And finally, Annalise understood. The bear wasn't a bear. It was another Fey creature, hiding under a glamour. All of them were under a glamour. There weren't twenty fine white horses anywhere in Lower Canada. And there were no gold ribbons or filigreed saddles.

They were trying to recreate the legends of their past, from their home country.

Abruptly, she felt an overwhelming pity for them all, with their pretend finery. They still had magic, yes, but they were much diminished from when they had first arrived on this continent.

Her feelings must have shown on her face, for the first rider nudged his horse closer to her, anger on his face, and the hounds began to growl, their feral red eyes narrowing as they crept closer to her.

Rufus barked, startling everyone. By the time the beautiful, angry Fey faces turned back to her, she was aiming the rifle squarely at the Fey man threatening her.

"I have to go now," she said calmly, though her heart raced and she worried she wouldn't be able to squeeze the trigger.

The Fey man looked down at her, his face a mask of grief and anger.

"You cannot kill us all," he said calmly. "You've already killed one of ours and you will pay, though I should die, too."

Suddenly, Annalise had had enough. Her father was dying while she wasted time here. He might already be dead.

"I haven't killed anyone!" she shouted, waving the rifle in a wide arc.

The bear growled at her.

"Liar! I saw where the little one fell but when I reached the spot, it was gone. You and your dogs were already running away. I chased you, but I didn't see where you left his body. Where is it?"

"If you mean the pixie," she said roughly, "he's fine."

Every single Fey, even the bear, flinched, as if she had used a foul word.

"Do you deny killing him?" said the bear, stepping closer.

"Oh, stop it," said Annalise crossly. "You're no more a bear than I am." She turned toward the Fey man who had first spoken. Her rifle dropped to point at the ice. "And your pixie friend is fine, though he shouldn't be, considering he must have fallen from a great height."

Throughout the circle, shoulders relaxed as hope overtook their anger.

"Where is he?" asked the Fey man. He dismounted and came to stand in front of her.

She found herself staring up into eyes as green as moss. He was very tall. It didn't help that she wasn't. And he was thin—much too thin. Those shoulders would never bear the weight of a canoe on a portage. But they didn't need to, did they? Not when the Fey had magic enough to allow them to fly through the sky.

The cold penetrated the layers of her pants and crept under her fur coat, and yet, the Fey sat their horses comfortably, bare-handed and bare-headed, with only a cloak to protect them against the killing cold.

Her small burden shifted slightly against her chest.

They flew through the sky.

"How did you lose him?" she asked finally. The pixie was a child, that much she knew. Surely the Fey weren't so different from humans that they would allow a child on such a wild ride?

Her bare hand felt numb. She could no longer feel the rifle in her hand. Frostbite would be setting it, but she dared not release her weapon. Not yet.

The Fey man lowered his gaze briefly, but then looked at her again.

"It was unintentional. We did not know the child had hidden himself in one of our bags until he fell out."

By all that was holy... Annalise shuddered, but the Fey man continued, oblivious.

"Elsgard," he nodded toward the bear, "was the only one who saw where he had fallen. By the time we circled back, he was gone and Elsgard was chasing you."

Hunting her, more likely. Annalise nodded, a plan slowly forming in her mind.

"Where is the child?" repeated the Fey man, crossing his arms over his chest. He wore a slit green tunic that seemed to be woven of fine wool and leather pants and boots. There was a sword in a jeweled scabbard strapped to his impossibly narrow hips.

Where is the child?

The child in question seemed oblivious to what was happening outside the warm cocoon of her fur coat. It had snuggled into her chest and now seemed to be asleep.

Annalise glanced at the overturned sled, the idea taking shape in her mind.

"Perhaps we can help each other," she said softly.

∽

Ste. Eulalie slumbered in the darkness of midwinter, the only sign of life the smoke pouring straight up from the chimneys in the still air. The streets of the village glowed like pale silk ribbons under the starlight but the homes seemed to hunch against the cold.

Annalise shouted "Whoa!" to Rufus but in the end, she had to stand on the brake to make the dogs stop on the ridge overlooking the small valley in which Ste. Eulalie slept. This close to home, they were anxious for their straw-lined boxes and a solid meal after so many hours of running on nothing but short breaks and small snacks.

But Annalise did not want to race into town without checking first if the Fey had held up their end of the bargain.

She brushed a mitten against her fur hood, making it fall back, and studied the village. She'd had to turn around and retrace her steps before finding where she had dropped the mitten, but she'd had no choice. Without the mitten, she would have lost the hand to frostbite. As it was, she might lose fingers.

The rifle was back in its sheath. It was a comfort to her.

She could see no movements on the streets below. Here and there, a faint light glowed in a window as a sleepless occupant made ready to greet the day, but otherwise, Ste. Eulalie slept, still hours away from dawn.

She couldn't see the doctor's home from this angle. She would have to get closer.

As one, the dogs raised their heads to the sky. Annalise looked up. High in the sky, a troupe of beautiful white horses flew through the air. They were too far for her to make out details, but she knew that a

Fey man or woman sat on each horse, and that red-eyed hounds accompanied them. The faint sound of baying drifted down to her and she shivered.

They were gone.

Mother used to tell her stories about these wild midwinter rides and what happened to the unlucky humans who met the riders. But those were tales from another time and place—a time when the Fey were powerful, a place where they belonged.

Replacing the fur hood over her head, she released the sled's brake and clicked her tongue. "Hike!" she cried, and pushed off with one foot when Rufus pulled against the harness. In moments, they were racing silently down the ridge toward the village.

It was easier without Father's weight in the sled.

Five minutes later, she turned the sled down the street where the doctor kept his practice, at the front of his house. A lantern glowed in the window of the clinic, and a bit of tension left Annalise's shoulders.

The doctor was up. Hopefully, he was tending Father.

"Whoa," she said softly and Rufus obediently slowed the team to a stop. There was no purchase on the frozen road for the brake, so she stepped off the runners and rummaged around the pelts in the sled until she found a sturdy rope. Then she walked around to Rufus.

"Good boy," she whispered, rubbing his face. "Just a little while longer and I'll take you home," she promised. He whined but seemed to accept her words. She slipped the rope around his harness and tied the other end to the post on the doctor's porch, securing the sled.

"You took your time," came a woman's voice.

Annalise turned to find the Fey man astride his magnificent horse. Next to him was a Fey woman, also sitting on a fine white horse. Both of them glowed with that strange white light that seemed to emanate from their skin.

"I don't fly," said Annalise tiredly. Now that she had finally arrived, exhaustion settled over her and she staggered briefly before regaining her balance. She didn't need the magical light to see the contempt in the woman's face.

"Our friend?" asked the Fey man. His face held no contempt, but neither was it friendly.

"My father?" countered Annalise. The cold seeped into her boots, freezing her feet. At least she could still feel them.

"We did as we promised," he said stiffly. He paused for a moment. "But I cannot promise that he will live. He is gravely injured."

A sob caught in Annalise's throat and she swallowed hard, refusing to show any weakness before them.

"You gave him a better chance than I could," she said finally. "For that, I thank you."

The man hesitated, then nodded solemnly, accepting her thanks.

"Our friend," reminded the woman sharply.

Annalise nodded, too, and took off her mittens. The cold immediately attacked her frostbitten hand but she would need both hands to unbutton the coat and untie the scarf.

The moment the coat was open, both the Fey man and woman dismounted and came toward her. The pixie, rudely awakened by the cold, stretched its tiny arms out and clasped Annalise's sweater, snuggling in closer to her warmth.

The Fey man looked down at the pixie, then blinked at Annalise.

"Was he there the entire time?"

Annalise shrugged, eliciting a soft protest from the sleepy pixie. She patted his back absently with her good hand.

"I thought he was dead at first," she said, changing to rubbing the pixie's back. "When I realized he was still alive, I feared he would die from the cold."

The Fey man reached out to touch the pixie, who opened his eyes and smiled in delight.

"Why didn't you give him to us when we first spoke?" demanded the female, clearly angry.

Annalise was too tired to argue, too tired for diplomacy.

"I needed your help," she said.

"You could have asked for it," said the male reproachfully.

Annalise's eyebrows lifted.

"Would you have given it?" she asked.

The male had the grace to drop his gaze but the female frowned.

"Why should we have helped, human?" she said.

Annalise smiled thinly.

"Exactly."

She tugged at the knot holding the scarf tied, trying to keep the pixie from squirming. Finally, the Fey male pushed her clumsy hands away and deftly untied the knot, catching the pixie when he tumbled out.

Annalise caught the scarf before it could fall to the snow and closed the fur coat over herself, unable to control a massive shiver.

"I must see to my father," she said. "And to my dogs." She made to turn away but the Fey woman stopped her with a surprisingly strong hand on her arm.

"You are very fortunate," she said softly. "In the old days, humans did not fare well when they met us on this night."

Annalise stared at her for a long moment. Finally, she shook the woman's hand off.

"These aren't the old days," she said. "And this is not the old country. Here, we help each other or die."

With that, she turned and clumped up the stairs to the doctor's porch, her feet feeling and behaving like lumps of ice. Before fumbling with the door knob, she looked over her shoulder.

The Fey man and woman were back on their horses. The pixie had found a home inside the male's tunic and he grinned at Annalise. A small hand worked its way out of the tunic to wave.

Annalise managed a wave, too, before weariness completely engulfed her.

ABOUT THE AUTHOR

Marcelle Dubé grew up near Montreal. After trying out a number of different provinces—not to mention Belgium—she settled in the Yukon, where people outnumber the carnivores, but not by much.

She writes science fiction, fantasy and mystery stories, and has 12 novels to her name. Her upcoming novel, *Epidemic: An A'lle Chronicles Mystery*, will be released in late 2018. Her short fiction has appeared in a number of magazines and anthologies.

Find out more about Marcelle at:
marcellemdube.com

f facebook.com/marcelle.dube.3
🐦 twitter.com/marcelledube
BB bookbub.com/authors/marcelle-dube
a amazon.com/Marcelle-Dub%25C3%25A9/e/B072LCS9R6

FAERY UNPREDICTABLE

DEB LOGAN

CHAPTER 1

I remember when my worst problem was that my parents were headed to the French Riviera without me. Boy, those were the good old days!

Back then—we're talking three months ago!—I had a mother and father who loved me, a decidedly weird grandmother who told tall tales, and Lexie, my very best friend who stood beside me as we started high school. So what if the parental units took a super fabulous vacation without me? We were a perfectly normal American family.

At least, I thought so at the time.

Turns out, we were as far from normal as it was possible to get, and now it was time to put on my big girl panties and walk straight into the lion's den of what I'd discovered was the other side of my heritage.

Because I'm definitely not just a typical American teen. I'm not even human anymore.

Nope, I'm a faery princess.

Truly.

For real.

My transformation began on my fifteenth birthday when Gran

introduced me to our family's guardian dragon, Roddy, and ended with my presentation to the King of Faery, Alberic, my too-many-greats-to-count grandpa on Halloween, or Samhain as the faery folk call it.

Yep. It's been a weird few months, but I'm adjusting...I think.

The doorbell rang, a five note fanfare that Dad had programmed when we bought this house. I took a deep breath, grabbed my powder blue fleece jacket from the back of the couch, and stepped to answer the summons. Roddy stood on the other side, his dark blond hair shining gold even in the dim winter sun that filtered through the shade of our wide front porch. Who knew jeans, hiking boots and a black leather jacket could look so sexy on a guy?

The sight of him warmed my heart and made me smile. Only six weeks ago he'd been a dragon, exiled from Faery since Rhiannon, the Faery king's daughter, had chosen to marry a mortal. King Alberic blamed Roddy for his daughter's defection. He cursed Roddy to life as a dragon and forced him to guard Rhiannon's family until her true heir should appear.

And who was that true heir? Why me, of course.

I'll never understand why fate chose me, or why it took as many centuries as it did for this heir-thing to materialize. I just know that I'm her heir and it's a genetic reality, not simply a political title I can decline.

On my fifteenth birthday, Roddy transferred his allegiance from my grandmother to me, and I discovered the truth about my heritage, that I was destined to not only take Rhiannon's place as Princess of Faery, but to become a full faery myself. Once I was presented to the royal court, I would no longer be human.

Great. Just what I always wanted: to lose my humanity and become part of a species I knew nothing about.

Roddy, in his guise of dragon, tried to prepare me for my presentation to the king, but he failed to mention that once I arrived in Faery, the king never intended for me to return to the mortal world. Of course, he also failed to mention that he, Roddy, was under a death sentence. Once I took my place in the royal court, his duty would be complete and the execution that had been deferred while the king awaited my arrival would be carried out.

It looked like King Alberic held all the power, but he hadn't reckoned on me.

I wasn't raised as a good citizen of Faery. I didn't know I was supposed to instantly obey the king's every whim. No sir! I grew up as a 21st century American woman. No king was going to dictate my life...or my dragon's death. I rebelled, and my rebellion nearly cost my life.

Incredibly, my bond with Roddy saved me, and Alberic, having nearly lost me before he'd even met me, released Roddy from his curse.

You can't begin to imagine my surprise when I discovered that my erstwhile dragon was actually a faery prince...and a really handsome one at that. Unbelievable!

And now the prince who had guarded my family as a dragon for generations stood on my front porch, ready to escort me to Faery. Christmas break had arrived and, according to the pact I'd negotiated with my many-times-removed grandfather, it was time for my first extended visit to Faery. The time had come for me to begin to learn my role as rightful heir to the High King's throne.

CHAPTER 2

R oddy and I stood at the center of a ring of enchanted roses, the air thick with their fragrance. Beyond the beautiful, if thorny, circle stood a castle, its windows shining in the morning light.

He held out his hand and smiled at me. I grabbed on like his fingers were a life preserver that would rescue me from certain death.

"Relax, Claire," he said, amusement coloring his words. "You've been to court before, you know what to expect. Besides, King Alberic loves you. He'll never admit it, of course, but he was thrilled with the way you stood up to him and demanded your right to return to your family. It proved you have the strength of will to rule."

I stared at him, eyes wide. "Really? I thought he was just humoring me because I nearly died."

"Well, there is that," he admitted with a shrug. "Come on. Alban Arthan is less than a week away and you have a lot to learn before the ceremony."

I sighed. "Great. I finally get a break from high school only to be forced into protocol school in Faery."

Roddy laughed and squeezed my hand. "Poor baby! Just think of all the little girls who dream of being fairy princesses. You owe it to them to enjoy this."

"Right," I grumbled. "Like any of them has a clue what they're wishing for. I think that falls under the category of 'the blessing of unanswered prayer.'"

"This is why I love you, Claire," he said, drawing me into bear hug. "You're such an optimist!"

He kissed me, and I forgot all my worries. If I had to give up my family and move to Faery to have Roddy in my life, the sacrifice would be worth it. I could grumble all I liked, but he was alive and well and back in his natural form because I was who and what I was.

Roddy lived. Everything else was secondary.

I broke our kiss and smiled up at him. "As long as you're with me, I can face anything. Even Grandpa Alberic. Come on. Let's go be royal."

At our approach, one of the roses bushes leapt aside and we stepped out of the threshold circle. An ornate black carriage pulled by silver stallions waited for us. Roddy handed me in and I settled beside a window, remembering my first carriage ride in Faery. Grandpa Alberic and his aide, Cadmar, had been with us on that journey. Well, I'd see them both soon enough.

Roddy bowed to the stallions, said, "To the castle," and joined me in the carriage. As soon as we were settled, the carriage moved forward.

"Seriously? No one's driving?"

"The horses know where they're going," Roddy said, his eyes twinkling. "Remember, Claire, you're in Faery now. This isn't Big Vista, Washington."

Well, duh! Can anyone say *understatement*?

It might be the middle of winter in my world, but in Faery the sun shone in a bright blue sky while perfect puffy white clouds scudded by. The grass in the meadow was an unbelievably vivid emerald green and littered with wildflowers of every color imaginable. If I'd expected a white Christmas, it looked like I was in for a disappointment.

As the carriage moved across the drawbridge and under the arch of the massive stone gate, I rubbed my hands down the denim of my jeans. Maybe I should have dressed the part, but I didn't own anything that I imagined a princess would wear. What did I know about being royal?

"Relax, Claire," Roddy said, noticing my nervous gesture. "You look fine. If Alberic wants you to dress in a certain way, he'll let you know...and he'll provide the wardrobe."

I nodded, licked my dry lips, and said, "I know. I just hope he doesn't expect me to suddenly become someone I'm not."

"Don't worry," he said, squeezing my hand. "I'm pretty sure you gave him a good idea of who you are and aren't at your last meeting. You're going to be fine, Claire. You were born to be Princess of Faery."

The carriage pulled to a stop before the wide steps leading to the main entrance. To each side of the huge carved wooden doors stood a knight in shining armor. Literally. Their armor gleamed in the morning sun like they'd just finished polishing it. The doors behind them opened and liveried footmen appeared, ran down the stairs, and opened the carriage doors. Before I could do more than blink, I'd been handed out of the carriage and escorted through the entry hall, down a wide corridor, and into Grandpa Alberic's study. Roddy strode beside me every step of the way.

Grandpa sat behind a large mahogany desk, its surface littered with important looking documents, maps, quills, and ink bottles. He looked up when Roddy and I entered the room, a wide smile softening his stern features. I grinned back at him, marveling again at just how deeply our family resemblance was written in our genes. His blue-black hair, fine boned face and clear, pale skin were the mirror image of my own. Even our eyes were the same shade of green, though his carried a depth of knowledge that I doubted I'd ever achieve. Looking at his unlined face and lithe body, it was difficult to imagine that he was old beyond my comprehension. How old? I had no idea, and I wasn't about to ask, but I knew he'd waited over a thousand years for his daughter's true heir to be born...and here I stood.

"Claire!" Grandpa exclaimed as he stood and came to meet me, arms open wide for a hug. "I'm so glad you're back. I can't tell you how dull life has been without our verbal battles."

Forgetting everything I'd learned about court protocol, I rushed to meet Grandpa and was immediately enfolded in a warm embrace.

"I'm glad to see you too, Grandpa," I said, my words muffled against the fawn-colored velvet of his doublet. I stepped back and looked up into his oh-so-familiar face. I'd only known him a short time, but he really did feel as much like family as Gran, who'd been part of my life forever. Maybe it was magic, or maybe blood really does tell.

Whatever! Grandpa was definitely part of my life now, and we were both anxious to make up for lost time.

"Prince Rhydderich," Grandpa said, nodding to Roddy while keeping one arm around my waist. "Thank you for escorting Claire home to Faery."

"It was my honor, sire," Roddy replied, executing a flawless bow with precisely the right amount of depth. I sighed inwardly, wondering if I'd ever be as confident in my courtesies as Roddy.

Grandpa inclined his head in acknowledgement of Roddy's bow, then smiled. "You're dismissed, Roddy. Your mother is in residence for the festival; go and find your family. I'm sure they're anxious to see you."

"Thank you, sire." Roddy glanced at me and grinned. "I'll see you later, my princess."

"Counting on it," I replied. "Say 'hi' to your mom and Bran for me."

"Of course," he said before turning and leaving the room.

Grandpa shook his head and held me at arms' length. "Really, Claire. We must work on your manners. 'Say 'hi' to your mom'? You were speaking of the Winter Queen!"

I shrugged. "Yeah, but I was also talking to my friend about his mother. Roddy knew what I meant, and he would've thought something was seriously wrong with me if I'd gone all formal on him."

Grandpa led me over to the hearth where a grouping of well-padded intricately carved wooden chairs stood before a blazing fire. I chose one with deep red velvet cushions and carvings of roses and vines. Grandpa settled in one carved with stags and hounds and sporting rich brown cushions.

"I suppose," he said, "but do try to limit your casual comments to family time. You can be familiar with Roddy when you are alone or the two of you are with me, but in front of courtiers, try to maintain a sense of dignity. There's been quite enough gossip about my heir and the heir of Winter already."

My eyes widened and I was glad I didn't have a drink to choke on. "People are gossiping about me and Roddy? Why?"

Grandpa narrowed his eyes, but seemed to decide I'd asked an honest question. "Because of who you are," he said, his tone suggesting he was explaining the obvious...which he probably was, "and the fact that Roddy has resumed his true form and walks the corridors of my castle."

I frowned. "Why does that lead to gossip about him and me?"

Grandpa sighed. "Claire, my entire kingdom knew that Roddy was under a sentence of death. Everyone knew that as soon as Rhiannon's true heir was returned to Faery, Roddy would die. But you're here and he's not only alive, he's been restored as Winter's heir. Obviously you did something to change my mind...for you're the only person in Faery who could have brought his redemption about. So just as obviously, he must be very special to you."

"Oh." Not my most brilliant come-back, but my brain was busy processing. I mean, I knew all of that, but ... "I guess I just never thought anyone would care enough to put those pieces together," I finally said, "or be interested enough to gossip about it."

Grandpa laughed out loud, a delighted sound that cheered my soul. "My darling, Claire! You are the most interesting thing to happen in Faery for centuries of your time. Everything you do, everything you say, even your smallest gesture will be of infinite interest to my subjects. To *your* subjects."

I startled, my mouth dropping open. I closed it with a snap, swallowed, and said, "Seriously? I'll be watched that closely?"

"What is the contraption the mortals use? Oh, yes. A microscope. Consider your life to be the focus of a microscope, Claire. Your people are curious about you. Everything about you. That is why you need to pay attention to your lessons with Ogham and Cadmar. Learn as quickly as you can. The sooner your actions are predictable and consistent with court etiquette, the sooner the intense scrutiny will abate."

"As long as you're an unpredictable faery," he continued, "the kingdom will watch your every move, wondering what you'll do next. Why, you've already saved Roddy's life and changed my plans for you. Both of those are things our people considered impossible. You're a full faery now, and yet I allow you to return to the mortal realm. Why? Because you bullied me into it. Of course people are curious about you!"

"I did not bully you," I said hotly, then more primly, "we negotiated."

He laughed again. "Of course we did! But no one else has ever forced me to *negotiate* something I'd already decided upon. You are a wonder in their eyes...and frankly, in mine as well."

Huh. Who knew that standing up for myself was such a novelty in Faery? Of course, these people were far older than they looked and had been dealing with each other for longer than I could imagine, so maybe my youth and inexperience would've made me unpredictable even if I hadn't been determined to save Roddy and live my life on my own terms.

At any rate, I'd pay attention to my lessons because I needed to understand this new world I was destined to live in, but I wasn't in a hurry to become predictable. I had the feeling that unpredictability might just turn out to be one of my most valuable tools. I just had to learn what was expected, so I'd recognize what wasn't.

Evidently, the first expectation I'd smashed to smithereens was that the High King never changed his mind. Good to know. And good to know that I could make the impossible happen.

CHAPTER 3

A routine established itself over the next few days. My faery maid, Elya, woke me each morning and helped me dress in one of the gorgeous gowns Grandpa had provided. As soon as I was presentable, which took remarkably little time considering I'd never have been able to figure out how arrange all those layers of cloth without Elya's help, I joined Grandpa for breakfast, a cheery way to start my day.

Next, I joined my friend Ogham, a handsome sorrel centaur who tutored me in magic, in his classroom. I'd come a long way in the few months he'd been teaching me and could now handle most basic spells and incantations.

When Ogham released me from class, I retired to my solar for lunch. I'd never heard of a solar until I visited Faery, but it turned out to be a pleasant sun-filled chamber that reminded me of a drawing room from a Regency romance novel. My own private reception room, with lots of large windows set in walls of some warm wood, like maybe cherry. The tile floors were covered with intricately woven rugs featuring Celtic knots and maze patterns, and the furniture seemed to change with the time of day. At lunch a large, a highly polished cherry dining table surrounded by beautifully carved chairs filled the space. At other times of day it featured comfy overstuffed chairs and couches artfully arranged in several conversation areas. I loved it. Especially when it was filled with people I was beginning to think of as friends: Roddy, Ogham, Bran, and various other faery folk I met on my visits to the Summer and Winter Courts before I was officially presented to Grandpa at Samhain.

The afternoons were my least favorite part of the day: protocol lessons with Cadmar. Grandpa's chief advisor was a tall, lean faery without an ounce of fun in his psychological make-up. He got off on the wrong foot with me early on by disrespecting Roddy, before I understood who Roddy truly was. Now that Grandpa had reinstated Roddy, Cadmar was a bit easier to take, but I still resented the way he'd acted in our first few meetings, which made our lessons a bit tense, and that was without even taking the subject matter into account.

So, cheerful breakfasts, fun mornings, entertaining lunches, and boring afternoons. No biggie; I could live with that. After all, I was a high school student. Especially since my evenings were reserved for Grandpa and Roddy.

The trouble began on the day before the festival of Alban Arthan.

I was enjoying lunch in my solar with Lady Meredith and Prince Bran and wishing Roddy could've joined us, when Cadmar entered the room. I knew immediately that something was up because the protocol master looked like a storm cloud had settled on his face.

Now, Cadmar's never been my favorite person and he always looks like someone stuffed a metal rod down his jacket, but we'd been getting along pretty well the last few days. Wondering what I could possibly have done wrong before I even got to his class, I stifled a sigh and controlled the urge to roll my eyes.

"Good afternoon, Cadmar," I said, trying to remember to phrase my comments appropriately. "Would you care to join us for lunch?"

Cadmar stopped across the table from me, bowed with a dignity I wasn't sure I'd ever learn, and said, "Thank you, Princess, but no. I've come to deliver a summons. Your grandsire, King Alberic, requires your presence in his study." He met my gaze straight on and added, "Immediately."

I swallowed, though my mouth was suddenly as dry as the Sahara. My heart drummed so loudly I could barely hear myself think, and my fingers froze to my silverware. What could I have possibly done? Grandpa had been fine last night. He and Roddy and I had played *Bows and Axes*, a board game that reminded me of a cross between chess and Battleship, and I'd lost spectacularly. A condition that always pleased Grandpa.

Forcing a calm I didn't feel, I placed my silverware neatly across my plate, wiped my fingers on my linen napkin, and rose. Nodding to Meredith and Bran, I said, "I'm sorry to leave in the middle of our meal, but duty calls."

As they murmured polite understanding, I walked around the table to join Cadmar, who offered me his arm. I declined his support and swept from my solar ahead of him. I knew the way to Grandpa's study; I didn't need a guide. The ringing of his booted feet on the stone floor told me Cadmar followed at the requisite distance, but the additional tramp of soldiers' boots failed to reassure me.

Why did I need an armed escort in the corridors of Grandpa's castle?

Something was seriously wrong, and I doubted I was the cause. I couldn't imagine doing anything to warrant such precautions.

When we reached the door to Grandpa's study, I paused to close my eyes, take a deep breath, and pull my thoughts under tight control. Cadmar took that opportunity to move past me to the door. I opened my eyes, exhaled quietly, and nodded to him. He opened the door. I stepped inside, and Cadmar closed the door behind me, leaving me alone with Grandpa.

King Alberic stood before the hearth, facing the merrily dancing flames. When the door closed, he turned to face me. If I hadn't already known something was wrong, I would've known it now. Grandpa's face was serious and drawn. For the first time since I'd known him, he looked old.

"Claire," he said, his voice quiet and somber. "Please, come and sit with me."

I didn't say a word. There are times to be boisterous and rowdy, or even sarcastic and flip. This was so not one of those times. Instead I walked across the room and settled in my favorite chair, the one with the red cushion and the rose and vine carvings. Grandpa perched on the edge of his seat, elbows on knees, hands clasped.

"I don't know how much Cadmar has told you about the upcoming festival, Alban Arthan," he said, then paused as if waiting for me to supply information. I took the hint.

"Alban Arthan, or midwinter, takes place tomorrow night. In my world it's known as the winter solstice, the shortest day of the year. After midwinter, the days begin to lengthen until we reach the spring equinox when day and night are of equal length. The days continue to get longer until midsummer, or the summer solstice, which is the longest day of the year. Right?"

He nodded. "From a human perspective, that's correct."

I frowned. "There's a difference between the human perspective and the faery perspective?" I asked. "I mean, the shortest day of the year is the shortest day of the year. It shouldn't matter which realm I'm in."

"Perhaps," he said, staring at his clasped hands, "but it does."

Silence reigned. Only the crackling of burning wood dared to break Grandpa's moody stillness. At last he looked up, sighed, and picked up the thread of our conversation.

"In Faery, magic is everything. Even the seasons change as a result of magic. I know that in the human realm where you were raised, people believe that science explains all, that the movement of the planets, the ebb and flow of the tides, the timing of light and dark are all based on scientific principles. Immutable principles."

He sighed again. "They're wrong. Their scientific knowledge explains their world only so long as Faery magic maintains its proper balance." He leaned forward and extended his hands to me. I laid mine in his and he grasped them tightly. "Something has happened that will disturb that balance. Something so catastrophic that both realms could find themselves locked in eternal winter."

I gasped and tried to pull away, but he held on tightly.

"This concerns you personally as well, Claire. Let me say it outright, then I'll explain as well as I can." He gazed into my eyes, and I saw sorrow and concern and steely determination reflected there. "The Wyrd Stone has been stolen and Roddy has been arrested. He is in the dungeon and you will not see him again. Do you understand what I'm saying?"

I yanked my hands from his, jumped up, and moved behind my chair. I wanted a barrier between him and me. I gripped the carved wood of its back and glared at the King of Faery.

"No!" I shouted. "I don't understand and I don't believe you. You're just looking for a way out of the deal you made with me. You want Roddy dead! You've always wanted him dead. I ruined your original plans and now you've found a new reason to persecute him."

I raced to the door, had my hand on the knob before I turned to throw my final barb. "If it's a choice between you and Roddy. I choose Roddy. Always."

I wanted to storm from the room, but Alberic was too fast for me.

"Stop!" he commanded, and I froze. He pointed at the door. "Lock."

A current of magic ruffled my hair like a summer breeze. I was trapped and I knew it. He released his hold on me, and I slumped against the door that was now useless to me until he chose to allow me to leave.

"Come and sit down, Claire." The king's voice was gentle, the words carried no command.

I stayed beside the door.

"Why do you think I commanded Cadmar to bring you here?" he asked quietly. When I didn't respond, he answered his own question. "Because I knew you would react this way. I know how close you are to Roddy, but you must believe me, Claire. I'm not trying to frame Roddy as your human friends would phrase it. He has been arrested because he is the only one with sufficient reason to do this foul thing."

"Yeah. Right. He's also the only faery who has lived after you decreed that he should die," I snarled. "You're just looking for a way to fix that little problem." I stepped away from the door and folded my arms across my chest. "What's your evidence? Why should I believe you, and why can't I see Roddy and hear his side of the story?"

"Think, Claire! We've held this ceremony for thousands of years... and the first time Roddy is back in Faery, the Wyrd Stone goes missing?"

"So? It's also the first time *I've* been in Faery for Alban Arthan, why haven't you thrown *me* in the dungeon?"

He sat down in his favorite chair, the one carved with stags and hounds, and scrubbed his hands across this face. "Because you have no idea what or where the Wyrd Stone is," he said in a resigned voice, "and you don't have an ancient score to settle with me."

I huffed. "And Roddy does?"

"Of course he does, Claire! I transformed him into a dragon and forced him to guard your bloodline for more of your centuries than I like to count. Because of me, he had to watch his best friend grow old and die in the mortal world. Because of me, he believed he would be executed the moment he presented you to me."

"Prince Rhydderich has more than sufficient reason to hate me, Claire," he said quietly, once again staring at his hands. When he glanced up, he motioned me to my chair, and this time I moved. Once I was seated, he continued, "There's one final mark against Roddy," he said gruffly, as if determined to get all the nastiness out in the open. "He is Winter's heir, and without the Wyrd Stone, Winter will remain ascendant forever."

I slumped against the back of my chair. "Okay," I said. "I can see your reasoning," I held up my hand to stop the comment he was about to make, "but you're wrong. Your evidence is circumstantial. You have no proof, only suppositions based on his title and your presumptions about his feelings. Just because *you'd* want revenge, doesn't mean Roddy does. I know Roddy, a lot better than you do now. Probably better than you ever did. He's innocent."

A horrible thought floated to the surface of my mind. I glared at Grandpa and growled, "Don't even think about torturing him to force him to give you information he doesn't have."

An expression flitted across his face and I knew I'd guessed the real reason Roddy was in the dungeon and the king had forbidden me to see him.

Putting all the steel I could manage in my voice, I said, "If you harm him, if you so much as touch him, I will go back to Big Vista and refuse to ever set foot in Faery again."

His face went stern and cold. "What makes you think I would allow that to happen?"

"Rhiannon accomplished it," I said, making my expression mirror his. "If she could escape you, so can I."

We stared at each other, both determined not to flinch from the confrontation.

Grandpa looked away first. I think I won because I was fighting for Roddy's life again, while he was just defending his right to rule. I had the greater stake in our conflict.

Grandpa turned, pointed at the door, and said, "Open!"

The door flew open, revealing Cadmar on the other side.

"Cadmar," the king commanded. "Hear and obey."

Cadmar went to one knee on the threshold. "Always, my king."

"Release Prince Rhydderich from the dungeon. Escort him to his chambers and seal him inside. None may enter his chamber except you, me, Princess Claire, and one knight of your choosing who will see to the Prince's needs while he is under suspicion."

Throwing a scowl at me, Cadmar rose, inclined his head to the king, and said, "It shall be done immediately, my king."

Grandpa flicked his fingers at the door and it closed behind the courtier.

"Does that satisfy you, Princess?" His voice was still cold, his expression grim.

"Thank you, Grandpa," I said, vowing to myself not to cross him again for anything short of a life and death situation. "Roddy and I will figure this out."

His frown deepened until I thought his face might crack. "Did you not hear..."

"I'm sorry," I interrupted. "I know Roddy is in prison. I just meant I'd tell him everything I learn and he'll help me figure it out. How much time do I have? Will you be looking for other suspects too?"

Relief lightened his features. "You...we all have until midnight of the Festival of Alban Arthan—that's tomorrow night—and yes, I will instruct Cadmar to search for others who might have done this terrible deed."

"Thank you, Grandpa," I said. I stood, moved to his side, and kissed his forehead. "We'll find the Wyrd Stone...and I'll prove Roddy is innocent. He doesn't hate you, Grandpa. He's not like that."

Grandpa caught my hand and kissed it. "I hope you're right, Claire," he said, his voice rough with emotion. "For all our sakes."

CHAPTER 4

R oddy turned when I stepped across the threshold of his chamber. An expression of joy and wonder lit his features and he rushed to hug me. I relaxed into his embrace, soothed by the strength of his arms and the steady beat of his heart. No way would I allow anyone—not the king, not some unknown thief—to separate me from Roddy.

"Claire! How did you do this?" he asked, but before I could say anything he hurried on as though he'd been waiting to talk, and perhaps he had. "I knew it had to have been you. Cadmar was livid when he released me from the dungeon and brought me up here. You're the only one I know who can upset him that much."

He pushed me to arm's length, but held onto my shoulders, his expression serious. "I didn't do it, Claire. I need you to know, to believe, that I'm not guilty."

"Of course you're innocent," I said, my eyes widening. "You didn't really think I'd believe them, did you?"

He relaxed slightly and hugged me again. When we broke apart, he kissed the top of my head and scrubbed his eyes. "No," he said. "Not really. But I worried. I was afraid I'd never see you again. Never get to tell you..."

"I know," I murmured. "Grandpa tried to forbid me to see you, but that didn't work out as he expected." I grinned. "He's got to get over thinking I'm just going to do what he says. Not going to happen," I said, shaking my head. "Not when I disagree with his command."

We walked over to the hearth where a grouping of three hunter green overstuffed chairs waited. Like my own chambers, Roddy's consisted of two rooms—a sitting room and a bedroom. A large fireplace occupied the wall between the rooms, opening into each so that one fire blazed in both. Besides the chairs before the hearth, the sitting room contained a walnut desk situated between two long, narrow windows, and a small dining table just big enough to accommodate two straight-back chairs. The stone floors were strewn with shorn sheepskin rugs.

I curled into one of the overstuffed chairs, while Roddy sat opposite me.

"Okay," I said. "We both know you didn't steal the Wyrd Stone, but we've got to figure out who did and get it back before it's needed for the ceremony."

"Yes," Roddy agreed. "Unless I want to spend the rest of my life in these rooms, we've got to clear my name."

I nodded. "So, tell me about this Wyrd Stone. I was so worried about getting you out of the dungeon that I didn't think to ask Grandpa."

"I appreciate that," Roddy said with a quick grin.

"You can skip the part about Alban Arthan and the length of days stuff. I've got all that. Just tell me about the stone. What is it...what does it look like...and why is it so important?"

A slight frown creased his forehead as he concentrated on my questions. "The Wyrd Stone is a magic artifact from our ancient history. It contains immense power and is used to control the turning of the seasons. Twice a year we unveil it in a sun ceremony. At Alban Arthan it turns the tide of days so that they begin to lengthen in preparation for the Summer Court's ascendance at Beltane. When it's used at Litha, midsummer, the days begin to shorten."

I shook my head. This all sounded like superstitious nonsense to me. "I don't know," I said. "I always thought the length was daylight was determined by the earth's position in relation to the sun. You know, as the planet orbits the sun...it's not a perfect circle. The ellipsoid pattern causes the daylight to vary."

"That's right," he agreed, "as far as it goes. What science doesn't understand is that the earth's orbit is controlled by the Wyrd Stone."

"Seriously?" I gaped at him. "You're telling me that some little rock in Faery makes the earth circle the sun? Roddy! That makes absolutely no sense."

He smiled and leaned back in his chair, steepling his fingers under his chin. "Think of it like this, Claire. If you had a radio-controlled plane, it would fly, but you'd control it from the ground with a radio transmitter. The plane would receive the signals and respond accordingly. If you stopped sending orders, the plane would fly in a straight line until it crashed into something, right?"

I nodded. I'd never flown an RC plane, but I understood what he was saying.

"The earth's orbit around the sun is like that. The Wyrd Stone is the transmitter, the earth's core the receiver. Twice a year, we adjust the earth's orbit with the stone. If the adjustment isn't made, the earth maintains its position relative to the sun and the length of days remains static."

He sighed. "I suppose the king thinks I did it because I'm heir to Winter and if the Wyrd Stone isn't found, the days won't lengthen and Winter will be eternal."

"Something like that," I agreed. "Of course he also thinks you want revenge against him for all those centuries you spent as a dragon in the human world guarding my family."

His eyes widened and he sat forward. "Really? He said that?"

"Yep."

"Well," he said, leaning back again. "If I ever get the chance to talk to him, I'll have to ease his mind." Roddy smiled at me. "After all, if I hadn't been a dragon assigned to your family, I'd never have known you...and you were worth the wait, Claire."

My cheeks warmed with a blush and a happy, shivery feeling

spread from my belly to the tips of my fingers and toes. Roddy certainly knew how to make a girl feel special!

The heady moment was broken when the door to Roddy's chambers opened and a faery knight stepped over the threshold.

"Excuse me, Princess," he said, standing rigidly at attention, "but Prince Rhydderich's evening meal has arrived. Will you be joining him?"

I glanced at Roddy and quirked an eyebrow. He grinned.

"Yes, I believe I will," I told the knight. "And you are?"

"Javan, your highness. Cadmar assigned me to assist Prince Rhydderich during his...uh...incarceration."

"Thank you, Javan. Please continue with your duties."

Roddy and I sat quietly while Javan arranged our meal on the small walnut dining table across the room. I noticed several pixies hovering outside the open door. They'd undoubtedly prepared and delivered our dinner, but were prevented from entering the room by Grandpa's geis.

The small, nut-brown creatures scrutinized Javan's every move, their large, dark eyes filled with concern as he arranged the dishes. One in particular seemed to be in charge. He twisted the hem of his apron in his long-fingered hands and hissed loudly whenever Javan set a plate or a spoon in the wrong position.

Javan, for his part, was sensitive to the pixies' instructions, glancing at them frequently for cues as to where items belonged.

At last the table was set and Javan, obviously relieved, stepped to the door, bowed, and left, shooing the pixies from the threshold as he closed the door.

Roddy rose from his overstuffed chair and held out his hand to me. "Shall we dine, my princess?"

I grinned, jumped to my feet, and took his hand, enjoying the warmth of his fingers on my own. "Let's eat," I said. "I'm starved."

The pixies had outdone themselves, and my mouth watered as Roddy seated me at the small dining table. Grilled trout on a bed of lemon and parsley, wild rice in mushroom sauce, a beautifully arranged platter of fresh fruit—including some I'd never seen before

—and a tureen of a hearty vegetable soup. Not to mention the most lavishly decorated cake I could've imagined, if baking and cake decorating was my thing, which it most definitely was not.

The frosting looked like it was spun from moonbeams with tiny stars twinkling in its sugary depths. Delicate rosebuds shimmered against a heavenly blue background while the whole confection seemed to hover above the raised dais of its plate. I couldn't begin to guess the flavors I'd taste when I had my first bite...and I really didn't want to wait until I'd finished the main course!

"Wow!" I exclaimed. "I don't think prisoners eat like this in the human realm. You must really rate with the kitchen staff."

Roddy laughed, and I smiled, pleased to have elicited that carefree sound.

"Well, I am a prince," he said, filling his plate with trout, rice, and fruit, "and the heir to the reigning monarch. Everyone wants to please royalty...at least until I'm proven guilty and banished from Faery."

"Which you won't be, because you're not," I said quickly, dismayed to see his light mood vanishing. I dipped a cup of soup from the tureen, inhaling a savory fragrance that sang of fresh, growing things, and turned our discussion to another topic. "You haven't told me what the Wyrd Stone looks like. How will I recognize it when I find it?"

He paused, a bite of flaky fish almost to his lips. "It's a brilliant blue stone about the size of your fist," he said, popping his fork into his mouth. He chewed, swallowed, and continued, "But you won't have to worry about recognizing it. If you get close, you'll know it."

I swallowed a spoonful of the delicious soup and frowned. "How?"

"It'll call to you, especially this close to midwinter. You'll hear its song and you'll be drawn to it. It's irresistible when it's ready to work its magic."

I nodded, set my soup aside, and filled my plate with tender fish, savory rice, and succulent fruit. I definitely needed to make friends with the pixies. After all, I was royalty too, and this was a better meal than they'd been feeding me. Of course, I wasn't in prison. Maybe they felt sorry for Roddy and were making an extra effort to please him.

"So, since we know you're innocent," I said between bites, "who would you suspect?"

He laid down his fork, wiped his fingers on a napkin of such fine linen it seemed a shame to soil it, and frowned. "Part of the reason I'm a suspect is because I'm Winter's heir. Since winter would continue if the Wyrd Stone couldn't perform its function, we'd benefit. But I can't believe that any of my family, or anyone under Mother's influence, would do such a thing. I also don't believe that anyone connected to Winter would leave me to take the blame for their actions. I've been gone so long, and everyone seems genuinely glad to have me home and free."

I pushed a piece of something that might have been pineapple except for its purple color around my plate, avoiding Roddy's gaze. "What about Bran?" I asked quietly. "He was heir in your absence... your return has pushed him back into second son status."

Peeking at him through my lashes, I saw him lean back in his chair and steeple his fingers beneath his chin.

"If he's upset, he's been doing a really good job of hiding it," he said. "I don't want to believe anyone in Winter has done this, but I suppose Bran would have the strongest motive...after me, of course."

I nodded. Bran was on my short list of suspects to investigate. I hoped for Roddy's sake that his brother was as innocent as I knew Roddy to be.

"Okay, leaving Winter aside, who else might benefit?"

"Well, there aren't all that many courtiers who are tied solely to the High King's court and I can't think of any reason one of them would do this. Your grandfather reigns regardless of whether Winter or Summer is in ascendance. His court is above the changing of the seasons."

"So that leaves the Summer Court, right?"

"Yes."

We'd finished our meal by that time, and I watched with an

unseemly anticipation as Roddy sliced the amazing cake. The frosting sparkled like sunlight on water or starlight in a clear midnight sky, its color shimmered through the visible spectrum, and very likely beyond. I could hardly wait to taste the airy confection that spectacular frosting contained.

I held my breath as Roddy lifted a slice of layered cake, deposited it on a gold plate, and presented it to me.

"Is this your first slice of celestial cake, my princess?"

I lifted my gaze from the enchanting cake to his face. "Is that what this is?"

He smiled. "It is. The kitchen pixies know it's my favorite."

I nodded, scarcely hearing his words. Celestial cake. Beneath the frosting, the cake was startlingly white. A white so pristine it would make the purest snowfall seem dingy and grey. Its aroma was intoxicating. A delightful mixture of nature's best: chocolate, honey, a garden full of blooms warmed by sunlight and a fresh spring breeze. My mouth watered in anticipation of the taste that would accompany that fragrance.

With trembling fingers, I lifted my first bite to my lips. A starburst of flavor exploded across my tongue, arousing a sensory experience in my whole body. The taste tickled my nose and tingled in my fingertips and toes. It warmed my belly and elicited a sensation of comfort and safety and...love. How extraordinary! A cake that tasted like love.

Faery was an amazing place.

"It's good isn't it?" asked Roddy, enjoying a bite of his own piece of cake.

"Good?" I gasped, barely able to speak. "How can you call this cake good? It's so far beyond good, it's...it's ..." my words stumbled to a stop. I had no words. I was incapable of rational thought. I closed my eyes and savored every delicate sensation of that indescribable dessert.

When the last crumb had disappeared, and I felt capable of speech again, I opened my eyes to find Roddy smiling at me.

"That was incredible," I said, as content as a purring cat.

"I'll be sure to have Javan tell the pixies how much you enjoyed your meal."

"Do that," I said, eying the remainder of the cake. "Honestly though, I'm not sure that cake should be legal. I mean, talk about addictive."

"Not to worry," he said. "The pixies are under strict orders not to make it too often."

With that, he opened the door to let Javan know we'd finished our meal. While the faery knight cleared the table, Roddy escorted me back to our comfortable overstuffed chairs. After that amazing meal, I felt a deep kinship for their stuffed status.

When all evidence of our meal had been removed and the door closed behind Javan, we returned to our earlier conversation.

"So," I said, "who do you suspect in the Summer Court?"

Roddy leaned back, elbows resting on the upholstered arms of the chair. "I don't know. It doesn't make any sense for anyone in the Summer Court to steal the Wyrd Stone during Winter's reign. If the stone doesn't exert its power, Summer won't return to ascendance. They have no motive."

His fingers drummed a tattoo against the chair, and then suddenly stopped.

"Unless..."

"Unless, what?" I asked, leaning toward him.

"Unless you were the motive."

"Me?" I yelped. "How could I be a motive for someone in Summer stealing the Wyrd Stone? I didn't even know it existed until today."

"Well," he said, a bit hesitantly. "It's just that it suddenly occurred to me that Idris might have a motive. I mean, everyone knows that you and I are close." He stopped, swallowed, glanced at me and then studied the floor.

"And?" I prompted.

"And, well, all the courts are gossiping about us and ..."

I threw up my hands in exasperation. "I don't see how people gossiping about us could be a motive for Idris to steal the Wyrd Stone."

"Fine," he said. "Here it is. He's a prince, too. If he's jealous of your feelings for me, he might steal the stone to frame me. That way he'd get rid of me and be able to make a play for you himself. You know he was interested at the Samhain Ball."

"Interested in dancing," I countered, my face blazing.

"No, Claire. Interested in marrying you, the heir to the High King."

"Then he's not interested in me, he doesn't know me. He's interested in the throne. Not the same thing at all."

"People could say the same thing about me," he said quietly.

The warmth of my blush died and I leaned forward to take his hands. "Then they don't know either of us," I said. "I fell for you while you were still a dragon, and you...well you know me better than anyone. Sometimes I think you know me better than I know myself."

I squeezed his hands. "Look at me, Roddy."

He lifted his eyes and gazed into mine.

"I know you care for me, not just my position as heir to the throne. You know how I know?"

"I think so, but I'd like to hear you say it."

"Because you cared for me when you didn't expect to live. You were my guardian and friend even though you expected Grandpa to kill you as soon as you presented me to him. But most of all, I know that you love me because your kiss, our bond, pulled me back into my body when I should have died."

I leaned closer and kissed his cheek. "Never doubt our love, Roddy. I don't."

Our lips were a centimeter from a passionate kiss when the door opened and Cadmar strode in.

Roddy and I jerked apart, but not before Cadmar noticed our proximity.

"Princess, your grandsire asked me to escort you to your chambers. You've spent far too much time in this miscreant's company."

"Watch it, Cadmar," I said, with a distinct growl in my voice. "You're on shaky ground."

"I'm only concerned for your reputation, Princess. I told your grandsire that you shouldn't be allowed to spend unchaperoned time with this...this ..."

"Don't finish that sentence, Cadmar. Not if you value your position at court."

He drew himself up to his full height, his silver hair sparkling in the light.

"As for the unchaperoned part, Roddy and I have been together for months in Big Vista. No one's been watching over us there."

Cadmar sniffed. "That was different. He was a dragon at the time. Now, however, it's highly irregular for you to be spending time in a man's chambers without proper..."

"He's under arrest," I yelled. "Where else am I supposed to see him when he can't leave these rooms?"

"I've offered my services as chaperone."

"No way," I cried, jumping to my feet and advancing on him. "You just want to spy on us. You don't want me to find the real thief. You just want Grandpa to have an excuse to execute Roddy after all."

I stepped close to him and poked him in the chest with my index finger. "Tell me, Cadmar. Did you steal the stone to frame Roddy? Did you take it so Grandpa would do him in and you wouldn't have to deal with him anymore? Did you?"

Cadmar's pale face whitened, but his eyes blazed. "How dare you?"

"Claire."

Roddy's quiet voice broke through my rage. I turned to find him standing beside his chair. He held out a hand to me and I strode to his side and grasped it.

"It's all right, Claire," he said, soothingly. "It's getting late. Perhaps it's time we said good night. Come see me tomorrow?"

"Of course," I said. "Wild horses couldn't keep me away." I glared at Cadmar. "Or even obnoxious courtiers." I squeezed Roddy's fingers and stretched to kiss his cheek, then swept from the room without another word to Cadmar.

CHAPTER 5

The next morning I sent Billow, a storm sprite I'd met at the Winter Court, to Cadmar to inform him that our lessons were at an end. At least until Roddy's name was cleared.

With that task accomplished, I almost ran to Ogham's classroom. The centaur who mentored me in the use of magic had been friends with Roddy for centuries. I knew he'd help me solve the mystery of the disappearing Wyrd Stone.

For being inside the High King's castle, Ogham's classroom was remarkably like the cave he'd been living in when I first met him. Rock walls, packed earth floor, huge fireplace, and a scarred work-table. Even the carved marble bench I'd rested on during that first meeting was the same.

I settled on the bench while Ogham chopped herbs at the table.

"So our friend is in trouble again," he said, somberly. "Tell me everything, Claire."

So I did. I told him how Grandpa had started by forbidding me to see Roddy right through to all our suspicions and suppositions.

"Not much real evidence to work with," he said when I finished my recitation, "and not much time to figure it out. Where do you plan to start?"

"I'm going to start with Bran," I said. "Figure out where he stands. If he's with us, he'll be able to help. If he's not...well, if he's not, he goes to the top of my list of likely suspects."

Ogham nodded. "I'll make a tour of the castle today. See if I can detect where the stone might be hidden. Finding it won't clear Roddy, but it will certainly ease the tension."

"Good plan. Meet me in my solar for lunch and we'll compare notes."

"Good hunting, Princess."

I nodded and left him to his work.

Where to find Bran? I knew he was somewhere in the castle; both the Winter and Summer courts were in attendance for the celebration, but the High King's castle was enormous. Especially now with magical spells laid upon it, expanding it to fit all the dignitaries. If I wasn't so angry with Cadmar, I'd be really impressed with his managerial skills. As it was, well, I was better off not thinking about him at all.

I could wander these corridors for a week and still not run across Prince Bran. I stopped, leaned against the cool stone wall and gazed out a nearby window at the endlessly fascinating landscape that was Faery. Magical castle...magical landscape that bloomed in midwinter...missing magical stone. Everything here was magical.

Including me!

I rolled my eyes and slapped my forehead with the palm of my hand. Of course! I didn't need to search the castle for Bran. I needed to remember who I was—a magical being, and royalty at that!

Closing my eyes, I reached within myself to the well of magical energy that pooled at my core, tapped it, and set my intention. *I need to see Prince Bran at his earliest convenience. Preferably now.* Releasing the magic, I sent my summons winging to Queen Maeve's youngest son.

A moment later, Prince Bran shimmered into existence a few feet from where I stood. Dressed casually in a leather vest over a snowy linen shirt and dark breeches, he was still unbelievably handsome.

My heart flip-flopped as he sketched a courtly bow and then cocked a questioning silver eyebrow at me.

Silver and gold, that described Maeve's sons. I'd first known Roddy as a dragon, a magnificent molten gold beast with mesmerizing emerald eyes. Now, in his natural form as a faery prince, my friend was golden-haired, his skin tanned to perfection.

Bran, on the other hand, was silver. His hair wasn't blond and it wasn't grey; it flowed around his face and shoulders like a stream of liquid silver, highlighting his grey-blue eyes and accenting his pale, porcelain skin. Bran was every inch the handsome faery prince.

"How may I be of service, Princess Claire?" he asked, his tone friendly, but a bit puzzled. Faery royalty rarely summoned each other with magic. Grandpa always sent a courtier to find me.

My cheeks heated under his quizzical gaze, while my heart thundered like a herd of galloping horses. I reached within, sought calm, and found it. I hadn't summoned Bran to admire his admittedly handsome face. I needed to determine his guilt...or innocence...in the matter of the missing Wyrd Stone.

"Thank you for coming so quickly, Prince Bran," I said, pleased by how calm and steady my voice sounded. "Will you walk with me? I have something I'd like to discuss."

"Of course, milady." He smiled, offered me his arm, and led me to a set of wide French doors that opened onto a stunningly beautiful formal garden. Flowers of every size and shape lined a maze of white-stoned walkways, a riot of color in what should have been the gloom of winter.

We stepped onto the path and I was immediately aware of hundreds of flower faeries watching us from beneath petals and leaves. I hesitated. This wouldn't do. I wanted my conversation with Bran to be private.

Bran felt my hesitance, glanced around, breathed a sigh of understanding, and whispered to me. "You can dismiss them, Claire. This is your domain."

"Oh," I said, an interesting mixture of embarrassment and relief warming my cheeks. "Of course. Thank you, Prince Bran."

He laid his free hand over mine where it rested near his elbow. "Please, call me Bran. We're practically family."

"Okay, if you call me Claire."

He inclined his head. "Agreed, Claire."

I smiled, took a deep breath, and surveyed the faeries in the garden. "Thank you all so much for making this garden such a pleasant place," I said, hoping my voice would carry to all the tiny creatures. "Another time I'd love to get to know you all, but today I need to have a private conversation with Prince Bran. Please leave and don't return until I go back into the castle."

A sigh of breeze wafted through the garden and when it stilled, Bran and I were alone.

"Nicely done, Claire," he said. "Not everyone treats the little folk with such courtesy."

I glanced at him in surprise. "Seriously? Well, shame on them. I'm very fond of the flower faeries. Especially the ones who inhabit our garden at home."

He nodded and led me to a marble bench beside a stunning rhododendron overflowing with the palest of pink blossoms. Once we were seated, he turned to me, his expression serious. "Now, how can I assist you, Claire? I doubt you summoned me just for a walk in the garden."

"No," I said. "I wanted to discuss Roddy's current, ah, situation. You know what's going on, don't you?"

His jaw tightened and he turned his gaze from me to his hands, clasped tightly in his lap. "I do," he said, his voice rough with...what? Suppressed anger? "I know that his association with you has once again led him into peril."

My breath caught and my heart constricted. I stared at him, open-mouthed. "What?" I cried. "You're blaming *me* for this?"

His hands relaxed and his shoulders slumped. He leaned forward, bracing his forearms on his knees. "No," he said with a sigh. "Of course not. Not really."

My pulse settled and I breathed a little easier.

"It's just that it's hard to see Mother so upset again," he continued.

"She's been closed off, stoic, for centuries. Worried and frightened and afraid to love anyone, even me, for fear her loved one would be snatched away." He looked at me and I saw deep pain reflected in his eyes. "She'd just begun to recover; having Roddy home whole and healthy allowed her to relax and be happy again. But now..." He stopped, too emotional to continue.

"I'm so sorry, Bran," I whispered. "You know I'd never do anything to hurt Roddy."

He nodded, returning his gaze to the grass at his feet. "I know," he said, quietly. "I've been a bit jealous since he's been back. Everything has seemed to go his way. He's Mother's heir again. He has King Alberic's favor. And," he gazed into my eyes, "he's got this amazing bond with you. I envy him your regard."

My pulse jumped and then settled as I saw the truth in this silver-haired faery's eyes. He admired me, but he loved his brother. Bran was not the villain of this mystery.

"But then I remembered," he continued, "the price he paid for what he was enjoying, and all envy fled. My brother has endured so much hardship in his life. He deserves all the happiness he can find."

"Thank you for your honesty, Bran," I said quietly, placing my hand on his arm. "I had to know the truth."

He startled and stared at me, wide-eyed. "Wait," he cried. "You thought...you couldn't have...you suspected *me* of stealing the Wyrd Stone and framing Roddy?"

I shrugged. "It was a possibility. I had to investigate."

His jaw dropped. When he closed it, a pallor of pain settled on his already pale features. "Does Roddy think so?"

"No," I said, shaking my head so hard my short curls bounced. "He agreed I should question you, but he knew you wouldn't do such a thing."

He breathed deeply, closing his eyes. "Good," he said. "I wouldn't want him to think me so disloyal."

I sat quietly, giving Bran a moment to compose himself. When he opened his eyes, he nodded to me. "How can I help?"

A warm glow settled in my middle. I had help. Roddy might be under house arrest, but Ogham and Bran were ready to help me clear his name. I might be a stranger in a strange land trying to understand the incomprehensible, but I had people who understood the rules to guide me.

I jumped to my feet and paced back and forth in front of the bench where Bran continued to sit. "Okay. We know Roddy didn't steal it and neither did you." I stopped in front of him, frowning. "So, who do you think it might have been?"

He leaned back, flicking away a rhododendron blossom that brushed his cheek. "No one in Winter," he said. "I know our court must look guilty, but everyone is so relieved to see Mother happy again that they'd never risk exposing either Roddy or me to harm. My people love Mother. They'd never do anything to cause her pain."

I nodded and started pacing again. What can I say? I think better on the move. "That leaves Grandpa's court and Summer. Neither of which would seem to have a motive." I plopped onto the bench beside Bran. "What am I missing?"

He shrugged. "Whatever it is, I'm missing it too. I can't see why anyone would steal the stone. It doesn't benefit Summer, and while you could argue that Winter would win, its theft is causing our queen pain, and the high king's court has no reason at all to steal it." His eyes met mine. "This makes no sense."

I breathed deeply, inhaling the sweet floral scent of the sun-warmed garden. Magic was in the air. I studied the flowers and the impressive structure of the High King's castle. I was heir to all of this. Castle, kingdom, and the magic that flowed through all of it.

"Fine. I've investigated you," I smiled at Bran, "and you passed with flying colors. Now I need to talk to Idris. Roddy thinks I might be a motive for Idris to misbehave."

Bran raised an eyebrow, and I felt an embarrassed flush heat my neck and cheeks.

"Yes," he said. "I can see my brother's point. If I may make a suggestion, Princess?"

"Of course."

"Don't summon Idris with magic—he's not likely to be as understanding as I—send a messenger instead."

"Oh," I said. "Did I do something wrong? I'm so sorry, Bran."

"Don't be concerned, Claire," he said. "I didn't take offense, but it is considered rude to summon as you did. Especially since your royal summons has a compulsion attached. Courtiers don't like being compelled."

Shame flooded my system. "Of course they don't. Most of my fights with Grandpa are about him trying to force me to do or not do something. I had no idea my summons had a compulsion attached. Thank you for telling me."

He nodded. "I thought as much. Let's go inside, that will let the flower faeries return. Once they're back, you can ask one to request that Idris join us for lunch."

We strolled back to the castle door and stepped inside. I watched as a breeze swept gently through the garden. When the leaves and blossoms stilled, I felt the gaze of hundreds of eyes settle on me.

"They're back," I whispered, and stepped over the threshold into the garden once more. "Is Una here?" I asked, holding out my right hand.

A tiny flower faery fluttered to me and hovered above my outstretched fingers. She was perfectly proportioned and about the size of my fist, with curly red hair and wearing a bright yellow Tinker Bell dress.

I smiled at her. "Thank you for coming, Una. Would you please find Prince Idris and ask him to join me for lunch in my solar?"

She bobbed a curtsy in mid-air. "Of course, Princess Claire. It is my honor to assist." She fluttered away on gossamer wings, and I returned to the castle corridor where Bran waited.

CHAPTER 6

Lunch with Ogham, Bran and Idris was a complete disaster. Summer's heir had never joined me for lunch before. His sisters had come a time or two, but I think Idris had been waiting for an invitation, and now that he had one, he seemed a bit miffed to find Bran there as well. The dark-haired prince's expression was surly when he nodded to me and he fairly glared at Bran. Ogham he ignored completely.

He was accompanied by a courtier, a young man named Keldan who I'd met once or twice. The faery knight was Idris's opposite in looks. Where the prince's hair was blue-black and his eyes a gorgeous sapphire blue, Keldan's hair was such a pale blond it appeared white, and his brown eyes were touched with gold. Following his prince's lead, he held his silence in a cool and aloof manner.

The pixies had outdone themselves, presenting us with an excellent meal of creamy potato soup with leeks and garlic, fresh crusty bread with real, melt-in-your-mouth butter, and a selection of every kind of cheese imaginable. But our conversation was stilted, even before I got around to asking about the Wyrd Stone.

"Excuse me," said Idris, his voice dripping with sarcasm. "Am I to understand that in addition to having my birthright stolen—for if the

Wyrd Stone is lost, Summer will never come to power again—you're actually accusing me of the stone's theft? Why would I steal the stone? And if you think it would be because I wish to blame Rhydderich, my next question is why would I wish to harm that miscreant you have chosen to befriend?"

Bran saved me from answering a potentially embarrassing question.

"Because my brother stands between you and the High King's throne," Bran said calmly, though his voice was deadly serious. "Roddy has Princess Claire's favor, and while he lives, you don't stand a chance of gaining her hand."

Keldan gasped, and Idris rose so quickly his chair toppled over. He didn't bother righting it, but strode around the cherry dining table headed for the door, Keldan hurrying to keep up. The prince stopped part way there, and turning to face me, said in a glacial voice, "I'm sure you're very charming, Princess Claire, but you are allowing your association with Winter to blind you more effectively than if you were lost in a blizzard. I am content to be heir to my own kingdom, poor that they may be in comparison to your own brilliant prospects."

He bowed to me, started to turn toward the door, then cocked his head and said, "See that you discover the whereabouts of the Wyrd Stone, for without it, my own prospects are bleak. Look to Winter, milady, for they are the only faeries who profit by the stone's loss."

With that pronouncement, Idris and Keldan left my solar.

"Well," said Ogham. "I don't know whether to take that as righteous indignation or bluster designed to disguise guilt. What do you think, Bran?"

Roddy's brother gazed thoughtfully at the door where Idris and Keldan had disappeared. "I've never liked Idris," he said. "We've been rivals over one thing or another since childhood, but I can't see him stooping to something like this."

"But," I broke in, "he didn't answer the question. He just deflected by asking his own, and did you see Keldan's face? He was paler than death. Doesn't that make the pair of them seem guilty?"

"Perhaps," said Bran, "or perhaps we simply caught Idris off-guard and he didn't know how to react other than to push the blame back at us. As for Keldan, he's probably never heard anyone talk back to Idris before. His pallor was undoubtedly shock."

"Bran is right," said Ogham. "I think Idris is an unlikely thief. However, if he wanted the stone stolen, all he'd have to do would be whisper the idea in the right ear...or ask Keldan to suggest the theft."

"Great," I said. "We're back to suspecting everyone in two courts. We'll never find the stone in time for the festival."

"Take heart, Princess," Ogham continued with a nod. "I believe you've hit on our direction. Forget the culprit. Find the stone."

"Yes," agreed Bran. "Once we have the stone in hand, the High King can discover the thief through his own arts. For now, we must search the castle for an enchantment powerful enough to mask the stone's signature."

"But what if it's not here?" I cried. "What if the thief has already sent it somewhere else, or worse yet, destroyed it?"

Ogham shook his chestnut head. "Unlikely, Claire. Bran is right, we need to be looking for a masking spell. The Wyrd Stone is too powerful to be destroyed by any but the High King himself, and most faeries would find it difficult even to move it from its appointed place." He nodded to Bran. "I salute you, Prince Bran. I hadn't considered a masking spell during my morning's fruitless search. I should have."

"Your words are gratifying, Ogham," Bran said, inclining his head toward the centaur. "Now, we need to organize this search, and we need more faeries."

He strode to the windows which overlooked the gardens where we'd talked that morning. After gazing out for a moment, he nodded and turned to me. "Claire, speak to the flower faeries. Ask them to join us in the search. Ogham, assist the princess in describing what the faeries should search for. We don't need to hear about every scrap of magical energy they detect."

"Excellent suggestion," said Ogham, joining him at the window. "What will your task be?"

"I'll return to Winter's quarters, assemble the storm sprites, and give them the same task. Between the sprites and the faeries, we'll find the stone."

His confidence was infectious. I felt more light-hearted than I had since Grandpa told me he'd imprisoned Roddy.

Ogham and I trotted off to the gardens, with him lecturing me about the proper way to explain the task to the flower faeries.

The tiny fae were as excited as Una had been to be of service to the royal line, and me in particular. Don't ask me how, but it seemed that I had become a favorite with the little people of the castle. One of the kitchen pixies approached as Ogham and I finished instructing the flower faeries and cautiously touched the hem of my gown.

"Yes?" I said, giving her my full attention once the flower faeries had flown.

"Your pardon, Princess," she said dropping into a deep curtsy, "but I heard your instructions, may we help as well?"

"We?" I said, looking around, for she was quite alone.

"The kitchen pixies, milady. We're very fond of Prince Rhydderich and would love to find some way to help him. May we search as well?"

Ogham answered for me. "Of course you may," he said, "but don't neglect your duties to the king to do so. Did you understand the instructions well enough to tell your fellows?"

"I did, sir," she said, bobbing happily in place. "We'll search in shifts so no meals will be delayed. Thank you, sir, milady." With that she disappeared down the corridor.

"Wow," I said, staring after her. "That was a great idea of Bran's. We've got even more help than I dared to dream of."

Ogham nodded. "And very effective help. The pixies and flower faeries in particular know the castle and grounds better than any courtiers ever could. And storm sprites," he shook his head, though he was grinning, "they're born troublemakers. If there's mischief afoot, they know how to find it...and join in. Fortunately, this time they're on the side of sanity."

"You really think this will work?"

"I do, Claire. It won't free Roddy, but finding the stone will allow the king to use other methods to determine the guilty party."

"Like what?" I asked. "Will he be able to see fingerprints or something."

Ogham laughed. "Psychic fingerprints, maybe. I don't know what method he'll choose, I just know that our king has ways of detecting such things."

"Gotcha. I'm going to go tell Roddy. I promised I'd visit him today, but I wanted to have something encouraging to tell him. I think this development qualifies."

"I do too. I wish I could accompany you, but I'm not included in the lucky few who can visit him."

Impulsively, I threw my arms around his waist and hugged my mentor. "Thank you for all your help, Ogham. I'll tell Roddy 'hi' for you."

CHAPTER 7

The search team came through for us. I was in Roddy's chambers telling him everything that had happened when Javan burst in.

"Princess," he said, bowing to me, then turned to Roddy. "Prince Rhydderich, I am commanded to escort you and Princess Claire to the king's audience hall."

"What's happened, Javan?" I asked, my heart beating a loud tattoo in my ears.

"I don't know, Princess," he said, his eyes darting from me to Roddy and back again. "I only know I'm ordered to escort you...now."

We hurried through the corridors to the Grandpa's audience hall. When we stepped inside, I marveled again at the majesty of the chamber. Tapestries depicting Fae creatures, dragons, and griffins adorned walls of polished stone. Warm wood floors inlaid with parquetry of every tree species and sprinkled with bits of gemstone and faery dust supported the courtier's feet. For the hall was rapidly filling with the denizens of Summer, Winter, and the High King's court. Javan escorted us to the far end of the hall where a raised dais supported two thrones. Grandpa sat upon the larger, an intricately carved seat with plush red cushions. When he spotted me, he gestured me to the smaller, a finely chiseled onyx chair padded in velvet of midnight blue.

I ascended the steps and took my place on the onyx throne. Javan and Roddy remained at the foot of the steps until Grandpa spoke.

"Prince Rhydderich, please take your place at my granddaughter's side. Sir Javan, you may take up your post at the door of the hall. Once all have entered, no one is to leave without my permission."

"Sire," said Javan. "I hear and obey."

Roddy looked bemused, but climbed the steps to the dais and took his place beside and just behind my throne. I caught his eye and smiled encouragingly. He wasn't in chains and he was standing near the king. Whatever was happening, it couldn't be too bad.

When all the courtiers had taken their places, a herald appeared in the entry, tapped his staff on the parquet floor, and announced, "Her Royal Highness, Queen of the Summerlands, Liannan, accompanied by her heir, Prince Idris, and her daughters, Meredith, Lady of Water, and Blodwen, Lady of Flowers."

Summer's royalty processed down the aisle to a raised seating area to our left. Each curtsied or bowed to us before taking their seats. Queen Liannan was resplendent in spring green, her red hair flowing down her back in artful cascades, but her iridescent eyes were hooded and cautious. She didn't know what was going on any more than I did.

Idris and Meredith both wore shimmering blue garb that accented their dark-haired good looks, but Blodwen fairly shone in a watermelon pink gown, her golden hair dressed in a riot of curls. She smiled at Roddy, and I remembered they had been childhood friends.

The herald tapped his staff again and all eyes turned to him. "Her Royal Highness, Queen of Winter, Maeve, accompanied by her son, Prince Bran."

Roddy's family walked solemnly down the aisle. When they reached the foot of the dais, Maeve dropped a careful curtsy before lifting her gaze, her expression sorrowful. Her eyes widened in surprise when she saw Roddy standing beside me, and a small gasp escaped her lips. She nodded to Grandpa, and moved to her seat in the box to our right.

Prince Bran also bowed to the throne, but he smiled at me and at Roddy, his features relaxed.

As soon as Winter's royalty were seated, Grandpa stood, majestic in garb of black studded with sparkling silver and blood-red garnets.

"I have called you here today to discover the truth regarding the recent theft of the Wyrd Stone." He paused while the room rustled with shifting feet and quiet murmurs. When the assembled courtiers quieted, he continued. "You will be pleased to hear that the stone has been recovered. A kitchen pixie named Mela detected a masking signature and alerted the centaur Ogham, who informed me. The stone has been restored to its rightful position and its power will be revealed in the ceremony of Alban Arthan tonight as planned."

He walked past me and stood before Roddy, placing a hand on his shoulder. "Winter will be gratified to hear that I have already tested the stone and found no trace of Prince Rhydderich or his magical signature upon it." He turned his gaze on Roddy. "My apologies, Prince Rhydderich, for any inconvenience you have suffered due to this crisis."

Roddy lowered his eyes and inclined his head. "Thank you, sire. I am relieved that the stone has been found."

Grandpa nodded and returned to his throne, where he continued to stand. "Now that we know who did not steal the stone, it is time to discover who did." He turned and held out a hand to me. "Claire, accompany me, please."

"Me?" I squeaked.

Grandpa smiled. "Of course, you," he said quietly. "Consider this a lesson in how to rule."

I placed my hand in his and rose, lifting my skirts carefully to avoid tripping as we stepped down from the dais.

"The stone has provided me with the magical signature of the culprit, as well as leaving its own imprint upon the person foolish enough to touch it without permission," he said as we walked among the courtiers of Winter, Summer, and our own court. Faeries stepped aside to allow us passage as we wove our way through the crowd.

Grandpa held my hand lightly, but even so, I was aware of a pulse running through his fingers, warming and cooling as we progressed, reminding me of the children's game of 'hot and cold.'

Grandpa's fingers steadily warmed as we approached a knot of courtiers standing near the box where Summer's royalty waited. We walked unerringly to this group, which parted until we found ourselves face-to-face with a pale and sweating faery knight. Keldan. The courtier who had accompanied Idris to lunch in my solar.

His eyes wide as saucers in a face the shade of curdled milk, Keldan fell to his knees before his king.

"Keldan, no," said Idris, shock apparent in every syllable. "I trusted you! How could you do such a thing?"

Keldan licked his lips and glanced at Idris, then focused on Grandpa. "Mercy, sire," he cried. "I meant no harm to you or your court. I would've returned it in time for tonight's ceremony."

"No harm?" Grandpa roared. "You caused an innocent faery, a prince of royal blood, to be thrown into a dungeon!" He paused as two faery knights approached and stood on either side of the disgraced faery. The other courtiers had moved away from Keldan, so that Grandpa and I now stood in an open space beside Summer's royalty, with Keldan on the floor at our feet.

At a gesture from Grandpa, the knights hauled Keldan to his feet and held him securely, one on either side.

"No harm," Grandpa shook his head and then turned to Queen Liannan. "This faery is your subject, Liannan, do you wish to take charge of his punishment, or will you leave him to me?"

Liannan turned cold eyes on her son's friend. "He has brought shame to Summer and put the entire kingdom in peril," she said. "I renounce him and leave his fate in your hands, my king."

Grandpa nodded, a satisfied expression on his face. "As you wish, milady. Come, Princess Claire."

Continuing to hold my hand, he led me back to dais, where we took our seats once more upon the ornate thrones. The faery knights

—I noticed now that Javan was one of them—pulled Keldan into place before us. Roddy, who had waited on the dais, placed a comforting hand on my shoulder.

"Keldan," Grandpa said, "for your crime, you are forever banished from Faery. You will wander the mortal realm from winter to summer until the end of time."

The disgraced knight cast one beseeching glance in my direction, but I thought of Roddy in prison and turned away. However, the punishment Grandpa had pronounced worried me. I leaned toward the king and, shielding my mouth with my hand, whispered, "Grandpa, I really don't think it's a good idea to turn this guy loose on the mortal world. I have friends and family there, remember?"

Grandpa looked thoughtful, nodded, and returned his attention to Keldan.

"Is there anything you wish to say before I send you from this court?" Grandpa asked. "Any explanation you wish to make?"

Keldan slumped in the guards' grip and lowered his eyes. "I have no excuse, sire. I meant no harm to Prince Rhydderich. I only wanted to disgrace him. To separate him from the princess so that she might take note of my prince's sterling qualities. I...I...did not think my actions through."

He straightened and met my gaze. "When I accompanied Prince Idris to your luncheon, Princess, I finally understood the pain I had caused."

He turned to Roddy. "My deepest apologies, Prince Rhydderich. I am ashamed that I did not confess at the lady's table as I should have done."

Roddy said nothing, but nodded to the disgraced knight.

Grandpa cleared his throat and we all looked at him. "I'm pleased that you show remorse and accept responsibility for your actions, Keldan. I am moved to amend your sentence."

I breathed a sigh of relief, and Roddy's fingers tightened on my shoulder.

"You are banished to the mortal realm, however, if you live an exemplary life there I will review your case in a hundred of their years. You may live in hope of returning to Faery."

Keldan's expression lightened and he inclined his head. "You are merciful, my king."

"I am," agreed Grandpa. "See that you deserve it." He waved his hand and a surge of magic swept Keldan from the room...and from Faery.

CHAPTER 8

The Festival of Alban Arthan was an especially joyous occasion. Even Idris seemed to enjoy the celebration, though he was devastated by his friend's treachery.

He approached Roddy and Bran and me as we stood at one end of the ballroom talking. "It seems I owe you an apology," he said, nodding to me and Bran. "Your suspicions were correct."

"Not quite," said Bran. "If you'll remember, we suspected *you*, not your knight."

Idris scowled. "Yes, well, it comes to the same thing, doesn't it?"

"No," I said, resting a hand on his arm. "It doesn't. He may have done it to advance your cause, but you didn't ask him to. You were as innocent as Roddy. I hope you'll forgive my suspicion."

His eyes widened and his expression cleared. "Of course, Princess," he said, then more quietly, "I hope we can be friends someday."

I grinned. "Please, call me Claire, and I think being friends is a great idea."

He grinned right back and turned to Roddy. "And you, Prince Rhydderich? Will you and your brother forgive me as well?"

Bran slapped him on the back. "If Claire calls you friend, I will

364

too. Just try not to get in my way when the games begin next summer."

Idris looked annoyed for an instant, then smiled and shook Bran's hand. He glanced at Roddy and cocked an eyebrow, waiting.

"As Claire said, there's nothing to forgive, Idris," Roddy said and held out his hand. "I'd be honored to call you friend."

The two princes clasped hands and grinned.

Bran motioned me to join him and we laid our hands across theirs. "This Midwinter got off to a rocky start," Bran said, his voice full of laughter, "but it's turning into the best one ever."

Idris grinned. "Indeed. The heirs to Summer and Winter have found friendship. That bodes well for Faery."

"Yes it does," I agreed. "I can't wait to see what happens next."

Roddy laughed. "Whatever it is, Claire, if you're involved it's sure to be unpredictable!"

ABOUT THE AUTHOR

Deb Logan specializes in tales for the young – and the young at heart! Author of the popular Dani Erickson series, Deb loves the unknown, whether it's the lure of space or earthbound mythology. She writes about demon hunters, thunderbirds, and everyday life on a space station for children, teens, and anyone who enjoys young adult fiction. Her work has been published in multiple volumes of Fiction River, as well as in *2017 Young Explorer's Adventure Guide, Feyland Tales, Volume 1,* and other popular anthologies.

Find out more about Deb at:
deblogan.wordpress.com

f facebook.com/deb.logan.750

g goodreads.com/deb_logan

BB bookbub.com/authors/deb-logan

a amazon.com/Deb-Logan/e/B005XGOP4I

THE STARS OF NEVERWHERE

T. THORN COYLE

W*ho was going to save Samuel Lee?*
That was where he was in the current story.

Things had grown so strange, he honestly didn't know if he could take it anymore. The stack of library books piled on the floor wasn't helping. Neither was his favorite playlist.

All he could do was return to the story inside his head. The one he'd been making up since he was seven and a half and the strange man had moved in next door. Samuel was ten now.

The man seriously creeped Samuel out. Samuel started crossing the street rather than cross in front of the cottage next door, certain the man would leap out and snatch him away one day.

"Just don't pay attention to him, Samuel," his mother said. "He's just a sad, angry man, and it has nothing to do with you."

She didn't know. The library books taught Samuel that parents were often oblivious to what was truly going on. Adults tended to see what was on the surface and missed the sideways places.

The sideways places were the most important things, Samuel knew.

They glimmered and beckoned and called. Things entered and did not return. Other things emerged.

Like the man.

∼

T he rain fell in steady, drenching sheets, the way it had been for twenty-five days, non-stop. It grew a little lighter at times and whipped up wind and trees in the middle of the night, but mostly, it was the same, straight down, a monochrome fall of wet.

Samuel didn't mind, except it made it harder to keep his books dry. And it obscured his view of the sideways places. He figured he should feel relieved by that, but he knew that not being able to see or hear whatever was there was worse than seeing and hearing. He could still *feel* something. He just had no idea what was there.

The man next door really had stepped out of the sideways places one day. That was the thing his mother didn't understand.

371

"Oh, he just moved his things in when we were gone that Saturday. Don't you remember? We went to see Spiderman, and out for ice cream after."

But Samuel had seen him. He had seen him slide through the shimmering air in his hunched black coat and slope-crowned, broad-brimmed black hat, with his skin as white as moonlight on birch bark, and his chin and cheekbones sharp as knives. The man didn't have much nose to speak of, and it was hard to see his eyes.

Samuel felt the man stare at him that day. It was the last sunny day before the rains hunkered down in earnest that year. The last day of Autumn before the Winter came.

The man paused, the top of his face shaded into darkness by the hat, the white lower half of his face gleaming, and looked—Samuel was sure of it!—straight into Samuel's eyes. Then the man scuttled around the back side of the house next door.

There was no moving truck. No car full of boxes. Just a man who stepped out from a narrow slit in the shadows into the sun.

Things were okay for the first year or so. The man scuttled out now and then, but mostly stayed in the hulking cottage that used to be cute, with neat little curtains and a tidy stoop. But month after month, the house took on a more gloomy cast, even at the height of summer.

Then the rains returned.

And the neighborhood cats began to disappear.

At first, no one noticed. They figured the cats were hunkering down under houses or deep in the bushes somewhere, waiting for a break in the downpour.

The break in the rain never came. And neither did the cats. They insisted on going out, morning, noon, or night. And they simply failed to return.

Their humans stood, holding offerings of tuna and kibble, on broad porches and back stoops, and called the cat's use-names off the balconies of the apartment complex on the corner. The shouted names and rattling of food boxes disappeared beneath the steady sound of falling water.

And Samuel Lee? Samuel played cards with his Oma, did his homework, played online video games with his best friend Hal, and went to school. He tried to not pay attention to the rapidly crumbling cottage next-door, to the winds that whipped the tree branches and rattled his windowpanes every night. He tried to ignore the steady drenching rain.

But most of all, Samuel tried to pay no attention to the man next door.

Oh, he still saw him. Samuel saw the man all the time now. Out of the corner of his eyes, the man was waiting. When Samuel stepped off the school bus in the afternoons, he saw the shadow of the man's hat and the rain that bounced off the brim. But when he turned to look, all he would see was a mailbox, or a tree stump, or sometimes nothing at all.

Who would save Samuel Lee? The story was at a standstill. All he knew was that he was in danger.

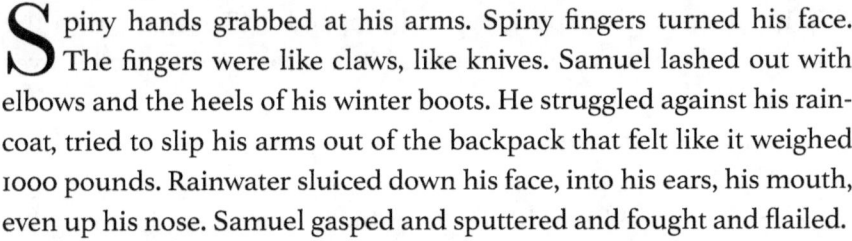

Spiny hands grabbed at his arms. Spiny fingers turned his face. The fingers were like claws, like knives. Samuel lashed out with elbows and the heels of his winter boots. He struggled against his raincoat, tried to slip his arms out of the backpack that felt like it weighed 1000 pounds. Rainwater sluiced down his face, into his ears, his mouth, even up his nose. Samuel gasped and sputtered and fought and flailed.

"Get off me!" Samuel couldn't see what had attached itself to him, but if he had to place any bets, he would bet it was the man. "Let me go!" Samuel kicked out again, this time connecting with a shin. The spiny hands didn't lose their grip, not for one second. Samuel's mind raced, trying to remember what he learned from the three months of kid's judo his mother had forced him to take the year before.

He went limp, and all the fight dropped from his body at once. Startled, the hands let go.

Samuel ran.

He ran all the way toward the tan brick bulk of the library, where he was supposed to meet Hal and work on their history assignment. Dragging open the heavy wooden glass doors he flung himself into the shadowed vestibule, and stood panting, dripping water on the gray mat covering the marble floor. He peered through one of the panes of glass, but all he could see were the bare maple branches, waving in the wind, some cars, and the steady rain.

Samuel swept the hood off his head, wiped his face, and entered the library.

The library had been one of his favorite places since he was small. He loved the smell of books, the quiet murmuring of the librarians, and the possibility that he just might find the answers he was looking for. He might even find out the answer to the question who would save Samuel Lee. But he was starting to doubt that. Especially now.

The rows of metal shelving filled with plastic wrapped spines of hardbacks made way to paperbacks, and finally, to the wooden study carrels. He could see the top of Hal's spiky blond hair already bent over some books. Hal was as much of a nerd as Samuel was.

Samuel quickened his pace until he was standing right next to Hal. He slung his backpack off, and dropped it like a weight to the floor. Then he shook himself out of his raincoat and draped it over the back of a wooden chair.

"Dude, you're soaked." Hal was always one to state the obvious. "You okay?"

Samuel dropped into his chair and leaned in close, lowering his voice, "I think that man tried to grab me."

"For real? The weird guy? What makes you think it was him? What happened?"

Samuel explained as best he could, but it sounded strange even to his ears. Hal looked interested, because nothing weird ever happened to him, but Samuel could tell he was skeptical. Skeptical. That was their word of the week.

"Maybe it was nothing. I don't know. But something grabbed me, that's for sure."

"Should we tell somebody?" Howell said. "Like the librarian? Maybe other kids are in danger."

Samuel thought about it for a moment, then shook his head. Who was there to tell?

~

He woke in the darkness. For once, the wind didn't lash the windows, and the rain had receded to a steady patter.

The man was in his room. Samuel could feel him. There was a disturbance in the air, the kind that let you know you weren't alone. And if he tried, he could hear someone breathing under the sound of the rain. Samuel lay very still. He tried to think of what to do. Should he yell? Call his parents?

That didn't seem right. Samuel didn't know how he knew it, he just did. The man was mysterious, and maybe he made the cats disappear, but Samuel hadn't heard any stories of children disappearing.

He made his decision. Quick as lightning, he reached out for his Buzz Aldrin lamp and flicked it on.

The man peered out from underneath his broad-brimmed hat, his eyes still in shadow, his cheekbones like knives.

"What do you want?" Samuel whispered.

The man cleared his throat. It sounded like rocks tumbling down the hills onto the highway. It was strange. Samuel realized he didn't feel afraid anymore. The old man wasn't exactly a friendly neighbor, and maybe he was still some freak from the sideways worlds, but he was also just someone who happened to be sitting in Samuel's bedroom in the middle of the night.

Yeah... Maybe it was a little weird. Maybe Samuel was a little bit weird.

"She thinks you're ready." The man's voice carried all the weight of winter. It was filled with long, dark nights, the feeling of ice on the back of your neck, and the taste of rain.

"Who? Who thinks I'm ready?"

The man shook his head, just slightly, enough to shake the edges of the brim of that dark hat.

"If you're willing, put on your shoes and come with me." The man stood, coat pooling around his ankles, white fingers emerging from the cuffs, face still half-shadowed.

Guess it's up to you now, Samuel Lee, Samuel thought. He flipped back his Crab Nebula comforter and swung his feet to the cold floor.

S amuel carried his shoes down the stairs, pausing in the kitchen to slip them on and lace them. His coat hung on a hook near the back door. The air in the kitchen was cold and smelled like spaghetti sauce. He was glad he'd pulled a sweatshirt on over his pajamas. Buttoning the coat up all the way, he stepped outside. It was dark. But the rain was letting up, which was good. Samuel didn't feel like getting soaked again. He'd had enough of that lately. Everyone complained about the rain, and not just the usual complaints, because it rained every winter. But not like this, the people said. Not like the last three years.

Not like since the man moved in.

"This way," the man said. Samuel followed him into the dark of the garden towards the back gate. The gate swung open quietly on its well-oiled hinges. Something skittered through the bushes. Opossum, Samuel figured. A yellow streetlamp marked the space between Samuel's parents' home and the man's cottage. The man slid around the pool of light, and it set the edges of his hat and coat gleaming. Samuel wondered why he didn't walk straight through, but he figured better follow whatever it was the man was doing.

That was what the stories always told you. When someone came from a place that wasn't earth, you either ran as fast as you could, or you did exactly what they did. Because you never knew what misstep might end up trapping you.

You never knew what thing you ate or drank or said meant that you'd never see your family and home again.

They walked behind the cottage, and Samuel stifled a gasp. While the cottage was falling down, the garden had flourished.

Secret hollows were covered in ivy. Japanese Maples brooded over stones. From a back corner, Samuel caught the slight trickling sound of a waterfall. And, in the center of it all, circling row after row of blooming roses.

Samuel moved toward them, sniffing their perfume. Then he saw that the bushes weren't quite right. Some of the bushes were in full bloom, others were tipped with delicate buds, and interspersed between them all were the bare rosebushes of winter, fat rosehips gleaming red in the mottled light and dark.

"What is this place?"

There was no answer, so Samuel just followed the man, who seemed to be leading him directly towards the center of the rosebush circles. Samuel understood now why the cottage was so neglected; all the man's attention must've gone back here.

There was an opening between one bush filled with deep red roses, and another of the winter bushes whose rose hips were bigger than any Samuel had ever seen.

His Oma put rosehips into honey and ate them all winter long. Samuel liked the combination of tart and sweet. Mama said it was the best way to get vitamin C.

Oma was never sick, so they both must be right.

"Where are you taking me?"

The man just flicked his spiny knife fingers forward. Samuel followed.

And there she was. He could swear she hadn't been there seconds before, but she was there now.

Surrounded by roses, hair pale as moonlight tumbled down her shoulders until it almost reached the ground. The ground that was covered with maple leaves, oak leaves, ginkgo leaves, and the petals of pink and yellow roses. The man bowed deeply, sweeping the broad-brimmed hat off his head for just a moment. Samuel could see he was bald. And then the man stood tall again, hat back on his head, face in shadow. Leaving Samuel to stand and stare.

Her face was all flat planes and hollows, her skin the color of the walnut dresser in his Oma's room. Three birch trees shook their silvery leaves, their bark as pale as her hair. Like the old man's skin.

"Who are you?" Samuel asked the question, but he knew. He knew exactly who she was. And the man? He must be some sort of messenger or something. Kings and queens always had messengers, didn't they?

She spoke. Her voice sounded the way Samuel imagined a glacier cracking would sound.

"I am the Queen of Winter," she said. "And I have been waiting for you."

It didn't explain the cats. Later that night, back in bed, that was the thought that flickered through Samuel's mind.

What happened to the cats?

The hems of his pajamas were damp around his feet. He shivered beneath the Crab Nebula comforter and burrowed more deeply into his flannel pillow. Out of all the things he wondered, maybe that was a little strange, but Samuel wanted to know. He had a hard time falling asleep that night, but he finally did.

She should have been terrifying, but she wasn't. Instead, Samuel found himself wishing that instead of a rose garden at night they were sitting in front of the fireplace in his favorite rocking chair, the one so big he could sit cross-legged in it, a book propped on his lap.

He would offer her the special hot chocolate his father made, the one with spices in it. She would like it, he was sure.

Instead, he stood shivering in the winter garden staring at the flat planes of her face, wondering why she called him there.

"I need the ones who see what isn't there," she said. "We always watch for the ones who pay attention. You've been seeing us for years, haven't you?"

Samuel froze in place, pinned like a beetle on a board. She was right. When he was five, he tried to tell his mother about it. She'd ruffled his hair and complemented his imagination. "But I'm not..." She smiled and told him to draw a picture.

So he did. He had notebooks filled with pictures that he would share only with Hal. Together, they made up stories about the sideways worlds and the people who lived there.

But he never thought to see one like this. Standing directly in front of him, with a voice like a glacier, and hair like the moon.

"I was never sure it was real," he said. "I mean, I only ever caught glimpses, you know?"

She nodded gravely. "That was by design."

Samuel shuffled his feet a little. His toes were getting cold. He cleared his throat. "So, um, the man, he said..."

"That I was waiting for you."

"Yeah."

"Follow me."

❧

Samuel didn't remember what happened after that. All he knew was that the man was carrying him up the stairs to his bedroom. The spiny white fingers helped him off with his boots and tucked him into bed, leaving Samuel awake with his thoughts.

❧

Night after night it happened. The man would wake him up, or sometimes Samuel would be reading, and the man would come. Samuel had learned to dress more warmly for bed. Sometimes it was raining now, sometimes not. And then the snow came.

The garden was white with it. Hushed with it.

Except for the ring of roses. The ring of roses looked as it had before. And there she was, with her moonlight hair and her walnut face arms crossed over her velvet chest.

"Are you ready this time?"

Samuel knew exactly what she was talking about. He nodded. "I want to go," he said.

And that was the truth; he *did* want to go. It had just taken him a while to work up to it. He finally figured out what had happened that first night. He had fainted. That was embarrassing, but oh well. The only thing that bugged him now about the situation was the fact that he hadn't told Hal. He just couldn't quite figure out how to talk to his best friend about it. Out of all the freaky stuff they discussed, this was a little too freaky.

But Hal would be pissed off that he hadn't invited him along. Maybe next time. After reconnaissance.

After Samuel had figured out exactly where this was leading.

He didn't see the doorway, the gateway, the whatever-it-was. One minute they were in the middle of the roses with snow sprinkling the garden all around them, and the next thing they were in a brick hallway—a corridor, the fantasy books called it. Torchlight sputtered and flared, lighting up the stones. Like, *real* torchlight. Iron rings bolted into the walls with flaming sticks thrust into them.

"Cool," Samuel whispered. He followed the long trailing velvet skirts of the Winter Queen. He could feel the man in the broad-brimmed hat behind. Samuel didn't know if that should make him feel safe or afraid. He shrugged. Might as well just go with it.

The hallway opened onto a vast hall with tall, vaulted ceilings held up by carved wood beams. There was an itching at the back of Samuel's eyes. He started to tear up. Then he sneezed.

Looking down at the flagstone floor he finally figured out where the cats had gone. There they were, dozens and dozens of them. Big orange bruisers, mottled tabbies, Siamese, even a Persian or two. They lapped at dishes of cream, reclined on fluffy cushions, or played with endless balls of red and yellow yarn.

Samuel laughed and laughed and laughed. The room was so huge his voice felt swallowed up. When he looked at the woman, she had a smile on her face.

"And that is why we called you here today. Our hob is sick. We need someone to care for all these cats."

~

"I don't get it," Hal said. "Why would the Queen of Winter need you to take care of the neighborhood cats? And why'd the cats run away in the first place?"

The boys were in Samuel's room, supposedly working on a science-art project. Popsicle sticks, glue, and construction paper littered the floor. The room smelled like the hot chocolate Samuel's dad had delivered half an hour ago. Samuel peered into his white mug. Yep. All gone.

"I'm not really sure. Not yet. None of it makes sense to me, though Strickleton says it 'will all be clear in time.' As if."

"Strickleton's the creepy guy next door? Why doesn't *he* take care of the cats?"

"I asked him that," Samuel replied.

~

Strickleton sniffed, a sniff that seemed too mighty to come from his tiny nose. His rocks-rolling-down-the-hill voice rumbled, "I," he said, "am the Gardener."

Just like that. Capital letter and everything. Gardeners, it turned out, did not take care of cats. Everyone in Sideways had a job and wasn't allowed to do anyone else's. And yeah, the hob who held the title of Cat-Herder was sick.

"You are perfect," the Winter Queen said. "We always offer gifts to the observant children like yourself. You shall grow up blessed, touched by our realms."

She'd paused then, and tilted her head his way. "Do you have a longing to be a poet?" she asked. "A bard? A painter, perhaps?"

"I want to be an astronomer!" Samuel blurted out.

The Winter Queen looked a bit disappointed at that. "Ah. I see. Well, the stars are nice, I suppose. We have different constellations here," she said. "We shall show them to you next time you come." The queen paused then, to drink deeply from a pretty golden cup. "If, that is, you agree to care for the cats for four phases of the moon."

Samuel rubbed at his eyes. He would really like to see the Sideways constellations. But there was the one problem...

"I'm allergic."

~

"So you have to help me!" he said to Hal. "You love cats, right? And didn't Moggie run away last year? I bet she's there! You could find her again. Bring her home!"

Hal didn't look too keen about the prospect.

"I don't know Samuel, you sound kind of crazy, you know?" Hal was gluing popsicle sticks together, trying to form a geodesic dome. "We're not little kids anymore."

Samuel paced the carpet in his small bedroom, from bed to desk, to the door. He skirted around Hal, waving his arms with excitement.

"Don't you see? All those books we've read, all the stories..." Samuel stopped and flopped back down on the floor. He leaned toward his friend, whose blonde hair was even more spiky than usual. Samuel wondered if Hal had accidentally-on-purpose rubbed some glue into his hair. "What if they're true?"

Hal sat down two triangles on a piece of newspaper to dry. "I don't know, Samuel. I have enough trouble getting my parents to let me come over to your house. You really think they're going to let me traipse off to wherever it is?"

"But that's the beauty of it," Samuel said. "They won't know."

S ure enough, Samuel convinced Hal to join him. Samuel figured if he brought someone to take care of the cats—though he still wasn't sure why exactly the cats had gone to the sideways world— then maybe, just maybe, as a reward, the Queen of Winter would let them both see the stars.

"Holy shit," Hal said.

"I know, right?" Samuel looked around the hall, still impressed by the vaulted ceiling, the crisscross of wooden beams, and all the cats.

He turned to the man in the slouch-brimmed hat. "Do we wait here?"

The man started to walk, threading a pathway through the cats. His bone white lifelike fingers gestured them forward. Hal looked at Samuel. Samuel just shrugged and loped after the man's dark coat.

Hal tugged at Samuel's coat sleeve. "This is like some Dungeons & Dragons stuff," he whispered. Samuel nodded again and kept moving. He just hoped this deal was going to work.

They entered a brick hallway lit with the same sconces, flames casting red and gold shadows everywhere. It was strangely medieval. Samuel wondered if all the sideways worlds were like this, or if it was just this one in particular. Maybe the Queen of Winter just liked it this way. He wondered if the torches were magical, or if there was a Torch-Lighting-Hob that took care of them.

Just as suddenly as the corridor began, it ended, this time opening into a smaller room. The ceilings were just as high, but the walls were close in, forming a cozy space. Fire crackled in an enormous hearth which was flanked by two wolfhounds who twitched their ears and slit opened their eyes. Checking for danger? The dog on the left sighed and closed its eyes again. The dog on the right stretched and yawned, then trotted over to a large comfortable chair where the

Queen of Winter sat, reading a book. Samuel would've expected a big tome with gilded edges, but it looked like an ordinary paper book from home. In her other hand, she held a half-eaten apple. The dog sat at her feet and whined. She looked up.

"Ah," she said, "I see you brought a friend to meet me." She held up the book. It looked familiar. "Do you like *A Wrinkle in Time*?"

It was one of Samuel's favorite books. "I love it."

The dark planes of the Winter Queen's face arranged themselves into what Samuel supposed was a smile. "Then I'm sure will be great friends."

She turned her eyes on Hal, who stood frozen to the spot.

"Are you the new Cat-Herder? You don't look like a hob. You look like a boy," she said.

Hal blushed, all the way from his T-shirt to his spiky blond hair. "Uhhh... Yes, ma'am. I'm just..."

The Queen tilted her head in question. Then she clapped her hands, "I know! You are a Bard! I can see it all around you. You must also be a friend of the Wind."

Samuel's jaw dropped. He stared at his friend, who only grew redder in the face. Hal sketched a shallow bow, then straightened up again.

"At your service, my Queen."

Wow. This sure was getting interesting, Samuel thought.

"How delightful," the Winter Queen said. "An Astronomer and a Bard." She turned to the man in the hat. "Well done, Strickleton. But what are we to do with all these cats?"

Strickleton moved forward, just as Hal burst out, "I'll take care of them!" Strickleton stopped in his tracks.

"Well, well, well," the Winter Queen said, "a Bard and a Cat-Herder combined. This is turning out better than I ever imagined. Would anyone care for some tea?"

～

And so the adventure began. Every evening between homework and bed, for four cycles of the moon, Hal would whistle at Samuel's window and off the boys would sneak to the hollow of roses in Strickleton's garden. Samuel studied the constellations in the sideways realm while Hal brushed five cats a night in turn. The cat-herding hob did not return, so the boys continued.

After six months or six days or six years of this, the Queen of Winter rewarded Samuel with the most clever and cunning telescope and astrolabe he'd ever seen. For Hal, she procured a lute.

The cats, it turned out, liked the cream from the Sideways world better than the cream at home. Plus, there was always a soft cushion or a warm hearth to be had.

Mostly? The cats hated the rain.

And so the boys grew up together, making music and gazing at stars. Years later Hal became both a rock musician and a poet of some renown. He raised Maine Coon Cats in his spare time when he wasn't recording or on tour.

And Samuel Lee? It turned out he didn't need saving at all. He fell in love nine times, helped to raise three children, and mapped areas of space no one even knew existed before.

He also wrote illustrated children's books. The title of his most beloved work was *The Stars of Neverwhere*.

It's still in print today.

ABOUT THE AUTHOR

T. Thorn Coyle is author of two contemporary fantasy series, *The Witches of Portland* and *The Panther Chronicles*. *The Steel Clan Saga*—a post apocalyptic epic fantasy series—is coming in 2020. Thorn has also written multiple books on magical and spiritual practice, including *Sigil Magic for Writers, Artists, & Other Creatives, Kissing the Limitless, Make Magic of Your Life,* and *Evolutionary Witchcraft.*

Thorn's short fiction, poetry, and essays appear in many anthologies, magazines, and collections, such as *Datura, Mandragora, Abraxas, Fiction River, Pulphouse,* and *Fantasy in the City.* They have produced four CDs of original music, been a professional dancer, and worked in numerous other interesting professions.

Thorn has taught workshops around the globe, runs a private coaching practice, and runs an online creativity school at Teachable called Lifelong Creative.

An activist and denizen of the Pacific Northwest, Thorn likes long walks, trees, whiskey, and tea.

Find out more about Thorn at:
thorncoyle.com

facebook.com/tthorncoyle
twitter.com/ThornCoyle
amazon.com/T.-Thorn-Coyle/e/B003VPM4HI
instagram.com/thorncoyle
bookbub.com/authors/t-thorn-coyle

THE KISS OF THE HORNED GOD

JAMIE FERGUSON

A cobblestone path wound under the bare branches of the trees in the city park. Holly stomped across the path, clenching her hands into fists, so tight her fingernails dug into the skin of her palms.

It wasn't fair. She'd been so close—*so close!*—to getting the research job at the arboretum at the botanic gardens. And now it was all gone, just like that, because some rich guy had donated a bunch of money so that *his* daughter—who was totally unqualified—could have the position.

She stopped in a small clearing and took a deep breath, trying—unsuccessfully—to relax and convince herself that losing this once-in-a-lifetime opportunity wasn't the horrible, life-shatteringly awful situation that it felt like. The air smelled like dead grass, dry wood, and the pine needles that crunched underneath her boots. Her throat tightened, and she gritted her teeth. She had to stay angry or she'd cry.

And if she started to cry, she wasn't sure she'd be able to stop.

The cool December breeze ruffled her hair, blowing a dark lock in front of her eyes. She bit her lip, tasting the faint salt-lime flavor from the margarita her friend Delia had bought her, after they'd heard the news about the job, in an attempt to console her.

But Holly had left the bar after finishing less than half her drink. There were only a few more days until Christmas, and the bar had been filled with festive people dressed in red and green, people who were far too merry to be around. And no amount of alcohol would ever get back the job she should have had. It could be years before another position like it opened up.

It wasn't as if that many places needed someone with a doctorate in woody plant ecophysiology.

She'd known it would be a tough field to find work in, but she loved trees. Sometimes she felt as though they were trying to speak to her, as if they were making sounds just outside the limit of her hearing, or as if the way their bare branches moved in the winter breeze meant something. None of that was possible, of course, but she felt happier working with trees than any other career she'd ever thought of.

At least she still had her job at the coffee shop.

Holly scowled around the clearing and brushed her hair back behind her right ear. It seemed awfully dark. As safe as this park was, walking around it alone at night didn't seem like a great idea. Yet it couldn't be that late—she'd left the bar before seven o'clock. She must have been walking for far longer than she'd thought. She should get home.

A branch behind her creaked, and she jumped.

She glanced around to see if someone was behind her, then froze. Instead of on a cobblestone path or dry pine needles, she stood on a patch of dry grass.

The path was nowhere to be seen.

A chill ran down her back. She had no idea where she was.

She'd entered the city park on the north side, just like she always did. The cobblestone path began a few blocks from her office, right next to the bar she had met Delia at. It was supposed to meander through the trees, gardens, and fields, then come out on the south-eastern edge of the park, right by her apartment building. In the winter evenings, the off-white globes from the lampposts along the path illuminated her walk home, and the glow of the city lights brightened the sky.

No lights were visible at all now. Not a single lamppost was in sight. The only light came from the star-filled sky and the crescent of the moon looming low on the horizon. The trees cast long, spooky shadows across the desiccated, silvery grass. The twinkling lights on the skyscrapers she saw every evening when she walked home were gone, as if the power had gone out everywhere in the metropolis.

But if there had been a massive power outage, she should be able to see the outlines of the buildings against the light from the moon—and she couldn't. It was as if the skyscrapers had vanished.

Or as if the park were no longer within the city.

Holly turned around but there were no lights behind her, either. The normal hum and bustle of the city was missing. The distant sound of car horns was gone, as were the ever-present smells of car exhaust, metal, and pavement. The only scents were of trees, and grass, and the cold winter earth.

She pulled her phone out of her pocket, but the battery had gone dead, which made no sense because she'd charged it earlier that afternoon. She put it back and took a few steps the way she'd come from—or at least she the way she *thought* she'd come from. She stopped, her heart thumping, no longer sure which direction was which.

The moon had been peeking over the horizon to the west when she'd left the bar, and she lived north of the park, so if she turned to her right she'd be heading in the direction of her apartment. Or reasonably close thereof.

Holly squared her shoulders and headed in what she thought— and hoped—was north.

She jammed her hands into the pockets of her coat and wished she'd remembered to bring her gloves. Her breath made little puffs in the air.

A band of clouds covered the sliver of moon, and, without the tiny bit of moonlight to guide her, there was no longer any way to tell if she was heading north. Assuming she'd been right about where north was in the first place.

She walked and walked under the light of the stars until she *knew* she should have hit the edge of the park—or at least run into one of the many paths that wound through it. This didn't make any sense. The park was no more than a mile or two long in any direction. Even if she were walking in circles, she should have seen *something* familiar.

She blinked back tears, unsure what else to do but keep going. The temperature had dropped. She wasn't dressed for being outside for this long—she had on her winter coat, but wore only a light blouse underneath. The wind had picked up, and kept blowing her hair in front of her eyes. She passed through a cluster of what looked like oaks, although she couldn't be sure in the dim light. It felt almost as though the trees were watching her, whispering to one another as she passed by. Tonight their whispers didn't feel like the tantalizing sounds she often imagined she could almost hear from other trees, but something darker, more sinister.

Her breath caught as she caught a glimpse of a soft, golden-yellow light off to her left.

The city.

Holly stopped, her heart thumping in her chest. Of course the city wasn't gone. That was ridiculous. This was only a weird, crazy power outage, and she just had to get back to her apartment. Whoever was making that light might know what was going on, and might be able to help her.

Or they might hurt her.

She bit her lip—why would she think *that*?—and squinted through the darkness at the orangish-yellow glow. It looked like two tall pillars of some sort—or were they trees?—framed the light on either side.

A small creak came from behind her, just like the one she'd heard earlier.

She caught her breath and looked back over her shoulder. The oak trees she'd just walked past seemed closer to her than they had been a moment ago, almost as if they'd moved toward her when her back had been turned, but of course that made no sense at all.

Neither did the fact that she couldn't find her way out of a park that normally took at most thirty minutes to walk through from end to end.

She shivered and took a step toward the light, and then another. The soft crunch of the dry grass under her boots sounded extra loud. She didn't want whoever was making that light to hear her coming.

She couldn't get the idea out of her head: What if it was someone —or *something*—bad?

She heard more sounds of branches creaking and rubbing together behind her. She swallowed and turned her head the tiniest bit, just enough so she could peek behind her out of the corner of one eye.

The oak trees stood several feet closer to her than they had a few seconds ago.

Holly gasped and sprinted for the light, her concern about making too much noise gone. Trees didn't *move*! Paths and lampposts and cities didn't *disappear*!

She ran as fast as she could through the forest—for *forest* it was now, there was no doubt about that.

In the city park the trees were spread out, with plenty of room to walk between them, have picnics, play ball with a dog. There were birch, ash, maple, cherry trees and more—all kinds of trees, and they ranged in age from saplings to older trees.

Here, the trees were planted closer together, were all old and tall, and every single one was an oak.

Another glance, and she could *see* them moving toward her from all sides, their roots rippling through the ground, their branches stretching out toward her. The lower branches of the oaks touched her, scraping against her coat, tangling in her hair as she ran by. She ran and ran, gasping for breath, her muscles burning.

And then she sprinted in between the two pillars and skidded to a stop, the light suddenly so bright she couldn't see where she was going. She threw up a hand to shield her eyes, then turned to look over her shoulder, her chest heaving as she tried to catch her breath.

Behind her stood two tall, narrow, grayish-green junipers—the pillars. Beyond them she could see the darkness of the forest and the now-stationary oak trees.

She looked at the ground underneath her boots. She stood on grayish-black granite flagstones. Not earth, not dry, dead grass, but stone. It wasn't the cobblestone of the paths that led through the park, but it was stone nonetheless. She had made it to *somewhere*. She turned toward the light, squinting until her eyes adjusted enough for her to see.

She stood in a small clearing forty or fifty feet wide. A ring of trees stood at the edges, juniper, pine, apple, and fir—but no oaks, which seemed odd, given how many stood in the forest just outside. The wind had stopped, and the air felt a good twenty or thirty degrees warmer than it had in the forest. In the center of the clearing a bonfire burned, surrounded by more of the grayish-black granite flagstones. Larger chunks of stone, also granite, were scattered about on the bare earth at the far side of the clearing.

Next to the fire, sitting cross-legged on the ground, sat a man.

Or at least Holly hoped he was a man.

Two curved black horns sprouted out of his head. His skin was the color of dark amber, and his eyes were light and piercing. A thick, furry hide—bear, maybe?—was draped around his shoulders like a cloak, and his brown trousers stopped just below his knees. Winding patterns of tattoos covered his bare, muscled chest. Sprigs of ivy wound through his long brown hair, and it looked as though he hadn't shaved in a few days.

She swallowed. He had to be wearing a costume. Those horns couldn't possibly be real. She'd lost her way and run into someone's strange idea of an elaborate game.

But the oak trees *had* been chasing her. She had no doubt about that.

The man smiled and rose to his feet. He stood at least a foot taller than she. Firelight glinted off a silver torc around his neck.

"Greetings, Holly," he said. His rich, melodic voice echoed in her ears.

How did he know her name? Who was he?

What was he?

"Um, hi," she said. Her eyes darted around the clearing. "Where am I? How do I get home? Who are you?"

"You are in the center," he said, waving a hand toward the line of trees that encircled them. "Where you are needed. You will return home when it is time. I am the Horned God."

Prickles ran down the back of Holly's neck. The center of what? What was she needed for? Did he really think he was a god?

What if he really *was* a god?

She shivered and glanced at the edge of the clearing. She couldn't see anything but darkness past the trunks of the trees that surrounded them. It was as if there was nothing at all on the other side of the trees. She could see the oak forest through the opening between the two junipers she'd run through. But why couldn't she see it between the trunks of the other trees?

She pulled her gaze back to look at the man.

"I don't understand," she said. Her voice broke on the last syllable. She rubbed her forehead with the back of one hand. "Please, can I just go home?"

"Do not be afraid," he said, his voice soft and kind. "You are safe here while time passes. Midwinter will be upon us soon."

Holly brushed a lock of hair behind one ear. The air felt strange, almost as if a storm were on its way, but there wasn't even the tiniest breeze—in spite of the fact that the wind had been blowing in the forest outside the clearing.

"Come," he said, gesturing to a thick log of oak that sat next to the fire. "Sit with me, and we will talk while we wait."

Wait? For Midwinter?

She glanced over her shoulder at the darkness of the forest visible through the two junipers, then walked over to the oak log. After a moment's hesitation—she had just been chased by a bunch of oak trees, after all—she sat down on one end. She glanced at the wood in the fire.

Every single log in the bonfire was oak.

The man sat down on the other end of the log. She tried not to stare at his horns, but her eyes kept wandering back up to them. It was even warmer this close to the fire, and the scent of the wood smoke tickled her nose. The night sky was pitch black, with not even a single star visible. Maybe it was cloudy. Or maybe the light from the fire was so bright it made it too hard to see the stars.

Or maybe there were no stars at all wherever they were.

She bit her lip, unbuttoned her coat and laid it on the log next to her, and tried to focus on the man's amber eyes instead of his horns. She knew she should be afraid of him, but felt oddly comfortable nonetheless.

"I am the Horned God," the man said. "Also called Cernunnos.

Ammon. The Green Man. Herne. Pan. Odin. I have been given many names, but none are my true name."

Didn't Pan have the bottom half of a goat? She snuck a peek at the man's feet. They looked like normal, bare feet. A little hairy, but human.

"What's your real name, then?" she asked.

The Horned God shook his head. "That I cannot tell you," he said.

"Okay," she said, although it wasn't really okay. He knew *her* name. "What *can* you tell me? Can you tell me why I'm here?"

"Holly rules from Midsummer to Midwinter," he said. "And then Holly and Oak battle, and Oak rules until Midsummer, when the cycle begins again. So it has been since the worlds were young, and so must it continue for all eternity."

Had he been here since the world was young? How many years was that? He didn't look that old—maybe thirty, maybe forty. He couldn't possibly be millions of years old.

Holly blinked.

He'd actually said since the *worlds* were young. Plural. How many worlds were there?

What on earth did that mean?

"But... I don't rule anything," she said. "That's all mythology. You know, the Holly King and the Oak King. I'm not a king."

He laughed, and she felt the corners of her own lips curve up.

"You are a symbol," he said. He waved a hand toward the two junipers. "Just as the forest of oaks you passed through is a symbol."

"I don't get it," she said. She shook her head. "What am I a symbol for? Am I supposed to do something to save the world? And if this happens every year, how come I've never been a part of it before?"

"You will save everything, and nothing at all," he said. "Death and rebirth, darkness and light. Everything relies on the continuation of this circle. You are here to represent Holly, by being Holly. When the moment of Midwinter arrives, something will be given to you, and the cycle will continue."

That didn't explain anything.

"I'm here as a symbol because my name happens to be Holly," she said. "And there's something I'm supposed to get at Midwinter, like a present. I guess you mean at the actual moment of the winter solstice?"

The Horned God nodded. Tiny clusters of lines fanned out from the corners of his eyes, as if he spent a lot of time laughing.

"Got it," she said. "When does that happen?"

Holly was pretty sure the solstice was today, but it could be tomorrow. She'd been so upset when she'd found out she hadn't gotten the job that she hadn't been thinking about anything else.

"In less than an hour," he said. Her eyes followed the shapes of the tattoos that wound across his bare chest. She wondered if the shapes meant anything.

"Do you do this every year?" she asked. "Find someone named Holly and lure them to this place until the solstice happens?"

He chuckled. "Every year is different," he said. "You are the first woman named Holly who has come here, to the center."

She stood up and took a few steps away from the log, looking at the trees, the flames, the pitch-black sky above them. She realized several of the stones on the far side of the clearing were arranged so that they looked like an altar, with one long stone resting on two shorter ones.

"You said we're in the center," she said, turning face to face him. "The center of what? Of all the—the worlds?"

"This is an ancient place, a hub through which power flows. I direct the energy so that the seasons continue to change, and light and dark remain intertwined."

"Is it hard?" she asked. "To direct the energy, I mean."

His eyes flickered, and his mouth tightened. "It is what it is."

"You've been doing this for thousands of years," she said. "Or more. Millions? You must be tired of it."

"It must be done," he said, then grinned. "Although this is the first time a dryad has been involved."

"A what?" She shook her head. "I'm not magic. I just like trees. I do research on how to help them grow stronger and be healthy. Or at least that's what I've been doing, but my post-doctorate ended last year, and it's been really hard to find a job in my field. That's all."

The frustration of not getting the position at the arboretum came back in a rush. She kicked at the edge of the oak log with the toe of one boot.

The Horned God rose to his feet and took a step toward her, and then another, stopping inches away. Her head came up to his chin. He placed his hands on her shoulders and met her gaze. The firelight cast shadows across his amber eyes. He had an earthy, musky smell, like the scent of a horse, or of a wild animal. She took a deep breath and tried to still her suddenly racing heart. She felt an almost over-powering desire to reach out and touch the black tattoos on his chest.

She closed her eyes, afraid he would kiss her...

...Hoping he would kiss her.

"This is my gift to you, Holly," he said, his deep voice dropping to a whisper. "It is Midsummer. Awaken."

He bent down and kissed her forehead, his lips warm and soft against her skin.

A tingling warmth flowed from the spot his lips had touched, trav-eling down her arms, inside her core, out to her fingers and her toes. It felt like a golden light flowing through her body, as though she'd been kissed by the sun.

Holly opened her eyes and looked up at the Horned God again. His expression was somber, almost sad. He brushed a lock of her hair back, his touch gentle, then stepped away from her.

Her shoulders felt chilly and bare where his hands had rested. He met her gaze and smiled. She must have imagined the sadness. He gestured toward the nearest of the trees in the ring surrounding the clearing.

"What do they say?" he asked.

Holly blinked.

The wheel turns. The year waxes. Summer comes.

Many voices, all saying the same words, over and over.

She turned to look at the trees, picking them out one by one as she identified them. The tallest fir's voice felt greener, darker; the junipers more prickly; the lone ash clear and smooth. Their words grew softer, then silent.

"I can hear the trees!" She clasped her hands in front of her chest and met the Horned God's yellow-brown eyes. "Am I really a dryad now?"

He chuckled. "You always were," he said.

"But...what does this mean?" she asked.

Did she have to live in a tree? What did dryads do? They were faeries of some sort, and were associated with trees, but she couldn't remember anything else about them.

"It means you can speak to trees," he said. "Nothing more. Nothing less." His eyes danced. "They've been speaking to you for years. You just weren't able to understand them."

She walked over to the fir that stood nearest her.

"Hello," she said.

Hello, Holly, the fir replied, its voice familiar.

Holly blinked as she realized the truth of what the Horned God had said. She'd heard the trees speaking before, but hadn't been able to identify their speech as words.

Now she could.

She pressed the palms of her hands against the rough bark of the fir's trunk and stared up through its branches, looking up through them to the black of the starless night sky behind them. She could sense the tree's age, its life, its sense of purpose. This fir, and all the other trees in the ring, were guardians. They kept the clearing safe—from what, she wasn't exactly sure, but she could feel the rightness of what they did, just like she could feel the rightness in her ability to speak with them. It was as if some piece of her had been missing, a piece she'd never even knew existed, and now that it had been put back in place she had become whole once again.

She pulled her hands back and walked to the next tree, and then the next. She touched each one's trunk, or a branch, or both. Every tree greeted her the same way the fir had. The last tree she greeted was an ancient apple tree with a bough of mistletoe hanging from one of its lower branches. She picked a sprig of mistletoe, twirled it around between her fingers, and then walked back to stand in front of the Horned God.

"Thank you," she said. "Thank you so much. I never even knew."

He nodded. A light breeze rustled the leaves of the ivy that twined through his hair. His horns didn't look scary at all. They looked like they were a part of him—as her connection with trees was a part of her.

Holly looked at the mistletoe in her hand. Was it coincidence that she'd picked it? Everything here seemed to have a reason, a purpose, whether or not she understood it. She took a deep breath, inhaling the Horned God's musky, earthy scent, then moved closer to him. Her heart thumped so loudly it seemed as though he must be able to hear it. One of the oak logs in the fire crackled. The air itself seemed energized, almost electric. She could sense the trees, reaching their limbs up, up, into space, or nothingness, whatever was in the sky above them. She took another step toward the Horned God and reached one hand up to touch his face, trailing her fingers down the side of his cheek.

He grasped her wrist and pushed her hand back, his grip tight, strong, and gentle.

"It's time to go home, Holly," he said, his voice deep and rough. He nodded at something behind her. "The trees will show you the way. The oaks will help you now that Midwinter has passed."

She took a deep breath and glanced over her shoulder at the two junipers, the gatekeepers to this place, who guarded the opening to the clearing.

Come, Holly, they said in unison.

"But I don't want to leave," she said. She furrowed her brow and looked up at the Horned God. "I want to..." She felt her face flush as she realized exactly what she wanted to do. She wanted to reach out and trace the patterns of the black tattoos on his chest, to ask him what they meant. To push back the bearskin from around his shoulders, to feel his hands against her bare skin...

"I am sorry, Holly," he said. "I must go now, to the Wheel of Stars." Holly stared at his hand, still wrapped around her wrist. She pressed her free hand on top of his and looked up at him. Above his head, just past the outline of his horns, she could see the soft twinkle of a few scattered stars where before there had been nothing. Why were there stars now? Why did she have to leave? Why did she feel this intense desire to be with a man—a god?—she barely knew?

"Will I ever see you again?" she asked.

He stood there in silence for a minute. She could hear the woody voices of the junipers beckoning her.

Come, Holly. Come.

"I do not know," he said finally. "But I hope so."

He raised her hand to his lips and kissed it, then loosened his grip. She bit her lip and stared into the Horned God's eyes. The stars behind him had grown brighter, their light glinting off the tips of his horns. The voices of the junipers had grown more strident, almost as if they were worried.

"Goodbye," she whispered.

She took a deep breath, and then grabbed her coat off the log and walked toward the junipers. She passed through them and out into the night.

A small cluster of oaks had replaced the oak forest she'd run through earlier. A light breeze rustled her hair, and stars filled the sky—far, far more stars than the few she'd just seen in the sky in the clearing.

This way, the oak trees said. *Follow the wind.*

Holly glanced in the direction the breeze blew. About fifty feet away she could see the familiar cobblestone path of the park winding its way through the dried winter grass. A lamppost lit the way.

She turned and looked back over her shoulder, through the opening between the two ancient junipers. The Horned God stood tall, his head raised high, his horns glimmering in the firelight. He looked strong. Powerful.

Alone.

The back of her hand felt warm and tingly where he'd kissed it.

Holly took a deep breath, then turned and headed for the lamppost, the path, and her normal life. Not that her life would ever be the same again. Thanks to the Midwinter gift the Horned God had given her, she could speak to the trees.

Her failure to get the position at the arboretum was frustrating, but she would find something else, something where she could use her newfound ability in order to help even *more* trees. What if she could find a way to help not only individual trees, but entire forests?

She glanced back one more time, but an empty meadow stretched out behind her, the grass silver in the moonlight. The two junipers, the glow of the bonfire, and the Horned God were gone.

She hoped she'd see the Horned God again. He'd given her a gift that was so wonderful, so amazing, so unexpected. She wanted to talk with him, learn why he had to do what he did...and feel his touch on her skin again.

Perhaps at Midsummer...

ABOUT THE AUTHOR

Jamie focuses on getting into the minds and hearts of her characters, whether she's writing about a saloon girl in the American West, a man who discovers the barista he's in love with is a naiad, or a ghost who haunts the house she was killed in—even though that house no longer exists. Jamie lives in Colorado, and spends her free time in a futile quest to wear out her two border collies since she hasn't given in and gotten them their own herd of sheep.

Find out more about Jamie at:
jamieferguson.com

facebook.com/jamie.ferguson.author

twitter.com/jamie_ferguson

instagram.com/jamie.ferguson.author

goodreads.com/jamieferguson

pinterest.com/jamieauthor

bookbub.com/authors/jamie-ferguson

amazon.com/Jamie-Ferguson/e/B004SVIP3G

DESTINY

KRISTINE KATHRYN RUSCH

Solanda walked the cobblestone streets of Nir, the capitol city of Nye, her tail up. She had a meeting with Rugar, the son of the Black King. He had sent a Wisp to find her, and it had taken the little creature nearly a day to do so.

Solanda was in her cat form, as she had been since the Fey captured this repressed country—and thus very difficult to find. The Nyeians had many faults—they were prissy, overdressed, and pasty-faced, not to mention abominably poor soldiers—but they did treat their animals well. She had found a family who fed her to excess, allowed her to roam outside, and pampered her as no cat should be pampered.

How appalled they would be if they ever discovered the golden cat their daughter had adopted was really a Fey Shapeshifter.

Solanda's tail twitched once in amusement. Every day she imagined eating her lovely tuna dinner in the glass plate that the family gave her, and then Shifting into her Fey form just to say thank you.

She didn't know what would appall the Nyeians the most: the fact that she was Fey, or the fact that she would be naked. She doubted any of them had seen a naked woman before: the wife managed to change her clothing one piece at a time, without ever taking it all off at once, and the husband didn't seem to think this unusual. He would probably be more shocked than his wife at the appearance of a naked Fey woman in his house. He would probably fall over in a dead faint.

Only the daughter, a girl of five, was redeemable. Esmerelda was a good child. She had to be. She was raised Nyeian. Her mother trussed her in layers upon frothy layers of clothing, making movement nearly impossible, and then yelled at the poor child whenever she did something natural, like running.

Sometimes Solanda thought she went back to that household at night because she felt sorry for the child. But in truth, she stayed there because they gave her fish properly deboned and they brushed her, and they put a warm cedar bed in Esmerelda's room. Esmerelda, good child that she was, never confessed to her parents that she often picked up the cat and carried her to bed, cuddling with her long into the night.

And Solanda would never tell anyone—Fey or Nyeian—that sometimes she purred when she slept, pressed against the little girl's back.

Shifters were supposed to be the coldest of the Fey, the most fickle members of a warrior people, incapable of real emotion, flighty, restless and completely self-absorbed. They also were supposed to take on the characteristics of the animal they had chosen to Shift into, so Solanda's fickleness—theoretically—was doubly compounded by the fact that she had chosen the cat as her alternate Shape.

Of course, it didn't matter how many times she had proven herself trustworthy. In the war against Nye, such as it was, she had done intelligence for the Black King. She had worn her cat form and slinked into Nyeian villages, soldiers' camps, and mess halls, keeping her ears open, and learning more than she should have.

Most countries that the Fey had fought had banned strange animals from military compounds. Solanda had heard that the Co had gone so far as to slaughter any strays, thinking they might be Fey reconnaissance. But the Nyeians had a fondness for cats, and while they kept stray dogs out of their camps, they fed cats on the side.

Solanda had spent most of the war the pampered resident of a Nyeian general's tent. He used to feed her bits of meat off his own plate while telling his staff his battle plans for the next day.

And then when he fell into his snoring sleep, she would go to the nearest Shadowlands and inform the Fey general of all she had heard. Toward the end of the war, she reported directly to the Black King, who shook his head at the stupidity of the Nyeians.

Conquering Nye was the first step toward world dominion. The Black King didn't say that, but Solanda knew that was his goal. The Fey were a great warrior people, but they only owned half the world right now. The Black King—and the Black Throne—wanted all of it.

Solanda entered the merchant sector of Nir, and silently cursed to herself. The merchants often shooed cats out of this area. Her presence here was suddenly noticeable, and she didn't dare Shift. She'd shock an entire community of Nyeians—which would probably be good for them.

Scents from the nearby vendor stalls caught her nose. Fried beef, more fish, some sort of vegetable something which turned her feline stomach. The fish was enticing. It almost made her forget that she was here because she had been summoned by the Black King's son.

Rugar had been her commander for part of the Nye campaign. He was an able warrior, frustrated under his father's tight leash. The problem with Rugar was that he believed himself to be the equal of his father, and he was not.

Solanda would rather work with the Black King, ruthless as he was, than with his less-talented son.

The tall stone buildings prevented the sun from getting to the cobblestone. The stone was wet beneath her paws from the morning rain. The air was thick and muggy, making the six layers of clothes the Nyeians wore look even more uncomfortable.

The handful of Fey who were on the street wore their traditional uniform—a leather jerkin and pants. The Fey were so much taller than the Nyeians that even if they didn't dress differently, they would be noticeable.

She ducked under some clothing stalls, past the buildings that housed the year-round indoor merchants, and turned on the street that led to the Bank of Nye. The Black King had taken over the building. It was four stories of gray stone, towering over the buildings around it—as close to a palace as there was in Nye.

She sighed heavily and crossed the street, climbing up the stone steps and staring at the large stone door. She'd have to Shift just to get into the place.

Then she saw a nearby window ledge. The window was open. She leaped onto the ledge and jumped to the stone floor inside. She thought this building unusually cold for a Nyeian structure. The house where she was pampered was made of wood, and had thick rugs on its floors. Every surface was soft, and the air perfumed.

Here the air smelled like chalk and the stone was chilly despite the heat. There were no guards in this room, although there should have been. It looked like it was someone's office—a desk in the center, chairs on the side for supplicants.

The door was open and led into a cavernous hallway. She heard voices and followed them. Several Fey guards huddled in an alcove. They were Infantry and young, tall even though they hadn't come into their magic yet. Their dark skin and black hair was a welcome sight. She'd gotten tired of looking at the pasty-faced Nyeians, and hadn't realized how much she missed her own kind.

"...fool's errand, don't you think?" One of the young men said.

"If it's so important, why doesn't the Black King go?" another asked.

"Blue Isle is important," said a young woman. "It's the only stop between here and Leut."

Leut was the continent on the other side of the Infrin Sea. The Black King wanted to go there more than anything. He wanted to conquer as much of the world as he could before he died.

"If we are going to conquer the world," the girl was saying, "we have to go through Blue Isle first."

"Then it doesn't make sense," the first man said. "Why send Rugar? He's not as good a commander as his father."

"Maybe," Solanda said in her most authoritative voice, "the best commander in the world has a plan that's too sophisticated for you to understand."

They all turned. They had similar upswept features, narrow faces, and pointed ears. Solanda had often thought that her people looked like foxes—most of them, anyway. Shifters, like her, often took some of the characteristics of their animals. Her hair and skin were more golden than dark, and she had the Shifter's mark on her chin—a birthmark that established who and what she was when she was in her Fey form.

But they couldn't tell now. All they could do was tell that a cat had spoken to them.

"Well," she said, sitting on her haunches and wrapping her tail around her paws. "Where do I start? Do I reprimand you for gossiping in the middle of the day? Do I tell you that I got into the building through a window that some careless fool left open and, if I had been some young Nyeian bent on assassination, I could have walked right past you and you wouldn't have noticed? Or do I ask that one of you poor, magickless fools get me a robe so that I can have my meeting with Rugar?"

They didn't answer her. She raised her chin slightly. Amazing how she could intimidate them, even though she was so very small.

"By the Powers," she snapped. "Get me a robe. And put a guard on the window."

She nodded over her head toward the room she had just come out of.

Two of the young men ran off toward the room. The third young man hurried off, presumably to get her a robe. That left the young woman.

"I really should report this," Solanda said. "Technically, you put the Black King's life in danger."

"From the Nyeians?" the young woman snorted. "You snarl at them and they run. They couldn't fight us in the war, and once they found out that they'd remain in charge of their businesses, they really didn't care that we took them over. Why would one of them try to get in here?"

"Revenge?" Solanda said. "We did, after all, slaughter half their army. Those young men were related to someone."

"Then that should take away half the threat, shouldn't it?" the young woman said. "After all, the Nyeians believe that only men are capable of fighting."

Solanda felt amused. "I have a hunch that belief has changed since they were defeated by us. What's your name?"

"Licia," the girl said.

"You haven't come into your magic yet, have you?"

The girl straightened her shoulder. Magic was always a touchy subject with Infantry. They were tall enough to show that they would get magic, but chances were if they neared adulthood and still hadn't come into their magic, their abilities would be slight.

"No," she said.

"You showed a tactician's mind. Why do you waste it gossiping with people who aren't worthy of you?"

413

The girl straightened her shoulders. "I don't normally guard. I am usually in the field."

"But there's no field at the moment, is there?" Solanda said. "What are you doing here?"

"Rugar asked me to come. He says his daughter needs more swordfighting training."

Solanda narrowed her eyes. Jewel, Rugar's middle child, was the most promising of all his raggedy offspring. She hadn't come into her magic yet either, but her height and her heritage suggested when her magic came it would be powerful. She was a good swordswoman now —Solanda had seen her fight in the last of the Nye campaign.

"Why would she need more training?"

Licia shrugged. "I suspect it has something to do with the fight Rugar had with his father this morning."

Solanda tilted her head to show her interest.

"They just left that room you came through. They were screaming at each other all morning long."

"About what?" Solanda asked, realizing that she was now gossiping. But she didn't want to go into a meeting with Rugar with less knowledge than he had.

"About going to Blue Isle. Rugar says he won't go without his daughter."

"Not his other children?"

"He didn't mention them." Then Licia smiled. "At least not at the top of his voice."

Solanda suppressed a sigh. The Black King favored Jewel. He felt that her brothers were idiots—and he was right. Their magic was slight, like their mother's had been. Rugar's entire life had been about defying his father. Rugar should have married a woman who had great magic. Instead, he had chosen someone he could control.

The young man returned with a flowing golden robe that was clearly of Nyeian origin. Solanda didn't ask where he had gotten it. She didn't thank him. Instead, she said, "Place it over me."

He did, blotting out the light. The robe smelled faintly of perfume and perspiration, but it clearly hadn't been worn in some time. The fabric was heavy satin—too heavy for a humid day like this—but she wasn't in the position to be choosy. If Rugar was planning something stupid, she wanted to meet him Fey to Fey. Psychologically, it gave her an advantage.

She Shifted, feeling her body slide into its familiar Fey form. Her body stretched and grew. Her tail and whiskers slid into her skin, her hair flowed down her back, her front paws became hands. She ended up in a sitting position, her knees drawn to her chest, the robe draped over her like a tent. Inwardly she sighed, and wished that there were a more dignified way of Shifting into clothes.

Then she slid her arms through the sleeves, and her head through the neck hole, letting the stiff fabric flow around her. It was a woman's garment, although she had no idea why someone would store one in a bank—or perhaps she did, and didn't want to think about illicit affairs among Nyeian bankers.

She lifted her long hair out of the garment's neck, and let it fall down her back. Licia bit her lower lip, and the other Fey looked down. They hadn't realized they were talking to the best Shifter in the Black King's army—at least, not until now.

Fools. Shifters were rare. How many of them would come into the Black King's dwelling and order Infantry around?

"Licia," she said, "announce me to Rugar."

The girl's skin colored slightly, but she moved in front of Solanda and led her down the hall. It got stuffier the farther in they went. Solanda was grateful that her feet were bare. The cool stone was going to keep her from melting in this robe.

Licia led her up a flight of stairs into a rabbit's warren of what had once been offices. Solanda smiled. Rugar was hidden here, in an obviously less desirable area of the building. The Black King had a thousand ways of showing his displeasure with everyone around him.

Licia knocked on a door at the end of the hall. Solanda stood far enough back that she wasn't visible from inside. She heard Rugar's gruff voice, and then Licia's response, announcing Solanda.

The door opened, and Licia stepped aside.

"I guess that means you're supposed to go in," she said.

Solanda stopped and put a hand on the girl's shoulder. She spoke softly so that Rugar couldn't hear. "If Rugar and his father are fighting," she said, "side with the old man. Rugar is not the future of this race. You're better off remaining in Nye with the Black King than going to Blue Isle with Rugar."

Licia nodded, then glanced over her shoulder as if she were afraid of Rugar. Solanda walked past her and through the open door.

Rugar stood in the center of the small room. He was medium height for a Fey, and his features had a predatory, hawk-like look to them. His almond-shaped eyes were the deep black that Solanda associated with the Black Family. It was as if the Throne echoed in their very essence. He had thin cruel lips, and an expression of permanent unhappiness.

For man in his fifties with grown children, he looked startlingly like a petulant child.

"You sent for me," she said, not disguising her lack of respect for him.

He clasped his hands behind his back, his father's favorite stance. "I'm taking an army to Blue Isle. You will be part of it."

She snorted. "I serve your father, not you."

Rugar glared at her. "He gave me permission to choose whomever I wanted from the standing armies in Nye."

"You have no need for a Shifter," she said. "Blue Isle is a tiny place, filled with religious fanatics who have never seen war. You'll sail in with your troops, wave a few swords, and be able to claim victory over an entire country in the space of a day. I'll be useless to you."

He shook his head. "I'm taking you, and a lot of Spies and Doppelgängers. I am to be military governor of Blue Isle. My father will launch an attack from there onto Leut."

Solanda narrowed her eyes and was glad she wasn't in cat form. She probably would have found an excuse to scratch Rugar, and that wouldn't have been good for either of them.

"Spies, Doppelgängers, and a Shifter," she said. "It sounds like an intelligence force. You won't need it if you conquer the country as quickly as you believe you will."

His gaze went flat. "I will need it."

She stared at him for a moment. He knew something and he wasn't going to share it with her. Spies made sense, even in an easily conquered country. They would find the pockets of resistance. But Doppelgängers had no place there. They killed their hosts and then took over the body, including the memories. Except for the gold flecks in the eyes, no one could tell them from their victims. Doppelgängers had a sophisticated magic—one that the best commanders used sparingly. And certainly didn't waste them on an already conquered country.

"You have no need for me," she repeated. "I stay with the Black King."

"You'll come with me."

"Your father said so?"

"No, but he will."

"Because he already acquiesced on Jewel?"

Rugar started. He hadn't expected her to know that.

Solanda raised her eyebrows and allowed herself a small smile. "I am good at gathering intelligence."

"And," he said, "as you pointed out, there's no need for intelligence gathering in a conquered country."

She nodded. "I'll go to Leut with your father, when he's ready. Until then, I'll relax here."

"Solanda—"

"Rugar," she said, holding up a hand. "You and I have no great liking for each other. I have a hunch your father is sending you to Blue Isle to get you out of his sight. I'd rather not be associated with you in any way. Right now, I hold your father's respect. I'd rather not change that."

Rugar took a step toward her. She could feel the violence shimmering in him.

She grabbed the doorknob. "Touch me," she said, "and I'll scratch out your eyes."

"You can't touch me. I'm a member of the Black Family."

She smiled. "I'm a Shifter. Unpredictable, irresponsible, flighty—remember? I'm sure the Powers would let this slide."

"But my father would not," Rugar said.

"Oh," Solanda said softly, "but I think he would."

She tried to see the Black King before she left the building, but he was nowhere to be found. His personal guards were gone as well. She decided she would find him in the morning, and went back to her life as a pampered Nyeian cat.

The home that she had chosen was a large one on the outskirts of Nir. It had two stories filled with more clutter than any home she had ever seen. Books of poetry, musical instruments, incredibly ugly paintings, and furniture everywhere. The only saving grace was that the furniture was comfortable and the kitchen had a cat door that she could escape through when the wife decided it was time for music.

Solanda slipped through the cat door, past the kitchen hearth. One of the three Nyeian servants was cleaning the pots from the evening meal. The air smelled faintly of roast beef, and Solanda's stomach rumbled.

Still, she didn't beg from the servant. She knew better. The idiot had kicked her "accidentally" once, and had the scars to prove it. But Solanda knew if she attacked anyone in the house too many times, she would be thrown out, and she wasn't willing to lose her rich dinners and soft bed just yet.

She blended into the hideous yellow wallpaper as she hurried up the stairs to Esmerelda's room.

Esmerelda sat on the edge of the bed, fingering a rip in her dress. She had a forlorn expression on her small face. Her brown hair hung limply around her cheeks, and a streak of dirt covered the pantaloons beneath the skirt.

Solanda had never seen Esmerelda look dirty before, nor had she seen the girl's hair loose at any time except bedtime.

"Oh, Goldie!" Esmerelda raised her voice in relief. She was speaking Nye, which was a language that Solanda hadn't known well when she moved into this house. Here her Nye had improved greatly, but she wanted to be fluent in it by the time she left.

The little girl launched herself off the bed and grabbed Solanda before Solanda could jump out of the way. Esmerelda wrapped her arms around Solanda and held tightly. Esmerelda had never done that before. If she had been a grabby little girl, Solanda would have been gone a long time ago.

So this meant, quite simply, that something was wrong.

Solanda let herself be held for a moment, then she turned her head toward the door and flattened her ears. Esmerelda, smart child that she was, understood both signals. She pushed the door closed, and then let Solanda go.

Solanda jumped on the windowsill. Esmerelda followed her, but didn't open the window like she usually did.

The room was hot and sticky. Solanda wouldn't be able to stay here too long if that window wasn't opened.

"I don't dare," Esmerelda said softly. "Mommy's really mad at me. She didn't even let me have dinner."

Now Solanda was interested, but she didn't want the story, not yet. She bumped her head against the window's bubbled glass.

Esmerelda bit her lower lip and shook her head.

Solanda placed a paw on the glass and meowed softly.

"Okay," Esmerelda whispered. "But if anyone comes, I'll have to close it."

Solanda almost nodded, then caught herself. When Esmerelda came close, Solanda bumped her affectionately with her head, and then watched as the little girl pulled the window open.

A cool breeze made its way inside. That was the other nice thing about this house. Esmerelda's room opened onto a large undeveloped area, so the smells of the outdoors came in strong. Breezes were unencumbered. Esmerelda's mother hated this, and often wished for close neighbors, but Solanda saw it for the blessing it was.

Esmerelda knelt down beside the window and put her elbows on the sill. She didn't touch Solanda, but she was still a bit too close. Her body heat was ruining the breeze.

"I been so bad," she said, "I won't get to go outside ever again."

Solanda watched her. The little girl had never been able to resist a cat's gaze. Solanda had never seen a child who was so very lonely. Esmerelda wasn't allowed to play—except with dolls whose clothing was frilly as the stuff she was trussed in—nor was she allowed to associate with the neighboring children who were, in her parents' mind, beneath her. She had lessons in poetry and music, art and dancing, but she liked none of it. What she really wanted to do was run as far as she could, and climb trees and learn how to swim.

She'd probably never get to achieve those goals.

"I was running this afternoon," Esmerelda said. Her face was wistful. She leaned her forehead against the glass. "Mommy was looking at fruit and I thought I could just go around the block, but she saw me. I guess she followed me."

Esmerelda had done this before, and it hadn't gotten her sent to bed with no supper. Solanda suspected the problem had something to do with the rip in the dress. Clothing was sacred, at least to this family. Solanda wanted to tear every piece so that this little girl could be free.

"She saw me fall." Esmerelda said, fingering her skirt. "She saw me hit a Fey."

Solanda stiffened. She almost asked who, and caught herself. Two near lapses in one conversation. She was getting much too relaxed with this child.

Esmerelda ran a soft hand over Solanda's head. Her touch was gentle again, as it had always been before.

"She said she was the Black King's granddaughter, and she yelled at Mommy for dressing me the way she did. And Mom yelled back. The lady said yelling at her was like yelling at all the Fey all at once."

Only one Fey woman could make that claim. Jewel. No wonder Esmerelda's mother was upset.

"And then Mommy told Daddy and he said that the Fey might hurt us. Because I ran." A tear coursed down Esmerelda's cheek.

And those fools were blaming the child for being a child. Solanda pushed against the girl's hand, and Esmerelda sniffled.

"I didn't mean to run. I just can't stay still sometimes."

Solanda understood that. She could never stay still. It was a curse of being a Shifter. It was the reason Fey wisdom said that Shifters were the most heartless of the Fey. Most Shifters did not have children, and most rarely stayed anywhere long enough to form a real relationship.

Esmerelda sighed. "I wish I was like you. I do what I want. Or like that Fey lady. She was nice to me. She didn't like Mommy though."

Neither did Solanda.

"She said children shouldn't be dressed like me. She said I ran into her because my clothing didn't let me run properly."

Probably true, Solanda thought.

"And that made Mommy really mad."

Esmerelda let her hand slide off Solanda's neck. She bunched her hands into fists and rested her chin on them, looking fierce and strong. Solanda felt her whiskers twitch in amusement. One day, Esmerelda's parents would no longer be able to control this child. If she was this strong, articulate, and intelligent at five, she would be impossible to control at fifteen.

Especially with all of the Fey influence around her.

"I wish I had magic," the little girl said. "Just a little bit. Then I could run and no one would know. I'd make myself invisible and no one would see me."

Solanda looked out the window, knowing her expression was too sympathetic for a cat. There was a ring of oaks at the edge of the lawn. They were blowing in the breeze. Maybe there would be another storm. Maybe this storm would finally cool the place off, although she doubted it. Nye's hot season was the worst she had encountered in any country she had ever been in.

"Esmerelda!" her mother's voice echoed from the hallway. "Why is your door closed?"

Esmerelda gasped and pulled down the window so quickly she almost caught Solanda's tail in it. Then she leaped onto the bed, stretching out. Solanda jumped beside her and curled up at her feet just as Esmerelda's mother opened the door.

The woman's face was flushed. She looked like a tomato about to burst. She was so tightly corseted that her body looked flat, and Solanda wondered how the woman could even breathe. She wore an evening dress of white satin that accented the redness of her face. The sides were lined with sweat.

"What are you doing?" she asked. Then she frowned. "How did that mangy cat get in here?"

Solanda growled softly in the back of her throat. She was not mangy. And the woman had never called her that before.

"I told you that you were supposed to be in here by yourself to think about what you did today. Things could have been much worse. Fortunately, she was in good mood. You know what those people can do? Why it's said they can cut the skin off a person with the flick of—"

Solanda yowled, and the woman stepped back, a hand over her heart. Esmerelda sat up, worry on her small face.

"Are you okay, Goldie?"

Solanda licked her right paw as if she had twisted it. She was not going to let that woman tell this little girl about Fey atrocities—even if they were true.

"Come on, Goldie," Esmerelda's mother said. "There's some beef for you in the kitchen."

Usually that would have gotten Solanda off the bed. But she could sneak down after everyone was asleep and take what she needed. Right now, she wanted to stay beside Esmerelda.

"Goldie," the woman said.

Esmerelda, good child that she was, bit her lower lip and said nothing. She didn't beg for the company that she obviously wanted.

"Goldie!" her mother sounded exasperated now. Then she shook her head. "Why do we put up with this animal?"

Neither Solanda nor Esmerelda answered.

Finally Esmerelda's mother sighed. "All right, she can stay. But I do expect you to sleep in that dress tonight and to think about how you could have hurt us all. That rip should be a reminder of the danger your misbehavior put us in. Nye isn't the place it used to be, child. Do something wrong, and those Fey will harm all of us."

Then she pulled the door closed, and Solanda heard the boards creak as she made her way down the stairs.

Esmerelda's fingers played with the rip. Solanda looked at it, then crossed the bed, took the skirt in her teeth and pulled. The rip grew. Esmerelda giggled, then covered her mouth. Solanda pulled harder. If the little girl had to sleep in these clothes, she might as well be comfortable.

Esmerelda ripped the pantaloons too, along the dirt line, giggling as she did so. "Mommy will think I did it when I was running," she said. "You're so smart, Goldie."

Of course she was. Solanda preened and allowed herself to be petted one more time.

Then Esmerelda looked at the door, her smile fading. "Sometimes I think Mommy doesn't want me. She wants somebody else. Somebody perfect."

Too bad she didn't realize that the child she had was better than perfect. Solanda sighed softly. Some people had more than they deserved.

～

The idea came to her in the middle of the night, in that hot and stuffy room. She could take Esmerelda away, and Esmerelda's parents wouldn't even know it had happened. But it would take the cooperation of the Fey Domestics.

Fey magic was divided into two parts: warrior and domestic. Warrior magic was designed for warfare. Some Fey magic turned its practitioner into a weapon, like the Foot Soldiers who had fingernails that could slice better than a blade. Domestic magic could not be used to fight any war. Domestics lost their magic if they killed. Their magics were healing magics or home-bound magics, such as spells that made chairs more inviting or fires warmer.

The next morning, after making certain that Esmerelda got

breakfast, Solanda slipped out the cat door. She went to the Domicile that the Fey Domestics had set up just outside of town. The Domicile had been built especially for the Domestics, and covered with various protection and healing spells. It was a traditional U-shaped building —with hearth and home magics in one length of the U, the healing wards in the other, and the middle section as a meeting place in between.

Solanda usually didn't seek out the Domestics. They always wanted to experiment with her—have her try on a new cloak covered with some sort of rain protection or have her taste a new food to see if it had an effect on her Shifting. The last time she had been in a Domicile had been when she had broken a paw jumping from a tree in one of the last Nye battles. The Domestics had mended the bone, and had given her a smelly ointment she had to apply in cat form. She had thought the stench alone would kill her.

As she mounted the steps to the center part of the building, she shook off her paws. Here she would not Shift to Fey form. The Domestics weren't as obsessed with power as Rugar was, so she didn't have to use her height as a reminder of the strength of her magic.

She pushed open the door and stepped inside.

The air was cool and welcoming. It smelled of a sea breeze. Bits of magic floated in the air. Spinner's magic. They were working on their looms. She could hear the hum just down the corridor.

A Baker entered, his fingers dusted with flour. They glowed. And she knew he had spelled the bread he'd been baking to remain fresh for as long as possible. It was a traveling spell, one most often used when troops were heading off to battle. She wondered if someone had requested it.

"I'm here to see Chadn."

The Baker nodded, then slipped through a door that led to the Healing part of the Domicile. Solanda hopped onto a chair. Her mood rose and she cursed, jumping down. She didn't need to be spelled, to wait, happy and contented, on a chair dusted with Domestic magic. Instead she paced the cool floor and wondered why she couldn't smell the baking bread.

Finally Chadn entered the room. She was a young Shaman, although the toll of her power had already turned her hair white. Her face was wizened, her mouth a small oval amid wrinkles. Only her eyes were bright—sparkling black circles of light in a ruined face.

She had been assigned to stay with Rugar during the war and she was happy to be free of him. Shaman were the most independent Fey: their Vision as strong as those of the Leaders, but their magic Domestic so they could not rule a warrior people. They were the wise ones, the advisors, supposedly the strength behind the Black Throne. The Black King required a Shaman of his son, but did not use one himself. He had dismissed his own, years ago, for disobeying him. It was one of many areas where the Black King broke with tradition.

"Solanda," Chadn said. "I had hoped to see you."

Solanda jumped on an end table and was relieved that her mood did not change. She sat on her haunches and looked into Chadn's face.

"I have a request," she said. "It's for a Nyeian child."

"A child?" Chadn sounded surprised. "Not a Fey child?"

Solanda shook her head.

"I had Seen you with a Fey child."

The Shaman's Visions—and the Vision that leaders like the Black King had—allowed them glimpses into the future. Some said that the glimpses allowed the Visionary to change the future. Others believed that the glimpses led the Visionary to that future.

Solanda's eyes narrowed. "I have not been with a Fey child."

Chadn nodded. "It was on Blue Isle. The child was a Shifter, and you kept her from death."

Solanda's whiskers twitched. "I told Rugar I would not go to Blue Isle with him."

"The future of our people lies with you, Solanda."

"And a child?" Solanda raised her chin. "Are you sure it was a Fey child?"

"Not entirely," Chadn said. "The child had blue eyes."

Solanda gave a soft grunt of surprise. She had heard of blue-eyed people, but she had never seen one. "The child couldn't be Nyeian?"

"She was Fey, and newborn. She had a birthmark on her chin. Only her eyes were strange, and perhaps that was because of the Shifting. I Saw you put your hands on her lips, and swear to protect her, raise her, and make her strong. Then I Saw her full grown, saying you had been the closest thing she had to a mother."

Solanda laughed, although inside she felt cold. A Shifter only swore to protect a child who held the future of the Empire. A blue-eyed child that Shifted? The center of the Empire?

"Visions can be altered," Solanda said. "I am not leaving Nye."

"You may have no choice."

"I'll always have a choice," Solanda said.

Chadn inclined her head toward Solanda as if giving in on that point. "What does the Nyeian child need?"

Solanda took a deep breath. "She is different from any other Nyeian I've seen. Strong, independent. She met Jewel yesterday and is being punished for it. I would like to remove the child from her family and bring her here, to be raised among us. She will be useful when she's grown. She will be part of the second-generation, the Nyeians that rule Nye for the Fey."

Chadn stared at her for a moment. "So take her. Shifters steal children."

"This one's mother will raise a fuss if she's gone."

"What mother wouldn't?"

"She'll come to us."

"And you can't prove to the Black King that we must keep the child."

"Not yet, anyway," Solanda said.

Chadn folded her hands over her stomach. "You want a Changeling."

"Yes," Solanda said.

"How old is the child?"

"Five."

Chadn sighed. "Have you asked the child if she's willing to leave?"

"Not yet. I wanted to know if I have help first."

"You will keep the child at your side?"

Solanda frowned. That wasn't a normal request. Shifters rarely kept children. They usually brought them to Domestics to raise. "Must I?"

"At five, it will be you she trusts."

Solanda shrugged. "Then she shall stay with me."

"And you will stay away from Blue Isle." Chadn said that not as a question, but as a statement.

"Rugar will not let a Nyeian child in his war party."

"So the child serves two purposes." Chadn's eyes narrowed. "Has she magic?"

"Of course not." Solanda laughed. "There is not magic outside the Fey."

Chadn frowned. "I am no longer certain of that."

"Because you Saw a blue-eyed Shifter?"

"Because I Saw a great war, coming when we least expect it."

"War is part of Fey life." Solanda jumped off the table and headed for the door. "I'll bring you news of the child tomorrow."

"I'll have Changeling stone ready," Chadn said. "But realize before you act, that this is for life."

"I already know that," Solanda said. "I have chosen well."

"I hope so," Chadn said.

Solanda went to the docks and sat on a fence. She loved it here. The Infrin Sea formed the most natural harbor on Galinas, and there was always some sort of activity. Toward the north end of the harbor, the Nyeian builders made the great ships. Those ships traveled all over the known world, and now Fey Domestics helped unload cargo that would go all over the Empire.

Ships from Blue Isle had stopped coming to Nye when news reached them of the Fey takeover. She would never see an Islander, never learn more about them than she already had.

And that would be all right.

For there were some things she couldn't discuss with Rugar's

Shaman. Like the prophecies that had been made by another Shaman at Solanda's birth, prophecies that claimed her legacy would be in the children she saved.

Children—not child, like Chadn had seen. Solanda would influence the life of more than one.

The breeze was cooler here, carrying with it the smell of salt and a tinge of dead fish. That smell made her stomach rumble. She tried not to think of the things she ate in her cat form, things she would find disgusting when she was in Fey form. Right now, raw dead fish sounded extremely appetizing.

But she didn't go in search of the source of the smell. She had some thinking to do. Prophecies and Visions made her nervous. She had no idea what to do with the information Chadn had given her. Because, at various points in her life, Solanda had been told by Visionaries that her future held contradictory things.

One Shaman had told her she had to avoid the Black Family for she would kill a Black Heir. Another Shaman had told her she would raise a Black Heir. And now Chadn had Seen her swear to protect a blue-eyed Shifter, a newborn who couldn't survive on her own.

Solanda bowed her head. The prophecy she never mentioned, the one her parents had kept silent, had come the day of her birth and she had never forgotten it. The prophecy was a cold one: she would die before her time, far from home, for a crime she did not regret.

The Fey did not believe in crime. They were constantly at war, so the crimes that plagued other races—murder, theft—were absorbed into the wars themselves. The Fey only punished two crimes: treason and failure. Both of those crimes were considered crimes against the Empire. Failure was a large crime, encompassing the failure to follow an order, or the failure to defeat an enemy in a prolonged battle.

Treason was any crime against the Black Family and was such a heresy, that it wasn't even discussed among rational Fey.

Both crimes bore the penalty of death.

It seemed to her that she would never commit crimes like that, that the prophecies had come because she was a Shifter, not because of her character. She wasn't as flighty or as difficult as anyone said she was.

And besides, she had to take care of Esmerelda.

She wished she could be there the morning that Esmerelda's parents discovered the Changeling. It would look like Esmerelda, even act like her—if stone could act like a living breathing creature. But it would only last a few days, and then it would cease to exist. They would think Esmerelda dead, when, in actuality, she was only gone.

Then, perhaps, that wretch of a mother would regret how she treated her daughter.

Esmerelda would live a life she couldn't even imagine now. She wouldn't have to wear six layers of clothes on the hottest day of the year, and she would learn how to live life to its fullest instead of remaining indoors and studying all the time.

Esmerelda would be the closest thing to Fey that a Nyeian could be—and for the first time in her young life, she would be happy. Solanda would see to that.

They would both be very happy.

Solanda returned to the house after dinner. Ultimately, she found she couldn't resist the dead fish that were piled near one of the docks. She had eaten herself sick, and then had to clean every inch of her fur before she even attempted the walk home.

Not that the house was home. In some ways, Esmerelda was.

Solanda used the cat door. Esmerelda's parents were talking softly in the parlor.

"Perhaps boarding school," the mother was saying. "If she is this incorrigible now, imagine what she'll be like when she gets older."

"Give it time, darling," the husband said. "She's still a child. She will learn, as we all did."

"It's just I despair of ever teaching her manners. You didn't see her with that Fey..."

Solanda had heard enough. She hurried up the stairs. She would talk to Esmerelda tonight. Tomorrow the Wisps would come, carrying a bit of stone in their tiny fingers. They'd fly in the open window, leave the stone on the bed and it would mold itself into a replica of Esmerelda while Solanda was leading the real Esmerelda out of the house.

Quick, neat, and completely perfect. The parents wouldn't have to worry about manners or boarding school. Esmerelda would get her heart's desire. And Solanda would have her reason for staying in Nye.

The door to Esmerelda's room was open. Esmerelda sat beneath a lamp, a long skirt over her lap. The air was stuffier than usual, and Solanda saw that the window was closed.

It had probably been closed all day. Sunlight had poured in, and the poor child had had to sit in the heat, working on some task her mother assigned her.

When Solanda got close, she saw what it was. The child was attempting to mend her own ripped dress.

The stitches were uneven, and Esmerelda had stitched the bottom layer of fabric onto the top. That would make her mother even angrier. Esmerelda's eyelashes were stuck together, her nose was red, and there were tearstains along her cheeks.

"Goldie!" she said, and let the dress topple to the floor. She was wearing another dress, equally inappropriate to the hot weather. She reached for Solanda, but Solanda jumped onto the windowsill.

She was not going to be hugged by a hot sweaty child—not, at least, until the window was open and the fresh air came inside.

Esmerelda glanced toward the door. She put a finger to her lips, as if she thought Solanda were going to give her away, and then called, "Mommy! Can I go to sleep now?"

Solanda froze in her spot. She didn't want to be seen in here, not tonight. She wanted to have her conversation with Esmerelda in private.

"Are you done with your dress, darling?"

"Yes."

Solanda looked at it. The dress was ruined. The poor girl would have an even more difficult day than usual tomorrow.

"Then blow out the lamp. Good night."

"Good night." Esmerelda pushed the door closed. Then she went over to the window and opened it.

A strong breeze came in, and on it, Solanda smelled rain. Maybe, after she spoke to Esmerelda, she would go outside. By then it would be raining, and she would be able to cool down.

Esmerelda put her hand over the lamp's chimney and blew. The flame inside the glass went out. Solanda blinked in the darkness, letting her eyes adjust. It only took a moment. There were clouds over the moon this night, and it was very dark.

Esmerelda went back to her chair. "I wish you knew how to sew, Goldie."

"I don't," Solanda said. "But I know someone who does."

Esmerelda let out a small yelp, and put her hands over her mouth. She peered around the room as if looking for the source of the voice.

Solanda had to go slowly with this. The child wasn't used to magic, not like Fey children were.

"I could take the dress to her tonight," Solanda said, "and by morning, you wouldn't even know there had been a rip in it."

Esmerelda's eyes were wide. She finally turned in Solanda's direction. "You can talk, Goldie?"

"As well as I can listen." Solanda jumped from the windowsill to the bed. The room had cooled down. The fresh air felt marvelous. "What would you think, Esmerelda, if I took you to a place where you could wear comfortable clothes, play with children your own age, run and jump and swim to your heart's content? What if I told you that you would never have to sew another stitch, have another music lesson, or sit in a corner when you've done something that your mother didn't like?"

Esmerelda looked for her, but clearly didn't see her. Cat's eyes were far superior in the dark. Solanda watched the child lick her lips, rub her hand over her knees, and then sigh.

"How long would I stay?" Esmerelda asked.

"Forever," Solanda said.

"Would I have to be a cat?"

Solanda laughed. For all her verbal sophistication, Esmerelda was still a child at heart. "No," Solanda said. "You'll stay just as you are."

"Would Mommy come?"

"No."

"Daddy?"

"No."

Esmerelda's shoulders stiffened. Her little body looked rigid. "Who would love me then?"

Solanda started. She hadn't expected that question. "I would be with you," she said.

Esmerelda was silent, as if she were thinking this over. "Where would you take me?"

"To my people," Solanda said.

"I'd live with cats?"

"No," she said gently. "With the Fey."

Esmerelda gasped. She held onto her chair as if she expected to be dragged from it.

Solanda wondered if she should have said that, but she had never taken a child before. Certainly she knew of no one who had ever taken a child of this age.

But Chadn had said she had to speak with the child, and the choice to come had to be the child's. There was sense in that. Esmerelda, at age five, would always have a memory of living with her parents. She needed a memory of her choice to leave them.

"Esmerelda," Solanda said. "I—"

"No!" Esmerelda screamed. "No!"

She launched herself out of her chair as if her voice had given the ability to move again.

"Help! Mommy! Help!"

Solanda's ears went back. She hadn't expected this from Esmerelda, not her sane, different child.

"Esmerelda, I only want to give you a better life—"

"Mommy! Daddy! Help!"

Finally Esmerelda pulled the door open and blundered into the hallway. Solanda followed, tail between her legs, ears still back. The little girl's screams echoed down the stairs. Her parents had reached her, and they both put their arms around her. Esmerelda was too terrified to be coherent.

Then the mother looked up the stairs. She saw Solanda, her gaze flat.

And Solanda realized she had no choice.

She Shifted, her body lengthening, her tail disappearing, her fur becoming skin.

Then she walked, naked, to the floor below.

Esmerelda's mother gathered her child in her arms and backed away. The father placed himself in front of his small family, arms out.

"You came from the Black King, didn't you?" the woman said. "To punish us by stealing our child."

"It's not about you," Solanda said.

Esmerelda peeked around her father, eyes wide. Solanda had never, in her entire life, been so conscious of her nakedness.

"Wh-what do you want?" the father asked. He was trying to sound brave. Like most Nyeians, he was failing.

"I had hoped to take your daughter, but it seems that she prefers this place, even though you treat her as less than house pet. It seems, for reasons I cannot understand, that she loves you."

"Of course she does," the woman said. "We're her parents."

"As if that's a divine right." Solanda stopped on the middle stair.

The family cringed below her as if they expected her to strike them with a lightning bolt. She didn't have that kind of magic. They had seen the extent of her powers, but apparently they didn't know that.

"She is a child," Solanda said. "She is to run and play. She is to have friends of her own age. She is to have comfortable clothing so that she can move without tripping. She is supposed to get dirty, to rip her skirts, and fall on her behind. She is to have some joy in her life. Do you understand?"

"I thought you Fey were supposed to leave us alone," the mother said. "I thought—"

"Be quiet," the father said.

Esmerelda clung to her father, her curiosity moving her closer.

"You will give her those things," Solanda said, "or I will take her from you. Do you understand?"

"Yes," the father said.

"You can't do this," the mother said. "You can't change our customs. The Black King promised you wouldn't."

"A promise made to a conquered people is worth nothing," Solanda snapped. "You will do what I say, or the child is mine."

"Mommy." Esmerelda reached for her mother. Solanda's eyes narrowed. Couldn't she see that her mother saw her only as a thing to be trained, to be forced into the right and proper life?

Probably not. It was too sophisticated a concept for her. The same innocence that allowed Esmerelda to accept a cat's speech, allowed her to believe that she was loved.

"Do I take her now?" Solanda asked.

"No," the father said. "We'll do as you say."

"But our friends—"

"Shut up," the father snapped. "Do you want to lose her?"

For a moment, the mother's gaze met Solanda's and in it, Solanda saw something she recognized, a coolness perhaps, a calculation. How would that woman have answered if she had been asked *who would love me then?* Would she have dodged the answer like Solanda had? Or would she have heard it at all?

"She will stay with us," the woman said. She sounded resigned.

Solanda felt a hope she hadn't even known she had die inside her. "Then I'll watch. You will treat that child as if she is more precious than gold. And if you fail, even once, she's mine. Is that clear?"

"Yes," the father said.

But Solanda did not take her gaze from the mother.

"Yes," the woman said.

Esmerelda had stepped to her father's side. She was still holding his leg. "Are you Goldie?" she asked.

Solanda gave her a small, private smile. "Only for you."

The little girl slipped behind her father again. Her answer was clear, too. She would stay, no matter what. And Solanda had done all she could.

So she Shifted back to her cat form. For a moment, she watched them all, tail twitching, then she ran up the stairs and into Esmerelda's room. She stopped for only a moment, knowing she would never return.

She leapt onto the windowsill, and sighed. She had just lost her excuse for staying on Nye. She was bound to the Black Family. She had to do as they wished.

Rugar wanted her to go to Blue Isle.

Where a Shifter awaited her care. A newborn child, with blue eyes. A child who would think her the closest thing she'd ever had to a mother.

Solanda looked over her shoulder. She heard Esmerelda's voice, high, piping, excited; the soft answers of her parents. Solanda had lied to them. She would not be able to watch.

She hoped they would take good care of her little girl.

Then she jumped out the window, and climbed along a tree branch. Maybe her future had been preordained. Maybe she had no choice. She would raise a Black Heir, maybe kill one, and influence children.

How different would tonight have been if she had told the child that she would love her?

She would never know. Perhaps that was the moment in which everything could have changed. Maybe she had just missed her only chance to save herself.

ABOUT THE AUTHOR

New York Times bestselling author Kristine Kathryn Rusch writes in almost every genre. Generally, she uses her real name (Rusch) for most of her writing. Under that name, she publishes bestselling science fiction and fantasy, award-winning mysteries, acclaimed mainstream fiction, controversial nonfiction, and the occasional romance. Her novels have made bestseller lists around the world and her short fiction has appeared in eighteen best of the year collections. She has won more than twenty-five awards for her fiction, including the Hugo, *Le Prix Imaginales*, the *Asimov's* Readers Choice award, and the *Ellery Queen Mystery Magazine* Readers Choice Award.

Publications from *The Chicago Tribune* to *Booklist* have included her Kris Nelscott mystery novels in their top-ten-best mystery novels of the year. The Nelscott books have received nominations for almost every award in the mystery field, including the best novel Edgar Award, and the Shamus Award.

She writes goofy romance novels as award-winner Kristine Grayson.

She also edits. Beginning with work at the innovative publishing company, Pulphouse, followed by her award-winning tenure at *The Magazine of Fantasy & Science Fiction*, she took fifteen years off before returning to editing with the original anthology series *Fiction River,* published by WMG Publishing. She acts as series editor with her husband, writer Dean Wesley Smith.

To keep up with everything she does, go to kriswrites.com and sign up for her newsletter. To track her many pen names and series, see their individual websites (krisnelscott.com, kristinegrayson.com, retrievalartist.com, divingintothewreck.com, fictionriver.com, pulp-housemagazine.com).

Find out more about Kris at:
kriswrites.com

g   goodreads.com/KristineKathrynRusch
f   facebook.com/kristinekathrynruschwriter
🐦   twitter.com/KristineRusch
BB   bookbub.com/authors/kristine-kathryn-rusch
a   amazon.com/Kristine-Kathryn-Rusch/e/B000AP6oYK

HOLLY VS OAK

REBECCA M. SENESE

The yellowish lights illuminating the poster blazed through the late afternoon twilight at such a piercing hue it made my eyes water. The piercing cold wind of early December didn't help either. I was standing on the frigid sidewalk, staring at the illuminated poster affixed to the main sports arena in Crossroad City and I still couldn't believe it.

Midwinter Extravaganza! One Night Only! In Person and Live! Holly vs Oak: the Final Showdown Exhibition!

I sighed. Was it too late to ask for vacation time?

Behind me, a car hissed along the street. As it passed, I heard the squelch of tires hitting slush. Before it could arc over the snow drifts and splatter onto my leather pants, I leapt into the air. Through the slit in my black leather coat, my blue faerie wings sprang forth, lifting me high above the sidewalk.

The slush splattered onto the sidewalk, right where I had been standing.

Instead of landing back in front of the poster, I let myself drift upward, riding the cold air currents, until the arena spread out below me. A huge concrete dome stretched over top, crusted with snow. It looked almost like a wintry egg. Three of the streets surrounding it were lit with yellow streetlights, twinkling under the bare branches of trees. The fourth led directly into the massive ten floor parking structure that supported the arena.

Not that it would be needed for the Holly vs Oak fight.

Faerie weren't known for their cars.

Already the city was packed with tourists, both normal and those crossing in from the Nether Realm through the Great Tear. The Great Tear had opened a rift between the dimensions of the normal world and the Nether Realm. Crossroad City sat smack in the middle in the normal world, serving as a way station between the realms. Magic was heavily regulated in the normal world; the delicate balance of the rift couldn't absorb a lot of magic on this side without catastrophic consequences. To help manage that, the Spells and Misdemeanours Bureau of the police dealt with any and all magical related issues.

And I was the lead detective.

As I hovered over the concrete dome, I spotted a cluster of twinkling lights flashing across from the right, heading north over the dome. I felt a spread of magic like a wind in the air.

Some idiots showing off for the normals.

So much for vacation.

I shifted and took off after them, aiming to intercept. My coat flapped around me with the force of my flight. Wind streamed through my long, red hair, flinging it back. As I got close, I unclipped the holster for my wand and got ready to pull it out.

Just a few feet ahead, I spotted them. A group of four faeries doing twirls and flips. Showing off, just like I'd thought. They were young, less than a hundred, dressed in the browns, and greens, and oranges of the South Faerie Court. Summer faeries. I wonder if they'd ever felt cold like this before.

I felt a smirk spreading across my face.

Maybe I should give them a real taste of winter. After all, I knew all about it as a seventh level princess of the North Faerie Court.

I got within five feet. They still hadn't spotted me. They were twirling end over end, laughing at the mist of their breath in the air.

I pulled out my wand, ready to give them a real taste of winter.

The ear piece plugged into my left ear squawked.

"Maeve, you there?" Trevel's deep voice rumbled in my ear. "I got some brownies creating mischief near the Incantation River. Could use some back up."

I could picture the troll holding his phone in his massive hand like it was a doll's phone. Trevel was my partner in the bureau and he could hold his own against magic. Calling for back up wasn't his usual style. He must need help.

Pursing my lips, I stared after the group of cavorting summer faeries.

They weren't *really* doing any harm. The ripple of magic I felt wasn't destructive, not enough to cause an issue with the Great Tear.

They were Just. So. Irritating.

I took a deep breath in and let it out slowly. The group drifted farther away. I let them go.

Just kids. Just goofing off. Never mind that it felt like an insult.

I grunted. That sounded like my mother talking, complaining about all things Summer Faerie.

I guess you could take the Faerie out of the North Court, but you couldn't take all of the North Court out of the Faerie.

Holstering my wand, I pressed on the ear piece.

"On my way, Trevel," I said.

Then I turned my back on the cavorting group of Summer Faeries and went to do my job.

Dispersing the brownies took a little over an hour. By that time, the sun had completely disappeared, plunging the day into full darkness. Trevel drove the Hummer back to the station and parked around back. As usual, the few officers who happened to be in the parking lot threw envious glances at the Hummer until Trevel stepped out of the driver's seat. The grey-skinned troll towered above the car. He wore a black tunic with his badge hanging from the breast pocket. His arms were bare as were his feet, but even stepping on the snow, he didn't seem to feel the cold.

I followed him, brushing snow off the shoulders of my coat. The harsh lighting inside made me blink as Trevel led the way to the service elevator, the only one strong enough to hold him. Even it creaked as it carried the two of us up to the eighth floor.

I was just imagining the rich scent of fresh brewed coffee when Trevel pushed the door open to our squad room and we found chaos.

A general rumble of voices filled the air with shouts, curses, and hexes. By the window, I spotted the blond head of Detective Lemmer as he bent over his desk, barely visible around a pair of wraiths. They both wore dark grey hoodies over black jeans. Narrow, skeletal heads bowed down toward the detective.

But the main action seemed to be taking place in the middle of the room.

Captain Hwon stood in the centre beside a hard-back chair. From the angle he stood at, I couldn't see who was sitting there, all I saw was the captain's impeccable navy suit. Even with his arms crossed, the fabric never creased for long. If I didn't know for sure he was human I would think he cast spells on his clothing.

His black hair shifted as he shook his head. His normally calm features were now completely impassive. Major warning sign for Hwon. The angrier he got the more impassive and still he became. It made the explosion of his wrath all the more impressive.

In front of him stood a group of three tall, black-robed figures. The hoods on the robed overshadowed their faces but I could feel the magic emanating from them.

I started shifting left, toward the coffee maker that sat on a small table to the side of the door leading into the captain's office. Maybe I could grab a quick cup and slip back out the door...

"We insist on better security," one of the robed figures intoned. The deep voice was ice cold, as deceptively calm as Hwon's demeanour.

Oh crap. I knew that voice.

So much for slipping out the door unnoticed.

I cleared my throat and stepped forward, edging past Trevel. As one, all three robed figures turned toward me. Another step and I could see around the captain. A figure wearing flowing light blue robes sat in the chair, doubled over, face in hands. Beautiful, ice-blue faerie wings sprouted from the back of the robes, but drooped in a lacklustre fashion that I knew was unnatural.

Some very wrong was definitely going on.

And naturally one of my relatives was smack in the middle of it.

I bowed my head at the three black-robed figures. "Uncle Ulvar, how can I help you?"

The figure at the far end threw back his hood. My uncle's narrow face appeared beneath a shock of red hair. A flash of delight crossed his face and was gone so quickly I wasn't even sure I'd seen it. He pursed his lips.

"We demand better security," he said. "The Holly King has been attacked."

The figure on the chair stirred and sat up. Despite his unlined face, the faerie looked old. White hair stuck up on his head. Greyish circles hung beneath his ice-blue eyes.

"I am all right," he said. His voice had a distant quality. "It could have been a misunderstanding."

I cocked an eyebrow in the captain's direction.

Instead of the dangerous impassivity, Hwon now looked at me with slight surprise on his face. It disappeared as quickly as it came.

"It appears there may have been an attempt to poison the Holly King," Hwon said.

I pursed my own lips to stop my mouth from dropping open. I didn't think there was anything in the normal world that could poison a faerie. Nothing that would have been by accident anyway.

My heart began to pound.

"We demand better security," Ulvar said. "A personal liaison to ensure the Holly King's safety. Maeve Hemlock will serve."

I could tell from the way Hwon's body stiffened that he didn't like being pressured. "I'm not sure..."

"I insist," Ulvar said, nodding at me. "She is faerie. She knows what needs we have. She is family. I trust her." Ulvar's eyes narrowed. "There is no one else here I trust."

Despite his impassive expression, Hwon looked unhappy. The slight crinkle near his eyes and at the corners of his mouth were obvious to anyone who knew him. As captain of the Spells and Misdemeanours Bureau, I knew he had been instructed in person by the mayor to make sure this exhibition fight went off without a hitch. It was vitally important to continue the good will between the normal world and the Nether Realms, and that good will in turn helped keep the Great Tear from doing any more damage, on either side.

But I also knew he had a limit to his patience, and those slight crinkles showed that he was reaching it.

And if he said the wrong thing, which was so easy to do around faeries, he could get into lots of trouble.

Before Hwon could open his mouth, I took a step forward.

"I would be happy to assist you, uncle," I said.

A smile flash across Ulvar's face. Of course he'd done this on purpose, thinking he could pressure me into it. I let him have a brief moment of glory.

"And my assistance will be all," I finished.

The smile faded a little on my uncle's face. He knew what I was saying; that if he accepted my help he wouldn't be able to ask any more of Captain Hwon or anyone else in the normal world.

I wasn't going to let him use this as political expedience at someone else's expense.

"Maeve," the captain said.

I gave a slight shake of my head, keeping my attention on my uncle. For a brief moment, I thought he might refuse. He got that stubborn jaw jut that my mother always did before she said no, but then his shoulders dropped. He gave a nod.

"I accept those conditions," he said.

"Good. First I would like to have one of our doctors take a look at the Holly King." I stepped around the captain and touched the Holly King's shoulder. "Then you'll give me a copy of your itinerary and where you've been over the last day. I'll have my partner check those places out." I glanced over at Trevel. He gave a nod.

"Then finally, I'll look over the current accommodations, make sure everything is intact."

"That will suffice," Ulvar said. "For now." He deepened his voice and tilted his head forward to look more menacing.

Sure. Menacing. The man who taught me how to catch floating fuzz balls in the Royal courtyard and fussed when I got too close to a stone wall and scraped my knee.

I let him have his performance.

"If that is sufficient, I would like to have a word with Detective Hemlock before she begins," Captain Hwon said. He gestured to his office.

I knew better than to refuse.

And fortunately, it seemed my uncle did as well. He merely nodded assent.

I followed Hwon into his office and closed the door behind me.

Unlike the rest of the squad room which always seemed awash in paper, Hwon's office was a study in simplicity. The surface of his oak desk held only a desk blotter, a phone on the right side and a closed laptop on the left. The walls were a yellow so pale it was almost white. The single adornment, other than the clock on the wall right of the door, was Hwon's certification as captain of the squad on the left wall. Behind his desk was empty. Nothing to stare at if he was reaming you out.

Even though the coffee machine sat right outside his office, the smell never seemed to permeate the room, which always seemed to have a slight odour of jasmine.

Hwon stopped at the corner of his desk and turned around to face me. His frown was more pronounced.

"I wish you hadn't done that, Mauve," he said. "That kind of favouritism was exactly what I was trying to avoid."

"It wasn't going to end any other way," I said. "They would have continued to complain and insist. This way you have someone on the inside."

"You didn't tell me your uncle was attached to the entourage of the Holly King."

"I didn't know," I said. "It all changes every year. The king and the guard surrounding him. It's a great honour to serve."

"Is that why you offered?" Hwon asked.

I blanched. "Great Tear, no. I hate that kind of thing. The manoeuvring, the double and triple meanings of everything. Why do you think I came here? It's so much simpler on this side of the Tear."

The crinkle lines around his eyes deepened but this time it was from the slight smile that curled his lips. "Really? Simple, here."

"You have no idea," I said and gave a little shudder.

Hwon sighed. "I'm still not happy about this, but you made a promise."

"And I can't go back on it," I said.

"No, you can't. But I want daily check-ins." He pointed to empha-size it.

"Of course. I'll contact Trevel daily."

"And me. I want to hear from you personally."

"I'll check in with you both," I said. "Don't worry, sir, they won't be able to tempt me back to the Nether Realm."

The crinkles deepened. "Just as long as you don't tempt them to stay here. One of you is more than enough."

I opened my mouth and then closed it. I wasn't sure if I'd been insulted or complimented. And didn't really want to examine it to find out which. I just gave him a final nod and braced myself to face my uncle.

Nothing showed up on the examination of the Holly King so I accompanied the group back to their suites at the Crossroad Enchantment, a luxury hotel near the stadium. I had only ever driven past the white sculptured towers, treated with something that sparkled multi-coloured in the sun. In the cold winter air, they twinkled ice-blue. Stepping through the sliding double doors and into one of the high-end suites was impressive.

Or would be, if I hadn't been raised in the North Court.

The white carpeting was sufficiently plush. The navy sofa and two matching armchairs were made of the softest leather. The brass fireplace was stylish and modern with a hint of tradition. Floor to ceiling windows gave a grand view of the city, showing a hint of Deep Pool Lake on the right with the Incantation River snaking its way toward the upper left.

Against the wall by the door was a squat, teak cabinet with three doors. I wandered over and opened the right one. It was a small fridge, stocked with different kinds of beer. I opened the other doors. Shelves of liquor bottles. Full size, not the little tiny ones, and no sign of a price list.

I didn't wanna know what one night in this room cost.

The Holly King bypassed the sofa and headed down a hallway on the left of the fireplace. As he passed, he snapped his fingers. Flame sprang up in the fireplace.

Two of the guards followed the King. The third came to stand beside me in front of the fireplace.

"I did not expect to see you," my uncle said. He let the robe slip down his arms, revealing a deep blue tunic over dark pants. They shimmered the way faerie fabric did in the light.

I cocked at eyebrow as I glanced at him sideways. "Oh really?"

"I did not expect there to be any trouble. This was to be merely an exhibition for the ritual of midwinter. Now someone has determined to make it something else."

He frowned, worry lines crinkling his face in places they never had before.

He wasn't lying. This had been unexpected.

I shifted so I faced him directly. He was my mother's younger brother but he had always acted older. Regal and responsible. He looked so much like her, but different. The slim line of his nose, the square jaw, the way his hair fell across his forehead, even the spread of his wings whenever he took flight. Memories from my childhood threatened to send me into a wave of nostalgia. I pushed it back. I had a job to do.

"Tell me how this all came about," I said. "And what's been going on since you got here."

Ulvar flashed a smile. "Still being the detective, Maeve? Questioning me?"

"I'm trying to get a handle on why someone would try to hurt the Holly King," I said.

The smile faded from my uncle's face. He turned to watch the flames dancing in the fireplace.

"There were some who were not happy about this exhibition," he said. "Some thought it undignified to perform the midwinter ritual here in the normal world."

The muscles along my back clenched, making my wings quiver. There were always those who thought any connection to the normal world tainted those in the Nether Realm. They wanted to pretend the Great Tear didn't exist, that by ignoring the normal world they wouldn't have to deal with it. But the Great Tear had happened and it seemed the only way to deal with it was to deal with each other. Anything less seemed to have an effect on the strange dimensional rift that cut a swath through our worlds.

"Did these someones do anything about it?" I asked.

Ulvar shook his head. "Nothing concrete. Vague whispers. Smokey enchantments. Just enough to make their displeasure known. I didn't take it seriously. I still don't, not really. It is the ones who say nothing that concern me."

Now it was my turn to nod. I knew what he meant. The ones who really disapproved wouldn't telegraph their actions. They would just take them.

"Okay. I'm going to ward the room and then I want to see your schedule over the next two days. Anything not urgent will have to be cancelled."

I held up a hand as my uncle opened his mouth to speak.

"We're not taking any chances," I said. "This is the first time we've had this here in the normal world and I want it to go smoothly."

Before he could protest, I turned away and headed for the windows. First step, make the room secure.

Then I would review everyone in it.

It took me over an hour and much concentration to completely ward the room. By the end of it, I had a headache that flowed from my forehead, over the top of my head, and down to my shoulders. My right hand felt cramped from clenching my wand. I shoved it back into my holster strapped to my thigh.

The flame still crackled in the fireplace. I turned away from it, toward the three-door cabinet. In the mini-fridge, I found a bottle of water. The seal cracked like the sound of an explosion when I twisted the top. I winced at it and then took a long swallow from the bottle. When I released it, half the water was gone. The vice tightening around my head seemed to loosen. Just a little.

I carried the bottle over to the windows and looked out over the city.

Snow had draped a white blanket over most of the buildings. Twinkling lights of red, gold, and blue hung in wires that crisscrossed many of the major streets. The Incantation River, a thick, dark line that split the city in two, was crusted with ice. Another few days and the skaters would appear. They thought they were risking the water not being frozen enough for skating but they didn't realize they risked more than that.

Because of the Great Tear, the Incantation River had a tendency to shift and change direction and location, with no discernible warning. No one knew what would happen if anyone was on the river when the next change occurred. So far, no one ever had been, but I knew some day it would happen. Someone would be on the river, skating, or swimming, boating, or maybe even fishing. Close enough to be affected by whatever great magic caused the river to shift and relocate.

I shuddered thinking about it. Would they be lost in the void between dimensions? Would they be thrown into the Nether Realm?

No way to know unless it happened. *Until* it happened.

"I have never seen such a place," came a voice behind me. "The lights are not magic?"

I turned my head. Pain stabbed up my neck. I managed to stop myself from blanching and merely winced.

The Holly King stood just behind me. He stepped forward until he was standing in front of the window with me. His pale skin looked a little less blotchy. His eyes looked a brighter blue. Whatever rest he'd managed had done him good.

"It's electricity," I said. "I don't know much about it."

"So many wonders," he said. "I fear I became overwhelmed with it. Before I was chosen the Holly King I had never even been to the North Court."

I turned toward him, studying him. "I thought the Holly King was chosen from the noble houses?"

"It has been opened to all for many years now." He tilted his head, studying me. "How long have you been here?"

I smiled. "In some ways, too long and others, not long enough."

He laughed. "A true faerie answer."

He turned back to look at the city lights, twinkling in different colours against the dark sky.

How many things had changed in the Nether Realm while I had been here? More than I had expected, especially in the North Faerie Court. The position of Holly King open to all in the North Court, who would have thought? That meant that the position of Oak King was also open to all as the South Faerie Court reflected the North and back again. Neither would enact something so revolutionary without the other following suit soon after.

Such a change opened up a whole new world of possibilities for suspects. Faeries were notoriously conservative and slow to change. Such a radical shift would disturb many. And then to arrange an exhibit fight here in the normal world, well, that could be too much.

I sighed. I had my work cut out for me.

I left the Holly King to his view and went to study the itinerary. If I had my way, we'd sit in this hotel room until the fight, but that wasn't possible. The whole point of the exhibition was to create awareness and acceptance between the two dimensions. That meant public appearances.

Which meant logistical nightmares for security.

Dammit, why hadn't I asked for vacation ages ago?

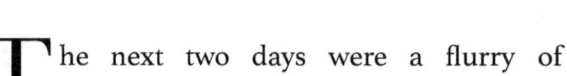

The next two days were a flurry of appearances. Press conferences in malls. Photo appearances on the steps of City Hall. More photo ops at the entrance to Black Forrest Park. A ribbon cutting at a dock on Deep Pool Lake, a dock that had been open for almost a year.

My head throbbed with the pressure of constantly scanning the crowds, searching for any trace of magic, trying to block out the residual energies from the magical creatures who were supposed to be there.

It was an impossible job.

But slowly the hours passed with the Holly King waving and smiling to the crowd. Spreading his wings and lifting up above them for a better photo.

Until the sun began to dip below the jagged edge of the city skyline.

"That is enough for today," Ulvar said. He touched the Holly King's elbow as they stood on the stairs to City Hall.

The Holly King gave a nod and began to back up the stairs, still smiling and waving to the crowd. He may have been from the backwaters of the North Faerie Court but he was working the crowd like a champ.

Finally when we reached the top of the stairs, he turned away. The faerie guard in their long robes closed around him. I brought up the rear.

The air seemed to sparkle with early twilight even though it was only four in the afternoon. The concrete stairs and the wide expanse leading to the multiple sets of double doors into City Hall had been swept of snow. The black marble was mottled with sprinkled dirt. There had been a big push in the city to get away from using salt because of the corrosive effect on car and on the concrete itself.

Sprinkled dirt helped some but not as much. There was still slipping hazards. It wasn't like bare ground was immune to being slippery.

Ground.

Dirt.

Summer.

Wait!

I leapt forward. Shoved past the first robed guard. Another blocked my way. I grabbed his arm, yanking hard. He fell back. The rich scent of earth filled the air. I caught sight of a swirl of blue fabric. Moving forward.

"Stop!" I yelled.

Heads turned toward me. The guard of faeries froze. A chill wind rustled the ends of their robes, giving the illusion of movement.

I'd done it. I'd stopped them.

Except the blue fabric was moving faster than the wind.

The Holly King took another step.

His feet flew backward, sliding on dirt that seemed to shuffle under his feet. I saw my uncle reaching, his lips moving in a spell.

Then the hard crunch of bone as the Holly King hit the pavement.

～

"Broken arm," my uncle said.

We stood clustered by the window in the hotel room. My uncle had his back to the magnificent view as the city lights twinkled beyond, oblivious to the disaster.

Captain Hwon stood on my uncle's left. A slight frown dimpled his lips. He wore a beige, knee-length, wool coat over his dark charcoal-grey suit. His black hair was perfectly in place.

"That doesn't sound too serious," Hwon said.

My uncle looked at me. "He does not understand."

I sighed. I had to play translator again. I hated having to translate cultural norms. It was too easy to screw up.

"It doesn't matter," I said. "The Holly King can't fight and he has to. It's a ritual. The Holly King and the Oak King must meet in battle at midwinter. They must be equally matched. To have one injured beforehand is to threaten the balance, not just here but in the Nether Realm."

The dimpled frown deepened. "Can't someone else fight for him?" the captain asked. "One of you?" He gestured to my uncle.

Ulvar shook his head. "We are sworn protectors. We are not eligible to take over for the Holly King. It has to be one unconnected to the guard."

"Then can't you call for a substitute from the North Court?" Hwon asked.

"It is too late," Ulvar said. "The fight is tomorrow. It cannot be delayed."

"We're screwed," I said.

My bold eloquence shut them all up. I stared out the window. The Incantation River was a dark line that zigzagged through the flickering lights decorating the city. From this high up, it was impossible to see anyone on the street, but I knew they would be there, hurrying along, bundled in winter coats. Some cursing the cold weather, others lifting their faces to the crisp, cool air. Most of them, regular people just living their lives. The disproportionate few trying to harness or exploit the energy released through the Great Tear.

Those dangerous few who threatened the balance, and the lives, of all of those regular people. The regular people I swore to protect. The few I swore to stop.

Now another threat had been dropped right at my feet.

And I knew what I had to do.

I turned my back to the window and faced my uncle.

"I will fight as the Holly King," I said.

And even as the words left my mouth, I knew I was really screwed.

The sound of the crowd was a constant throbbing hum in the dressing room of the main sports arena. I felt like I was deep underground, in some bomb shelter. The dressing room certainly exacerbated the feeling with the grey concrete walls and the concrete floor. Bland, beige area rugs had been tossed onto the floor but I could feel the hardness of the concrete through them. Framed photos of the Crossroad City Trailblazers decorated the wall above a lumpy, faded, burgundy sofa.

Opposite that was a dressing table, complete with a huge mirror surrounded by blazing lights.

Revealing me, dressed as the Holly King.

The frosted blue outfit moulded to my figure like a sheet of ice. It had originally been intended for a male faerie, but the fabric had certainly woven itself around me in a way that accentuated my figure. Streaks of white rippled down when I moved. Over top, I wore the blue robes with a tall, white collar that looked like it was made of wings carved of ice. Against the blue and white, my skin looked even paler than normal. The blue of my wings, usually a deep, rich colour, now matched the blue of the robes, looking ice cold.

My blazing red hair had been pulled back, braided, and tucked into a tight bun at the base of my skull. Strings with beads of white had been wrapped around my head, looking like a mix between a crown and snowflakes. Somehow it drained my red hair of colour, making it look frosted.

I had never looked more like a Winter Faerie and it felt decidedly weird.

Over the rumbling of the crowd, I heard a knock on the dressing room door.

I turned away from the mirror.

"Come in."

The door swung open and Trevel ducked as he entered. He stayed hunched as he stepped into the room, his shoulders almost brushing the florescent lights hanging from the ceiling. His bend head created a pool of shadows across his face and chest but I could still see the widening of his eyes as he looked at me.

I pointed a finger at him. "Not a word."

He held up his hands and shook his head. "They sent me in to get you. Maeve, are you sure you want to do this?"

"Want to? No. Have to? Yes," I said. "Who else are they going to get at such short notice? It has to be a faerie from the North Court. It can't be one of the guards. There isn't anyone else."

Shadows deepened on Trevel's face as he frowned. "I don't like it. The summer faeries have been sabotaging this fight and you're playing right into their game."

"Don't, Trevel. I'm nervous enough as it is."

"Maeve..." he said.

I held up my hand. "Stop. I expect you to stop fretting about me and keep an eye on everything else. You're my back up, right?"

He straightened as much as the lower ceiling would let him.

"Of course," he said.

I nodded. "I'm going undercover, that's all."

Saying it out loud actually helped. I wasn't the Holly King, I was just acting the part. Setting up the sting. And Trevel would have my back.

That gave me some comfort. Enough to let my heart slow from the steady gallop to a more reasonable pace.

I picked up the Holly King's sceptre, a rod of blue with white streaks spiralling down it. At first it felt cold as ice, then seemed to meld to my hand. A surge of magic tingled through me, leaving my wings quivering. I gave a nod and we left the dressing room.

As soon as we passed through the door, the wall of sound hit me, vibrating along my nerve endings. The sound seemed to go on and on as if no one needed to stop for breath, just an ending hum of chants and cheers.

The large hallway angled upward and the yells led the way, increasing in volume with every step. Cool florescent lighting created a twilight zone of dim lighting with no shadows. Ahead, I spotted a whiter light, expanding as the sound expanded.

It opened to fill the auditorium.

The noise was deafening. The stadium was filled with people, rows and rows stretching upward and disappearing into darkness above the hanging lamp that shone on the ring in the centre. It was set up like a boxing ring, a few stretches of rope separating the fighters from the onlookers.

The path led straight to the side of the ring. People hung over either side, cheering, jeering, yelling. The air held the bite of a chill but as I stepped onto the path, I felt the heat radiating from all those bodies.

The yeasty stench of beer floated like a cloud, punctuated with the smell of popcorn and burnt hot dogs. It made my stomach curdle. Bile burned the back of my throat. My legs trembled as I walked. It felt hard to pull the stuffy air into my lungs. I gripped the sceptre so hard my fingers ached.

My shoulders tightened with every step. The crowd seemed to get louder and louder as I moved toward the ring. How could this many people fit in this space? How could there be any air?

Stop it. I was giving myself a panic attack. I forced myself to look straight. Stop looking at the sides, stop looking at the people. I was here to get to the ring. I was here to be the Holly King.

That was all I had to do.

As I stared at the off-white canvas floor, my breath came a little easier. My shoulders loosened. My fingers stopped throbbing.

It was going to be all right.

Then I spotted the Oak King.

He was tall for a faerie, probably six feet or more. His body was shrouded in browns and greens that shifted in the light like the dancing of leaves in a breeze. He carried a staff of brown that looked like a bent branch but I could feel the energy pulsing from it even across the arena. Leaves made a living crown on his head, reflecting the vibrant green of his wings.

He leapt into the air, soaring over the ropes, and landed in the centre of the ring.

My stomach tightened again.

Okay, so he looked formidable. That was the whole point, wasn't it? The Oak King and the Holly King battled on midwinter, until summer overtook winter and the days became longer. This was just an exhibition fight, just ritual. Nothing really to worry about.

Nothing at all.

But I wasn't gonna let any Summer Faerie upstage me.

Still halfway to the ring, I leapt into the air. My wings unfolded behind me and I angled myself so they could catch the light. From the gasps below, I knew they glittered like blue jewels. The blue and white of my costume only accented their look.

I aimed for the ring, drifting through the air like a snowflake. As I descended, I noticed the tight lips of the Oak King. He didn't like being upstaged either.

Tough cookie. This was my town.

And I was gonna give them a show.

I landed on the canvas floor and felt the slight give of the fabric. As was custom, I held out my left hand toward the Oak King, palm up. He stepped forward, extending his left hand, palm down. I could feel the energy tingling between our hands without them even touching.

I lifted my sceptre and slammed it down on the mat.

A loud boom filled the room, drowning out the crowd.

The cheers and yells stopped. Silence descended.

Time for the show.

I looked at the Oak King. High cheekbones, a square jaw with dimpled chin. Soft hazel eyes. Light brown hair the colour of fresh earth. His eyes narrowed as he glared at me.

I lifted my chin.

"The land sleeps in winter. Let it slumber," I said.

"The land yearns to wake," he said. "I will wake it."

"So it shall be," I said.

"So it shall be," he said.

We clasped hands. The shock of magic took my breath away. Around us, the crowd seemed to shimmer. I thought I heard loud gasps.

This was an exhibition, right?

The Oak King broke contact first. He stepped back, surefooted. He twirled his staff, holding it out with both hands, ready to engage.

Of course, he'd trained for this, knew what to expect. My legs still felt wobbly from the energy.

I grabbed my sceptre in both hands. Bent my knees.

Let's do this.

The Oak King leapt into the air. I tried to follow, but he spun to the side. His staff lashed out. Slammed into my left upper arm.

Pain and energy burned through me. I staggered back.

He twirled the staff. Ended up holding it by the end. He swung again.

Aiming for my head.

I threw myself down. Landing on my back.

The staff soared a few inches from my face.

This was no exhibition fight.

I rolled to the right and sprang to my feet. My hand tightened on the spectre and I felt its power surge up my arm. I gripped it in both hands and feined a swing toward the left.

The Oak King darted to the right.

I used my momentum to pull my right hand back, clenching my fist. Then I punched and caught him on the chin.

He staggered back. A look of shock crossed his face. The leaves on his head rustled as if startled.

Obviously he hadn't been expecting something so unmagical.

I could have gone in for the kill but this was an exhibition. As the Holly King, I was supposed to lose. Summer was to triumph over winter at midwinter. But I wasn't gonna make it easy for him and I wanted him to know it.

From the way he held his staff a little closer to his body, I figured he got the message.

We circled each other, both holding our staffs between us. Magical energy crackled in the air around us, heightening my senses. I could smell the sweat and mingled stench of a dozen different perfumes in the air from the crowd around us. Heat from the lamp above shimmered on the top of my head along with the press of heat from the multitude of bodies. Yet the costume of the Holly King seemed to wick away the worst of the heat, leaving me as cool as a winter breeze.

The Oak King darted right. I turned to meet him. But then he was gone.

I heard the soft rustle of wings.

I glanced up.

I caught a glimpse of brown and green, shimmering in the light, before he landed on me.

My back slammed into the mat. My breath whooshed out of me, leaving me gasping. My vision darkened, seemed to twinkle. A flash of brown caught my eye.

Coming down at my head.

I managed to roll to the left.

The staff slammed into the canvas mat an inch from my head.

I breathed in deep, gathering the winter wind to me. Cold sank into me, freezing me. I clenched my left fist then swung toward the Oak King.

But not in a punch.

At the apex of the swing, I released my fist and blew out. Winter wind surged through me. Freezing cold flashed over him, driving him off me and back across the canvas ring. The leaves on his head curled. The brown and green of his costume faded in colour, looking almost frosted.

As he struggled against the wind, I used the spectre to help me stand. My body felt achy from slamming into the mat. Gathering the wind and expelling it also took energy.

Fortunately, the Oak King looked like he was feeling the effects too.

He shook off the wind, slamming the end of his staff into the canvas mat. The wind died immediately. After a moment, the leaves on his head unfurled. The colours of his suit deepened again, like a blooming in spring. He glared across the space at me, grinding his teeth. Then his lips pursed. His precursor to taking flight.

I leapt first.

My wings sprang out, grabbing the air and sending me upward. The Oak King faltered, then jumped after me.

The green of his wings shimmered in the light. I didn't have much time to admire them as he dove toward me, staff aimed like a spear.

I twirled, darting around him. As he passed, I swung out with my spectre, hitting the staff right above his grip.

An explosion of light burst forth, blinding me. I yanked myself back, aiming upward and behind. I knew the direction would carry me away from the Oak King, give me a chance to recover.

The moist mossy smell of fresh earth told me I wasn't far enough.

Shapes were just starting to fade in through the white as I closed my eyes. I pulled my arms in tight to my body, then kicked out with

461

my right leg. My wings folded, heightening the sudden spin. Within a few seconds, I could feel myself twirling like a top.

I sucked air in deep into my lungs, pushing my belly out as far as it would go.

Then I pushed it out.

Cold air swirled around me. I could almost feel frost on my fingertips. I readied my spectre to blast the air at the Oak King...

Something slapped my wings. My twirling faltered. I lost momentum. Cold air dispersed. A flash of brown passed over my eyes. The sudden impact of the Oak King's staff slammed against my back.

My wings crumpled. I fell end over end. Down... down...

The off-white of the canvas mat grew in my vision.

I was going to smash into it, possibly break one of my wings.

Almost a death knell for a faerie.

I murmured as fast as I could. Waved the spectre in front of me.

And felt a cushion of cold air catch me just before I slammed into the mat.

It slowly deflated. I got my feet under me and stood on the canvas, using the spectre to steady me.

The roar of the crowd crashed over me. At the far end of the ring, I caught the worried look on my uncle's face. His brow crinkled. He was probably imagining how he was going to explain this to my mother.

I bet he wished he was in the ring now.

Then I caught sight of the original Holly King standing beside my uncle.

His lips were pressed tight together as he glared across at me. Was he angry that he'd lost his chance to fight in this exhibition?

Or was it something else?

A different look crossed his face, something I wasn't able to identify, as the Oak King landed on the mat in front of me.

Now that I looked closely at him, he wasn't directly in front of me but off to the right side. Far enough that he was able to glance over at the original Holly King without being too obvious.

Wasn't that interesting?

Traditionally, neither the Holly King or the Oak King were allowed to have any contact before the midwinter fight. Secrecy was so strong they didn't even know who each other were.

But these quick, split second glances told me they did know. And had actually met.

And come up with a plan.

A plan I was ruining.

No wonder the Oak King looked pissed.

Maybe they hadn't planned on actually taking the Holly King out. Maybe it had been a mistake. But why the threats then?

I didn't have all the pieces yet. I was going to have to get them if I was going to be able to bring this fight to its successful conclusion.

The Oak King raised his arms, lifting his staff into the air. I could feel the gathering of his magic. The rich smell of earth surrounded me.

I leapt forward and tackled him to the mat.

We landed in a tangle of limbs. The rough texture of his costume scraped against my hands like rough bark. His staff bounced against the mat and rolled away. For a moment, he wouldn't be able to use magic.

He was heavier than me. Stronger. Already I could feel his hands closing on my upper arms, getting ready to shove me away so he could retrieve his staff. I pressed my cheek against his, bringing my mouth close to his ear.

"What was the plan with the other Holly King?" I whispered.

The Oak King froze. I could almost hear the echo of his pulse over my own.

Before he could move, I grabbed my spectre. With one motion, I slammed it down on the canvas mat beside us.

"Freeze!"

Around us, the entire auditorium froze. Silence descended. I had taken us out of time, between the beats of our hearts, for a fraction of second. Even with the concentrated assistance of the spectre, my spell wouldn't last long.

I pulled back from the Oak King so I could look him in the face.

"Spill," I said. "What did you cook up with the Holly King?"

He shook his head. "I do not know what you are talking about."

"Don't lie to me," I said. "I saw the look you two gave each other. He didn't look exactly pleased that I was in the ring. Were you going to throw the fight? Is that it?"

He shook his head again and tried to pull away. I lifted the spectre, wagging it.

"Don't make me use it," I said.

"You were not supposed to be in here," he said.

"So I figured," I said. "Who was?"

He pressed his lips together. He didn't want to answer.

Tough cookie.

"Look, tradition is that you win this fight," I said. "You can still do that, but I'm more than willing to make you work for it and give you some scars to remember me by."

The muscles along his jaw tightened. I gripped the spectre tighter. He had trained for this fight but I'd been working on this side of the Great Tear for a long time. I knew a few tricks that would take him off guard.

Finally he sighed. "All right. No one was supposed to take his place. The fight was to be forfeit."

Now it was my turn to shake my head. "Why? You're set to win the exhibition fight anyway?"

"We did not want to fight," he said. "Not *here*."

Now I got it. The exaggerated threats, the Holly King taking a spill. It had all been planned to prevent an actual fight. The forfeiture would still have satisfied the midwinter change toward summer with the Oak King claiming victory, but they wouldn't have had to sully the event on this side of the Great Tear.

Except they hadn't counted on a member of the North Faerie Court being so readily available, especially someone as high as a seventh level princess.

Well, I wasn't exactly thrilled to be tangled up on the floor of a canvas mat with a guy who smelled just this side of a manure pile.

"I assume neither of you let either Court know about your little plan," I said. "Would be a shame for it to come out now. A disgrace for the entire Faerie world."

The Oak King turned a sickly shade of green. "You would not tell on us?"

"Not if you finish this fight properly," I said. "And when you return to the South Faerie Court, you stand down. Allow the Summer Court to rule in your stead."

He pressed his lips together so tight they looked bloodless.

"Better decide. This freeze is going to end..."

Cheers exploded around us. We slid back into the timeline as if no time had passed. With a grunt, the Oak King shoved me away and dove for his staff.

I jumped to my feet, gripping my spectre, as he rose, holding out his staff. His gaze flicked toward the original Holly King then back to me. He tucked his chin, giving me the briefest of nods.

A deal then.

He swung his staff, calling down a warm wind. I let it sweep me into the ropes on the side of the ring.

The rest of the fight lasted less than five minutes. We gave a great show of flashes of light clashing. Cold wind buffeted and losing to warm breezes. It ended with the Oak King sweeping my spectre out of my hands and me landing on my back.

He lifted his staff above his head, claiming victory for the South Faerie Court, for the rising sun and the coming summer.

The crowd exploded with cheers. The cold white light from the lamp shining down shifted into a golden glow, expanding the light up the entire auditorium. The beginning of a new day. The midwinter shift from winter toward summer.

I climbed to my feet and bowed alongside the triumphant Oak King. As we waved to the crowd, I caught his occasional nervous glance in my direction. I pressed my lips together to prevent the smirk from rising.

After several more bows, we exited the ring. As I crawled under the rope, following the Oak King, I nodded to him. He gave me a nod back. He would remember our deal. I would be checking on him. To have a princess from the North Court calling him out would be more disgraceful than relinquishing the Oak crown.

My uncle came up beside me as I headed back down the hall toward the dressing room. The press of people on either side didn't bother me anymore. As we headed down the sloping hall I felt a headache begin at my temples. My whole body ached from the fight, both physical and magical. I wasn't used to casting spells like that. Even in my day job, it was usually one spell to stop someone, not casting over and over.

Plus I missed the comfort of my own wand. The spectre was powerful but not attuned to me. My wand made my own magic feel effortless. But it never would have withstood the assault from the Oak King.

As we passed out of sight of the crowd, the cheers faded into a rolling roar. My uncle tossed back the hood of his robe and put his arm around my shoulders. A feeling of coolness spread through me, easing the knots in my back and numbing the throbbing at my temples. I felt a sleepiness coming over me. The aftereffects of the fight.

I leaned against my uncle. He steered me into the dressing room and closed the door. I reached up and pulled the crystal crown from my head.

"You did a wonderful job," he said. "I knew you would get them to finish the fight."

I blinked at the mischievous smile on his face. My sleepiness faded.

"Wait a minute. You knew they wanted to sabotage the fight, that both Kings were in on it."

Ulvar shrugged. "I suspected it."

"That's why you insisted on me helping. You knew you could push me into it if something happened to the Holly King."

I jabbed my finger at his chest. He captured my hand and patted it.

"I knew you would do the right thing, Mauve, the honourable thing for both our Courts, for both our Realms. These boys have tunnel vision believing we can be separate from this world. With the Great Tear, we must learn to live together or it will tear our worlds apart. You know that better than anyone. I knew you would find a way to make it work."

Manipulated. Machinations. Even though I knew my uncle meant the things he said, there were still other layers underneath. All the crap I'd left the North Faerie Court to avoid.

"Don't pull this stunt on me again," I said. "You may be my uncle but this is my town and I'll not have you bring that faerie crap here. Understand?"

He grinned. "I understand."

It wasn't exactly an agreement but with my uncle it was the best I was going to get. He was nothing if not the quintessential, shifty faerie.

He reached past me and picked up the crystal crown I had dropped onto the sofa.

"Just one more thing before I go," he said.

I crossed my arms over my chest. "What's that?"

"Your mother wanted me to get a picture of you, and I did not get a chance before the fight."

He held out the crown toward me.

Was he kidding me? I could see from the sincere look on his face that he wasn't. I could refuse and let him take the heat from my mother.

But giving in to this might just come in handy at some other point in the future.

It never hurt to have a faerie owe you a favour, even when he was already your uncle.

I took the crown from his hand and balanced it on my fingertips.

"I'll pose for you on one condition," I said.

Ulvar's eyes widened in surprise. Then he sighed and nodded.

"Let me guess," he said.

"No, you won't have to," I said. "I'll be sure to let you know when I'm collecting." I placed the crown on my head and then tilted to give the best angle. "How's this?"

My uncle pursed his lips. "Not quite what I was expecting but it will have to do."

Truer words had never been spoken about me before.

And may not be again.

I grinned wide for uncle as he prepared to take my picture. The things we do for family.

ABOUT THE AUTHOR

Based in Toronto, Canada, Rebecca M. Senese survives the frigid blasts of winter and boiling steams of summer by weaving words of horror, mystery, science fiction and contemporary fantasy.

Garnering an Honorable Mention in "The Year's Best Science Fiction" and nominated for numerous Aurora Awards, her work has appeared in *Fiction River: Superpowers*, *Fiction River: Visions of the Apocalypse*, *Fiction River: Sparks*, *Fiction River: Recycled Pulp*, *Tesseracts 16: Parnassus Unbound*, *Imaginarium 2012*, *Tesseracts 15: A Case of Quite Curious Tales*, *TransVersions*, *Future Syndicate*, and *Storyteller*, amongst others.

Find out more about Rebecca at:
rebeccasenese.com

facebook.com/Rebecca.M.Senese

twitter.com/RebeccaSenese

goodreads.com/Rebecca_Senese

bookbub.com/authors/rebecca-m-senese

amazon.com/Rebecca-M-Senese/e/B004LYV91A

A LAST MEAL FOR THE HOLLY KING

STEFON MEARS

The cabin. Jess and I bought it not long after we got married.

Stupid purchase, really. I mean, we were kids. Twenty-five years old, and barely making enough to get by. We lived in a one-bedroom apartment, for Pete's sake. We were the last people who should have taken out a mortgage to buy a vacation cabin off in the Oregon woods.

But Jess' dad was a realtor, and Jess grew up learning the business. Even if she hated it. Even if she never wanted to sell a damned house, no matter how much money she could make doing it.

She loved accounting, so that was what she did.

But she *knew* real estate. And she knew bargains.

The cabin was a bargain. Mispriced way under market value. Solidly built. Over fifty years old. Maybe a thousand feet from the Willamette River.

Jess was convinced it would be the place we took our kids every summer. The place we hid away every chance we got, once those kids were out of the house.

We never had those kids. We tried. Lord knows we tried. But the one time the pregnancy caught, well, it went wrong.

Badly wrong.

The doctor was gentle about telling us we'd never have kids.

Turned out the doctor told Jess more than that, but she'd kept it from me. Didn't tell me about the internal damage she'd suffered when it all went wrong. That the hours it had taken us to get her to a real hospital—from that damned cabin—had left their mark deep inside her.

"Don't worry about it, Stevie," she'd told me, ruffling my hair the way she did whenever she wanted me to drop a subject. An old habit. One she'd started back when we were freshmen in college, and she didn't want me worrying about the ex-boyfriend living on her dorm floor, only two doors down.

Truth was, that big lunk Lester hadn't been anything to worry about. She was more than over him, and he was into some new girl every other week.

Set the precedent in my head. When my blond curls got ruffled,

Jess was telling me the truth. That what she told me when she ruffled my hair and said those magic words, that was something I really didn't have to worry about. It was something I could put out of my mind, and never think about again.

Didn't matter if it was how we were going to make ends meet when we were living paycheck-to-paycheck. Didn't matter when her dad decided I was the devil incarnate and he forbade her to marry me. Didn't matter when some cute guy at work had the hots for her.

She'd just play with my curls, smile that smile of hers, and say, "Don't worry about it, Stevie." And within a few weeks I'd see proof that I'd never had anything to worry about in the first place.

Jess only lied once, when she ruffled my hair.

It was five years after the pregnancy—ten years after we bought the cabin—that the bill came due on the one hair-ruffling lie Jess ever told me.

That was six weeks ago.

Her funeral was five weeks ago.

Only three hours ago, I finally got the rest of our friends and families to leave me alone. Gave them a promise I didn't intend to keep about visiting for Christmas in a few days.

They meant well. They all did. My friends. Her friends. Our friends. Our neighbors. My parents. Her parents. Her grandparents, for Pete's sake. Even my brother—who I heard from once a year—and her two jet-setting sisters.

Everybody meant well.

Everybody was *there* for me. All I had to do was call.

Everybody but the one person who mattered.

Everybody but the only person who could make it all better.

Everybody but Jess.

Took me three hours to get to the cabin from Portland, in our red Subaru Outback. Another purchase I hadn't thought we could afford. But Jess had been right about that too.

Was almost sunset when I left. Pitch dark now.

And now I'm just sitting here in the front seat. Listening to the ticking of the engine, and the muffled sounds of a few brave western meadowlarks, still singing in the Douglas fir trees that are every-where around here.

If I rolled down the window, I could hear them better. Maybe some of the stellar jays too, with their cries that sound kind of like crows, but not quite. If the meadowlarks are still up, maybe the stellar jays are too.

Jess always loved the stellar jays. Liked to say they were blue jays wearing helmets. I used to doodle images of stellar jays taking off their helmets for her, in different places. On the moon. Atop Mount Everest. On the eighteenth green at Pebble Beach Golf Course. Wherever.

Jess kept at least a dozen of those drawings. They weren't my best work, but she still had four of those doodles up on the cube walls of her office when I went to collect her stuff.

Those four are on the seat next to me. Along with her favorite blue-green scarf that brought out her eyes. The one she wore even in the summertime, because it was "silk, and beautiful" and because I gave it to her.

If there are any stellar jays out there, I could hear them clearer if I opened the windows.

I could also get the woodsy smells of this part of the forest. The smells I know almost as well as I know Jess' smells, long as we'd been coming out here.

But I keep the windows closed. Just a little bit longer.

Because with the windows closed, I can still smell traces of Jess' favorite spicy perfume, from the time she spilled half a container on the floor of the front seat. Over a year and a half ago now.

She'd wanted to clean it up, but I hadn't let her. Insisted I wanted to keep the smell.

Sitting here right now, I'm half-glad I did and half feel like a fool. But I can't stop sniffing.

Well, maybe there's another reason I'm sniffing, but that one doesn't matter. At least, it won't matter for long.

The cabin.

I'm back at the cabin, one last time.

And no, I didn't pack a change of clothes.

~

I finally drag myself out of the car. Don't bother locking it. There's no one around to steal it. Hell, even in the height of tourist season, we never saw anyone close to our cabin.

But now? In late December?

The woods are empty, but for the birds and squirrels. Grabbing what they can between rains. Especially with snow likely by the new year.

Even the deer are smart enough to have found shelter by now. And the coyotes and raccoons too, though I'm more likely to spot one of them around here. Even if it were snowing, I'd probably spot a coyote. They're crazy like that.

Biting chill in the air. Cuts right though my heavy jacket. Probably should have worn my long johns, coming out here. Something a little more under the heavy jeans. Wasn't like I intended to freeze to death.

At least I had on wool socks. Jess always insisted on that. "Before the hiking boots go on, first the wool socks." If she said it once, she said it a thousand times.

Jess was the native Oregonian. I grew up down around the San Francisco Bay Area. Place called San Mateo. When I first met Jess, I thought hiking was something done in sneakers and a tee shirt, so you didn't overheat when you started sweating.

It was our first spring break at OSU when Jess took me hiking in the Oregon backwoods for the first time, and I found out what real hiking was like.

She never let up on that. Always called me her city boy. As if she was born in the deep woods or something, instead of a Portland suburb like Tualatin.

I walk around the cabin carrying a can of gasoline, blazing a bright LED flashlight to conduct the customary check and make sure everything is in order.

The cabin stands two stories tall. Some two thousand square feet.

Faux-log exterior, and as I pad along the wet fir needles, I wave the beam of light to make sure nobody's broken any of the dozen windows. Make sure the generator hasn't been fucked with, and that the well pump is still in good working order.

I pour gasoline into the generator, while the scent offends my nose. Only a few gallons. Won't need much, after all.

Once it coughs to rumbling life, I get the pump working, and run the outside tap until I'm sure the line is clear.

Water's freezing, but nobody's messed with the pump, or the generator, or the house.

That's good. Jess loved this cabin so much. Even after ... what happened with the baby. I'd wanted to sell it the next day, but Jess wouldn't hear of it. Insisted we keep coming out here. "Make good memories to overwhelm the bad one."

It worked for a while, but it will never work again.

With that sunny thought in mind, I head inside. Flick on the lights. Little fake candles scattered around all light up, warm incandescence, and not too bright.

The inside keeps up the illusion that this is an actual log cabin, instead of a fancier place crafted to look like a log cabin. Has the rich yellow-orange look of weathered old wood. Big heavy crossbeams along the ceilings. Smells of weathered old wood too.

Jess had tried to explain that to me once, but all I took away from it was that there was enough real wood inside the place to keep the illusion alive, and that my imagination supplies the rest.

We have a faux bear skin rug in front of the huge stone fireplace. Still enough chopped wood in the iron frame beside it—my handiwork, those split logs—to last through the whole of the winter.

I get a fire going before I check out the rest of the bottom floor. Still making sure no one's been in here.

The crackling warmth feels good on my face and hands. Brings a misty smile to my face. Jess was always so proud of my fire-making skills. Used to joke.

"Ugh. Cave man make fire. Good."

Every time she did that, I'd throw her over my shoulder to show her what else a cave man could...

I turn away from the fire.

Other throw rugs all through the place. The only thing that obviously gives the lie to the log cabin pretense—apart from the fact that there's an upstairs, or the properly plumbed bathrooms—is the kitchen.

Real log cabins don't have refrigerators or electric stoves and ovens. Or recessed electric lights, for that matter, but they're set inside pretty realistic fake candles and such.

Looking around the place, I doubt we could afford it even today. What with the way the market's gone nuts. But a decade ago? Should have been impossible.

But Jess found a way.

She always did.

Almost always.

I drop my backpack and fall to my knees on the faux bear skin rug. Run my hands over it. Wonder if she washed it after our last visit, or if I could still smell her...

I can't. She washed it.

I fall asleep there anyway.

~

The beef jerky I'd eaten on the drive to the cabin had tasted good at the time. Teriyaki. Tasty.

But when I wake up the next morning, it tastes stale in my dry mouth. And like chemicals, which I probably shouldn't think too long about.

My neck is kinked up, and my back is sore.

A whole night on my belly on the bear skin rug. I guess I should count myself lucky that the fire just burned itself out, instead of leaping out onto all this wood and burning the place down around me while I slept.

Would have been an appropriate ending for me, really. Taken out by the cabin that killed Jess.

No. Stop it. The cabin didn't kill Jess.

I make my way to my knees. Roll my neck around slowly. Shrug off my heavy coat. I'd been sweating in my sleep—in the coat and right in front of the fireplace—and now the inside was wet. And so was the rug, where my face and pits and hands had been.

I shiver in the chill now. The fire's been out a while.

I consider building another, but don't. Instead I dig into my backpack. Dry swallow a few ibuprofen tablets, then dig out a peanut butter and honey sandwich. One of two. Whole wheat bread. The good stuff, not some cheap major brand knock-off.

That was one of my contributions to our diet, and Jess ate it up. Literally. She'd grown up on the major brands of bread, and had no idea how tasty the real stuff was. Or how much better for you. Well worth the cost.

But I can't get the whole thing down without some water, so I dig out one of my three plastic bottles of water. Pint bottles, from the drive up.

I down the bottle and the sandwich, and still my belly rumbles for more.

"Tough," I say. "Hike first, then the next sandwich."

I need one last hike. Not just to get my blood going, and maybe work out a few kinks.

No, I want one last memory of this cabin. Maybe being the best that the woods can be around here. One last memory of the place that Jess loved so much, before...

I grunt as I get to my feet. Try to work out that kink in my neck a bit. It's spread to my jaw now. At least it feels like it. Hope the ibuprofen kicks in soon.

I stop in the john to relieve myself, but don't look in the mirror. Not even when I wash my hands.

I pull my coat back on, grimacing at the wet spots, head out the front door then. Locking it out of habit, and laughing at myself when I catch it.

I leave it locked anyway. What the hell.

I pick a direction then and start out. I double-check my good compass to make sure I know which way I'm going, and start.

At first, it's just plodding along. My stiff, sore body unhappy with this much movement. My boots scuffling and squishing through the places still damp from last night's rain. The fir needles like a carpet underneath me, for the most part. Making my steps soft and quiet.

Well, quiet for me, anyway. Jess always said I stomped through the woods like a herd of elephants.

I work my way through the Douglas firs to find the game trail near our cabin. Jess said it's a deer trail, but I was never sure how she decided that.

If I follow it east, it leads to the river. If I follow it west, it heads into the foothills.

The foothills is a longer hike, but the river is prettier.

I was going to do it at the cabin, but the river seems like an appropriate place to me. Yeah, it isn't what I planned on, but this way it could look like an accident.

Might be easier on the families that way.

So I turn east, and have to watch my knees along the way, because the ground slopes toward the river, and going down with a twisted knee out here all alone would suck. Make everything more difficult.

There's thicker underbrush on both sides of me here. Lots of ferns, and other plants I don't know, but Jess would.

Drier through here, under a thicker canopy from the fir trees. My boots make a more satisfying crunch with every step. Not to mention that all that underbrush is hiding more animals. I can hear them every so often, moving around in the underbrush.

I can hear more birds along here now too. Crows and meadowlarks, mostly. I try to spot a few stellar jays, but don't have any luck.

I do see a bird I didn't expect though.

A wren.

Beady little thing, compared to the crows. Pale gray, with darker wings. Not many wrens in Oregon. I only recognize it because Jess spotted one on that first hike together, and she called it a lucky sign.

It must be lost, but I can't help but follow it now. Jess' lucky sign. It's heading toward the river too.

I try to keep pace with it. Risking my knees. Hurting my neck every time I look up to track it, and gritting through the pain because I like the idea of there being something all the way out here that's just as lost and lonely as I am.

When I lose sight of it, I damn near start crying. Have to stop, huffing and puffing for breath, my face all hot and my skin itching under my coat and the heat of exertion.

I just lean against a tree and hang my head a moment.

Of course the wren got away. What was I going to do anyway? Catch it?

I roll my stiff neck one more time, hissing at the jabs of pain at key spots, and start hiking again.

The river isn't far away now.

~

Lots of wild grass between the trees and the river here. Greenish now, from all the rains, instead of the amber color it is in the summertime.

And right now, it's all wet. Maybe there was a little local rain overnight, or maybe it's just wetter here, close to the river.

My boots are squishing already, coming around that last tree and looking at the damp grass between me and the river.

The Willamette is broad here. Maybe a hundred yards across. Maybe more. Jess and I used to kayak along it sometimes. Never all that fast, not along here. Nice and safe for kayaks.

Should have thought to grab one from the cabin. If I'd thought about using the river that way.

Doesn't matter now.

The sky is gray-blue, mixed from dark rain clouds all the way to blue patches. As though trying to promise a break. Clarity. A little sunshine on my life.

As if.

I can hear the dull, soft roar of the river's rush. I look forward to it getting louder and louder as I get closer.

I draw one more deep breath, reassuring myself that my knees are as bad as I think. Playing catcher in college, that was a long time ago. I've been much better to my knees since then. Haven't dislocated them once, since then.

They pop anyway as I squish closer, and every time my boots slip in the mud, I grit, and seize, and squeak at the pain in the kinks in my neck and shoulders.

But I keep my feet and get closer.

Soon enough I'll be able to climb out onto our rock. That should be dry enough to be safe, at least. Toward the land side of it anyway.

Properly speaking, our rock is a boulder. Bigger than my Subaru, it juts out of the ground and out over the river.

Jess and I used to fish from the rock, sometimes. When we wanted to pretend we had a shot at catching something. Neither of us could fish worth a damn, but sitting out on that rock with Jess was a lovely way to spend a summer day.

We didn't come out to the rock in the wintertime, of course. But the whole family knows about the rock. Knows what a spot it was for me and Jess. Wouldn't surprise any of them if I went out to visit it one last time, even in the wintertime.

And if I "happened" to slip off that rock—wet as the river side would likely be from rain and river spray, especially without the summer sun to burn it off—well, that was an end they could tell themselves was accidental. Even if they might suspect otherwise, deep down.

I almost reach the rock when I realize someone's already sitting on it.

Can't get a good look yet, but already anger boils around in my belly.

How dare someone be on *our* rock? On today of all days?

I'm half tempted to shove the interloper into the river.

I don't try to soften my steps either. I stomp right out onto the rock, tracking mud. Even call out, "Hey!" nice and sharp.

I mean, if it shocks the interloper into the water that wouldn't be *my* fault, would it?

I admit though, shame burns through me all the way to my face, the moment I call out. I'm not the kind of guy to do something like that, and Jess wouldn't have approved.

Of course, she wouldn't have approved of the other thing I have in mind for today. But then, Jess lied to me about the condition that led to her death, so she doesn't have any stones to throw on that front, as it were.

The interloper doesn't turn around. Just raises a brownish, wizened hand.

The interloper's dressed in mostly dark brown clothes, but accented with forest green. Heavy stuff, like he might live out here in the woods and knows how to keep warm.

And even though I can't get a good look at the interloper yet, it feels like a *he*.

I want him to turn around. Show some surprise. Maybe say something. Maybe even get mad at *me* for interrupting his solitude. Give me an excuse to get righteous.

But he doesn't. He just sits there, almost like he expected me to join him.

So I do, out of spite.

I can see his face now. He has what my mom always called Celtic features. Just like our Scottish-Irish family has, but I don't think he's a relative. It's just that he has the right kind of jaw to be Scottish— heavy, with a cleft that I could see even past his scraggly, snow-white beard. Right kind of cheekbones too.

Scraggly, snow-white hair, around his nut-brown tan, falling down to his shoulders. With a sprig of holly tucked in just above his right ear.

He has a lean frame. Not skinny, but more like a life of work has made him wiry strong.

This is an old man, but up close I'm not sure I could take him.

I sit down beside him.

"Morning," I say.

"Yes," he says. "You are."

"I beg your pardon?" I say, astonishment giving me formal tones.

"I could feel it before you even got out of the woods. Mourning."

"Well..." I start, but don't know what to say next, so I just trail off.

"What a pair we are," he says.

"What do you mean? A pair?"

He turns and looks at me, his eyes so vibrantly green I start shaking and have to clasp my elbows to stop.

"What a pair we are," he repeats. "Both due to die before sunset tomorrow. But I'm going to rage and fight like hell, while you're going to ... what? Just fling yourself in the river and freeze or drown, whichever comes first?"

"I ... what..."

"I. What," he mimics, his tone getting sharper. "Say what you want to say."

His tone snaps right through me, and words fall out of my mouth before I can stop them. "Jess was my world. Jess was everything. And now she's gone. What's the point of going on? Might as well just end it now, and stop wasting resources that everyone else could profit from. And what do you mean you're going to die tomorrow? What do you mean fight like hell? Who's going to kill you?"

"Mmmm," he says, tugging at his beard, and I only just realize he's not wearing gloves. I'm not either, but, I mean, he's an *old man*. Complete with the weathered wrinkles. "Still more in there, isn't there? Interesting. That usually gets everything out like you've got food poisoning."

"Food poisoning?"

"Terrible way to die, that," he says. "Freezing and drowning are both better." He shrugs. "If you think there's a *good* way to die."

Bitterness in his tone that time. Bitterness I'd been hearing in my own voice for the past six weeks. But hearing it now, from this old man, it snaps through just as hard as his other words had. But even deeper.

Once more, words fall right out of my mouth.

"We were skydiving. Stupid thing, really. But we'd promised

ourselves years ago. Every year we had to do something new. Some-thing we'd never done before. And skydiving, well, it just sounded more exciting than exotic cuisine, or some kind of safari."

I shake my head, tears leaking out of my eyes now. The first tears I've let myself shed since it happened, and I'm only half-aware they're escaping. I'm still in the middle of the words I'm saying to a stranger who has no business hearing them.

"Skydiving. It was my idea. We'd tried one of those trampoline places last year, and Jess kept teasing and teasing me that I didn't have the courage to bounce as high as she did. But if I'd known... If she'd told me..."

"But she didn't," the old man says, his voice gentle. "Keep going, son. Get it all out."

"Damn it!" I punch the rock, just to distract the emotional pain with physical.

Doesn't help. I damn near don't feel it. Just a distant buzzing and pulsing from my knuckles. Even though I know it should hurt. Too wrapped up in the pain welling up inside me. Overfilling me like a balloon. Sure I'd pop any second now.

Every bit of my insides feels shaky and angry and tight.

But then I start talking again, and the words coming out of me almost seem to deflate me as they go.

"She didn't tell me! She didn't tell me about the long-term damage. The risk of a rupture. The doctor told *her*. Showed me right on the damn chart, the day she died. Showed me the *day and hour* he told her. Like it was high blood pressure or something. That sharp stupid tone in the smug bastard's voice. Like he thought I was going to sue him for malpractice or something, and his little *chart note* gave him a get-out-of-murder free card."

"Was it murder?" the old man asks, voice still soft, but compelling.

"No. Yes. Maybe. I don't know." I shake my head, spiking pain from my kinked neck, echoed in the throb of my knuckles. My body still shakes like I'm caught in a whirlwind and might end up in Oz. "Not on his part. He'd done his damned duty. Maybe not even on Jess' part. Maybe she'd forgotten. Hadn't thought about how jarring the landing would be, even a good landing. And her landing, it wasn't exactly textbook."

"But..."

"But damn it! If she'd told me, *I* would have remembered it. *I* would have known. I would have stopped her. Hell, I wouldn't have let her do the river rafting we did two years ago. That could have gone wrong. Or the—"

"Maybe that's why," the old man says, in that soft, compelling tone. "Maybe she didn't want to stop living just because she *might* die."

"But she did! She died! She left me!" I hang my head forward. So far forward I almost fall into the river, but a very strong hand catches me by the shoulder and pulls me back.

"Easy there," he says. "Don't want to do that now."

"But—"

"She took a risk, didn't she? She died, yes, but she died doing the things she loved, with the man she loved. Didn't she? How many people can say the same?"

"But she *died*," I say, drawing that last word out like it's going to spiral down a drain and disappear, and take me with it.

"And I'm going to die tomorrow. What do you say to that?"

That snap to his tone again. Makes me look at him. Stare deep into those green, green eyes. See such sincerity that I can't stop myself from saying, "Don't."

That gets a smile from the old man. "Don't have a lot of choice in the matter." He cocks an eyebrow at me. "And who are you to talk? You going to tell me you weren't planning to throw yourself in this river? And that's assuming you don't just hike back to your cabin and eat your gun."

"How did you know about..." I shake my head. "Don't die. Look. I can see the life in you. You're three times as vibrant as my grandparents, and they're likely to live another fifty years. If some bastard thinks he's going to kill you, don't be there."

The old man chuckles. "Not that simple, my boy. Tomorrow's the winter solstice, and that's the day it has to happen. He knows it. I know it. Not like this is the first time anyone's danced this dance."

That makes no sense to me at all. I shake my head again, ignoring the pain.

And for a moment. Just for a moment. I see a way to find a little meaning in my life. Not much, and not enough to last long. Not without Jess.

But more than enough to see me through another day or two.

"Look," I say. "No reason you can't have one last good meal, right? Come back to the cabin with me."

"You mean that?" the old man says, one white eyebrow high as a bird flies. "You want to cook me a last meal?"

"I do," I say. I stand, take his hand, and pull him to his feet. He comes up so easily I don't think he needed the help.

"Come on," I say, "my cabin's this way."

I lead the old man back through the woods along the deer path, and he moves so quietly through the trees that I have to keep checking that he's still with me.

More animals on the hike back. I swear. It's almost like every bird and squirrel and every little fuzzy woodland creature wants to come by and pay his respects to the passing of this little old man.

I wonder once in a while if he needs a break, but every time I turn to ask, he's moving along as easily as I am. Maybe more so. So I just shake my head and stop worrying about it.

I need something to talk about though, besides death, so I ask the only thing I can think of, as I watch yet another meadowlark dip as it flies past.

"I spotted a wren earlier. Any chance you saw it?"

"No," he says with a chuckle. "Can't say I did."

"I'm surprised," I say. "Every other animal in the forest seems to want a look at you."

"Well," he says, "animals are notably sensitive. Often more so than humans, I find."

I don't know what to say to that, so I let us lapse into silence. Fortunately, he seems to be all right with silence, and it's not all that much longer before we get the cabin.

"I don't have much food," I say as I unlock the door and swing it open.

"Of course not," he says without a trace of judgment in his voice. "Why would you?"

I gesture for him to enter, then flick on the lights. In the summertime we don't need the lights during the day, but with the winter overcast, well, I just can't take that many shadows right now. Not here.

I watch him take the place in. The pretense of it being a log cabin seems to amuse him, as does the faux bear skin rug. He likes the wood though, running his hands along the walls and floor. He likes the stone of the fireplace, too, from the way he caresses it.

"A lot of love went into building this place," he says reverently. Then looks at me, expression totally neutral. "A lot of love since then, too."

"Yeah, well, we came here a lot."

I start a fire, as much for something immediate to do as to chase a chill out of the air.

"I can tell," he says. "You two spent a lot of time in this room."

"What are you?" I ask. "Some kind of psychic reader or something?"

He chuckles. "Not quite."

"So you're not going to tell me my future?"

"Depends," he says, and his eyes catch mine and hold them while I'm still holding a log I'm about to add to the kindling that's finally caught. "Do you have one? In this world, I mean?"

I don't answer. Just add a couple of logs, then stand up and make a show of taking off my coat.

"Can I take your coat?" I ask.

"No need," he says. "I never get too hot or too cold."

He settles down onto the faux bear rug and stares into the fire, like he's reading the future in it after all.

I turn away to go start preparing lunch. Or maybe it's dinner. I've lost track of time, but that doesn't seem to matter.

I'm not sure it matters to him, either. The way he stares into that fire, I'm pretty sure he's forgotten I'm even here.

"Wouldn't happen to have any logs of oak, by any chance?" he asks without turning.

"Sorry," I say. "Fir's a lot easier to get close to the cabin."

"Pity," he says. "Smart, of course. And I can tell all of this was split from fallen trees. Still. I would have savored the smell of burning oak today."

I almost—*almost*—ask him what that means. Why that is. But the question dies on my lips. I'm not sure I really want to know, and I'm not sure he'll tell me anyway.

I wander into the kitchen to see what we have left over from our last trip out here, around Labor Day.

Nothing in the freezer, of course. It would have gone bad. Nothing in the fridge for the same reason.

But maybe in the cabinets...

Ah. Here we go.

"Do you like chili?"

"Love it," he says.

"Good, because it's the one thing we have plenty of." I pull out four cans, then add the fifth and final. Not sure how long it's been since the old man last ate, and it's not like I have a reason to save any.

In the back of the cupboard, passed the canned peas and corn, I spot something else though. Something left from earlier in the summer.

"Do you like brown bread?" I ask.

"Of course," he says.

"Good," I say, pulling it out. "Not many people like bread that comes in a can. We don't have any butter though."

"Honey will be fine," he says.

I scowl at his back. Honey is the only condiment we keep here.

Not like it's going to go bad, and neither Jess nor I were ever big on things like ketchup or mustard.

I reach into the upper cabinet for a jar of locally grown, clover honey. Came from a little stand on the side of the road, near where we leave the freeway to come to the cabin, that shows up every spring and stays into the early summer, depending on how productive their bees are.

Doesn't take too long to put the food together, and while I do I rummage around in the cabinets to see if we left anything else we might want right now. A two-liter of soda would be nice, so I can offer the guy something other than water...

Or this.

From the back of the top shelf of the cabinet behind the refrigerator I pull down a bottle of Stag's Breath scotch.

I stare at it for a moment. I hadn't known it was here. I didn't buy it. Stag's Breath is easy to find in Scotland, but not all that easy to come by in the States. It's a honey whisky, and a personal favorite.

Then I see the sticky note on the back of the bottle.

Happy half-birthday, Stevie. This is your reward for being a good boy and coming out here with me so I can enjoy a proper January snow.

The bottle gets hard to read for a moment. It's blurry for some reason.

∾

The old man and I sit at our—my—little kitchen table. Only big enough for two people, but that was all it ever needed to accommodate. On the rare occasions Jess and I brought friends out here, we just ate casually around the fire.

The smell of the spicy chili—extra spicy because I found Jess' cache of chili powder—has my belly rumbling so hard I swear it had almost given up on ever getting more food and has been trying to devour itself.

How long ago was that peanut butter and honey sandwich?

I pick up my spoon to dig into the chili, but pause when the old man bows his head for a few mumbled words of prayer.

I let him finish then, instead of digging straight in, I reach for the whisky.

"Afterwards, for that," he says. "Let's just enjoy the chili for itself."

I frown, but grab my spoon and dig in.

The old man eats with real gusto. Like he's a starving graduate student or something, and this is the first food he's seen in months. I mean, I'm hungry. But this guy's done with his first bowl before I'm halfway finished, and he's already ladled more into his bowl before I can offer to do it for him.

I slice him a few hunks of brown bread, still cylindrical from its packaging. I put the honey next to his plate, so he doesn't have to ask for it.

Have to do something to make myself feel like a proper host.

But the old man does act like a good guest, making sounds of pure pleasure as he eats. Even as he drinks, as though our filtered well water is fancy, imported bottle water from some exotic, untouched location.

And the brown bread. When a slice of honeyed brown bread touches his tongue, the old man's eyes close in rapturous bliss.

I frown at that too. I mean, I like brown bread plenty. Developed a taste for it as a kid. My dad's from Boston, and he grew up with it, so he always wanted it once in a while when I was growing up. Became like a treat for me.

But this old man, he acts like the brown bread with honey is manna from heaven.

I can only shrug and eat. I'd been a bit worried about maintaining a good dinner conversation, but clearly the old man doesn't need or want any of that.

He eats exactly half of the chili and brown bread. When I offer to heat up some veggies, he shakes his head and puts one hand on his belly.

"No need," he says. "The fare is more than sufficient to its task. You have my gratitude, and that is not a small thing."

Something about the simple sincerity of his words touches me. I find myself smiling. My face warming, just a little.

For the first time in weeks, I actually feel good for a moment.

The moment passes, of course, but I try to pretend it hasn't.

"So," I say. "You're ready for the whisky?"

"Ah," he says. "The perfect complement to the fine dinner."

I pour each of us a measure into tumblers from the cupboard.

"To your health," I say. "And to your *long life.*"

That makes him chuckle. "And to yours. Both health, and *long life.*"

Those last two words. They echo inside me.

I flash on a scene. Me, lying on my death bed.

I'm old. Older than my parents. Maybe older than my grandparents.

But I'm the grandparent now. Two generations of my progeny surround the bed. Four kids—three boys and a girl—and their spouses. A good dozen grandchildren.

I don't recognize where I am, but I know I'm at home.

"It's okay, Dad," my eldest son says. He's a good looking boy. In his forties now, but fit as a fiddle, with a full head of hair. Just like his old man was at that age.

Harold. His name is Harold. Funny. I always thought I'd name my first son Jonathan.

"Go on if you're ready." Harold smiles then, and I see myself and my father and my grandfather in his smile. "But if you aren't, snap out of it already."

I want to chuckle, but my body doesn't believe me. I want to say something, but my lips won't move.

I realize then that my eyes are closed. I can see my family and my room. But my eyes are closed. Why is that?

Suddenly I'm back at my table in the cabin, holding up a glass of Stag's Breath and looking into the shockingly green eyes of the old man across the table from me.

"What was that?" I ask. Or maybe I demand it. Or maybe I just try to demand it, and my mouth only makes it a question.

I'm not too sure of a lot of things right now.

"A possibility," he says. "Not a certainty, of course. And nothing that will happen if you throw yourself in the river or eat your gun."

"But... I had kids. I don't have any kids."

"Not right now. No. You don't."

I drink down a long pull from my glass. Savored the honeyed flavor of the scotch. Smooth and delicious, and distracting me from...

...from whatever that was.

The old man only sips his scotch. Or at least, that's what it looks like. Still, I note he's going for a refill while I still have scotch in my glass.

I toss it down and hold up my glass.

The old man smiles. Tilts his head. "You sure?"

"Yeah," I say slowly, noticing again the sprig of holly stuck behind his right ear. "What's with the holly?"

"Don't you like holly?" he asks, and I swear his voice is laughing at me.

"Sure, but Christmas isn't for a few days, and that's not exactly a wreath."

"I'm not Christian," he says with a shrug. "Think of it as a signature of sorts. I'm probably the only man you'll ever meet who keeps a sprig of holly behind his ear."

That seems so obviously true that I just give him a grimace, like it's a bad joke.

He chuckles and sips some more scotch, so I join him.

And that's when he tells me the story.

Now, I've been told a lot of stories in my day. From the time I was tiny and all those stories started "once upon a time..." all the way through the whoppers that the guys from work tell about their weekends. But this old man's story, it isn't like any other story I've ever heard.

He doesn't so much tell it. Except that he *is* telling it. I mean, his lips are moving and words are coming out, and all that jazz.

No, it's that I don't so much hear the story as experience it. Remember it, as though it all happened to me, just the other day.

As soon as he starts talking, I'm not me anymore, and I'm not sitting at a table in a faux log cabin, drinking scotch with a strange old man I picked up beside the river.

No, in this memory, I was a wren. Just like the little one I'd seen earlier on my hike.

I was a wren, and I was flying through the cold air of winter, but singing songs of joy because the cold was my time. It was my world. The trees I knew were evergreens or leafless. The seeds I knew were cold and hard and tasty. Everywhere I tapped my beak for worms or insects was cold and hard—perfect, in other words—and my food tasted all the better for it.

Until the day of the robin.

It seemed a day like any other. Shorter, I do admit it. Shorter than any other day of the year. Still, I flew and I ate and I sang out my joy.

But as I winged from one tree to another, I spotted the red breast of the robin.

My enemy? Yes, and no. It was a strange relationship. I knew I'd fought a robin once, when I was young. I remembered that. But now I was an old wren, and this robin was fresh and young. And it wanted the worms and seeds and bugs I ate. It wanted the best places for nests.

It wanted the warm time. Wanted the warm time to come. Wanted to end my delightful cold days.

The robin and I fight. He for the warm time, and I for the cold.

When I was young and fought the old robin, I was fresh and strong and exulted in my victory.

This time, it was the robin that exulted.

I lay dying on the forest floor. On a death bed of fir needles.

～

My eyes snap open.

I must have fallen asleep on the table. In the middle of the old man's story?

The old man!

I jump to my feet, then lurch heavily. My legs still asleep. My neck still kinked from my night on the rug. Most of my muscles tense.

But my table is clean. All the dishes washed and dried and put away.

My bottle of Stag's Breath exactly half-full, and capped, sitting in the middle of the kitchen table.

And the old man is gone.

"No," I breathe.

I scoop up my coat on the way to the front door. At least I'm still fully dressed.

I slam the front door behind me. Don't take time to lock it.

It's been raining. Ground muddy, and the air smells like rain. Like maybe the gray sky's not done yet. The air cold, but that won't matter long.

I start running. Fast as I dare on the mud.

The river. Have to get to the river. The old man was waiting there. That's got to be where he went. Got to be where he figures on getting murdered.

The woods blur past me. My thoughts only on the old man. Only on hoping it's not too late. Can't tell what time it is, not past the thick layer of rain clouds. The cold wind cuts my face as I run. Tries to freeze my heaving lungs.

I haven't run like this in ages. The little jogging I do to stay in shape, that's nothing like this.

Running downslope in the mud through the trees.

I expect to trip at any moment, when I take time to think about that. But even then I don't slow down. Don't worry about the kink in my neck. The ache in my knuckles. The stitch trying to take hold in my side.

I just keep panting for breath. Putting one boot in front of the other. Soaking my shirt and jacket lining with sweat. Soaking my jeans. My good wool socks.

I just keep running.

Have to get to the old man. Have to reach him before it's too late.

Can't let him die.

I finally do make it to the river. Shivering and shaking and breath-less. A cramp in my stomach hurting as much as my knuckles, as much as the kink in my neck. My hair matted to my forehead now.

Every icy breath stings my lungs on its way down.

No sign of the old...

Wait.

I try to laugh, but I don't have the breath.

He's right there. Sitting on the edge of Jess' and my rock. Just like he was yesterday.

Still trying to laugh, but not managing much more than a wheeze, I work my way down to the rock, and out onto its harder, if still rain-slicked surface.

"Careful back there. Don't want to fall in."

That's not the old man's voice.

I stop walking right where I am. A wave of cold passes through me that has nothing to do with the wind, or the spray from the river.

The man sitting on the edge of the rock turns to look at me. And now I see the differences.

His clothes, still dark brown trimmed with forest green, but lighter weight. Spring fare, not winter.

And he's young. College age, if that. Too young to even have a beard, by how smooth his face is. Strong though. Wiry strong, like the old man.

Chestnut brown hair, halfway down his back. No sprig of holly behind his ear, but he does have a few oak leaves tucked into the same spot.

"Oak," I say, still only with enough breath for my words to come out as little more than a harsh whisper. "He wanted oak for the fire last night."

"I don't doubt it," the young man said, laughter in his voice. "When my time comes, I'll probably want a holly log or two myself."

"You killed him." Simple accusation. I don't have the air for proper indignation, no matter how I feel about it.

"I did," he says, admitting to murder with a casual nod. "It was his time. Mine will come in its turn."

"But—"

"But indeed," he says, and now he meets my eye.

This young man. His eyes are the same vibrant green as the old man's were. Makes me see the similarities in their features.

The old man's murderer is ... what ... his grandson?

The young man shakes his head.

"Not quite," he says, as though I'd said those words aloud instead of thinking them. "But let's not talk about me right now. Let's talk about you."

"But—" I try, and he silences me with a raised hand that shuts my mouth without my trying.

"Don't interrupt me when I'm being magnanimous," he says. "It's bad form."

He rubs his hands together. Fine, strong hands, and just as tanned as the old man's were.

"Now," he says. "You offered my predecessor a meal and shelter, did you not? You even tried to help him evade his destiny." He chuckles. "Believe me, you're happier you didn't succeed on that score. Not that he would have tried to flee. He knew better."

I open my mouth to say something. I'm not even sure what. But the young man just raises an eyebrow and I think better of it.

"Good," he says with a nod. "Now. As I was saying, you were a marvelous host, and even if your reasons might have been misguided, your intentions were good. And since this is a time of new beginnings, I offer you one *now*."

That last word hits me in the chest like a sledgehammer. Knocks me to one knee.

Realizations echo through me.

In the forest around me, trees and bushes die, clearing the way for new life to grow. Animals die, feeding other animals, or even just feeding the soil. This is the way of the world.

Lives end. But *life* goes on.

Jess. Jess could have died on any day of her life. A car accident. A plane crash. A mugging gone bad. Any one of a thousand, thousand ways.

Jess didn't *try* to die. She just died.

Her life ended. But maybe my life can go on.

If I don't just snuff it out.

By the time I can blink away my tears and say something to the young man, he's gone. I think I hear the song of a robin in the distance.

Exhaustion overwhelms me. I collapse across the rock for a time, my head pillowed on my arms. But to my surprise, I'm not nearly as stiff or sore as I expect, when I finally sit up. The kink in my neck is gone, and my knuckles feel pretty good. Almost like I never punched the rock. There's even a hint of sunshine through the clouds above me. A trace of blue among the gray.

My stomach rumbles. I need to head back. Eat the other sandwich in my backpack.

Then I'll have to head back home. I didn't bring enough food to stick around. Plus, I could really use a change of clothes. One thing the cabin doesn't have is a washer and dryer.

I'll make sure to shut off the generator and the pump before I go, though. Put everything away. Lock up the cabin.

Maybe I'll come down next month. See the winter snow in the deep woods, the way Jess wanted. Finish that bottle of Stag's Breath.

Then, I don't know. But at least I know the cabin will be ready when I am.

Jess would have wanted it that way.

ABOUT THE AUTHOR

Stefon Mears grew up in California, Middle-Earth, and Amber. He went to U.C. Berkeley intending to major in Genetics, but the call of storytelling compelled him to graduate with a B.A. in Religious Studies (double emphasis in Mythology and Ritual). He later earned an MFA in Creative Writing from the Northwest Institute of Literary Arts, with a Fiction major, and has published many short stories, poems and essays.

Stefon has been an invited guest at a major Vodou ceremony in New Orleans, taught classes in the Brazilian martial art of Capoeira, spoken on a panel at one World Fantasy Conference and given a reading at another, and engraved his own set of Norse runes.

Stefon has worked as a professional audio engineer and played straight pool for money. He is an avid, lifelong fan of the San Francisco Giants. He lives in Portland, Oregon, with his wife and three cats, and when not writing he can often be found playing roleplaying games.

Find out more about Stefon at:
stefonmears.com

facebook.com/stefon.mears

twitter.com/stefonmears

bookbub.com/authors/stefon-mears

amazon.com/Stefon-Mears/e/B008FQUU0Q

BRIDE THIEF

BRIGID COLLINS

L et it never be said that Chelsea Hewitt was a poor friend.

Though her heart writhed like a trapped squirrel, Chelsea gathered the full skirts of her bridesmaid dress—*that's all it is,* she kept reminding herself—and hobbled in her stockings over to the full-length mirror on the far side of the venue's dressing room. She let the skirts fall, then smoothed them down with hands that had gone clammy.

She was afraid to look, even though it wasn't actually a wedding dress. It was, but it wasn't.

She *wasn't* endangering herself by going along with this ridiculous tradition for Jennifer.

Like any good bridesmaid, Chelsea had gone to the bridal salon with Jennifer and helped her friend pick the perfect dress. But when Jennifer requested she get fitted for a second gown of the same style, Chelsea had suffered a split-second mini-panic.

"Did you forget who you're marrying?" Chelsea had asked as the seamstress looped a measuring tape around her. *And did you forget how I bawled on your shoulder while you helped me burn the few photos from my disaster of an attempted wedding?*

"It's a family tradition," Jennifer had explained. "The ladies always have their attendants dress the same. It confuses evil spirits bent on stealing brides away on their special day."

"What about Danielle?"

"Danny's attendant will wear a tux, just like her. Please, Chels, I know this is a big ask after Alexa's vanishing act. But you're my best friend. I don't want anyone else standing with me, or wearing an equally gorgeous dress on my day."

It was for sure the hugest ask Chelsea had ever been dealt. And if it had come from anyone else, Chelsea would have told them where to shove their extra wedding gown.

Taking a shaky breath, she forced herself to look at her reflection.

The white dress fit better than she'd expected. Oh, she hadn't doubted the seamstress would do good work, but still. She twisted about for a better look.

This one suited her more than the one she'd worn three years ago, although that one hadn't puckered slightly at the front. Then again, she hadn't been wearing a ring from a long-broken engagement around her neck just yet.

The old burn of humiliation flared in her chest, and loneliness echoed in all her empty spaces, but she put a hand over the lump of the ring in her bodice, re-gathered her strength, and shoved the doubts deeper inside herself. Jennifer was the bride today. She needed Chelsea to keep it together. The dress suited *Jennifer,* and it was mere coincidence that it worked for Chelsea's build as well.

Of all Chelsea's friends, Jennifer alone had never judged her for holding onto the ring Alexa had given her. That in itself made Chelsea more willing to break her own vow never to don a wedding gown again. And with the way Danny and Jennifer constantly batted their lashes at one another, she didn't have to worry about anyone being left at the altar today.

Chelsea was happy for them, and she was honored to stand up for them. But she wished it wouldn't make her so aware that there was no one batting their lashes at her anymore.

Enough beating herself up at the mirror. Just because Alexa had done a runner on her didn't mean some other woman wouldn't recognize what a gift Chelsea's affections were, and said woman wouldn't feel the need to pressure her into trying another walk down the aisle.

Nodding to her reflection, she adjusted her bodice so it lay a little flatter, slipped her shoes on, and called to the photographer who waited to take her pre-ceremony photo.

"I'm ready."

"Then do emerge." The voice was not the photographer's, but an unknown woman's. Its melodic tones warmed Chelsea's ribcage like a gulp of mulled wine, but also sent shivery prickles rushing over her skin.

Following the voice took no effort. In fact, even though Chelsea stood in the hallway, she couldn't remember leaving the dressing room.

She blinked.

The photographer lay slumped against the exposed brick wall. A woman stood over him, turning his camera over in hands that crawled with frost.

The moment Chelsea appeared in the hall, the woman lifted her eyes from the camera. Her gaze drove into Chelsea like a blast of wintery night air, slicing her to bits with frosted edges. A hunger lingered in the darkness of the woman's eyes, insatiable, a void that intended to pull Chelsea in whole.

She *wanted* Chelsea. More than that, she desired her.

The woman let the camera clatter to the floor, and the lens broke with a sharp crack. But Chelsea found she couldn't flinch.

This woman was not human. The knowledge frightened Chelsea, made her throat burn with the need to scream as she fought to recoil from the woman's fingers, which curled as if to caress her face. It made her breath turn cold in her lungs as the word *faerie* drifted into her mind.

But Chelsea's blood stirred like it never had for Alexa, even in their good days.

Tall and willowy, the faerie woman wore a flowing, silvery garment with white fox-fur trim that sparkled with icy crystals. Her hair, black as a veiled night, hung loose, but a laurel of holly and mistletoe held it out of her alabaster face. The same frost that covered her hands curled over her sharp cheekbones and along the edges of her lips.

From the chapel behind Chelsea came the strains of the chamber quartet warming up.

"What is your name, mortal?"

Chelsea tried to break free, willed her mouth to form any word but her own name. But her body was not hers to command, and the harder she fought it, the tighter the chains of the faerie woman's power wound about her, until...

"Ch-Chelsea."

The relief of giving in wrenched a sigh from her. Why had she struggled so, and against one who saw what a lovely bride she made?

This was what she'd been wanting ever since Alexa abandoned her.

Unfurling a flirtatious smile, she stepped closer to the beautiful woman. "My name is Chelsea. What's yours?"

The faerie's face split in a wide grin, revealing sharp, blood-blackened teeth.

Quick as a snake striking, the faerie snapped her outstretched arm around Chelsea's neck and ground icy fingers into the back of her skull.

Chelsea had no time to scream before, with a sickening lurch of movement, she found herself somewhere else entirely.

Chelsea's head throbbed. Snowflakes light as feathers brushed at her cheeks and melted through the lacy sleeves of her dress. Gasping at the cold, she opened her eyes, only to find her vision blurred from a lingering dizziness. Her breath clouded in the space above her lips. A few of these clouds dissipated before she realized that she lay cradled, not in a comfortable bed, or even the rough branches of a tree, but in the arms of the faerie who had stolen her away.

They were moving through a forest of leafless birch and larch, silent but for the rush of wind through the boughs and the soft cackle of the ice-white pixies that darted in and out of shadows. No crunch of snow underfoot marked her captor's motion, and no footsteps jostled her as she lay against the woman's bosom.

The combination of pain and chill broke the trance-like spell the faerie had cast over her.

"Let me go," she said, thrashing. One of her shoes flew off her foot and disappeared into the darkness of the forest.

The faerie woman tightened her grip. "The Winter Queen is most pleased by your timely bridal preparations, and she awaits your arrival in her Court. You are accorded a great honor on this winter solstice, mortal Chelsea."

A tingle of power zipped through Chelsea's body when the faerie spoke her name, and her thrashing subsided.

Stupid, Chelsea thought. *You never give your true name to faeries!*

And of course the lady had never given her own name in return, so Chelsea had no means of retaliation. But it was too late to fix that moment of weakness now, and besides, how else was she supposed to react when the most beautiful woman she'd ever laid eyes on asked for her name?

Not to mention the fact that she was up against a bona fide evil spirit. She'd thought Jennifer's silly superstition was just that. She'd never expected her role as decoy bride would actually be called into service.

Jennifer would be frantic if her only attendant didn't show up for the ceremony. Chelsea had to find a way to escape, but she couldn't very well tell her captor that she'd got the wrong bride. That would defeat the whole purpose of wearing this stupid dress in the first place, and even if Chelsea was wishing she could go back in time and give her friend a flat "no" in that bridal salon, she'd never want to put Jennifer in danger.

"Take me back," she said, "I'm developing cold feet."

"Then you oughtn't to have kicked your shoe off," said the faerie. "But you'll grow used to the chill of the Winter Court."

She continued through the forest, gliding like a silent specter along an unseen path in the snow. The land rose and fell in gentle hillocks, and through the clasping branches overhead, the stars twinkled in the cloudless night sky. The scent of wood smoke drifted on the air, crisp and stirring as it mixed with the cold.

They crested a hill, and the source of the smoke came into view. In the valley below, still too distant to make out details, a host of faerie creatures cavorted around a pale fire in a clearing. A white-blue glow hung in the branches, and Chelsea realized it must come from a swarm of pixies.

Abruptly, the faerie released her grip on Chelsea's legs. Chelsea yelped as the ankle-high snow soaked through her fancy shoe and stockings, as well as the train of her dress. The faerie's arm around her shoulders only made her shiver harder.

"I require the token now," said the faerie.

"Wh-what token?"

The faerie brought her face close to Chelsea's. She wore a soothing expression, and her holly berry breath misted cold over Chelsea's forehead, almost sweet enough to make Chelsea forget the earlier image of her bared teeth. Her free hand came up to cup Chelsea's cheek.

"The token your mortal lover gave you to initiate the bridal ritual."

Chelsea's heart thudded hard enough to set the ring beneath her bodice rattling on its chain. The ring Alexa had abandoned along with Chelsea was all that gave her the strength to combat her fears and self-doubts. Would handing the ring over entangle her in this faerie's grasp even more?

Did she have a choice?

Probably not. Even if her captor didn't compel her to obey, Chelsea had to continue the ruse long enough to keep Jennifer safe. Hopefully her friends had the presence of mind to go on with the ceremony without her.

Her hand shook as she pulled the chain out. Staring into the blackness of the faerie's gaze, she yanked on the ring and snapped the chain.

Letting the chain slither through her fingers, she held the ring out, and the faerie took it and stepped away. It was a cheap thing—more because Alexa had been broke at the time than as any foreshadowing of Chelsea's lonesome stand at the altar—but it sparkled in the starlight as the faerie hefted it in the palm of her hand.

The faerie frowned.

Despite the cold, sweat slicked Chelsea's hands. What would happen if this dangerous creature could tell the ring symbolized a broken engagement?

The wind sighed in the trees, and a faint trill of a pipe echoed from the revelry below.

"Its power is heavy," said the faerie. "It will do."

Closing her fingers over the ring, she put it in one of her billowing sleeves. Then she clamped a hand around Chelsea's wrist like an icy manacle.

"Come, mortal Chelsea. Your queen awaits her bride."

Though the summons left Chelsea helpless to disobey, and the ring she usually relied on to grant her strength lay in the hands of her captor, she swore she would never become this queen's wife, not even if the lady displayed more beauty than the one who had snatched her away in the first place.

T he glade was alive with light and shadow, and music resonated among every snowflake that drifted lazily through the air. A long, low table carved of a wood so dark as to be nearly black ran along the far side of the clearing, spread with food fit for a mead hall feast. The smells rising from it, savory meats and succulent fruits dripping with honey and spices, set Chelsea's mouth watering even as the sight of the gathered faeries sent a shock of cold horror through her heart.

Knobby goblins, looking like piles of rocks and dirt come to life, sank their tiny, sharp teeth into their helpings of meat, which were cooked so rare the juices ran down their fronts like rivulets of blood. Beside them sat a group of masculine figures, all dressed in the furs and leathers of huntsmen, but each with a different animal's features on their heads. One wore a crown of shedding antlers, draped with reddened tatters of loose flesh.

A pair of bards lounged on silken cushions at the base of a large, gnarled tree, one strumming his lute, the other counting beats before she resumed playing her pipe. The melody tilted and bent, oddly disjointed from the countermelody, but the beautiful faeries who danced in the field between the musicians and the table appeared to have no issue keeping step. They whirled and curtseyed, bowed and leapt, all while pulling the most gruesome visages at their partners.

Overhead, the branches were festooned not with free-flitting pixies as Chelsea had assumed, but with elegant cages full of them. The tiny creatures hissed and screamed whenever the jostling of their cellmates pushed them against the bars.

Beyond both table and musicians, a throne chiseled from ice sat on a raised stone dais. Holly and mistletoe grew around the base and wound around both arms, but the seat was empty.

While Chelsea and her captor approached the glade, the gathered faeries continued about their revelry as if the two of them did not exist, but the instant her captor dragged her beyond the last barren tree, every fearsome creature in attendance ceased what he or she was doing and dipped into a low bow or a sweeping curtsey.

"Hail, Queen of Winter, Regent of Ice, Most Beautiful Gem of the Winter Court," called the bard with the lute. "And hail to her chosen mortal bride."

"Hail," chanted the gathered faeries.

Chelsea gaped up at her captor. *"You're* the Winter Queen?" Couldn't the woman have had enough decency to be upfront about this part of her identity? What kind of marriage did she expect to have here?

Chelsea's captor ignored her and gave the court a stately nod, then glided forward, pulling Chelsea along with her. The faeries moved aside for them, still prostrating themselves to their ruler.

Chelsea's feet crunched through the snow. Hers were the only footprints that marred the otherwise pristine field.

The Winter Queen did not release her hold on Chelsea's wrist until the two of them had mounted the stone dais.

"Mortal Chelsea, you will sit here while the ceremony commences," she said, pointing to a spot just to the right of the throne. The tingle of power trilled through Chelsea once more, and she felt her knees bending of their own volition, until she knelt at the queen's feet like a trained dog.

While Chelsea gnashed her teeth and struggled in vain to stand, the queen turned to face her subjects and swept up a large chalice from where it rested on the arm of her throne.

"My friends," she called. Her voice rang with tones even more melodic than those that had first lured Chelsea to her side.

That moment seemed so long ago now, Chelsea realized. Just how long had she been within the realm of faerie? How much time had she already lost?

But the queen continued her address. "Tonight, on the cusp of the turn of power amongst the Courts, we of the Winter Court have cause to celebrate! Though the solstice oft marks the waning of our power, by tapping into the power of a mortal bridal bond on the stroke of midnight, we shall finally have the strength to oppose those of the Spring Court. We shall strike their foul robins from the sky, and we shall cause the filth of their blooms to wither into dust. Snow and ice shall cover the Realm as is its right!"

The fey folk cheered, and the sound grated at Chelsea's ears.

The queen held up one pale hand to quiet the crowd, then brought the chalice to her lips and drained it in a long, slow swallow. Finished, she lowered herself into the throne and placed the empty vessel back on the arm.

Her face darkened, and a tear fell from each of her eyes. They froze into crystals on her cheeks, where the flickering pixie-light sparked off of them.

"Now, the opening ceremony must begin."

The lute player struck a chord, and Chelsea gasped as sadness threatened to engulf her. Though she hardly knew why, tears ran down her own cheeks.

A hush fell over the crowd, and the antlered huntsman stepped forward, a faerie maiden on his arm. Her waves of red hair tumbled loose over her shoulders, and, like the queen, she wore sprigs of holly in her hair. A pair of gossamer dragonfly wings twitched against her back. Her sheer dress of beaded frost clung to the curves of her body, leaving little to the imagination, but her youthful face remained shuttered to any who might try to read it.

The queen gestured to the huntsman, and he approached her with a somber bow. He took the empty chalice from her throne, keeping his face pointed towards her feet as he did. Then he held out his hand, palm up, as if to ask his liege lady for a dance.

The queen pulled Chelsea's engagement ring from her sleeve, held it aloft so it glinted in the pixie-light, and then dropped it into his waiting hand.

Chelsea's knees ached where they pressed against the stone dais, but the pain didn't match the burn of fear that flashed over her when the huntsman closed his fist around that ring. Somehow, despite the fact she'd snapped the thin chain that had kept the ring secured by her heart, the phantom weight of it tugged against the back of her neck as the huntsman returned to his waiting faerie maiden and slipped the ring onto her left hand.

The maiden curtseyed to him, and as she rose, he moved to stand behind her. His arms came around her, cradling her like a lover, and he pressed the chalice against her belly, just below her breast.

Then he drew his knife from his belt. A cruel talon of a thorn, its edge glowed black in the mingled light of fey fire and caged pixie. The maiden rested her head against the huntsman's shoulder with a sigh.

Chelsea wanted to look away, to close her eyes, to do anything to block out her vision. But she knelt, transfixed as she had been by the Winter Queen's voice, as the huntsman drove his thorn knife into his maiden's heart and caught the blood in the chalice.

There was enough that the chalice overflowed, and spatters of blood blossomed on the snow by their feet.

Carefully, the huntsman lowered the maiden's still body to the ground. He left his knife buried in her chest, the hilt pointing up towards the stars, and carried the chalice to the end of the table farthest from the throne.

By the time he'd passed the chalice into the grasping hands of the first eager goblin, his face had settled back into cruel passivity.

The chalice made its way along the table, and each and every faerie in attendance drank deeply of the maiden's blood.

The Winter Queen leant over the side of her throne to whisper in Chelsea's ear. "I have waited so long for you, my mortal bride. Now that you are here, you see that I am willing to do anything for you. I will even spill the blood of my own in your name, Chelsea. Surely that is more than your mortal lover could offer you?"

She ran her fingernails through Chelsea's hair, and Chelsea shuddered. The queen's touch was so cold it burned, but Chelsea's reaction came from the truth the queen spoke.

Alexa had never been willing to do much for her beyond the basics. Everything that their relationship had been, good and bad, had come from Chelsea.

But a thread of wariness glimmered deep in Chelsea's heart, down amongst all the swirling doubts she'd kept chained up behind that old ring, and she clung to it like a drowning woman. Was the Winter Queen—the one who hadn't bothered to tell Chelsea who she was in the first place, and who had used the knowledge of Chelsea's name to control her—truly spilling her own people's blood for Chelsea's benefit? Or had that maiden's death been in pursuit of expanding the Winter Court's power?

The huntsman returned to the throne, his silent footsteps eerie. The ragged, fleshy tatters on his antlers twisted and swayed in the breeze when he bowed to the queen once more and offered her the chalice.

The queen cupped it in both hands, lifted it to her lips, and drank as she had earlier. Her throat convulsed with every swallow, and a flush colored her cheeks, as if what she imbibed were the headiest of wines.

Stopping cost her visible effort. She gasped as she lowered the chalice, her breast heaving as if at the height of passion. Her obsidian eyes blazed bright like the stars above.

She turned to Chelsea and smiled. Blood ran from her lips and down her chin in thick lines, and her pointed teeth glistened with fresh wetness.

"Stand, my beautiful bride Chelsea. The last is for you. Drink, and our love shall be eternal. Eat of our food, and you shall want for nothing. Bind your hand with mine, and I shall be your slave."

Chelsea stood. Her legs tingled with the queen's power and with their own numbness after so long against the stone, but she lifted her arms to take the chalice of her own volition.

The Winter Queen had not used Chelsea's name in those final three commands.

She cupped the chalice as the queen had done and peered into the depths. Though every faerie in the glade had drunk from it, and the queen had practically guzzled her own serving, the chalice remained half-full. The smell that rose from it was sharp, and it made Chelsea's eyes water. But it also made her aware of her sudden, desperate thirst.

She deserved someone who would worship her, who would kill for her. She *wanted* that.

The phantom chain she'd felt earlier dragged at her neck, and she lowered her head until her lips nearly touched the rim of the chalice.

But the thread of wariness she still clung to pulsed. No, no. She wanted what Jennifer and Danielle had. True love. Mutual respect. Someone who wouldn't abandon her when it was convenient. *That's* what she deserved.

She was done letting beautiful women push her around and making a fool of herself in front of everyone.

She yanked her head back up, and as she did, the phantom chain dissipated and scattered on the breeze like so much pixie dust. Then she tipped the chalice over and let the remaining blood pool on the stone dais. Steam rose from it in thick curls, and a hiss went up from the faerie court.

The Winter Queen made no sound, but her face grew sharp and shadowed. She did not look at the spilt blood, did not blink as the steam swirled before her eyes.

She raised a hand, palm out and fingers crooked towards Chelsea. Power gathered there, pulsing and giving off a dark sort of light. The wind kicked up, blowing from behind the Winter Queen, setting her dress and black hair whipping about her body. It sounded like a hoard of banshees, and for all Chelsea knew, it actually was.

She didn't intend to stick around to find out.

Not bothering to gather her skirts, Chelsea darted away from the throne and under the arm of the huntsman when he tried to stop her. The dead faerie maiden still lay in the middle of the clearing, with the thorn knife still protruding from her breast.

Chelsea snatched the knife up. She whirled about, sending drops of blood flying in an arc around her, and held the knife out to defend herself.

But when she faced the throne once again, she found the huntsman cowering before her, as did every other faerie in attendance.

Only the Winter Queen remained upright and maintained eye contact, though she slowly lowered her arm. The shadows on her face had shifted from cold fury to steely wariness.

Chelsea liked that.

She extended her arm a little more, pointing the bloody knife at the queen. "I'm not a doll to be turned this way and that. I'm not interested in marrying someone who hasn't earned my respect, and who doesn't respect me back. You don't even respect me enough to tell me your name, even though you know mine."

The Winter Queen stepped off the dais. "Mortal Chelsea—"

"No! I don't care if you know my name. No one holds power over me any longer."

Then she turned and ran, her feet flying over the unbroken blanket of snow, and the full skirts of her ridiculous decoy bridal gown flowing around her. She held the thorn knife close against her chest as if her life depended upon it.

The last of the blood on the blade seeped into her bodice, leaving a dark red smear over the place where her old engagement ring used to hang.

She felt free.

Somewhere along the way, her other shoe fell off. Branches snagged at her dress, tearing her skirt and her lacy sleeves, but none of that slowed her down. She ran and ran, until the sparkles of pixie light faded and darkness closed in.

She ran until suddenly her feet weren't crunching through snow, but padding along a carpeted hallway. Her breath still rasped harsh in her ears, but the unearthly sounds of the faerie realm gave way to the gentle lilt of the string quartet beginning the wedding processional.

The wedding party stood lined up and ready to enter the chapel, and at the back of it, looking as frantic as Chelsea had imagined, was Jennifer.

The dress really did look stunning on her, Chelsea thought.

But Jennifer gaped at Chelsea, her eyes running up and down Chelsea's body, taking in the damaged dress, the surely tangled mess of her hair, and the bloody knife Chelsea still held in her fist.

"What on Earth—where have you—what happened?!"

Chelsea glanced down at the knife—the proof of her victory over a truly evil spirit on her friend's wedding day, and a way cooler accessory than the mini bouquet—then smiled back up at Jennifer.

"Just being the best damn friend you've ever had. Now let's get you down that aisle."

ABOUT THE AUTHOR

Brigid Collins is a fantasy and science fiction writer living in Michigan. Her short stories have appeared in Fiction River, The Uncollected Anthology Volume 13: *Mystical Melodies*, and the *Chronicle Worlds: Feyland* anthology. Books 1 through 3 of her fantasy series, Songbird River Chronicles, are available in print and electronic versions on Amazon.

Find out more about Brigid at:
backwrites.wordpress.com

 twitter.com/purellian
bookbub.com/authors/brigid-collins
amazon.com/Brigid-Collins/e/B010BJQBN4

THE GIVING YEAR

ALEXANDRA BRANDT

EITHNI

This would be a Taking year.

It had been a long time—decades—since the last one. But this year, there had been signs. The timing was right. The wise women and the Head of the Gull Clan—and, most importantly, the clan gossips—all agreed on this.

The whispers followed Eithni everywhere she walked.

Especially now, as the days reached their darkest, as the frost daily made glittering shards of the brown grass along the paths. Already the long, deep nights had told Eithni she didn't have long.

Because, as much as she wanted to shut them out, she believed the whispers.

This would be a Taking year, and Eithni would be the one Taken.

She walked now in the dark, placing one foot in front of the other on the path she refused to fear. It was slow and careful going, hindered as she was by the thick layers of wool and fur-lined hide wrapped around her feet and body. All she could hear was the crunch of the grass beneath her and the sound of her own breathing inside the cloth around her face. The air was sharp, prickling the inside of her exposed nose.

The horizon before Eithni slowly began to lighten as she walked, black to dark blue to green, but overhead the brightest of the stars still burned, cold and clear. Too cold for snow.

The wise women predicted equally clear skies seven mornings from now, when the Light would come.

Perfect conditions. A perfect candidate. All signs pointed to success.

And a successful Taking, when the gods would welcome the human supplicant into their realm, would be followed by a year of Giving. Such things were long overdue on Gull Island. As the old hens had been saying for half a year now, hardly caring whether Eithni was in earshot or not. Even knowing this was her year to welcome the Light. Her year to step into the chamber of the gods... and offer herself up to them.

Did the old hens think that Eithni, too, would long for a Taking year? That she would welcome it with open arms?

Inside the wrapped hide and furs, Eithni's fists clenched. It was a long, cold walk from her home, from the clan settlement. Alone in the semidarkness, she had no distractions from her own troubled mind. Nothing outside of careful footing and tumultuous thoughts.

Anyone in her situation would view the Solstice with some fear. It was to be expected. Even other years, when signs of the gods' attention were nonexistent, the young woman or man chosen to bring in the Light of the coming year would still feel a tremble of anxiety the night before.

In those other years, the chosen youths returned, a little disappointed that they had not found favor with the gods, yes—but even more relieved. Eithni knew, because she had aided and observed the last three, knowing that it was likely she would be chosen for the ceremony soon.

But in those days, she hadn't thought her year would be any different from any other.

She wasn't even sure if *this* year was different because she had been chosen...

Or if she had been chosen *after* the Wise Women knew it was a Taking year. If she had been chosen *because* it was different.

No one would tell her which was true.

But oh, it mattered.

Yes, that was the hard, cold point at the heart of the storm inside her head. The one thought Eithni couldn't shake loose. Even more powerful than the fear of the Solstice and the dawn of the new year.

Did her own people *want her gone*?

Tradition dictated, of course, that the Solstice Ceremony would always be performed by the clan's best and brightest of youths, in hopes that they would please the gods.

Common wisdom knew the gods favored supplicants talented in the arts, or skilled in craft, or simply the most beautiful to behold.

Eithni could not argue against her suitability on those counts. Gull Clan men and women were frequently blessed with fair faces and forms, with glossy dark hair and fine, fair skin, and eyes of blue or green or gray—or all three colors together, as in Eithni's own case. And in anticipation of pleasing the gods, all Gull children were trained early on in music and storytelling, crafting and artistry.

Eithni's own talent, stone carving, was unusual enough to be notable. And, perhaps, unusual enough to be the reason she was singled out this year.

Or one of several reasons.

The gods favored the unique, the different. So the wise women might argue, if she ever dared to ask them. But beneath that question would be another: *Am I too different to ever comfortably belong to the clan? Is that why you chose me for a Taking year?*

Did Eithni really want to know the answer?

She shivered and pulled the furs tighter around herself. Ultimately, the answer didn't matter.

What mattered was this: would she do it?

Would she welcome the dawn?

She kept her feet steady in the half-light, steady on the grass-lined path. Ahead, a mound loomed, black against the greening sky. Eithni wasn't supposed to be here, not now. But she needed to *know*.

She straightened her back and raised her chin. She was a child of the clan, same as anyone else on this island. She would be without fear. She would dare what no one else had dared before her.

What did she have to lose?

She rounded the dark side of the cairn, a dome of tightly stacked flagstone, grown over with frosty grass, barely visible now in the pre-dawn twilight. The work of the ancients who had come before.

Like the standing stones overlooking the sea to the east, the structure carried the weight of ancient powers and mysteries. The wise women said in the days of the ancients, the gods had walked the ground. When they left, the ancients raised stones, tall and strong and sharp against the sky, and built their chambered cairns, in hopes of drawing the gods back.

Instead, on a certain day—a certain moment—of the year, they opened doors.

Or at least this one did. And now, that only seemed to happen once every few decades or more.

As to why, the gods were silent. The only signs of their favor or disfavor could be read by the wise women, read in the earth and sea and sky.

Eithni smiled grimly. She had some questions to ask of the gods. If it came to that.

But first she had some questions to ask of herself. And the answers—she hoped—lay within the Sun Chamber, the chamber of the gods.

She turned and faced the opening of the cairn. Dawn was nearly upon her; the light was silvery now. In the weak almost-morning light she could finally see it: the one thing always in the center of her thoughts.

The frosted grass was a shroud, a cold mist blanketing the mound. In summer it would look green and inviting. Not today. Two arms of stone and grass reached toward her, framing the long rock-lined entrance.

Beyond that, the ancient doorway into the hill, dark and unknowable. It only led to more stone and shadow: another long, low tunnel that led to the inner chamber.

A passage to a doorway to a passage to a doorway. The wise women would tell Eithni there was meaning in that. The ancients had crafted it so.

Eithni could never think beyond the knowledge that when the time came, she must walk each passage and enter each doorway *alone*. Then the final chamber...and the final doorway, if the gods willed it.

But as the dawn broke behind her, and the frost-covered grasses began to glitter like knives, and the sun stretched its first long lance of pale gold into the low, dark passageway, Eithni pushed herself forward.

It wasn't Solstice yet. She had nothing to fear.

She crouched at the doorway and followed the shard of light into the shadows, though she had to bend nearly double to do it. She paused, pressing her lips together. She untucked a hand from her furs to brush her bare fingers against the walls. They were rough stone, icy cold.

Her mouth was dry. She moved forward again, trying to focus on keeping her head from hitting the stones above it, and wishing her heart would stop hammering.

At last—why did so short a distance seem so endless?—she stumbled into the inner chamber. The Sun Chamber. Chamber of the gods.

It was a surprisingly large room, built of large slabs of flagstone, tightly joined. The room seemed equal parts heavy strength and echoing space. Perhaps it was made more so by the deep shadows shrouding the edges, filling the vaulted ceiling.

Her eyes were drawn to the sunlight creeping along the floor, just touching the far wall.

She stepped out of its path. She couldn't look away from the illuminated slab of stone on the wall, the slowly growing patch of pale, honey-colored light.

When had she decided to fear the sun?

Inch by inch, the light filled the opening behind her. Filled the shape on the far wall, a rough echo of the passage she had just left. Not quite a perfect square, yet.

Would it become a doorway in seven days?

Would she step through?

"I'm not afraid of you," she said under her breath, testing the words for truth. They didn't make it past the wrapping around her face. They didn't feel real. None of this felt real.

She tugged down the cloth at her mouth and took a deep, shuddering breath. The air in here was cold, although not as icy as the outside had been.

No one was here to see or hear her. She took her hands out from the furs again, moved slowly to the wall, and planted herself in front of the golden square.

Her bundled form threw a shapeless, bulky shadow over it.

There. Just light after all.

She put both hands on the wall and shouted.

"I. Am. Not. Afraid!"

As the ringing echoes faded away, a voice spoke from the shadows.

"Who are you?"

SABLE

Sable waited until the last of the lightlords moved beyond the sight of her post, then tugged the visor of her deer skull helm back up over her forehead. She leaned her back against the heavy slab of stone and lifted her face to the low-lit sky, breathing the perfume of dew-drenched flowers.

She smiled. Violet and heady blooming rosemary and countless others. Each of the lightlords had a stake at the Stone Door, which meant Sable now guarded the heart of more than a score of gardens, each a little piece of a lord's realm. And could enjoy the richly scented benefits.

When the lords weren't around, at least.

Sable was not fond of the deer skull, despite its impressive looks. It was her job to look impressive, of course. She and Umber both. A matched pair of hartkin in dappled armor, broad of shoulder, well-muscled, carrying twin leaf-bladed spears. With gleaming antlers growing from their heads...or at least the illusion thereof, on Sable's part. Her brother was hart, she was hind. Her antlers were branches bound in her tawny hair. His were real.

She glanced over at her brother, who still wore his helm. His head was cocked in her direction; he appeared to be studying her in the predawn light.

"You don't think the lightlords will return today." It was a statement, not a question.

"They won't." She was counting on it, in fact. Her liege might think she was here for the prestige of guarding the Door on the eve of the Solstice, but prestige had nothing to do with it.

She was here for knowledge, first.

And someday: change.

Umber, now—Umber was here because Sable could never have gotten this post without their 'matched pair' feature. He didn't mind the prestige, of course, but he was loyal to his sibling first, his liege second. That was the most important thing.

She probably owed him for this. There was a good chance she would be getting them both into trouble at some point in the next seven days.

Umber was still examining her, the set of his shoulders unconvinced.

Sable stretched her neck from side to side, working out the kinks. "They've no reason to come back. Nothing interesting has ever happened in the days leading up to the Door opening. Besides, everyone wishes to feast and make merry somewhere there aren't quite so many rules. At any rate, putting us here, now, it's just a formality."

Umber grunted. "It's only been a formality for the past two decades because none of the lightlords' courts were due for a human. But now..." he shrugged.

She mirrored his shrug with her own. "Can you remember there ever being an actual need for guards at the Door before? Even on years when a Taking was due. It's all for show. Just like the midnight ceremony."

And what a relief to be done with *that*. The ceremony last night, giving their liege lord formal possession of the Door—and the human who would come through it in seven days—had been one thing. The celebration that came after, lasting the remainder of the night, had been quite another.

But now she and Umber were alone, the celebration would continue in the domain of her liege, and the night was fast fleeing.

She had chosen this for a reason. To learn everything she could about the Stone Door and how it operated—beyond what everyone in the Summer realm casually knew, that is—and get that information back to the Daylight Order.

And the sun would be rising soon...in both this realm and the human world.

Sable felt her pulse begin to race. Would it feel different, touching the edge of a world she'd never seen?

She watched the sky. "It's rising," she murmured.

The skull helm suddenly felt especially stiff and heavy and cumbersome. Out of place. On an impulse, Sable lifted the helm from her head entirely, although she took care not to jostle her carefully entwined antlers. She looked at her brother, a touch defiantly.

Umber shook his head slightly, but lifted his hands to tug at his own helm's visor. Sable caught a glimpse of a quirked smile in her direction before he, too, turned to watch the horizon.

Sable pressed her hand against the stone behind her. "Seven days," she whispered.

The first gleam of sun edged over the horizon. The stone vibrated slightly.

Her eyes widened. She turned to peer at it. No one had seen fit to mention... Perhaps it was nothing.

A whisper of sound caused one of her long, sensitive ears to twitch. It came from the Door opening, behind the sentinel stone.

It sounded like footsteps.

She wasn't allowed to enter the chamber where the true Door would form. She shouldn't even enter the long, low tunnel that led to it. Of course, she had been planning on ignoring that edict eventually...just not *first thing*.

Ah, well.

She stepped around the sentinel stone.

"Sable? What are you doing?"

She waved a hand at her brother. "Shh, I'm listening." The footsteps sounded like they were in the passage. Or the chamber beyond it. She edged in further.

The light of the sun touched a small part of the passage before her.

Silence hung for a moment. Several moments.

Then a voice came from the depths of the passageway: *"I. Am. Not. Afraid!"*

It was slightly muffled, as if from a distance or behind a wall. But even so, it was a shout of defiance. Female, and young.

Sable gasped and stumbled. Struggled to find her voice. "Who are you?"

An equally startled gasp echoed faintly in the tunnel. Sable peered down it, but could see nothing.

The voice again. "I—I thought I was alone—who are *you*?"

Why would someone inside the chamber think they were alone? Why would someone be in the chamber in the first place?

Sable cleared her throat. "I am the guardian—"

"Sable?" Umber's voice behind her. "What in all the stars—"

"Oh, *hush!*" Sable whipped around, glaring. "There's someone *in* there."

Her brother opened his mouth, then shut it. He was smart enough not to argue and make further noise. He lifted one shoulder and gestured toward the tunnel, his message clear. *Go on and investigate, then.*

Sable nodded and turned. If she was going to do her job properly, she would clearly need to enter the passage. It made sense from the outside, if she had to justify herself later.

Although best to never mention it at all.

But this...this was even better for her *own* purposes. The possibilities danced in her head. If she found something she could tell the others...

The passage was empty.

Greatly daring, Sable went to the end of the it, to the entrance of the inner chamber itself, although she was not bold enough yet to step inside. The light from the sun partially illuminated the back wall. It was enough sunlight to see there was no woman or being in that room. Not anywhere.

Still...she couldn't help it. "Hello?"

There was only silence.

EITHNI

Eithni stumbled through the cairn's passageway and back into the light, heart stuttering. She had heard *voices*. But there had been no one in the cairn but herself. Anything else was impossible.

No one was permitted to come here until Solstice, and even then, no one would enter the chamber but Eithni herself.

But then, perhaps she wasn't the only one in the clan to break the rules.

She peered back inside. Though the shaft of sun was once again slowly retreating, passing up and out of the tunnel, everything was better illuminated now in the cold morning light. If someone moved within, she would surely be able to see them. Wouldn't she?

Did she dare go back inside?

I am the guardian, the voice had said. The voice had been a woman's, someone Eithni didn't recognize. But of course it had been faint. A human? Someone from the clan?

But...

The voice had seemed to come from the stone itself. The wall of the inner chamber. Where the light of Solstice would touch. How could it be human?

A...god, then? A servant of the gods?

Deep within her fur wrappings, her hands shook. The sun was above the horizon now, but no warmth touched her.

Eithni had said she wasn't afraid. It had been half-lie, half-truth, then.

Now? She was terrified.

She didn't know how long she stood at the entrance. Long enough for her feet to go numb.

In the end, she broke. Hunching her shoulders, she turned her back to the morning sun and fled toward the village.

She couldn't do this after all.

~

She changed her path to approach home from the opposite side, knowing that people would be well awake by now, doing whatever they needed for continued winter survival, preparing for the ceremony, and so on. She hoped no one would be near enough to see the direction from which she'd actually come.

Eithni might have told herself she had nothing to lose by breaking the rules at the cairn, but she didn't want to test the truth of that, either.

If she could avoid seeing any other humans at all until reaching her own house, so much the better.

But it was not to be.

"Bright day to you!"

That voice. Eithni's gut clenched and she thought about hurrying away, pretending she hadn't heard. Maybe Derilei hadn't recognized her in all her heavy wrappings yet.

"Eithni? Is that you?"

Of all the things Eithni wanted in this life, talking to the woman she had once loved was the very least of them. Why else had she been so careful about avoiding Derilei this past year? In such a small clan, it was a feat worth noting.

She had thought Derilei wanted the same thing—to avoid contact, to avoid remembering. The other woman had fairly rapidly found herself a husband, after all. After...

Eithni tried not to let her shoulders stiffen as she turned to see the bundled form of her one-time companion. She tugged the cloth down from her mouth, as was only polite. "Bright day," she said evenly.

Derilei stood with her cloth-wrapped hands at her mouth, her lovely face bare to the cold. She had successfully—or unsuccessfully, in the eyes of the wise women—completed the Solstice ceremony two years ago. The experience had brought Eithni and Derilei closer together than ever...until it suddenly hadn't.

"Oh, Eithni," Derilei whispered now, her blue eyes wide. "I...just wanted to say..."

That you're sorry?

That you know you might be the reason I was chosen for this —privilege?

Another question Eithni never wanted answered.

Derilei sucked in a breath, let it out. "You—you're a gift. The Gull Clan doesn't deserve you."

At those unexpected words, Eithni looked at her. *Truly* looked at her.

There were tears in Derilei's eyes.

"I...don't know what to say to that," Eithni finally said. The least she could manage was some form of honesty. Her thoughts had suddenly become a tangled mess. What did Derilei want from her?

"Eithni, I'm sorry—"

"Bright morning!" A male voice, interrupting. Cheerful, or perhaps forced cheer.

Galam, of course.

Eithni nodded to the husband of her one-time lover, wondering, as she so often did, how much he knew. How much he, in particular, would be glad to see Eithni gone.

At the moment, Eithni would gladly be anywhere else.

Even the realm of the gods?

"Bright morning to both of you," she said with a false smile, and turned and fled down the path to her home.

Eithni's father was in the workshop, despite the cold. Stone carving was not a winter trade—have a care for numb fingers— but no one seemed to have told Edarnon that. He peered at a sketch in the weak morning sunlight, muttering to himself.

Eithni hesitated. He would most certainly have noted her bed was empty when he arose this morning. Whether he would say anything about it or not was another matter. Edarnon was not one for talking, unless it was about his craft.

Sometimes that was a blessing.

"Have a look at this, would you?"

She blinked at the thin, flat piece of wood suddenly thrust under her nose. The charcoal sketch of a name-stone.

One question answered, at least: her father didn't care where she had been this morning.

She looked down. Edarnon had a sure hand, born of years of experience. The complex arrangement of symbols could have been a jumbled mess, but each element was distinct from the other. The clan names were images she didn't recognize, although they referred to both a woman and a man, judging from the mirror and axe decorating the base.

"Who are they?" She asked.

"Never mind that. Southerners." Of all the people in Gull, it seemed only Edarnon Stone-Carver ever ventured beyond the island, for months on end, working on name-stone commissions by other Clan Heads. Sometimes even princes, it was said, although he never mentioned specific names.

Eithni had hoped one day to join him, in lands she had never seen, accepting commissions of her own. Surely there would be a place for a woman stone-carver, if she was gifted enough.

Now, she supposed she would never know.

Her father broke into her thoughts by shaking the piece of wood in front of her.

"This needs to be something special, Eithni. New name-stones have to be more impressive than the old ones. That's the Southern way." He dropped one shoulder. "It needs your eye, child."

Eithni took the sketch, hands suddenly trembling. What would father do without her?

Looking at him out of the corner of her eye, seeing the angle of his shoulders, the crease between his eyebrows, she thought he was asking the same thing.

"This face is well-balanced just the way it is," she said, turning the image. "But you could add patterns to the sides..." she shaped the idea with her hands. "What goes on the back?"

"Hunting scene." He pulled another sketch from the table, and a blank piece with a stick of charcoal for Eithni. And they got to work.

Soon, the morning had passed so quickly and easily that Eithni almost forgot what had come before.

And what lay ahead.

Right up until the moment when her father put his hand on her shoulder and said, gruffly, "Ah, child. The gods will—" He swallowed, "—would surely be lucky to have you."

She dropped the piece she had been holding. Too much. It was too much.

"I..." Her throat was suddenly dry. "I have to go talk to someone."

Those questions, the ones she'd been hoarding, carrying deep inside, *afraid*...it was time to ask them at last.

SABLE

Sable spent the better part of the day in and out of the passage, never quite venturing into the forbidden chamber. She never heard another sound, and certainly never saw anything.

At some point, Umber had rolled his eyes and resumed his post, muttering something about *one* of them needing to take some responsibility. Sable chose to ignore him.

The voice had been real.

The more she thought about it, the more she wondered.

Had she heard the voice of a *human* on the other side of the true Door?

Someone actually from the human world? Perhaps the veil between their worlds was thinner here, so close to the opening at Solstice. But in all of her research, no story, written rule, oral tradition, nor anecdote had made mention of anything like this.

A thrill of excitement went through her. If her guess was true, she had discovered something new. Something no other denizen of the Summer realm had ever seen or known.

Or, at the very least, had ever decided to mention.

This was exactly what she needed. What she had come for. This was bound to be important for the purposes of the Daylight Order. But she wanted—needed—more proof.

And she knew just how to get it.

"Umber. I need you to do something for me."

"Of course you do." His smile was crooked, but good-natured. His eyes—amber brown like his name—twinkled under the deer-stripe running to his curly brown hair. Sable allowed herself a small smirk —her brother had tossed his helm to the side by mid-day.

True to Sable's predictions, no lightlord had come near. The feasting and celebrations were all happening in their liege's court, after all. Nothing for them here, where the rules were too strict for proper carousing.

"I need to go to the Mirror. Urgently."

His eyebrows shot up. "Leave your post? That's...bordering on suicide. I thought you *wanted* to be—"

She flapped her hands at him. "It's for the job. I need to investigate the...dawn...occurrence. It has something to do with the human realm, I'm positive of it."

None of that was a lie. She couldn't lie to Umber, not really. It wasn't in their nature. But selective truth-telling, now...

He shook his head. "You're not supposed to use the Mirror, either. It's not for the likes of us."

"It's important, brother." She met his eyes squarely, let him see how utterly serious she was. Like her sibling, Sable was named for her eye color. Where his were golden-brown, hers were deep and dark. Liquid, like a deer's.

And, she had on good authority, quite difficult to refuse when she turned her full gaze on a person.

Unless that person was Umber. "It's a mistake. If I'm caught glamouring a fake Sable here," he pointed at her post, where she was *not* currently standing, "Then I'm as much a lawbreaker as you are. These are some of the more *serious* laws, I might add."

Sable clenched her jaw, weighing her options. She could try to argue, to wear him down. But the day might be over by then, and the lightlords' feast wouldn't last forever. Come twilight, at least one of them would surely wish to use the Mirror for himself. And who knew when she would have another opportunity like this?

Oh, her brother was going to be so *angry*...

She flexed her fingers and huffed out a breath. Before Umber could so much as twitch, Sable blurred her form into that of a deer, and cleared the entirety of the Stone Door's mounded bulk in a single leap. She knew he wouldn't dare give chase. *Someone* had to keep guard, after all.

She could hear him cursing as she bounded away into the forest beyond the lightlords' gardens.

~

The Mirror was one of the wonders of the Summer realm, although it didn't look it. A seemingly innocuous small pool of glass-clear water, thickly hedged by ferns and tangled branches, the foliage rich and green as gemstones, and impossible to pass through.

You could only approach the Mirror one way, through a pair of great stones, ones surely as old as the Door. Possibly even of the same origin.

Because the pool wasn't actually a mirror, despite its name. It was a *window,* into the human realm. And by law, only lightlords could use it. The last time Sable had been here, it was on guard duty for her liege. She had stood just outside the great stones, ears swiveling to catch the sounds from within.

Now, Sable would just have to be very, very careful.

The air was redolent with the scent of herbs and magic as she approached in hind-form, her black nose and long, tawny ears twitching. There was a deep hush around the Mirror, as if it waited for something.

It awaited her, then.

She dropped hind-form as she passed between the stones. She had a feeling the pool would not respond to her as anything other than her most true self. Not that a hartkin's shape-changing ability wasn't a part of who they were, inside and out. But broad shoulders, strong arms, supple hands and fingers and tawny hair—that was the form Sable loved most, and so it was her truest self.

She saw that self now, in the Mirror, and saw the resolve in her own eyes. Lightlord she was not, but she could still work her will upon this tool.

The water rippled, clouding, and then stilled. Sable knelt beside it.

"The other side of the Door," she murmured.

I t took some time to find the right way to ask for what she wanted. And to find *who* she wanted. Several times she doubted herself: her ability to wrestle the Mirror into submission, her assumptions about the truth of the morning's happening. Perhaps it had not been a human there after all.

But finally she was getting somewhere. The key lay in backtracking, in seeking images of what had transpired *at dawn* in the human realm.

No easy task. But now, at last, she could see the person who had shouted her fearlessness into an empty chamber:

A bundled human form, quickly emerging from the human equivalent of the Stone Door and out into the weak morning sunlight.

The human realm looked *cold*. Of course it would be. It was midwinter there.

The human was naught but a mass of furs and hide, tightly wrapped to keep the cold at bay, Sable assumed. She found herself slightly disappointed. "Follow," she whispered to the Mirror. The figure walked quickly, stumbling on the stony ground, heading toward what Sable assumed to be the human's village.

Sable could hear no sounds, despite pushing at the Mirror with all her stubborn strength.

Ah—maybe she needed to change her approach. "The same human. At the *current* moment."

"...broke the rules today, Conchenn," a woman's voice said, rippling from the pool. Sable leaned closer, seeing the speaker at last: a young woman, as Sable had guessed. Not terribly long out of girlhood. Still warmly dressed in woolens and furs, but with most of the bulky outer layers now shed, revealing a slim but surprisingly strong figure, long dark hair, and pale skin.

Sable willed a closer look.

The human's face was solemn, a smooth oval with a high forehead, slender nose, and high cheekbones. Large eyes the color of the sea.

The girl—the woman—she was so very lovely. Sable felt her breath catch in her throat.

"I thought you might," another voice drifted up. A much older woman's. "Young Eithni. Always doing things her own way."

The younger woman ducked her head, flushing.

Eithni. Now Sable had a name.

"Still," the older woman—Conchenn?—continued, "Former mentor or not, I am surprised you admitted it to *me*."

"So am I," Eithni said, under her breath. The old woman didn't seem to hear her, but the Mirror caught it just fine. Sable smiled. She liked this girl already.

Eithni raised her voice. "I can't keep pretending everything is all right. I can't just...blithely march on to this ending, not without knowing..." she trailed off.

"Knowing...?" Conchenn gently prompted.

"The truth." The girl looked at the woman. "Which came first for you wise women, Conchenn? Selecting me? Or seeing the signs of the gods?"

The gods? Ah, that would be the lightlords, then. Manipulating the humans for their own gain. Further confirmation of how things stood between the Summer realm and the humans...as if Sable needed *that*.

But she filed that knowledge away almost absently, absorbed as she was in the conversation in the Mirror.

In the human girl's question, and the weight that it seemed to carry.

The older woman sighed. Sable moved her vision from Eithni now to see the other woman's hands, wrapped around a steaming cup. They were wrinkled and weathered, with wrists tattooed in patterns Sable had never seen before. She supposed this was what a wise woman looked like.

"I think you already know the answer to that, Eithni."

The girl's hands trembled. "You read the signs first," she said. "And you wanted me gone, and so you chose me."

Sable felt a knife of pity. What a terrible thing to believe. How much worse if it were actually true.

And *this* was the human who would pass through the Door in seven days? This lovely, brave girl with tears shimmering in the corners of her eyes?

The old woman set her cup down. "That's not the truth. Not the whole truth."

"The *whole* truth—"

Conchenn raised her hand, and Eithni fell silent. It was clear the wise woman carried power here. "I care very much for you, child. I don't *want* you gone from here. You haven't made things easy for yourself here, true—"

"As if I can choose who I am," Eithni half-whispered.

"—*But* that is not the first consideration when selecting our candidate for welcoming the light. Which you should well know already."

"To be 'pleasing to the gods?' Any number of Gull youths could—"

"No," Conchenn said, gently. "They could not. Not with a spark like yours."

Sable found herself agreeing. The lightlords—her liege—would *love* this human girl.

What a terrible, terrible thing.

Eithni was silent, but not for long. "Why, then," she said slowly, drawing a careful breath and licking her lips, "why must the Gull

Clan sacrifice one of our own to please the gods? Why not send someone they...wouldn't want?"

"Have a care, Eithni," the wise woman said, warning clear in her tone. "Who would dare cheat the gods?"

Then she took Eithni's hands in both of hers and leaned forward, lowering her voice so that even Sable had to strain toward the Mirror to hear it. "We *need* to please the gods this year. We need a successful Taking, or the Gull Clan may cease to exist as we know it."

The girl drew a sharp breath. Sable found herself holding her own, forgetting to breathe entirely, in fact. Her mind swirled with new information, connecting it to all the things she already knew. And her heart ached for this Eithni woman, caught in a role she didn't want.

If Sable could only—

She suddenly froze. Behind her, beyond the twin stones, she heard approaching voices.

Lightlords.

EITHNI

Trembling, Eithni raised the cup of the Conchenn's herbal tisane to her lips, trying to collect her thoughts and emotions. Her free hand traced circles on the wood of the wise woman's table. It was worn smooth by age, dark and heavy.

The Gull Clan may cease to exist as we know it. What could Conchenn possibly mean by those words?

The gossips all had their own versions of why the clan was in dire need of a Taking, or rather in need of the Giving that followed. The Giving would save them from poor crops, sickness, rumors of invaders to the South, rumors of invaders to the West, the encroaching sea, any number of things.

But the old hens always complained about these things. It had been hard for Eithni to consider any of them seriously *this* year.

The Gull Clan may cease to exist as we know it.

She took a swallow of the tisane. It had gone cold and bitter. Eithni felt cold too.

"Why do you say that?" she forced herself to ask. She didn't want to know. Didn't want to know any of this.

But she had come for the truth.

"I'm going to tell you something the Wise Women and our clan leaders know, but isn't widely known otherwise." Conchenn's voice was pitched low, so that Eithni had to lean forward again to hear it. "The Gull Clan hasn't always been its own entity. We were once Orcadi."

Orcadi was the Boar Clan. The cluster of islands to the East, Eithni remembered, although she realized she knew little else about them.

"On the Orcadi isles, there are great wonders. Immense rings of stones that far outshine our own standing sentinels. A mound like our own cairn, but three times its size. All within sight of each other. Places of power, sacred to the gods. But the Boar Clan fears them."

Eithni raised her eyebrows. "Surely they worship the gods too?"

Conchenn dipped her head. "They worship the gods in name. But not in action. Not the way we do."

Maybe that is no bad thing, the rebellious spirit inside Eithni thought.

It must have showed on her face. "Child, the gods have favored us in ways the Orcadi could never dream of. It's no coincidence that the Gull pays tribute no one, not the Orcadi king nor any other. Nor do we follow the law of Brude, the high king to the South. The Boar is under this Southern king's thumb, but The Gull is free."

The Gull is free. That was a saying Eithni had heard her entire life. So this was what it truly meant?

Still. Eithni lifted a shoulder. "But what do the gods have to do with...politics?" She wished she had made her father talk about his travels, had taken more of an interest in such matters before now. But her obsessions had always been art, and stone carving, and then Derilei—*ah, Derilei!*—and stone carving again.

"Many generations ago, before my grandmother and her grandmother, we owed fealty to the Orcadi king and paid tribute in men and goods. But our island was poor and our numbers few. We couldn't spare our sons for the Boar's skirmishes with the South."

She reached out and put her hand on Eithni's.

"And then, we were saved by the gods. Because unlike the Orcadi, we chose not to fear the sacred places of the ancients."

Eithni frowned. "I don't understand."

Conchenn sighed. "The chamber, Eithni. In Orcadi, their great cairn is sealed shut and they dare not open it. Ours, open and active, is a doorway to the gods themselves. And so the gods favor us. We prosper, and we are kept safe and hidden from all who would seek to make us theirs."

Eithni took her hand from Conchenn's. She closed her eyes, running her fingers along the carved sides of her cup. If all that kept the Gull Clan safe was the favor of the gods, then she had no choice.

She opened her eyes.

"I'm going back to the chamber tomorrow," she said. Her expression dared Conchenn to challenge the statement. The other women merely sighed and dipped her head in acknowledgment.

Eithni rose. "If I'm to do this, I must not be afraid."

She did not mention the guardian. But now she realized she *must* speak with that voice. It was her only chance to know the truth of the gods before she gave herself over to them.

And she had new questions.

SABLE

Sable broke her contact with the Mirror and quickly shifted to hindform, hoping it would be enough to disguise her. Lightlords could sense a glamour if they drew close enough, but the hartkin's second forms were no illusion—and mostly indistinguishable from a real deer of the Summer realm.

Her ears twitched, telling her that the voices of the lightlords were possibly far back enough on the path that they might miss her emergence from the twin stones.

In any case, she couldn't remain here.

Sable forced herself to move. She made her leap erratic, away from the Mirror, hoping no one would see where she'd truly come from.

Startled shouts accompanied her sudden movement.

She made for the underbrush. With her heart hammering so, she hardly needed to fake the panicked flight of a deer disturbed by intruders.

She felt the brush of lightlord magic as she moved, shivering across her back. What manner of spell it might be, she couldn't say. Something to halt a deer in flight? Something else?

She couldn't afford to find out.

A real deer would stop immediately, just outside the range of its perceived threat, and stand perfectly still in the undergrowth. For natural predators, such an action would be effective. But a lightlord would not be fooled. Sable had to keep running, a risky action in itself.

If the lightlord in question was her own liege, the dangers were even greater.

She didn't dare to look.

Even after the shouts faded behind her, Sable didn't stop moving until she neared her goal, slowing herself at the edge of the woods, where the boundaries of the Stone Door's place of power were marked by the richly scented gardens of the lightlords.

She forced herself to pick her way through them slowly, quietly, keeping to the bowers and taller greenery. She didn't know what she would find once she reached her post. Best to approach in hind-form and hope to catch Umber's eye so he could merge his glamour with her true self.

If he had done what she thought he would, that is.

The enormity of the risks she had taken suddenly stole her breath away. What had she been *thinking*?

She hadn't, really. Sable had always been more a creature of action than thought. Often *calculated* action, certainly, but no time wasted on long contemplation of consequences.

Especially not consequences that reached beyond the immediate dangers. Such as the one that struck her in this moment, causing her to go completely still among the garden greenery.

If she were caught now, what effect would that have on her mission? On the Daylight Order as a whole?

It could be far worse than any personal repercussions.

She had been charged with gathering knowledge on one of the most important symbols of lightlord power and dominance: their control of the portals into the human world. If she did her job right, and her people found what they needed, they could finally put that kind of power in the hands of everyone in the Summer realm, not just the corrupt, elite few.

But now Sable could lose her post, and depending on her ability or inability to effectively wheedle or prevaricate, she might either find herself enslaved, imprisoned, or put to death. But that was only half of the problem.

Should the lightlords discover her rebellion against their edicts prohibiting the use of yet another of their 'sacred' privileges—the Mirror—what kind of questions might follow?

And would those questions lead back to the Daylight Order itself?

Sable forced herself to start moving again, picking her way through the ordered chaos of another lightlord garden. Her guts screamed at her to just get it over with and leap through it at the same speed she had left, but the rational part of her mind locked that feeling away.

Another part of her mind continued to gnaw on what she had just seen, and what her next move might be.

With a sinking feeling, she realized the information she'd gathered just now at the Mirror wasn't even the right kind of valuable. The Daylight Order didn't *need* further proof of the lightlords' evil, of their manipulation of human communities. It wouldn't make a grain of difference, except as personal vindication for Order members, perhaps.

As much as Sable wished to know the threat that the human woman's clan—*Eithni's* clan—faced if they didn't please 'the gods,' it wasn't relevant. In fact, aside from any knowledge she could gather at the ceremony itself, at the moment the human would cross over, Sable would be best served by forgetting about Eithni entirely.

She would need to keep reminding herself of that.

Because even now, despite everything, she wanted to go back to the Mirror and see her again.

~

"That was a stupid thing to do," Umber hissed.

If any gods truly existed—and Sable had her doubts—they must have smiled on the siblings today, for she had emerged from the gardens without trouble, and no one appeared to witness her transition from Umber's illusionary guard duty to real.

Umber's savage glare notwithstanding.

She didn't blame him for his anger. She had forced him into this position, knowing she could rely on him to help her despite himself. It was a shoddy thing to do to her own brother.

A dangerous thing.

She didn't regret it nearly enough.

Even knowing she wasn't out of danger. Even knowing that no lightlords might have come after her *yet*—but that had no bearing on whether they would in the future.

But she wouldn't tell Umber about that, or anything else that had happened at the Mirror. He was already worried enough. And he already disapproved of 'whatever it is you get up to' with the Daylight Order.

The less said, the better.

So in response to Umber's '*What were you thinking?*' Sable only said, truthfully, "I'm so very sorry I put you through that." He would forgive her eventually. He always did.

She did not add, *'and I won't do it again.'*

She couldn't promise that.

Her nerves didn't stop humming until well after nightfall. She and Umber spelled each other on their watch in silence throughout the night, a night which Sable knew from her research grew uncommonly longer the closer one drew to the Stone Door during the height of the humans' Winter. Something about the human realm affecting the Summer realm at this nexus.

Another fascinating aspect to this place. It was as if her own realm's mornings and evenings were aligning with the humans'. For a purpose even the lightlords didn't truly know, Sable would venture to guess.

And it all met at the center, on the humans' Winter Solstice.

When a human could cross over into the keeping of a lightlord who didn't deserve her, who...

No, best not to think about it, or about Eithni at all.

S able's resolve on this matter utterly failed as the new dawn approached, as the mist wreathed the gardens and the dew formed at her feet.

Despite herself, every sense she possessed now bent toward the opening at the front of the mound, where she had heard the voice yesterday.

Would she possibly hear it again? Would Eithni return? Sable wished she could have stayed to hear the rest of the conversation with the wise woman. She wished...she wasn't even sure what she wished. All she knew was some kind of irrational longing, growing as the colors of the morning twilight grew on the horizon.

Then she heard it, faint but distinct: *"Hello...guardian?"*

Sable's heart thundered. But she shot a glance at Umber, who had awoken well in advance of dawn and joined her, still deep in disapproving silence within his masked helm.

Now, his ear twitched and he looked at her sidelong. "Are you going to answer?" His voice was so carefully neutral, she didn't know what he was thinking.

But she knew her response to his question, all the same.

She ducked into the passageway.

"I seek the guardian," Eithni's voice sounded again from deeper within, firmer this time.

"I am here," Sable responded.

EITHNI

"I am here," came the voice. Eithni's breath caught. It was the same as yesterday: a female voice, she was sure of it.

Eithni planted her feet firmly, pressing her hands against the wall where the light had formed. The stone beneath her bare fingers was numbingly cold, but she didn't care.

She wouldn't run away this time.

"I am Eithni of the Gull Clan," she said clearly, into the stone. "I welcome the sun in six days, and I have questions of the gods."

No, no—far too strong! Potentially insulting, even dangerous, to sound like that. She hastily added, "...as a supplicant. I seek to know my path, if the gods will it."

Would it be enough?

"I am not a god," the voice said. Was that a note of hesitation? No censure or harshness, at least. Eithni let her shoulders relax slightly. *"I am Sable, kin to hart and hind, and watcher of the Stone Door. I...may not have what you seek."*

Eithni's lips moved silently as she tried to understand what she'd heard. Kin to hart and hind. A deer spirit? Something else?

But not a god. Maybe no use to Eithni at all. Still, she wouldn't know until she asked more.

And she certainly couldn't leave now.

But she took far too long trying to form her next question. She didn't know how to proceed. How did one cajole a servant of the gods into helping you? She hardly believed she was speaking to one at all.

The voice broke into her paralyzed silence.

"Still—if there is any...that is, ask your question and we shall see."

It suddenly occurred to Eithni that the voice sounded...not necessarily human—there was an odd, echoing quality to it—but like a *person*. Not a powerful god or guardian.

A woman, just like Eithni. With a name—Sable, the voice had said. Perhaps this Sable was a deer spirit, yes, but not so different from Eithni herself.

"I don't know where to start," she found herself admitting.

"You said you wanted to know your path? I can't answer that, but—you may ask me something else. If you wish."

"I've never spoken to a servant of the gods before."

"I have never spoken to a human before," the reply came, a bit wry.

Eithni found herself unexpectedly smiling. "I hope the experience does not disappoint," she said, and then caught herself. Was she attempting to *banter*...with an unknown spirit, or being, or deer maiden, and from the realm of the gods, no less? This was madness.

"I do not think it will, Eithni of the Gull," came the surprising reply, warm and humorous. Followed by what sounded like a quickly indrawn breath.

The words, the sounds, were somehow clearer now. Eithni raised her head from the stone, shifting herself, and saw that the pale honeyed light had grown stronger, covering most of the space before her.

Was the connection to the other side also stronger because of this?

But perhaps that meant the connection would fade, once the sun moved from the passage. If such was the case, Eithni needed to pull her scattered thoughts together quickly.

She needed to ask something important, something relevant.

No more strange behavior. No more forgetting the nature of the...*being*...on the other side of the conversation.

Of course, she couldn't ask the most important question of all.

Will my sacrifice be worth it?

Or, put a different way: were the gods deserving of the tribute the Gull Clan would give them? Would they honor this supposed promise they made to her people?

And what would become of *her* once she gave herself to them? Would it be slavery?

...And if so, how could anyone say 'The Gull is free?'

Eithni didn't know how to ask any of those questions, without risking the wrath of beings she didn't truly understand.

But perhaps she could gain a clearer knowledge of her own fate, if she asked the right questions in the right way.

"Tell me this, if you can," she finally said, drawing a deep breath, "what becomes of one who finds favor with the gods and crosses into their realm on Solstice?"

Silence.

"I...can't say," the voice responded, slowly. Eithni's mind still stubbornly seemed to insist it belonged to a woman. It made her want to know what the owner looked like, however irrelevant that information might be.

It made her want to look into the other woman's eyes and ask that question again.

"Are you saying you don't know the fate of humans who—" *sacrifice themselves* "—give themselves over to the gods?" Eithni tried desperately hard to keep her voice steady and calm, while her near-frozen hands clenched and unclenched painfully.

"...No."

A long pause, while Eleni tried to understand if it meant 'I don't know,' or if it meant 'I'm not saying I don't know.'

It mattered more than she wanted it to.

"I'm sorry," said the voice again.

And then, quietly:

"This was a mistake."

SABLE

Sable backed away from the wall, away from the accusation beneath the other woman's words and tone, so carefully controlled.

She could picture the look on Eithni's face. She had seen it in the Mirror: those luminous green-gray-blue eyes turned upon the old woman Conchenn, piercing straight through her with their truth.

"Are you still there?"

How could Sable have been so stupid as to think she could escape that fate? She didn't need to see Eithni's eyes now to know she had earned everything that must be showing in them.

"Guardian?"

She should have known the human woman would ask questions Sable didn't dare answer. Not when everything still depended on what must happen in six days.

"...Sable?"

She should never have answered that voice at all.

Umber waited at the entrance, arms crossed. But his scowl died in an instant when he looked at his sister's face.

"What happened?" he asked, quietly.

"I made another mistake," Sable said. The sun had risen now, enough that the shaft of light in the entry to the Stone Door had begun to drift out, allowing the shadows to return to the chamber inside.

Sable picked up her deer-skull helm from the ground and carefully fitted it back onto her head, avoiding her brother's gaze.

"Do you want to talk?" he asked, as the silence stretched out further.

Yes. But not to him. Umber didn't need to know her mission, or how she had inadvertently jeopardized it...in more ways than one. He didn't need to know her doubts and fears.

Everything was too tied up in things she must keep secret, for his safety and her own.

And, if she was honest, she didn't want to admit all her mistakes to him.

She didn't want to admit she had begun to care about a human woman she'd had no business ever speaking with in the first place.

~

"The human woman is at the Door again, Sable."

Sable lifted a shoulder defensively. She had awaited this new dawn—only five away from the human Solstice, now—with dread forming a cold knot in her stomach. She knew her rigid

550

posture gave too much away under the keen eye of her brother. "What of it?"

"She's asking for you. By name."

Sable had placed herself further away from the doorway than usual. She had even started humming some old tune from her childhood, over and over again, just in case.

And now Umber had to ruin it.

"I can't control what she does. Put your hands over your ears if it bothers you," Sable said waspishly.

Out of the corner of her eye, she could see Umber lift his helm visor and try to catch her eye. She stared straight ahead, knowing it was childish, but not knowing what else to do.

"You don't need to snap at me," he said, his voice cool. "You caused this. You should fix it."

"I shouldn't have spoken to her at all."

"It's too late to take that back, and you know it."

She turned to look at him. "What would *you* have me do?"

She threw it out like an accusation, but Umber was ready for it. He met her gaze with raised eyebrows. "Sable, I don't even know what you've already *done*."

Sable took a deep breath. She really didn't want to do this. But it was better than this war with herself, better than trying to cover her ears against the chance of hearing the voice inside the Door, while her own rebellious body strained to listen anyway.

She took the easiest approach she could think of. "Your hearing is as good as mine. What did you overhear of my conversation with the human woman?"

Umber frowned. He glanced into the doorway, ears flicking back and forth, then glanced back at Sable. When she refused to even look in that direction, he sighed and came over to her.

"I could hear your part better than hers, other than the beginning. Let's see...she thinks the lightlords are gods, and wanted to know her path. You told her your name, which seemed unwise...I think you might have been flirting. Then she asked a question I didn't hear, that you couldn't—or wouldn't—answer. And you came out of there looking like you had ruined someone's life. Do I have it correct?"

"Fairly...you thought I was *flirting*?"

"A little bit, yes."

"That doesn't make sense."

"Not particularly," he agreed easily. "But you often do things that don't make sense."

She punched his arm and scowled, but her mind was already elsewhere. What exactly had transpired during the conversation yesterday to make Umber even think...that? She had shied away from thinking about it at all, but that might have been a mistake.

Had she been flirting?

With a human woman?

Were those feelings she'd had, seeing the woman in the mirror—were they more than just simple admiration for someone so defiant, and intelligent, and...utterly lovely?

"Oh, Umber. I think I am in trouble."

"I know," he said, watching her, "but why?"

And then she told him everything.

She first told him, over his protests, about her role in the Daylight Order, helping to gather knowledge of places of power only used by the lightlords. Sable was a quick thinker, so when their liege had been awarded the next human for his court, Sable had seen an opportunity to get close—and by necessity pull Umber in too—just to get a shot at the Stone Door during the most important time of the year...

During the most important *year* in a long time.

She told Umber how too many good opportunities had lined up, giving the Order their first real chance at learning the lightlords' secrets of the Door...too good for Sable to change anything *now*...

And she had been certain that the voice inside the chamber of the Stone Door was another opportunity she shouldn't pass up, and maybe she'd been right at first, but she realized now that the Mirror had been purely to satisfy her own curiosity, and now it might be the choice that would ruin everything, *even if* Sable never got found out...

Because, she just realized, she cared far too much about what happened to Eithni.

Maybe more than she cared about her mission.

And if she talked to the human again, she might find herself telling Eithni the truth about the lightlords, about everything, and then the human would flee and the ceremony—the one thing the Daylight Order *needed* in order to steal the secrets of the Door— would come crashing down.

And Sable would never see Eithni again.

"Among other things," Umber said, once he had recovered from the onslaught of Sable's words and the implications they carried. "You will also get us both killed...or worse, punished. And that's just one thing."

Sable felt cold. Of course. Anything she did to ruin the ceremony would get them *both* punished. Umber's innocence in the matter wouldn't make the smallest difference—lightlords didn't embrace concepts like reason or mercy.

"I'm sorry, Umber," she whispered. "I dragged you into this mess and you had nothing to do with it."

Umber smiled crookedly. "I knew you had an ulterior motive and that it was caught up in this Order of yours. And I know you've done it before, too. And it always worked out previously—by the time I figured out you were up to something in the Diamond Forest—"

"—You knew about that?"

"Yes, and it worked out very well for both of us that time, with no one the wiser. I figured you would be smart like that again, here. And this," he gestured around them, "was an opportunity *I* didn't want to miss either."

Sable's shoulders sagged. Despite their intent, his words didn't absolve her at all. "I don't know how to make anything 'work out very well' for us this time."

"I think you were right—you can't talk to her again. The human."

Except...the knot in the pit of Sable's stomach doubled as she realized something she had perhaps known all along.

The light hadn't fully left the tunnel yet—a sliver still remained.

Sable pushed past her brother, toward the mouth of the Door, and this time let her sensitive ears strain for the voice they wanted to hear anyway.

Was there still the faint sound of calling within?

Umber grabbed her arm. "You don't want to do this, remember?"

She pulled away from him, shaking her head rapidly. "You don't understand, Umber. You don't understand *her*. She thinks long, and thinks deep. That conversation we had...I didn't handle it right at all. If I *don't* talk to her again, she might leave anyway."

EITHNI

Eithni tried to fight the disappointment weighing her limbs, creeping in like the damp chill of the air. Like this mist-ridden, cloud-blanketed, damning sky.

She had been so determined not to give up. To keep pushing, no matter what.

This was her *life*, after all.

But now she was no closer to knowing her future than the day she first decided to break the rules and enter the cairn. In some ways, her situation was worse than before.

She had gotten *close* to something yesterday, or so she had thought. But it was all silence now, and she surely had been here long enough for something to happen by now.

But the silence could be the result of the cloudy sky—her timing could be off because of the light changing too gradually, or, as she had wondered before, it might be the lack of sun to light the wall and trigger the magic.

Or it could be that this Sable person, the guardian servant of the gods, had decided to abandon Eithni.

If true, the idea stung. For a moment, Eithni had thought there was a spark of camaraderie between them. But the guardian had never owed Eithni anything to begin with.

It had been audacious indeed to think the gods—or their servants —would answer to Eithni at all.

Still. She clenched her fists. "This isn't right," she said to the empty air. As far as final attempts at contact went, it was perhaps less diplomatic than it should be.

But this silence *wasn't* right, even if it was how things had always been done before.

If the Gull was to be truly free, every member of the Gull clan needed the freedom to choose. *Especially* the one sacrificing herself.

And from the meager piece of conversation with the guardian yesterday...was Eithni willing to chance everything based on knowledge that left her *less* confident in her future?

And if she chose...

If she chose to *leave* before the ceremony took place?

What then?

She squeezed her eyes shut for a moment, wishing she was someone else. On some other island, in some other clan that had no special arrangement with the gods. Orcadi, perhaps.

Because maybe it was better to be under the thumb of a ruler to the South, or to pay tribute to a larger clan, than to sacrifice one of your clan's own children every few decades.

A dangerous thought.

She turned to fold herself into the passageway to the outside once more, wondering where her loyalties lay. Where they *should* lie.

Then, behind her: *"Eithni of the Gull? Are you still there?"*

She whirled. It was the female voice—Sable's voice—again. The magic still *worked*.

"I am," Eithni said, her voice cracking. She rushed back to the wall, still bathed in semi-darkness.

"Good," came the other's voice, sounding breathless and very faint. *"I don't know how much longer..."*

Eithni strained to hear the rest. "Longer...?"

Silence again.

Eithni was growing to hate silences.

She slumped forward, resting her head on the stone. Had there been something about 'the light' in there before she lost the thread?

If the magic relied on the timing of the light, as Eithni had first believed, then perhaps the light that *would* have been there today continued to mark the door, despite the clouds.

But if so, why would Sable have waited until the end of that short space of time to speak with her? Surely the guardian would know better.

Or perhaps it still had something to do with the cloud-cover making things fainter and more tenuous. This magic was uncharted ground for Eithni, and she wasn't about to ask Conchenn for knowledge the wise woman wouldn't approve and probably didn't even possess.

It didn't matter, in the end.

She had other, more pressing, questions. Which would have to wait...again.

But of a certainty, Eithni would be back tomorrow.

This time, the sky was clear. The stars were out, in all of their cold brilliance. Eithni's mind, too, was clear, and her heart light and fierce. The guardian Sable would speak with her again after all.

The mound was still dark when Eithni arrived. She had hastened here too soon, well before sunrise. And of course there was no rushing the sun. But she crouched and made her way into the chamber anyway. She would be able to start speaking the instant the light first touched the wall, and not a moment wasted.

Today Eithni could finally get her answers—or at least, answers *enough*—if only she asked the right questions.

And she *would*. She must. She had only four days left.

Or...perhaps fewer than that, with the wise women and the Head beginning to grow watchful. She had seen it in the clan Head's glance yesterday, sidelong and silent, and in the candle in Conchenn's window this morning. Watching Eithni slip out of the village once again.

No one had forbidden her anything, yet. But there was always the chance. There were plenty of hours left in the day.

The light in the passage began to grow, and her heart beat faster. She was ready. Her first question was already on her tongue.

The minutes were agonizing in their slowness.

The first light touched the wall, and she amazed herself at her own swiftness there, bundled form and all. She didn't know if touching the stone with her bare fingers actually made a difference, but it felt right, somehow. She was a creature of the stone herself, after all.

"Guardian Sable?" she asked, working hard to keep her voice calm.

Two heartbeats. Three.

"*I am here,*" the voice said, and Eithni allowed herself to breathe. The sound was still faint, but that should change as the light grew stronger. Eithni hoped. She wanted to read the emotions of the other woman, if she could.

She hesitated. The last exchange had ended abruptly, and hadn't been much to begin with. And the *real* exchange between them before had ended badly. Eithni had devoted so much time to planning how she would approach the guardian. But now that she was here, it felt...not quite right.

"I am sorry if I caused you distress," she found herself saying, instead of her carefully planned speech. "Perhaps I wasn't a good 'first human experience' after all."

"*Oh—I—*" Pause. "*I am sorry too. I did not handle things well...*" the voice trailed off.

"Perhaps we could start afresh?" Eithni suggested. It seemed like the right thing to say, although she didn't know what it meant in practical terms. Or where it would take her.

"*I would like that, Eithni of the Gull.*"

But maybe it would be better this way.

"Good," Eithni said, and found herself smiling. She suddenly knew just what to ask. "What is the realm of the gods like?"

SABLE

"Ah," Sable said, smiling, "*that* I can answer." Not completely satisfactorily, but enough for truth.

She might even enjoy this conversation.

Because the part of Sable that longed for this human woman, despite all logic, had instantly noted—with some satisfaction—the warmth evident in the other's voice through the stone. The way that Eithni had spoken to Sable as if she were a person, a fellow woman, not some mystical divine being.

Despite all the dangers, Sable *wanted* that kind of connection. She shouldn't, but she did.

"First, we don't call it the realm of the gods," she said, easily sidestepping the question of gods for now. She hated having to bite her tongue every time Eithni said that word. The lightlords didn't deserve to be called that. But she didn't dare correct the human woman.

This would be a delicate dance already.

"We call it the Summer realm. The people who live here...there are all kinds." No, no, she shouldn't elaborate on that. "The land itself...it's beautiful...and, I think, strange to you humans. There are no seasons here, just Summer eternal. There are forests and mountains and rivers and lakes like the human realm, but no seas. Not like yours, anyway."

She frowned, realizing she had no true way to compare her own realm with Eithni's. She had never been in the human realm. No one, aside from select lightlords, had crossed the *other* way in a thousand years.

"*But do you...like it?*" came the response, and Sable realized she hadn't really described her home at all. Not in the way Eithni would want to hear it.

For a moment Sable had forgotten that the other woman wanted to know about the Summer realm because she would soon be in it.

For the remainder of her human life.

Sable's mood fell, and she rubbed the side of her head. Eithni was clever, asking Sable for opinion now instead of description. How could she answer?

She knew how she should. How she *must*.

It had to be the truth.

May the gods and Umber forgive her.

"Often," Sable said. "But not always."

EITHNI

This was exactly what Eithni wanted, and exactly what she feared.

"The Summer realm is a bright jewel. But...it's hard and sharp-edged in much the same way."

Sable's voice sang with truth, now. The connection had grown stronger, and so had the emotion. *"What you call the gods, we call light-lords, and they are powerful, but indifferent to the rest of us beyond the ways that we can serve their ends. Don't look for mercy, although the light-lords can be indulgent when it suits their whims. They are fond of music and artistry, and—they are very fond of humans."*

The words came out in a rush, as if the woman on the other end needed to get them all out at once. But Eithni couldn't take the time to analyze that.

A chill shot through her body. Somehow, deep down, she had known it would be like this. That the gods would be like this. Beautiful and cruel and terrifying.

This was what she had needed to know. Hadn't wanted to know.

She swallowed. "Fond of humans...how?"

A long pause.

"Humans are a delight and a curiosity to—many of us in the Summer realm. And especially those humans with talents in craft and art, song and dance. But..."

Eithni shifted in the following silence. "Please. I need to know the truth."

"They do not...value individuals, beyond what entertainment and enjoyment they can provide. Lightlords make humans into their own creatures, their own playthings." Hesitation. *"I am told it is a blissful life, being*

a human in a lightlord's court. But...they will change you into someone—something—other than who you are."

It took a moment for the words to sink in. *They will change you.*

Eithni snatched shaking hands from the stone wall, backing away. *This* was what the gods demanded? She wrapped her arms around herself, feeling another, deeper, shuddering chill from her toes to her crown.

She almost missed Sable's next words: *"And I would not want that for you, Eithni of the Gull."*

It was spoken softly, but with the light now filling the wall, every sound came through clearly. The guardian's voice was full of emotion...emotion Eithni suddenly thought she recognized.

It was not unlike the way Derilei had sounded, telling Eithni the clan didn't deserve her.

Did this guardian—this Sable creature—*care* for her? For Eithni, a mere human she had never truly met?

"Why would you care what happens to me, guardian?" she found herself asking, her voice equally quiet. It wasn't a diplomatic question. But now it seemed more important than anything.

The pause was longer, deeper this time.

"I suppose...because I like you."

A simple enough answer. Too simple.

"But why? You know nothing of me."

"That's not entirely true." Another pause, awkward this time. *"I have...watched you."*

The rapid succession of confused thoughts and emotions following that statement made Eithni suddenly wish she could sit down.

Sable was a guardian, a creature of the gods—or lightlords, Eithni supposed—and might have every right to watch a human during a Taking year. Many people of the Gull thought the gods watched all the time, in fact.

But the gods weren't what Eithni's people thought they were. And Sable was no god. And it wasn't particularly fair that she should have knowledge of Eithni—what had the other woman *seen?*—with no way for a mere human to gain equal ground. And for the past handful of minutes, Eithni had foolishly begun to think of herself and the guardian as equals—Sable herself had been the one to make the connection personal, hadn't she? But...

It was too much. Everything was too much.

She didn't want to know any more; she wanted to know everything. She didn't want to have to think about this, any of it, but that was impossible.

The silence stretched.

"What do you mean, watched me?" Eithni finally asked. She couldn't think of anything else.

Another pause from Sable. Eithni allowed herself a small, crooked smile at the discomfort she could only assume the other woman felt.

"After I heard your voice that first time, I wanted to know more. I went to a place within the Summer realm, a window that lets the lightlords look into the human realm."

That answered another question, about the gods watching.

"And then I found you, when you were speaking with the wise woman. And...I found I cared about the outcome."

"You cared," Eithni said slowly, wonderingly. "What do you mean?"

"You were so full of—I just—I don't know how to say it. There was pain there, and fear and bravery, and you asked questions that mattered, and I—I thought you deserved better."

Echoes of Derilei again.

"What I deserve doesn't matter," Eithni said, and didn't try to hide the touch of bitterness that came with the words. "The Gull matters."

"I don't believe that," Sable said, and the warmth in her voice brought unexpected tears to the corners of Eithni's eyes.

"But tell me—I was interrupted before I heard the end of the conversation with the wise woman. What did she say to you, that brought you here again?"

Eithni hadn't planned to speak of the Gull, or of anything that Conchenn had said. With another being of the Summer realm, another guardian, she wouldn't have dared. But Sable wanted to know, and this was so very different from what Eithni had expected... and so Eithni told her everything.

About the Gull being 'free' because of its special relationship with the gods—and all that came with that so-called privilege.

And if the telling of it showed a touch of resentment, of questioning the justice of the gods, Eithni didn't bother to hide it.

They had moved past dancing around the truth, the two of them.

SABLE

The light began to move from the wall—and with it, Eithni's voice, and her account of the Gull and their old pact with the Lightlords, began to fade as well.

"I think our time is coming to an end," Sable said, loath to interrupt the other woman's words. The story's significance was not lost on her, especially as a member of the Daylight Order.

But she wanted to make sure of an even more important thing. "I want to talk to you again. Will you come tomorrow?"

Eithni's reply, very faint now, nonetheless came quickly: *"Yes, I will."*

~

And she did.

For the next three days, Sable rushed to the wall at first light. Umber stopped asking questions entirely now, merely looking thoughtful when Sable emerged, watching the expression on her face —always a mixture of joy and despair.

Eithni was so lovely in every way, and the connection felt *real*. Real in a way they both yearned for.

They were kindred spirits: in pushing against the established rules, in questioning...and yet they approached it so very differently. Sable, quick to take action, and Eithni, more inclined to think long, to push to the questions at the very heart of things.

But neither of them found answers for the most important question of all.

What would they do?

The coming day of the Solstice loomed between them, resurfacing at odd moments.

"Sable, are you...a woman?"

"I am a female hartkin. I suppose one of my forms is like yours—my favorite form. But I think I would look strange to you—there is quite a bit of the deer in me too."

"I have difficulty picturing this."

"As to that, I am sorry. I have seen your face, but you won't see mine. It's not fair, I know."

Pause.

"Will I not see you when...if...when I step through the door?"

Longer pause.

"I—I don't know. Yes. But you would not be there for me, but for my liege. The ceremony, everything is controlled by the lightlords."

And the thought was a slow, twisting knife in Sable's gut.

And by the long silence on the other end, she knew it was the same for Eithni too.

Sable barely remembered to worry about the implications of the Solstice, and whatever would ultimately transpire then, in regards to her own mission for the Daylight Order. All she could think of was this: what *should* Eithni choose...and in that choice, how could Sable live without her?

For there was no happy ending, either way.

EITHNI

Snow.

The wise women had predicted cold, clear skies on the day of the Solstice. They hadn't said anything about snow having fallen the night *before*. But here it lay now, and even though there was no moon, the starlight reflected ghostly blue on every surface.

Eithni stood outside her door in the frigid air, breathing the sharpness into her nose and mouth. Dawn—*the* Dawn—was still a long time coming, but Eithni had only a scant few minutes before the wise women came to prepare for the ceremony.

This might be the last time she would ever see Winter.

She knelt and put a bare hand to the snow, scooping it up with fingers not quite yet benumbed. The melting water provided a sort of icy focus. If she concentrated on the bite of it, pooling in her hand, she needn't think of anything that was to come.

But the moment was far too short.

Conchenn and the others arrived, already clothed in garments the color of ash. A girl, several years younger than Eithni, came with them. Eithni knew that both the girl, Muire, and another, a boy named Caltram, now filled the role she had taken before—assisting the one welcoming the dawn, in anticipation of becoming that person in the next year, or the year after. There was no shortage of youths for candidates, some younger, some older.

But none of them need worry about a Taking year, not for a long time.

If Eithni did her duty for the Gull today.

She turned and let them into her home. Muire approached her, smiling, bearing the ceremonial gown—two gowns, actually—a lighter, softer garment of green beneath another of thick cream wool. Summer, blanketed by Winter. When the human supplicant crossed over, she would cast off her heavy garments in favor of dress more fitting of her new home.

If she crossed over.

Eithni let the women help her into the clothing, her mind already far, far away, deep in a decision she still hadn't made.

Would it be so terrible for her to lose herself to a lightlord's whim in this Summer realm, a place Sable spoke of with both love and loathing?

If Eithni fled her duty, she would never be welcome in the Gull anyway. Conchenn, Derilei, the whole village would hold her in contempt. She would go into exile, likely to never see even her father again.

She would lose those few tethers to her human side, the life she had known, regardless of what she chose.

And the Summer realm had Sable in it. Sable, who saw Eithni and loved her as she was. Eithni was as sure of this as she was of anything.

But in the Summer realm, she would have no freedom to exist as she chose. She might never see Sable again. Or worse, she might see Sable every day and have no will of her own.

To lose herself like that...

Eithni had never before wished to change who she was. Her reputation for being 'difficult' and 'wayward'—she acknowledged it, wore it like an unlovely but comfortable garment. Even her desire for Derilei, unsanctioned, ignored, suppressed by her own people.

Only once, in that conversation with Conchenn, had Eithni wondered for a moment what her fate might have been, if only she had been a different, more accepted member of the Clan.

And now?

She had no answers to anything.

But it also seemed she had no choice. Really, the thought of leaving had been an illusion from the beginning—where else would she go, in the dead of Winter? Gull was an *island*.

This she told herself, as Muire and the women helped her wrap herself in a protective layer of heavy furs and take up the lantern to lead the procession from the village to the hill.

It was better this way. For the Gull. For Sable, too.

For everyone, perhaps, but Eithni.

SABLE

The night was so, so long in ending.

It wasn't nearly long enough.

Today, the advancing dawn would bring an end, or a beginning. And neither would be what Sable wanted. Neither would be fair, or good, or *right*.

She hated the lightlords. She hated them for luring the Gull clan into this arrangement in the first place...although she would never have met Eithni without it.

But that would have been better—for Eithni. Maybe better for Sable too.

Try as hard as she might, she couldn't find a way to fix this.

Unless.

Oh, if only she *dared*.

"Umber," Sable said quietly, her heart in her throat. "Forgive me."

Her mind started working rapidly, trying to chase the dangers, the complications, the repercussions all the way to their end, as Eithni would.

Umber turned his full attention to her. "You're going to do something stupid." In the dark, behind the helm, she couldn't read his face properly, but his voice held no accusation or rancor. Only affection.

Sable swallowed.

"Oh yes. I think I am going to do something very, very stupid."

❦

The throng gathered now. Lightlords and their entourages, crowding in their respective gardens, all facing the doorway of stone in the half-light. A slight, warm breeze ruffled the shadowed banners and trappings of folk the size of trees, or thin as reeds, or small as birds, and everyone in between.

Sable's own lightlord took his place ahead of all, a short distance from the entrance.

She and Umber faced him, each sinking to one knee. If their liege was proud to show the matched pair of guardians, in their deer skull helms and branching antlers, it did not reflect on his face, which held nothing but avid anticipation of the dawn.

This close to their lightlord, Sable and Umber were unable to even glance at each other. But Sable's body vibrated with tension, and she knew her brother's did too.

The sky grew lighter before them. Slowly the lightlords turned, their people with them, to face the dawn as well.

Sable looked at Umber, who inclined his head ever so slightly. They must wait for the sun, but they would be ready.

EITHNI

The women were singing.

They sang every year, once they passed the standing stones that marked the path to the cairn, turning toward the sea. Eithni sang her part with them, despite everything inside her. She could not throw off the years of Gull tradition, not here. Not with the long line of her people snaking behind the procession, listening, watching the dip and sway of the wise women's lanterns.

Eithni knew this song by heart. But this time, the words were like heavy stones in her belly.

Now lifts the darkness
We welcome the light
Our best we bring
Our gifts we receive
Thus will end the longest night...

But Eithni was the offering they brought. She hoped the gifts the Gull received in return would be worth it. She hoped they choked on the blessings of the gods...the *lightlords*.

Eithni couldn't turn from her position at the head of the procession to look behind, to see if she could find her father's face, or Derilei's. But she wondered what she would see. Tears? Resignation? Nothing at all?

No, No. She would see *something*, and her task would be harder for it. Better to not even be tempted to look.

She walked carefully, looking ahead to the approaching mound, ghostly in its new, white shroud. Outside of the circle of light from the lanterns, the snowy drifts along the pathway now seemed to give off a pale light of their own.

The sky was beginning to lighten.

~

The singing ended.

They stood now in a circle around the cairn, rows upon rows, but for a broad snow-covered path left free before the entrance.

All of the Gull, arrayed to welcome the light.

And Eithni stood before them all, facing the horizon. Trying not to look at the faces of the people lining the path the sunlight would soon take.

She was not alone. Conchenn and the other wise women, young Muire and Caltram, all stood in a semicircle to either side of her, before the arms of the entrance to the cairn.

Torches and lanterns had all been quelled. The people of the Gull turned their heads toward the brightening sky. It seemed as though all held their breath in the frozen air.

The first gleam of sun edged over the horizon. Eithni trembled as the lance of golden light traveled down the snow. She turned away from its blinding eye, and moved to the side to allow it entrance to the chamber.

Then the wise women and youths helped her remove the heavy furs and hides, until she stood in the chill sunlight in her cream-colored wool gown, trying not to shiver.

All lifted their arms to the sky and sang once more, welcoming the blessings of the gods. Greeting the new dawn. Eithni opened her mouth and pretended to sing as well, pretended her eyes weren't burning with suppressed tears, pretended her throat wasn't so tight now that no sound could possibly emerge.

And the song ended, and Eithni entered the cairn, alone.

SABLE

At the first gleam of light, the lightlord entered the passage to the chamber.

Sable and Umber followed, as was their duty, along with four others of the lightlord's entourage. Sable tried not to think of being trapped in that room with their liege. Escape might be possible, but it would not be easy.

Sable and Umber stood on either side of the chamber, allowing their lightlord and his people to fill the room. Large as the space was, it felt far too crowded with seven beings in it—nothing like the quiet intimacy of just Sable and the wall, and the voice on the other side.

Magic began to fill the chamber, as the light grew.

Sable could feel it now—more powerful than it had been any of the days before. She was counting on the strength of that magic. The occupants of the chamber were silent, watching with bated breath as the square of light began to take shape.

What if Eithni wasn't on the other side of it?

What if she was?

It didn't matter. Sable knew what she had to do.

She looked at Umber. He tensed, prepared. At the right moment, the moment she took action, he would escape the room under glamour, masked by the magic and by the confusion of the moment. It was a terrible risk, but the only way Sable could think of to make sure her brother stayed alive.

The magic flared brighter, and the door did as well.

Sable surged forward, amid the shouts of the lightlord and the others in the room. She moved faster than she ever had before.

She leaped through the door.

EITHNI

Alone in the chamber, heart hammering, Eithni watched the light grow. Her breath came in gasps and her entire body trembled, with cold and with fear.

Brighter than ever before, and more complete, the square of sunlight flared gold-white, once. Twice. The stone behind it disappeared, leaving only light.

The door.

Eithni drew a shuddering breath and braced herself to take her first step.

Shouts erupted through the light, and Eithni stumbled back as something—no, someone—leapt through. Eithni's first impression was of a deer—no, a human, tall and lithe, with antlers—

It was Sable. It had to be.

The shouts grew louder on the other side, and the tall figure turned quickly to face the door, spear pointing into the light. "Stand behind me," the other said, with Sable's warm, beautiful voice.

Eithni's hands went to her throat as she pressed herself against the wall. What did this mean? What was the guardian doing?

Saving her.

Defying the lightlords.

Eithni clenched her fists and willed the door to close, before the beings on the other side could come through and do something terrible to them both.

How many seconds, minutes, could the magic last?

And Sable—if she went back through, would she go to her death?

"Enough," came a voice from the other side. Sable gasped and flew back, as if thrown, hitting a slab of stone on the other end of the chamber. Her spear clattered to the floor. Eithni's heart flew into her throat.

An unearthly hand, long and pale, emerged from the lighted doorway, clenching. *"You dare defy me, hartkin?"* the voice hissed. *"I will come fetch the human my—"*

"The door is closing!" Eithni shouted. "The light is fading!" It might have even been true—the bright white flared again, perhaps as a warning. But more important still, if the lightlord believed it...

The hand withdrew. *"Your kin will suffer for this,"* the lightlord said, and Eithni didn't know if the threat was for Sable, or for herself.

A final flare, and the door became a patch of sunlight once more. Eithni could still hear the turmoil of voices on the other side. But no one could come through the stone.

Eithni ran to the form now collapsed against the chamber wall.

"Sable," she breathed, reaching for the other woman. "Please be alive."

The deer-woman's lanky, broad-shouldered form didn't look

broken, but the antlers Eithni had seen...they were destroyed, lying in pieces by the woman's hand. Eithni knelt beside Sable, looking closer.

The deer-woman's tawny hair was thick and springy, and didn't appear to have any blood matting it anywhere. Had the loss of her antlers not caused any damage? Eithni knew nothing of the nature of...what was the word? Hartkin.

Sable's skin was golden-brown, much like her hair. Unlike a human, her ears were long and furred, and a broad stripe of deeper color—more brown than tawny—extended from between her long-lashed eyes to her hairline.

The other woman had been right to predict that Eithni would find her strange. But beneath the strangeness, there was something deeply appealing. The bones of her face were strong and well-shaped, her mouth generous.

She began to groan and move. "Wait," Eithni whispered. "Just wait a moment."

Sable's eyes flew open, and Eithni drew a quick breath. The eyes were like the woman's name, deep and liquid-dark, and utterly captivating.

"Eithni of the Gull," Sable said, and her full mouth quirked into a smile. "We meet at last."

Eithni couldn't help but smile in return. "Guardian Sable." Her smile fell. "Are your injuries..."

"I will be fine." She began to shift, sitting up gingerly. "Sore, but fine. Eventually."

Eithni helped her stand and lean against the chamber wall. Sable looked past her to the place where the door had stood. "The light has almost moved on," she noted.

Eithni's turned to look. Her insides clenched. "You...can't go back, can you?"

"Do you want me gone?" The tone was light, but when Eithni turned back to Sable's face, she saw the question there.

"No—no! I just can't believe you are here. But—you must live among humans, now. Even if for only a year..."

"Or longer."

"...how could you want that?"

"The Summer realm needed shaking up. The lightlords needed defying. I can't think of a better way to accomplish this than to break all the rules for a human woman who deserves much better than her people—and mine—had in store for her."

Eithni took Sable's hand in both of hers, her heart full, head racing. She could not picture the shape of the future, but for the first time, the thought didn't terrify her. "I think I love you, guardian," she found herself saying, her face grave. "But I don't know what that means."

"I hope it means I can kiss you," Sable said, with a heart-stopping smile.

Eithni's eyes widened. "You knew...I have desired—loved—a woman only?"

"I only guessed. And hoped you might, with me."

Eithni smiled, and kissed her. It was warmth in the cold, light better than the sun, sweeter than the coming spring.

When she drew back, her mind was at peace.

"Let's bring the truth to the Gull," she said. "Tell them about the lightlords. Tell them the old ways must change. And..."

She rested her forehead against the warmth of her hartkin's brow. "Let's go to them as we are. Who we truly are."

It was risking everything—changing things thus, demanding acceptance. But Eithni was ready to try.

"Yes." Sable said. "I am with you. For everything." She stood away from the wall, and if she winced a little, at least her movements were unhindered. The light had moved from the place where the door had once stood, and the sound of singing now rose outside of the cairn.

The people of the Gull were preparing to leave, and would soon be checking the chamber to verify Eithni's disappearance.

They didn't know what was to come.

Eithni and Sable took hands, drew deep breaths, and prepared to welcome the dawn.

ABOUT THE AUTHOR

Alexandra Brandt spent most of her childhood dressing up in fairy wings and parading in front of the mirror telling stories to herself. Not much has changed: she still loves a good costume, and tells herself stories every day.

Her short fiction appears in *Fiction River* and other anthologies, and has made it onto *Tangent Magazine's* 2017 and 2018 Recommended Reading lists. "We, the Ocean," her story in Fiction River #22: *No Humans Allowed*, was described as "inventive, heartbreaking, and wholly original" by Hugo award-winning writer and editor Kristine Kathryn Rusch.

When not writing, reading, or debating worldbuilding details with her writer husband, Alex writes marketing copy for a medical practice and does graphic design work, including freelance book cover design. She occasionally sings in a choir, and always welcomes any excuse to sit down and play tabletop games—from D&D to board games to cards.

Find out more about Alex at:
alexandrajbrandt.com

facebook.com/AlexandraBrandtWriter

goodreads.com/AlexandraBrandt

amazon.com/Alexandra-Brandt/e/B01N307Z7I

bookbub.com/authors/alexandra-brandt

ABOUT A PROCESSION OF FAERIES

Midwinter Fae is the second volume in the anthology series A Procession of Faeries. If you enjoyed this collection, check out the others—and follow the series on Facebook!

 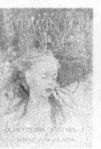